**Praise for the Novels
of Pam Rosenthal**

The Slightest Provocation

"A novel to savor and read again and again."*

"Perfect for those who like their historical romances sexy, smart, and with a dash of sharp wit." —*Booklist*

"Thoroughly grounded in history and threaded through with breathtaking sensuality, this intelligent, well-crafted romance takes readers on a fascinating journey and will appeal to those who appreciate a bit more history with an erotic, literary touch." —*Library Journal*

"Emotionally raw, sophisticated . . . beautifully written, unflinching, and seductive. Rosenthal's prose is elegant and vital at once, filled with tiny, probing observations and literary allusions one moment, rampantly sensual play and soul-rending marital battles the next . . . easily one of this year's best." —**The Contra Costa Times*

"[A] sensual romp amid one of England's most exciting time periods. Readers cannot help but be enchanted with the historical details, lusty passions, tender romance, and the healthy dollop of intrigue that spices up every page. A must-have for all historical lovers!" —Romance Junkies

"Rosenthal crafts a tantalizing tale about a fiery love-hate relationship that defies the boundaries of love. Her strong characters' fierce desires will leave readers panting." —*Romantic Times*

"Pam Rosenthal's writing is extraordinary. Fans of Laura Kinsale and Julia Ross will adore Rosenthal's ability to humanize her characters—to render their emotions and reactions realistic to a fault, while maintaining a warmth that makes them sympathetic. Kit and Mary breathe." —Fresh Fiction

continued . . .

"What a wonderful, challenging, envelope-pushing, smart, and astonishing book."   —Dear Author . . .

"An erotic, romantic, sensitive, and provocative story with fascinating relationships and characters set inside a richly illustrated historical backdrop amid turbulent times . . . a must read!"   —*Romance Reader at Heart*

The Edge of Impropriety

**Winner of the Romance Writers of America's
2009 RITA® Award for Best Historical Romance
One of *Library Journal*'s "Best Romances of 2008"**

"A sharply insightful, realistic look at some of the darker, often glossed-over aspects of Regency society. A delightfully 'improper' read."   —*Library Journal*

"Rosenthal smartly leavens her always elegant writing with just the right dash of wit, and her latest lusciously sensual historical romance is nothing less than sublime."
                    —*Chicago Tribune*

"Rosenthal does a lovely job with the love scenes—at turns bawdy and sensual. [She] solidifies her reputation as a name to watch in the historical romance genre."
                    —Erotica Readers & Writers Association

"A steamy historical romance with substance and style."
                    —Fresh Fiction

"Rosenthal [is] always looking for new ways to burn up the pages and keep your mind focused on characters and plot, not just her wonderfully erotic love scenes . . . an exhilarating adventure filled with untamed passion, intrigue, and wild escapades in and out of bed." —*Romantic Times*

ALSO BY PAM ROSENTHAL

The Edge of Impropriety

THE SLIGHTEST PROVOCATION

PAM ROSENTHAL

SIGNET ECLIPSE

SIGNET ECLIPSE
Published by New American Library, a division of
Penguin Group (USA) Inc., 375 Hudson Street,
New York, New York 10014, USA
Penguin Group (Canada), 90 Eglinton Avenue East, Suite 700, Toronto,
Ontario M4P 2Y3, Canada (a division of Pearson Penguin Canada Inc.)
Penguin Books Ltd., 80 Strand, London WC2R 0RL, England
Penguin Ireland, 25 St. Stephen's Green, Dublin 2,
Ireland (a division of Penguin Books Ltd.)
Penguin Group (Australia), 250 Camberwell Road, Camberwell, Victoria 3124,
Australia (a division of Pearson Australia Group Pty. Ltd.)
Penguin Books India Pvt. Ltd., 11 Community Center, Panchsheel Park,
New Delhi - 110 017, India
Penguin Group (NZ), 67 Apollo Drive, Rosedale, North Shore 0632,
New Zealand (a division of Pearson New Zealand Ltd.)
Penguin Books (South Africa) (Pty.) Ltd., 24 Sturdee Avenue,
Rosebank, Johannesburg 2196, South Africa

Penguin Books Ltd., Registered Offices:
80 Strand, London WC2R 0RL, England

Published by Signet Eclipse, an imprint of New American Library, a division
of Penguin Group (USA) Inc. Previously published in a Signet Eclipse trade
paperback edition.

First Signet Eclipse Mass Market Printing, May 2010
10 9 8 7 6 5 4 3 2 1

For Michael,
by my troth

Prologue

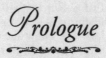

1771, 1817

In March 1771, a son was born to Emilia and Walter Stansell, the Marchioness and Marquess of Rowen, at Rowen Castle, near the village of Grefford, in the southeast corner of Derbyshire.

A very pretty boy, the marchioness thought. And very like his lordship. She traced the infant's cheek with a timid finger. He wasn't sleeping as peacefully as he had been a few minutes earlier. Ignorant of babies as she was, it seemed clear enough to her that he'd soon be awake.

The birth had been quick, and rather less dreadful than she'd been led to expect. Her husband was delighted. Not that he'd ever been anything but excruciatingly nice to her during the ten months of their marriage, but this time his smile had seemed genuine.

And now the baby *was* awake, mewling piteously and waving a shapeless little fist in the air. Poor little thing, he looked hungry. No one had told her anything about feeding a baby. But then, no one had told her much of anything since she'd been wed and packed off to be Lady Rowen of Derbyshire. She'd quickly become pregnant; the only other time she'd seen her husband so happy was on the morning she'd announced her condition to him.

"Capital, Emilia." He'd taken her on his lap and kissed her forehead. "Well done," he told her.

She'd wanted to protest that in sad truth, she hadn't *done* much of anything. But instead she put her arms around his neck and clung to him. Feeling rather like a little girl than the lady she knew she could be, she told herself that everything would be all right now.

She still told herself that sometimes, but less often.

Still, it was impossible to be unhappy with this lovely little boy in her arms. Look, he was hungry; his mouth was moving like a kitten's. She felt the most remarkable sensation in her breasts, which had grown hard, and moist at their tips.

"But what are you doing, your ladyship?" She'd never liked the housekeeper at Rowen.

"He's hungry. . . . Aren't you, pet . . . little Wat, little kitten . . ." How soft his cheek was, how vulnerable his smooth little pink gums, and what an interesting feeling in her breasts—the need to love and care for someone became palpable reality, a piquant tugging at her flesh.

"His lordship has engaged a wet nurse for Viscount Sherwynne."

She must mean the baby, Emilia thought, as the housekeeper tugged at the bell rope.

A nice-enough-looking girl entered the room, curtsied to Emilia, and stared at the Belgian lace on her pretty bedgown. She appeared rather less interested in the baby; but then, Emilia thought, she was probably quite familiar enough with babies already. Her breasts were bigger than Emilia's, her hands looked capable, and the little viscount seemed happy enough once he was sucking.

The milk and her tears dried up, and her menses started again a few weeks later. This was why she wasn't to nurse the child, she was told—for his lordship wanted another son, to ensure the continuance of the marquisate, and as soon as possible.

How simple things were, Emilia thought. She remembered a joke she'd overheard, about how the London Marriage Mart wasn't much different from the Smithfield market for livestock. It was true after all; people had probably said of *her* that she'd been bought like a broodmare.

She tensed her shoulders now at the familiar polite knock on the door of her bedchamber. His lordship would be visiting her almost every night, until she was indisputably with child again.

But on this particular night, before she opened her legs, Emilia wrested a bargain from her husband.

"As soon as I've given you another boy, you will never touch me again," she told him. "For you don't really like me that way. I used to feel very bad about it, but now I've stopped caring so much.

"Because I've got to care about myself—well, if *I* don't, Walter, who will?" Much later, she'd be amused to learn that a great sage had first enunciated that question, as a universal statement of the human condition. More exciting, though, to come upon it as she had, propelled into the glittering darkness of philosophy by force of her desires.

The excitement had emboldened her—not only to say what she had, but (which seemed even more daring) to call her husband by his Christian name. He was thirty-five years old, just short of twice her age, and before now she'd always called him *your lordship*.

"It's not that I couldn't enjoy having you in my bed," she continued. "I think I could have, you know, if you'd liked me."

Eyes wary, he waited quietly to hear what else she had to say.

Her stomach twisted, for until that moment she'd cherished the faintest of hopes that he'd protest that she'd simply been imagining things. Ah, well. She took a deep breath and continued.

"Just know, Walter, that there will be other men, and if there are other children, you will give them your name. I've heard the gossip, after all. I'm not the only noblewoman in England in this fix. I shall manage as well as many ladies, and perhaps rather better than some have done."

No doubt she was still addled by the exigencies of giving birth: postpartum depression, a modern reader might call it. Whatever the reason for it, her boldness might have spelled disaster, if a chance phrase had not turned the tide in Emilia's favor.

For when she had referred to *the gossip,* she'd only meant the stories everyone repeated, about certain great ladies and their lovers. The ever-cautious marquess, however, had taken her words to mean that she'd somehow found out about the highly inappropriate personage he did, in fact, like very much in bed.

He masked his fear with a show of affability. For he could be quite affable, though you wouldn't have thought so if you'd first learned of him from his nearest country neighbor, the wealthy brewer Joshua Penley.

But we will hear more of Mr. Penley later.

In any event, the marquess decided that there was nothing to be done about it. He'd have to trust his wife with his secret. He felt oddly confident that he could, for in truth, she was an unusually reasonable and level-headed young woman. Excellent at her duties: she'd overseen the estate carpenter's restoration of some precious ancient paneling; this year she'd be supervising Mr. Brown, the landscape gardener. Had a touch for charity and good works too: the tenants and cottagers had quickly grown fond of her. Most important, she'd given him a fine, healthy heir. But babies were fragile. The marquess feared for the continuance of his line.

If she can produce another Stansell son, her husband thought, *there isn't much more I need ask of her.* Just another boy, to ensure the orderly and legitimate progression of inheritance.

He didn't relish the thought of forcing himself upon her. Why *not* promise her a little future pleasure then, to take as she would, quite as he would continue to do?

Because lovely as she was—small and slender, with fascinating green eyes and a luxuriance of silky black curls spilled on the pillow—the unavoidable truth was that he *didn't* like her that way.

He did insist, though, that when the time came she cuckold him with a gentleman (or if she must, more than one) of unexceptional status.

And she—silently reminding herself that nature maintains its own aristocracy of value and virtue—had no difficulty promising this, if he would give her authority over the hiring and firing of the upper servants. Life would be easier and better, she thought, if she had people about her whom she could trust.

After which promise she bent her rosebud lips into a smile with just a twist of bitterness at its corner, graciously lifted her thin lawn nightdress, and parted her legs . . .

. . . Nine months later to the day presenting him with baby William, who looked every bit as much like his lordship as little Walter, though Will turned out kinder and a bit more intelligent than his brother Wat.

The couple honored their promises to each other, more or less, over the years. Emilia kept her husband's secret—after she'd finally guessed it, with some amusement—rather better than she'd kept her own. For there *had* been a lapse: one mysterious attachment on the marchioness's part had been cause for discussion among the gentlemen in their clubs and ladies in their drawing rooms (with some consequent unpleasantness at Rowen). Emilia had to take some rather extreme measures in order to divert the world's attention—but on the whole she managed it quite well.

And so, as Belle, Kit, and Georgy followed their less exuberantly conceived brothers into the world, the marquess gave them his name without protest. Without much affection, it was true, but then, he had very little affection for anyone except that inappropriate personage he continued to love until he died, sometime after his second son, Will, was killed in Spain.

⚜

Emilia—now the dowager marchioness, and resident in Paris since the autumn after Waterloo—doesn't usually devote much thought to her late husband. But this morning she's entertained a caller whose presence has brought back the events of almost half a century ago. *So many years gone by,* she thinks, *just fancy what a story it would make.*

She's still beautiful: a bit plumper, the luxuriant black curls striped with silver, cut shorter and caught up in a becoming Grecian knot. Her smile, above a decidedly more rounded chin, takes an ironical curve as she thinks of her first sweet baby rather comically grown to the stodgy Ninth Marquess. She raises her chin, remembering her moment of bravery, the depth of her need. Do all stories begin at a moment of great need? But Emilia doesn't know about all stories. Only her own.

She thinks of other stories, ended too quickly or never really begun. Of her other children: Will, buried in Spain; beautiful, proper Belle, all but buried in Mayfair (at least to Emilia's mind); Georgy, a charming rake, rather as one would expect.

While as for Kit, her third and most troublesome son, now *there's* a story: people in the countryside still like to talk about how the third Stansell boy ran away with Joshua Penley's youngest daughter, Mary. Kit has survived the war—thank heaven for *that*—and with some distinction too. But Kit had been a fighter since childhood—his elopement made the marquess angrier than anything Emilia ever managed to do. Emilia isn't surprised by Kit's success in military affairs. What continues to plague her is his difficulty at love.

She's always liked Mary. She liked Mrs. Penley as well; in fact, Emilia had confided a few interesting things to her, a decade ago upon the occasion of the young people's elopement. Not that the two women were ever friends. A pity, but such a thing would have been impossible.

Ah yes, Mary's call this morning has brought it all back, and most particularly the story of Kit and Mary, the sadness of their marriage ending in separation. Still, Emilia hasn't given up all hope. It had been agreeable to be able to do the young woman a favor this morning. Emilia herself will be returning quite soon to England. The story isn't over yet.

Chapter One

NORMANDY, MAY 1817

The road was smoother here, winding closer to the city gates. The borrowed traveling carriage wasn't jolting so fiercely on its springs; Lady Rowen's coachman had managed to coax the exhausted horses into a gentle trot. Peggy, the maid, had fallen asleep on the backward-facing seat, head lolling against blue velvet, mouth slightly agape, apple cheeks glowing from the day's rain and wind.

A Dutch painting.

Mary Stansell, née Penley, congratulated herself on the justness of her observation. Oh yes, very much a Dutch painting, all earthly flesh, rich textile, and pure, transcendent light.

She smiled at her own cleverness. And then she frowned uncertainly.

Did the Dutch do moonlight? In truth she had no idea; she'd seen so many paintings this year that they blurred in her memory.

The clouds had lifted. Mary wiped her breath from the glass to stare up at the moon shedding its beams through the coach's window. After a beastly hard day of travel, the pale illumination made a pleasing composition from a muddle of objects on the floor—baskets, books, and parcels; maid's and mistress's muddy boots; and (hell and botheration!) a ragged strip of muslin trailing from beneath Mary's skirts.

She'd stepped through the hem of her petticoat; poor Peggy would have to stitch it up when they arrived at the inn.

Her mouth twisted. Poor Peggy indeed.

No, that was unfair. It was hardly the maid's fault that they were short of fresh linen; it hadn't been *Peggy's* idea to wait so long, and then to quit Paris so suddenly, with no time to send the last bundle to the laundress. The girl had done what she could to keep things nice along the journey's way. And she was certainly entitled to an innocent flirtation.

If *innocent* was what one might properly call the curve that had suddenly and completely reshaped Peggy's soft baby lips. Mary watched in fascination as a flush started somewhere at the base of the plump neck, rosy bright pink spreading upward now, beneath the freckled cheeks' surface. Blissfully unaware of moonlight and mistress both, her young chambermaid was in the thrall of a delightfully wicked dream.

Or was Mary simply imagining it, projecting, as though by magic lantern, her own unruly desires onto the screen of Peggy's wide, guileless countenance?

It was a diverting notion. Because she'd had it on no less authority than Mr. Shelley that she was sadly deficient in imagination. He'd told her as much last summer, when she'd declined to continue traveling with him and the rest of his household.

Ah, but you see, he'd protested, *we are not* merely *a household.* Warming to his subject, eyes sparkling beneath his wide brow, pale schoolboy curls stirred by the wind off the Swiss mountain lake, he spoke of idealism, a leap into mankind's future, the imagination's mortal reach beyond the bounds of petty conventional morality— with himself, his beautiful beloved Miss Godwin, and

Miss Godwin's rather earthier stepsister, at the center of their new bold Eden.

Tactfully, she'd swallowed back the response that had at first sprung to her lips: that it hardly took imagination to see who had the most to gain from all this rampant idealism. Checking her words was a hard-won skill; a decade ago she might have delivered a rebuke stinging enough to redden the young genius's pretty ears. Since then, however, she'd learned the art of gentle refusal, the helpless shrug and self-deprecating smile. *I'm sadly bound to my obligations, sir; just think of all the precious letters of introduction I've got, expeditions arranged, sights and monuments to visit.*

As you like, madam, he'd replied. A brief pause to recover his equilibrium, and he'd launched into an elaborate disquisition on poetic spirit and inner vision— capabilities, he feared, that were rather beyond her petty limitations.

It had been a stimulating lecture, though she might have gotten equally good conversation if she'd stopped back with Miss Godwin. Still, she listened obligingly, while the wind off the lake turned chilly and the light of the poet's intellect bade fair to burn deep into the night. He might have chosen a gentler way to frame his argument. He probably would have, if she'd been better able to hide her amusement.

Give me another decade, she thought now, *and I'll master the extra measure of control.* No need to ask for the decade, of course; it would come whether she liked it or not. And by the time it did come, by the time she was forty . . .

But she'd just had a birthday; she was thirty-*one* now, and (as though to illustrate the passing of time) had recently acquired a pair of small, gold-rimmed, oval reading spectacles. There had been letters of birthday congratulation from England, and one from Matthew Bakewell in France; he was studying the wonders of Jacquard weaving in Lyon. Too delicate to ask whether she'd finally seen her estranged husband, he'd simply written how much he missed her company, was counting the days to Midsummer Eve when they'd be together, and looked forward, finally, to a resolution of their complicated situation.

After nine years of separation from Kit Stansell, she wanted some resolution as well. Something simple and settled, with a man as fine as Matthew.

Just be happy with Miss Godwin, she'd exhorted young Shelley. *Leave aside the fantasies of communal love, and for God's sake get rid of the stepsister.*

Leave aside all the fantasies. And the memories as well.

❧

A gentle snore bubbled from Peggy's open lips. The coach swayed, righted itself on its springs, and turned onto a smaller road. The inn was close by the city gates; they couldn't have too much farther to travel.

On the whole, Mary thought, Percy Shelley had been quite correct in his assessment of her. She loved poetry, liked poets, and was clever enough with words herself, but the poetic temperament was as little her forte as the ironic was his.

Irony, a penchant for exaggerated self-scrutiny, perhaps, and a small skill at observation—as if it would take any skill to discern what was going on between Peggy and Lady Rowen's handsome footman, Thomas.

What *had* taken skill was ignoring it. Easier before today: the good weather and smooth roads had helped. The coach Lady Rowen had lent her was so well sprung and comfortable that Mary had been able to occupy herself with books or her journal, when she wasn't staring out the window, reliving her peregrinations: Rome, Florence, Venice; Greece and Turkey; the Alps; and castles along the Rhine.

Since Waterloo, every Englishman and -woman who could afford it was touring the continent, trudging up mountainsides, gaping at monumental ruins, buying up nearly everything else, and—according to Lord Byron anyway—rendering the place utterly uninhabitable.

Mary had found it quite delightfully habitable; she'd spent a wonderfully entertaining year, moving at a brisk pace with a series of charming companions. The only annoyance was the occasional stupidity of being cut, by widgeon-brained people one could avoid in London but might unexpectedly bump up against at Ephesus or Pompeii. Small matter. Her separation from her husband was stale news; her association with the Shelley party, respectable if a bit outré; her latest less-than-respectable liaison managed discreetly and recently brought to an amicable close.

Anyone she might actually want to be acquainted with was happy to know her, for she made a charming tourist—earnest and inquisitive, amused rather than annoyed by the inevitable mishap; frightfully well-informed and endlessly appreciative of whatever there was to be seen.

Today's plaguing mood was an aberration, no doubt brought on by all the rain. Peggy and Thomas had been most circumspect, but there could be no ignoring them with everyone so jumbled together by the weather. A formidable storm had blown in; a lesser coachman than Mr. Frayne might have refused to start out this morning.

Perhaps he'd been overzealous. A pity to work the horses so harshly. But he was proud of his skill, and (like all of the dowager marchioness's servants) devoted to doing his best. He was also—when given the rare chance to converse with two-legged creatures—more than a little bit pompous and long-winded.

Big arms folded beneath his voluminous cape, he'd whistled through the gap in his teeth, decrying the bloody hellishness (begging the lady's pardon, perhaps he should say the *capriciousness*) of the elements. But seeing as it was such a first-rate vehicle the marchioness kept, and what with Lady Christopher wanting to get home to England as soon as possible, he thought he could see them through.

Clutching his top hat in front of him in an exaggerated show of decorum, he'd promptly ruined the effect by his insinuating pronunciation of *Lady Christopher,* all but winking to show that he knew a thing or two, being so long in the family's service. Though of course he'd never breathe a word of it.

Ah, well. Better-bred people had said and done much worse. The brewer's daughter had learned to respond affably to a title that felt (more than ever in her current circumstances) like fancy dress. The woman estranged from her husband was quite accustomed to being quizzed.

The storm, Mr. Frayne. Do go on, sir.

Well, then. He drew a breath.

The local people were of the opinion that the storm was like to pass by nightfall. Not that you could entirely trust them Frenchies and their stories. Still, it looked that way to him as well.

It'll be a hard day for sure (he seemed to be concluding his remarks now), but if my lady and the little maid is willing to trudge through the wet an' the muck alongside the coach when we comes to some o' the biggest hills—well, then, ma'am, you can lay your trust on Thomas and me to do for you.

Thomas had nodded with great seriousness, and Peggy had beamed up at him proudly.

Good. Then we're off. (Mary had begun to turn away.) Thank you, Mr. Frayne.

With lu-u-u-ck, Mr. Frayne had added (the latter syllable stretched almost to the breaking point of ponderous slowness, to signal that Mary must turn back and hear him out), you'll be sleeping in an honest English bed tomorrow night, Lady Christopher. One more night on French soil, and by tomorrow I'll be putting you on the Dover-Calais packet, safe and snug and more or less in one piece.

Yes. Thank you very much indeed.

In one piece. More or less. Well, with a lot more mud on her skirts and a lot less food in her stomach, since the vehicle's jouncing and lurching had caused her to lose her luncheon several hours ago. And with bruises on her feet, from wet shoes rubbing through bunched stockings.

At least her insides had ceased their churning. She'd even felt some pleasant twinges of hunger. Tonight's inn was reputed to have an unusually good kitchen; Lady Rowen had made particular mention of it. They should be arriving quite soon and in very reasonable time under the circumstances.

Mr. Frayne had badgered and cajoled the horses through rain and wind and muck up to their fetlocks, while Thomas handed Mary in and out of the carriage with great ceremony, holding the green umbrella over her as though she were a precious, delicate parcel, even as he sent the occasional fleeting smile back over his shoulder at Peggy splashing along behind.

Absurd to have felt those twinges of envy, of a couple of servants' evident happiness. Absurd, self-indulgent . . . *ignore it, Mary*. Orangey light was flickering through the coach windows—from hearth fires, in houses along the road. They must be approaching the inn.

Peggy yawned and rubbed her eyes with round little fists reddened from the rain. She looked very young, as indeed she was: eighteen, hardly older than Betts, Mary's niece at home.

While Thomas must be nearly a decade older, well over six feet tall, and quite excessively handsome; he'd doubtless cut quite a swath during his own employer's tour across Europe. He did seem to care for Peggy, though. Would he continue to do so if she became pregnant? In the event, of course, Mary would do what she could to help. But it was a pity to leave it all to fate—and even worse to trust to nature.

"You can't do a thing about it." Her sister Jessica had said this years ago, when Mary and Kit had first been married and Mary had consulted her two older sisters about a wayward scullery maid.

"Jessie's right." Julia was two years younger than Jes-

sica, equally opinionated, and particularly voluble in the
Scots intonations she'd adapted since her marriage.
"We've both tried to teach them, and so did Mama. Of
course, nothing's entirely trustworthy, but they and their
young men think it's indecent even to *try* to improve their
chances against nature. 'Them things is just for hoors,
Mrs. MacNeill,' was what my chambermaid told me when
I broached the subject with her. And then, remembering
the contents of *my* nightstand, she added, 'Well, hoors
and eddicated ladies, I guess, beggin' yer pardon, Mum.'
Which showed me *my* place quickly enough."

"Only be sure that Kit's keeping *his* . . . eyes to himself," Jessica had added. She'd blushed—they all knew
about Arthur's misadventure with a maid, during Jessie's difficult recovery from a miscarriage some years
past. The affair was completely smoothed over, but
Mary had rushed to hug her eldest sister nonetheless—
the exuberant gesture, she thought now, rather sullied
by a youthful, callow presumption that such a thing
could never happen to *her*.

Jessie had laughed and generously returned the hug.
"Not that Kit could have eyes—*or* anything else—for
any woman in the world besides you."

The light through the coach windows had turned a
bright, smoky yellow—gas lamps, she supposed, to
mark the inn. They'd arrived without her noticing it.

Calls of greeting mingled with the admiring whistles
and halloos such a fine traveling coach inevitably called
forth. Torches and lanterns guided their way through
the porte cochere and through the yard to the inn's
front door. Glare and rattle and cry made a pleasant
diversion from her echoing thoughts and memories.

Mr. Frayne brought the horses up smartly, Thomas
leaped down from beside the coachman to hand Mary
out, and Peggy gathered up the jumbled objects strewn
around the seats and floor during their filthy, exhausting, but—thank heaven—now completed day on the
highway.

Her last night on French soil.

Of course, *he* hadn't made much effort to see her either—they'd missed each other in more than one capital city. Missed or avoided—she'd heard talk of an Austrian baroness. Perhaps she should have lingered a bit longer with the Shelley party. Or better still, with her companion in Milan. Not that he'd necessarily be paying attention. But (in the event that he *were*) just to show him that she *could* . . .

❧

Defiantly, she lifted her chin against that last notion. Shaking Thomas's hand from her arm and hurrying with light steps toward the inn's front door, she held her head so high and her back so straight that no one watching would have thought her anything but entirely confident and rather haughty, if a bit disheveled.

And almost beautiful, the dark-haired gentleman observed silently, from among the inn yard's shadows.

Almost, but not quite. Too energetic, perhaps. The brown eyes too bright, set too wide above her cheeks.

Alighting onto the cobbles—the swirl of snuff-colored skirt, white petticoat, and dark red cloak affording him a precious moment's glimpse of muddy boot and slender ankle—her movements were too quick for any classical notion of beauty.

Too quick, too willful, too complicated, and yet too lacking in mystery. *Just see her marching across the yard with that ridiculously endearing little triangle of torn white cloth fluttering behind her.*

It reminded him of a bit of stage business—comic soubrette brought low by her unmentionables. Or a white flag of surrender fluttering over a battlefield. Surrender easier to go after than forgiveness.

He lit a cheroot, from a torch stuck in the inn yard wall. Foolishly, he'd thought she'd be arriving much earlier. The weather . . . he should have known better; a soldier should always take account of changes in the weather.

The coachman had gone inside now, to get some supper for himself. It would be a while until she came down to eat; she'd be needing a good wash, perhaps a rest, and doubtless some repair work in the petticoat area. He'd grown finicky about matters of dress during his service in Paris and at the Viennese court. And so he was surprised to discover that—at least in the little matter of the petticoat—he rather hoped she'd leave things as they were.

Chapter Two

Peggy was clever with a needle; she'd quickly stitched up the torn hem after helping Mary scrub away the worst of the grime and dressing her in dry stockings, clean shoes, a fresh gown of pale green chambray, and a soft India shawl around her shoulders.

"But I can brush my own hair," Mary told her now, "after I lie down for a little rest."

The inn was as charming and comfortable as Lady Rowen had pronounced it, the landlord affecting the requisite astonishment to hear them drive up: *sacre bleu,* and after such a day of rain and wind. But it was all for the best; in good weather, his establishment was often full up to the garrets. He'd shrugged his shoulders admiringly (the gesture gone a bit stale with repeated use, but English tourists would expect a soupçon of Gallicism from him). You English with your *très formidable* coachmen, spitting through their teeth like fierce beasts. *Eh, bien,* no wonder they have such a mortal hand with the horses.

Still clucking over the charming barbarity of the occupying nation, he'd led them up the stairs to a simple chamber, walls freshly whitewashed and lace curtains swaying at the half-opened window. A young woman brought clean hot water and a bar of lavender-scented soap. Thomas did a splendid job of banking up the fire. Her books and portable writing desk were near to hand.

Stretching her neck and curving her back like a pampered housecat, Mary cast a greedy eye over a high, wide bedstead and thick feather bed. *Just a little rest,* she thought—a little stillness and serenity in which to anticipate a good meal—*and it will be as though today's spell of bad humor never happened.*

"Yes, dear, I'm sure I'm all right," she told Peggy now. "Run downstairs and have your supper. If you hurry, you can catch up with Thomas. Just make sure he's told the kitchen to save some food for me."

The girl didn't need to be told twice. A brilliant smile, a lightning-quick curtsy, and she scampered down the back staircase, while Mary propped herself up against the pillows and cast her eyes over Jessica's latest meandering, cross-written, and much-underlined letter.

A troublesome daughter, recently become a beauty:

. . . . *So* tall, *like Mama, so graceful and willowy and with Mama's "goddess excellently bright" quality that none of* us three *ever quite managed, though I daresay we're all* quite all right *in our* ways.

I thought of sending her to town, to give the two of us a respite from each other. I might have asked her aunt Lady Grandin to take her, but Philamela's coming out right now, and Philamela isn't the prettiest *of girls; her mother wouldn't have wanted such a lovely cousin within eyeshot—bad enough having to hide Phila's sister, Fannie, when suitors come calling. Maybe we'll bring her out next year, Betts and Fannie have always been good friends, they'd be* charming together *and this year we'll content ourselves with a cozy, merry country time for midsummer.*

Or so I try to tell her, when we manage to speak at all. When she's not running over to Rowen, to make insipid conversation with the young marchioness, who encourages *her to be a ninny, I fear.*

A host of responsibilities, to her estate:

. . . When I'm not half distracted by accounts.

And to the neighborhood as well:

. . . And when I'm not worn out trying to help the people in the village, as Mama would have done and as they rightly expect *of me—but hungry children make me weep, the present Marchioness Susanna Stansell does her charitable duties most ineptly, and damn and double damn, Mary, I still miss Arthur so terribly. Two years, I can't believe it. It's bloody, sodding* awful *how much I miss him, Mary. . . .*

Her eyes had smarted a bit at that, even while she smiled at Jessie's awful language. The family joke was that the Penley women needed to withdraw after dinner in order to spare the delicate sensibilities of the gentlemen at table.

I am *all right,* she thought, *and I'm doing the right thing too.* The least she could do, to hurry home after lingering too long on the continent. Jessie and Julia had taken care of her when she'd needed it. It was time she did her part for Jessie.

Very kind of Lady Rowen to have remained her friend all these years; profoundly generous to lend her the coach. What good fortune to be making the trip so comfortably, with coachman, footman. . . .

And now this marvelously comfortable bed. A very big one too, for just one person. Which tended to lead one's thoughts in a certain direction. *Besoin d'aimer*— the need to love. She'd learned the phrase in France, though it was probably Peggy and Thomas who'd brought it to mind today. One of the strongest of needs, even if people wouldn't think it of a lady.

Whereas no one would wonder if a gentleman traveling alone might be thinking of more than his supper right about now. He'd be wanting warmth, consolation, diversion. And if none of the maids suited, he'd inquire whether any of the local girls were pretty and in want of a bit of blunt, with a consideration thrown in for the landlord's recommendation. No need for a gentleman to travel without all the requisite comforts, while Mary would have to depend upon a particular book she'd purchased in Paris.

As always, Peggy had buried *Les Bijoux Indiscrets* on the bottom of the pile on the nightstand. Perhaps she'd picked up a bit of French on their travels, and had guessed what Monsieur Diderot had meant by a woman's "indiscreet jewels."

Or perhaps Thomas had. In any case, it wasn't a book to read at table—a habit Mary and her sisters all practiced when they ate alone, and to hell with anyone who might deem it vulgar. She picked up Mrs. Wollstonecraft's *Letters Written During a Short Residence in Sweden, Norway, and Denmark,* and put her spectacles in her reticule.

Yawning and stretching, she swung her legs over the side of the bed. It was getting late, her hair still needed brushing, and—*besoin d'aimer* or not—she also wanted her supper.

❧

The dining room was almost deserted. And Thomas, who usually watched over her while she ate, was nowhere to be seen. She glanced at her pocket watch; the inn's other patrons would be in bed by now. Perhaps Thomas was on his way up the back stairs, to watch over her things. He must have decided that she'd be safe enough with hardly anyone to bother her down here.

The lights had burned down. With or without spectacles, it was much too dark for reading. But the glassware and linen in front of her were clean, and excellent smells still issued from the kitchen. There's a last capon on the spit, the serving girl told her. We saved it for you, madame, as Monsieur Thomas requested. It's fat and crispy, basted with brandy from Calvados, its juices drizzling into a pan of good local onions, turnips, and potatoes.

Will you have some, madame?

She nodded eagerly.

And will you be drinking cider or wine?

Cider, she was about to say, when her eye caught a glint of ruby across the room in the direction of the fireplace. Seated alone at a small table, face and body almost obscured by the shadow of low ceiling beams, a man was holding up a glass of wine, quite as if he were toasting her health.

Ah. Yes. Well.

She could barely make out his features. Surprising, then, the strength of her first impressions: a powerful material solidity, excellent tailoring and very good linen, a taste for mischief and a flair for the theatrical.

Her last night in France.

Ridiculous.

Dangerous.

And thank heaven she hadn't taken out her spectacles.

He held himself muffled in darkness, wineglass between long, elegantly squared-off fingers, its stem angled so the dark red liquid would catch the firelight.

"Wine," she told the girl standing at her elbow. "A small pitcher of red wine, *s'il vous plaît.*"

It would only be polite to return his toast.

And impossible to shy away from his challenge.

She raised her glass, he nodded, and they sipped their quite passable Bordeaux with rectitude and calm conviviality.

Her eyes must have adjusted to the room's dimness. She could make out a few more details, even in the flickering light of a few low candles.

His chair was tipped back against a plastered wall, but even so, she could see thick black hair curled charmingly over his forehead. The sharp edge of a high, white collar, under a well-tied, almost dandyish cravat.

Perhaps she *should* have let Peggy brush out her hair. It usually fell into a fetching enough mop of ringlets, but with today's rain and that awful wind . . .

The food the serving girl was setting down in front of her looked wonderful. A large leg of the chicken and a slice of the breast as well, hot and glistening from the spit.

She took a bite—oh, Lord, she was sad to be leaving France. The sauce especially, made with apple brandy . . . she hadn't realized quite how ravenous she was.

Was he smiling over the rim of his glass?

She'd probably wolf down the food without doing it justice.

On the contrary. She felt herself eating it most extremely slowly and deliberately, under the steady greenish gaze from next to the fireplace.

His eyes were still in shadow. She'd felt their color rather than actually seen it. Lichen on rock, under a brook's swift-moving water. Winter barely turned to spring.

He must have finished his supper. But he didn't appear in any hurry, refilling his glass now from the pitcher in front of him and evidently content to watch (certain things, it seemed, remaining quite unchanged. She'd been so interested in the ways he'd changed that she'd quite taken for granted the ways he hadn't).

Well, then. For she still had a pretty mouth, with gracefully bowed lips, a single dimple in the right corner, and small, even white teeth. She looked well when she was eating, even something as dodgy as spaghetti. She remembered a midnight supper in Italy, with a highly amused Lord Byron and his glowering Venetian mistress.

Very quickly, she flicked her tongue over her lower lip to catch a stray bit of carrot. A sip of wine, to cut the food's richness. A long swallow, dark perfume swirling at the back of her throat.

The sauce was splendid. She mopped up a bit more of it with a crust of fresh bread and ate it slowly.

Her belly was starting to feel full—the next few bites would be for the pure pleasure of it. Just one more mouthful now; she needed to save some room. One wouldn't want to come through Normandy and not sample every inn's own particular apple tart. Especially an inn that Lady Rowen had recommended.

Though this wasn't exactly the moment to be thinking of Lady Rowen.

The serving girl had returned to see if she wanted any dessert.

Oui, s'il vous plaît, mademoiselle.

With sauce Chantilly? Sweetened fresh vanilla whipped cream sauce?

Bien sûr. And, um, *beaucoup.* Lots of it, *s'il vous plaît.*

A bit embarrassing, to be so straightforward about one's greediness. But not so embarrassing that she'd do without the extra sauce.

He'd put down his glass and made a quick, almost peremptory gesture—no abashed, tentative *s'il vous plaît* for him. The girl hurried to bring him his own large slice of the tart, with its proper little dab of cream. Placing it on the table in front of him, she twisted her sharp gamine face into an expression compounded of admiration (for monsieur, at least) and impatience, it being all too clear that this wearisome pair of *anglais* were going to be taking their time over their *tarte tatin,* and that it would be far too long before she herself could quit work and get to bed—alone, *hélas.*

Yes, it is rather a pity, Mary thought. *But that should teach you, mademoiselle, even to think such thoughts about my monsieur.*

If so he could accurately be called.

The morsel of tart passed through her lips in a cloud of fluffy whipped cream and dispelled the little moment of pique. The food deserved her full attention. Or as much of her attention as she could spare from the sight of his mouth moving slowly above that dazzling high collar.

The food and wine's taste, texture, and perfume melded perfectly, sliding past her tongue and down her throat. She paused to watch him bring his fork to his lips again; he'd moved closer to the table now, and she could see, rather than guess, that he was looking into her eyes.

She felt herself tempted to eat more and more slowly. To flirt with downcast eyelashes from behind a napkin pressed to her lips, as though from behind a painted fan in a box at the opera. And then, almost as an after-thought, to bring another bite to her mouth, sucking sweetness from the apples and raisins, sinking her teeth into buttery crust, licking up any unctuous morsel of cream that might have stuck to her lips.

At this rate, they'd be here all night.

Which would be unfair and rather cruel to the serv-ing girl—even if she had been a bit impertinent.

She put a few *sous* on the table, took a candle to help guide her way back upstairs, and rose slowly from her seat.

❧

He caught up with her at the bottom of the stairs.

"Mary . . ." She'd been trying to imagine what it would feel like to hear him speak her name. It was more difficult than she'd expected. As though in a dream, she turned to face him.

". . . Wollstonecraft's *Letters Written During a Short Residence in Sweden, Norway, and Denmark.*"

Book in outstretched hand, he looked cordial and entirely at his ease. "Splendidly composed by an emi-nently reasonable creature. And an excellent choice for a lady traveling alone."

"Yes," she heard herself say. "Yes, I admire the au-thor excessively. I was named for her, you know."

He bowed slightly. "Indeed," he said. "And are you an equally reasonable creature?"

If she were, she wouldn't be speaking to *him*.

But the best means of self-defense were to take the offensive, wasn't that so? And just as well, because she had a question of her own.

"Is it a coincidence," she asked, "that we're both here tonight?"

"Alas, it isn't. I planned it when I heard you'd be traveling through here. Not the least bit coincidental . . . what say we call it fate instead?"

She laughed, in part with relief—surely she could manage *this* sort of nervous chatter. "All right. Certainly. Let's agree that we were fated to meet here. Because if it's fated, we're hardly responsible for the consequences."

He nodded. "Exactly so."

They were silent for a few instants now, considering each other from a shorter distance than across the dining room.

"You kept your hair short," he said. "I should have thought you'd go back to those elaborate braids and coils you were so fond of."

"They never really suited me; this is so much easier. And I'm a bit surprised at the dandy you've become." He'd also put on about a stone of muscle; the clothing he wore tonight would have overwhelmed the raw-boned young man he'd been, all sinew and nervous energy.

"The French have very clear expectations of what an English gentleman should look like. Mustn't disappoint 'em while we're occupying their country."

"No, I suppose not. *I'm* a bit disappointed, however. I should have liked to see you in your uniform."

"Sorry, too late. Cashed out quite suddenly."

She supposed she should ask about his plans. Or tell him of hers. She found that she didn't wish to have that conversation at the present moment. Nor did she wish that anything existed outside of the present moment.

"Do you think this is wise?" she asked.

But he also knew how to parry a question with one of his own. "Were we ever wise?"

She reached to take the book from him.

"I'll bring it," he said. "And look." He raised his other hand. "I've got another bottle of the Calvados, too, that you liked so much in the sauce. You manage the candle, Mary, and lead us up the stairs."

It seemed a very long way to her bedchamber. Long enough to convince herself that a certain giddiness was entirely to be expected, with all that food and drink in her. She wondered what Thomas would think, when she arrived at the door of her room with *him* at her side.

Not that it mattered. "Go to bed, Thomas," was all she'd need to say.

But Thomas was nowhere to be seen. Nor, when she threw open the door, was Peggy waiting to help her to bed.

Her companion nodded. "I told Thomas you wouldn't be needing either of them tonight."

"You spoke to Thomas?"

"When I called on my mother in Paris. The day after she promised you the loan of her coach. And then again just before you came down to supper."

She opened her mouth indignantly.

"No, don't blame her ladyship. She had no part in it; she was angry enough at me that I hadn't gone to see you. As for tonight, well, I worked the whole thing out with Thomas. He's a good, loyal fellow."

An angry pounding started up from one of the neighboring bedchambers. They shouldn't be disturbing their fellow lodgers by talking out here in the corridor. Kit turned a dour, puritanical-looking face in the direction of the noise and put a finger to his lips.

She thought of the tiny gesture he'd made downstairs and how it had brought the serving girl running. At Rowen, the servants were equally attentive, as though honored to feed and dress the neighborhood's first family. Most natural thing in the world, she supposed, for him to describe it as loyalty.

But *she* wasn't as loyal as that. Nor as complaisant.

He was speaking so softly that she found herself obliged to lean forward in order to hear him. "A pity," he said, "to pull little Peggy out of bed at this late hour, wouldn't you agree?"

As though it were all a rather bouncy bedroom farce.

For what if she'd demurred back there at the bottom of the stairs? Hadn't he considered that she might have murmured a polite "No, thank you"?

Of course not. He'd taken it all as rather a lark—this business of men and women, of urgent desire, and of a stupid, passive, even servile eagerness to forget the wrongs of the past. As though it should be an easy, rather jokey matter for her to fall back into bed with him.

She shrugged.

It had been an exhausting, confusing day. It was her last night on the continent.

"Indeed," she replied—a little too loudly; the pounding started up again. She found it difficult to control her voice; at this moment she was finding it difficult to control—or even to comprehend—a great many things.

She whispered, "Quite unnecessary to fetch Peggy, now that I've got *you* to undo my stays for me."

Her mouth had taken an ironical curve, but her hand was firm around her husband's as she drew him into the room and shut the door behind them.

Chapter Three

❦

The pounding had ceased. She folded her shawl over a chair by the window while he prowled about the room, picking up stray items and laying them down again. The air seemed to hum. His nervous energy had a familiar resonance; they might have been back in her bedchamber in Curzon Street. He'd deposited the bottle on the dressing table and was fiddling with the books atop the bed stand.

"Diderot, eh? Lying supine beneath the witty lady who wrote *Pride and Prejudice.* An excellent arrangement, don't you think, for the both of them?"

If she weren't careful, she'd laugh along with him.

"Come here," she said, "so I can look at you more closely."

In truth, to do more than simply look: she'd have to employ all her senses, to encompass the fact of his presence. Her lips trembled, parting to take a deep, heady breath of him. As once she'd taken greedy, icy gulps of water from the brook at the border of Rowen and Beechwood Knolls.

He'd taken hold of both her hands. Holding them down at her sides, his own large, strong hands about her wrists. They exchanged a tiny, conspiratorial smile; she gazed serenely upward, to take his measure.

•

The curtains stirred in a sweet salt breeze. A serene, temperate night; one wouldn't guess at the ferocious weather they'd been having just a few hours earlier. The fire burned low and even, its mellow warmth spreading upward around their legs.

Time was when the two of them would fall asleep like puppies on the floor, in front of just such a low, comfortable fire. Sated by some newly discovered pleasure, exhausted and beguiled by some elaborately contrived private diversion, congratulating themselves on one or another highly athletic position they could almost believe they'd invented. Housemaids and butler would have gone to bed long before, or might even be beginning their workday, if Lord and Lady Christopher had made a really late night of it.

Shaking her hands free of his, she lifted her fingertips to trace the lines of his face: curl of lip, bump at the bridge of a nose broken so many years ago, swoop of eyelid fringed with straight, thick black lashes.

Difficult to cease her explorations, even more difficult to turn away. "I meant it," she said, "about my stays."

"I'm quite at your service," he replied, "but we'll have to start with your dress, won't we? Such a sweet pale green . . . it's very pretty on you."

She turned to allow him to get to the hooks at her back.

"Pistachio green, it's called." Uttered so softly that she doubted he'd heard her.

A ridiculous state of affairs in a civilized nation—how had it come to pass that a lady was unable to get out of her clothes without assistance? If assistance was what you'd call what he was offering.

Peggy would have had the buttons and hooks undone in a trice. But Kit wasn't bad at it. (*Of course he isn't bad at it,* she reminded herself. *It's not as though he hasn't unhooked a lady's dress during the past nine years.*) He fumbled now and then, cursing good-humoredly at the dress's formidable array of hooks, the buttons being more for show than function. Still, he had marvelously deft hands for a gentleman. When he'd been bored, he'd sometimes amused himself by carving little birds or animals out of wood.

She'd burned all the ones he'd left behind.

His breath—slow and warm on the back of her neck—came more quickly now, a low, cool whistle of triumph at getting through all those fastenings. She glanced sideways at the window, at their reflections against the black night sky. He was grinning, a slightly chipped right front tooth catching a ray of moonlight just an instant before he bent his lips to trace the curve of her nape. The tip of his tongue, rough as a cat's, began its nimble descent down the bumps at the top of her spine.

Her dress would have slipped down around her if she weren't holding it up, her hands on her breasts, the chambray falling in uneven folds—high around her shins in front, drooping down to the floor behind her, from the V it made, open to the middle of her back.

He'd lowered her shift around the tops of her arms, his lips continuing downward to her shoulder blades at the verge of her corset.

Her wings, he'd once said. If she'd had fairy wings, they'd have sprouted right there. Like water lilies, from those pads of bone and muscle.

You're a poet, she'd exclaimed, like Ovid. Don't tell my brothers, he'd responded—so quickly that they'd both laughed at how scandalized he'd sounded.

He must be surprised, she thought, at how primly she was holding the dress about herself. The two of them had been so careless back in Curzon Street. Returning home late at night, you could trace their path through the house by a trail of discarded garments—coat and waistcoat, cloak and lace mantilla. . . . Neckcloth and petticoat like snowdrifts on the entryway's black marble floor.

His hands had crept around her, to grasp hers, prise them open and cause her to loose her hold on the fabric. *Oh, all right*. She sighed, and so, it seemed, did her gown, expelling a puff of air as it fell to the floor about her feet. Impatient and untidy as she'd ever been, she kicked the heap of cloth out of their way.

He cupped her breasts through the stiff fabric of her stays.... No, wait, there'd been a sudden loosening—he'd taken a lucky tug at the drawstring; his inquisitive, leisurely fingertips moved closer to her skin, taking the time, she thought, to remember the shape of her nipples, which were stiffening at an alarming rate. Caressing her through her shift—she was wearing an old one; damnable to be so short of clean undergarments; the silk had once been very fine but now it was almost threadbare—he could be touching her through a cobweb.

She must have leaned back against him. Her naked shoulders chafed against his coat; she could feel his hips, his belly—no use denying it, she could feel his cock—hard against her, through her petticoat.

"My stays," she repeated, in a more temperate voice than she'd have thought she could manage. "Please, they're awfully tight about my waist. The ... supper I ate, you know."

Forcing herself to take a step forward, she put an inch of space between their bodies to stop him, in any case, from continuing to press himself, in that disreputable, near-irresistible way, against her arse. Arms akimbo, she pushed her hands hard against the sides of her waist to relieve the tension of her flesh against the laces up her back.

"Ah," he murmured. His fingers had crept upward from her breasts to the shoulder straps, held fast with ribbon. No, not held fast, not now. She wiggled her shoulder blades, but he wouldn't be distracted from unknotting the strings at her waist.

"Ah yes, the supper you ate. I'd forgotten—no, in truth I've never forgotten—what a picture you make while you're enjoying your food. Press a bit harder for a moment, will you, so I can get a little slack on this loop...."

Much better, thanks . . . do you know, Mary, that watching you eat, I found myself envying the capon?"

She smiled despite herself. "I expect there's rather a smutty witticism to be made from that."

"I should have thought you'd have made it by now."

"But you see," she told him, "what a staid, well-governed, and circumspect lady I've become."

Or at least a less vulnerable one.

He snorted with laughter and then took a breath—"Ah, got it. No more need of your help, thank you, Lady Chris . . ."

But she could already tell that he'd gotten it, by the sudden easing of pressure about her torso, not to speak of the impatient breaths he was drawing while he waited for her—to? Well, that was rather the problem, wasn't it? She'd hoped that this step of her hastily conceived strategy would have become clear to her when the need arose. Though in truth she remained unsure. . . .

But she wasn't really obliged to do anything, was she? Even with the laces undone, she could keep her hands at her waistline and hold the garment's stiff canvas in front of her, as a sort of shield.

Hands firmly planted, she turned to face him. Her voice (she hoped) would issue light and abstracted, as if attentive to other concerns.

"Yes, well, my thanks for your assistance, Lord Christopher. Couldn't have managed without it, but as I'm sure must be shockingly evident, I've had a most tiring day. . . ."

His face darkening, jaw tensing, eyes slowly comprehending.

". . . And so," she continued, patiently now, as though to Mr. Frayne at his most irritatingly voluble, "as I won't be needing you for anything else tonight . . ."

He snarled. "That was . . ."

You've got the advantage, she told herself. *Have the courage to use it.*

She dropped her hands and let the length of boned canvas tumble to her feet.

"... low!"

"No, they're not," she informed him (and rather coolly too, she thought). "They—and I as well—have weathered the years quite admirably, thank you."

⋅⊱⋅

The hell of it, he thought, was that she was right. Her breasts bobbled high as ever on her torso. *Admirably* (yes, he rather thought so) and insolently too, the nipples still dark and erect, the firm roundness of her flesh entirely discernable through that utterly disreputable shift.

Less girlish, a bit fuller than when he'd seen them last (*hell, have I remembered her body so precisely, over the span of nine years, a large number of battles, and a larger number of women*? Distressingly, it seemed that he had). But a little additional fullness was certainly nothing he'd take exception to.

"That was mean, rotten, and unworthy of us both," he said.

At least, he thought, she had the decency to look a bit shamefaced. Still, "You were entirely too self-confident," she said. "Cocky, one might even say."

"Yes," he replied, "I expect I was. Whereas *you* weren't quite so confident of yourself as you pretended to be."

For if she had been, she wouldn't have been so quick with those last comments. Nor would she have hesitated—even for an almost indiscernible instant—to show herself.

Elegantly proved, Kit. As well it might be, for he suspected (or hoped, at least) that he was still the British nation's leading authority on Lady Christopher Stansell, née Mary Artemis Elizabeth Penley, at her willful, furious best.

"You shouldn't have doubted yourself," he added. Because it was true. And because it seemed rather to confuse her to hear him say it. Well, then, he'd take his pleasure from her discomfiture—and simply from gazing at her.

The years had added an inch or so of flesh to her waist. The corset had left some angry marks for him to kiss away. . . . Or so he'd imagined himself doing, perhaps just about now, after reaching around her to get the petticoat off and lifting the shift above her head directly afterward. Finally able to bury his face in her belly, the additional inch of flesh entirely welcome under his mouth . . . unless, of course . . .

"What are you smiling at?" she asked.

"I wasn't aware of smiling—a grimace, more like, produced by the ragin' discomfort, don't you know, that you've effected upon me. But I *was* wondering whether you wear those indecent, mannish new undergarments some ladies have taken up nowadays."

"Drawers?"

"Please tell me you don't."

⁂

The idea of having to worry about an additional cumbersome item of intimate linen struck her as surprisingly funny, while his relative good humor over her bad behavior struck her as simply surprising. Perhaps not so flattering as she would have liked. But likeable for all that, and a reminder that beneath all the anger and pride he'd once been a rather genial, and quite amusing, young man. She'd forgotten those aspects of his temperament. By the end of their time together his geniality hadn't been much in evidence, his jokes long gone. The good humor and silly, outré quizzing he'd loved to do (*drawers?* for it seemed he could still catch her unawares)— all that, she'd believed, were gone forever.

Drawers? She shook her head and gave him a level stare. "No, I don't."

⁂

She supposed (later, upon reflection) that she'd put out a hand then, as a gesture of conciliation or even apology. From which it reasonably followed that he'd taken it in his own, their fingers interlacing.

But as for how she had found herself so tightly and precipitously clasped against his front—in truth, she wouldn't be able to render a complete account of it. Though she was pretty sure it wasn't entirely his doing, now that his coat, waistcoat, shirt, and cravat were all pressed so importunately against her flesh, not to speak of his doeskin pantaloons, with all their buttons below.

Disagreeable, him being so covered up: she should do something about it.

In a moment. After she managed to gain control of the trembling that had started up somewhere between her belly and her knees, causing her to grasp and cling, not merely from the violence of her desire but from a commonsensical fear that her legs would give way. That she'd lose her balance if his mouth continued so warm, so eager and inquisitive, so apple-and-raisin sweet and so . . . well, so *all over* her lips and jaw and chin, leaving her no choice but to trust to the impressive new musculature in his limbs and shoulders.

So be it. Let him hold her upright, even while he continued to kiss her so roughly and juicily and altogether adorably. His lips had slid down her neck. Leaning back into his arms, she arched her spine, loosed her hands from around his shoulders, unbuttoned his waistcoat, and unknotted his cravat. The happy result being that only his linen shirt and her threadbare shift lay between them now.

A bit of a chafing sensation, actually. But she rather liked it. And more than liked the effect of his fingers touching and molding her nipples through it.

He pinched her. She squeaked rather gracelessly, and he laughed and gave her a great, smacking kiss—and a smack on the rump for good measure.

There'd been a time, years ago, when his hands had been too big for the rest of him. Tonight they were exactly the right size, and the one that wasn't playing with her breast had curved itself around her bottom now, pressing her so firmly against his belly and thighs that she could have no doubt (even if she hadn't caught a delicious glimpse) of how extravagantly eager he was for her. And even if their intertwined bodies' lurching progress toward the bed was proceeding far, far too slowly.

Not that she had any right to criticize, since the fact that they were moving at all was mostly his doing.

Yes, darling, she told him silently, *yes, I'll help. In just a moment. As soon as I pull your shirt from where it's tucked into the waistband—ah yes, lovely . . .*

Wait, she'd found a button, which by dint of much tugging, she'd succeeded in getting open. . . . Oh, dear, actually she'd ripped it from the fabric and sent it skittering across the floor. . . . At exactly the instant her calves collided smartly with the bed frame (which should have been painful but wasn't), and just a second before she felt herself lifted up and bounced onto her back and bum and . . .

How long had it been since she'd seen that particular smile of his? Amused and aroused, egotistical and overbearing . . .

Delightful, the simple pleasures of a good firm bed beneath her and his warm breathing weight on top.

And the satisfying certainty that all she really needed to do was lie still and smile back at him.

"Oh yes, much better," he told her. "Much better indeed."

He raised his weight onto his arms and dipped his head, licking her neck and throat and then nibbling her breast through the thin silk. Nettle cloth, the fabric was called—odd how certain words came unbidden at the most inopportune of moments. Was it actually made of nettle? It didn't feel like it—it felt smooth and sweet. Everything was sweet; he was feasting on her as though she were apples and cream.

She shouldn't have been so surprised by the quick updraft of sensation that had grabbed hold of her. . . .

. . . swept her into a vortex . . .

. . . and caused her to scream like that.

Though she might have expected that, before she'd

quite recovered her senses, he'd have contrived to lift her petticoat (all the while keeping his eyes upon her face) to enable her to rub her quim (no, no drawers, absolutely not!) against the bottom of his belly, to open herself and receive the quick entry of his cock, to moan and gasp, grasp and tighten her very wet and slippery self around him, and then (for he'd pushed her a few inches backward on the bed) to dig her heels into the mattress, so she could move in rapid, rough arcs, in rhythm with his thrusts.

His thrusts or (one might say) his pummeling. If one were able to say anything at all, if one could stop howling and mewling, groaning and giggling—and acting so utterly delighted with this abrupt and utterly undignified . . .

She hadn't expected to lose herself again so soon.

Expectations be damned. Pleasure was what mattered, losing and then finding herself once more, just in time for him to give way to his own excitement. He spilled himself outside of her (which was generous—not to say skillful) before collapsing so heavily that for a moment she thought he'd gone right to sleep.

She rather wished he had.

For now they finally *would* have to attempt a conversation.

Chapter Four

⁓⁓⟡⁓⁓

He was quite certainly awake; she could tell from how he was breathing. And how he was moving too—inch by sweet inch, just as she was, their intertwined bodies striving for a more harmonious alignment of limb and torso. She always loved this moment, the humor of it, the graceless intimate shifting about to make provision for the awkward extra arm that inevitably gets in the way of postcoital bliss. Until at last he'd gotten his body curved around hers, her head fitting (perfectly as ever) into the space below his clavicle.

Her thoughts drifted back to Curzon Street.

" 'Ere you are, gov'nor," the hackney driver would sing out, "and my compliments to your lady too." She and Kit had been favorites among the town cabbies: running, laughing and half-unbuttoned, up their front steps, they'd fling large coins behind them, all breathless eagerness to finish what they'd started on the way home. Though they might have to wake the servants to let them in, for they frequented such raffish parts of town that they'd sometimes lose their keys and purses to pickpockets.

Astonishing that the house had never been robbed. And that all they'd lost was each other.

Perhaps if they hadn't behaved so badly . . . she

should be regretting it. But instead she felt herself almost drunk on unbearably sweet nostalgia. A sigh escaped her lips before she could bite it back. He dropped a kiss on her forehead.

Had he guessed her thoughts? And could he also remember how much fun they'd had?

"I want you again," she said. "Soon. Before we begin remembering . . ."

He stopped her lip with a fingertip, laughed, and took her hand. "No chance that I could forget how demanding you are."

Just as well to turn it into a joke. There'd be no suppressing the memories, but she supposed there was no reason to speak about the horrible parts.

"Soon," he agreed. "Give me just a few more minutes."

A few more minutes would be quite acceptable, even nicer, perhaps, than the times when he'd been ready for another go-round before she'd entirely caught her breath. And maybe by the time they'd quite finished with each other, they *would* be too tired for conversation.

She snuggled against him while he kissed the inside of her wrist. And then her palm. Very softly, and oh, very nicely indeed, his lips and tongue insinuating themselves into hidden places where one wouldn't have thought there were any.

"And I'm not so demanding as all *that*," she protested happily. "I'm perfectly content. . . . Well, it's perfectly nice. . . ."

She wasn't quite sure what he'd contrived to do with his tongue just then. No, not his tongue—it was his teeth, and whatever he'd done had caused her to gasp and forget to finish her sentence.

She only knew that she wanted to do something equally nice for him. To trace the sinews of his neck with her lips; sniff, snuffle, and lick at him; nibble at his ear.

Of course, things would be nicer still if there were no obtruding buttons or wet and sticky layers of clothing interposed between their bodies. But on the whole, these were very minor inconveniences.

She wriggled a bit and settled her other hand into the little arch at the small of his back. Good. Excellent, in truth. He breathed deeply and let out a ragged chuckle.

"This wasn't at all how I planned it, though," he said. "I'd imagined us sipping our Calvados and exchanging compliments. . . ."

The bottle on the dressing table, next to her journal and portable writing desk. She'd utterly forgotten.

As she slipped away to get it, she could hear him re-arranging himself in bed. Backing up against the head-board, he'd propped his head against the bolster to watch her.

"Well, I do have some news," he said.

"Hell." She was fiddling with the cork.

He laughed. "Bring it here. I'll do it."

"It's coming, just give me a moment."

He sighed comfortably. "I was going to tell you later, but maybe we could drink a toast to . . . to a possible new career for me. You see, I've got a letter recom-mending me . . ."

Perhaps if she used the tail of her comb to wedge it out, or the little knife she used to trim her pens. . . .

But she'd missed a bit of what he was saying.

". . . a talent for organization and intelligence. You'd laugh to see how neatly I file my papers nowadays and how many details I have at my fingertips. An army needs to communicate—about supply routes, enemy movements, all of that—and it seems that I enjoy that sort of thing. And since I'm going to need something to do, now that there's peace, and Wellington will be end-ing the occupation soon enough anyway . . ."

He spoke quickly now, a little too carelessly. "Of course, there are still a great many details to attend to. I can't leave immediately. And I'm a bit nervous about it, if truth be told. . . . Letter of introduction to Lord Sidmouth."

She raised her eyes from the bottle.

"Oh, I know," he continued, "the Home Office

doesn't *seem* like much, shockingly small staff and what all. But there are important things to attend to. I don't wish to alarm you, but there's been rioting in England this last year. Anarchy. Insubordination. And now that there's peace on the continent, order and, um, legitimacy restored, it seems to me that one ought to be bringing all that home, where it's needed as well. For there's been a serious report to Parliament, about certain dangers."

She'd put down the brandy bottle somewhere after *Home Office,* and had completely forgotten about prising out the cork when he'd gotten to *order* and *legitimacy.*

For if he'd practiced for days—and perhaps he had, she thought sadly—he couldn't have found a worse way of putting it to her.

He *didn't wish to alarm her.* Yes, she expected that's what one *would* say to a lady who didn't read the newspapers. An understandable error: she'd been a very giddy young thing during their time in London. How could he know that she'd had a few thoughts, developed a few opinions since last they'd seen each other?

Perhaps if she spoke carefully, if she reasoned deliberately, if she simply *tried* hard enough, she could explain that it was hardly anarchy for a propertyless man to petition to vote. Or to claim the right to distribute literature, assemble with his fellows to discuss it.

In any case, she had to say *something.* He was already manifestly disappointed by her silence.

Slowly, reluctantly, she began, "But you must know that there's been a terrible harvest. Famine in some places, unemployment, soldiers returning home without pay. Men are angry, even in the . . . in *our* village.

"They believe themselves misgoverned," she continued. "They want to remedy it, by helping elect the Parliament. They petitioned all over England. They collected a million signatures, and their shameful government refused to look at it."

Perhaps the words *our village* had come out too sentimental. She didn't care. She'd first laid eyes on him there; it *was* their village. Unfortunately, he'd probably paid more attention to *shameful* and *misgoverned*.

Had she really needed to plunge them into argumentation?

She watched his mouth harden while he fiddled with his clothes and then swung his legs over the side of the bed.

Couldn't she, perhaps, have waited?

He'd been away for so long, fought bravely, risked his life for his country. It would be stupid to expect him to understand all at once.

But now that she'd begun . . . well, in truth he *ought* to know that the government he'd fought for had claimed the right to lock people up indefinitely without bringing charges against them—since last February, after the petition had been delivered.

She wasn't good at political discussion—a woman didn't get much practice. She could write things down clearly enough, but in the heat of disputation she tended to become overexcited, forget to watch her language.

She tried to calm her voice, which seemed to be shaking.

"Jessica's been writing me about the people in the village. They need so much; it's been so difficult. And of course Richard says . . ."

"Of course. Richard." He was staring down at her from where he stood, speaking stiffly through pinched, whitish lips.

⁂

So much for *that,* he thought.

So much for telling his exciting news to the person he most wanted to tell it to.

How many times had he imagined . . . *you see, I'm not such a scapegrace anymore, Mary.*

Spoken modestly, of course, with an ironic twinkle . . . *quite the responsible officer, don't you know . . . even Wellington agrees, in fact he . . .*

He'd been an idiot. He deserved whatever radical claptrap . . .

No, he didn't.

He didn't deserve to hear his government slandered.

Nor to hear whatever bloody *Richard* had to say.

It felt better to pace around a bit. *Better* being a relative term. It felt like hell.

She'd wrapped her shawl about herself and had begun her own pacing, in the half of the room nearest the fire.

Of course. She *would* take that half of the room, just as he'd become conscious that he was freezing, his hands in particular. Probably because there wasn't much blood in them—nor in any of his limbs, his vital fluids having reasonably assumed they'd be needed elsewhere just about now. He thrust his fists into his waistcoat pockets so precipitously that a button popped off and rolled under the bed.

How many more damn buttons am I going to lose tonight?

He'd pick it up later; right now he didn't relish the thought of scrabbling around on his knees while she vented her spleen at him.

For suddenly, they weren't talking about politics at all. If you could even call what they were doing *talking*.

Lecturing. Hectoring. Reviving vicious old arguments and raking over horrid old events.

"Yes, it *does* still hurt," she was saying. "Even after all this time. Of course it does. One doesn't forget a husband's cheating and lying, staying out nights whoring, and sometimes not coming home till noon. Not to speak of pretending to love me and then not touching me for weeks—as though I were . . . hideous, repulsive. After that first year when we'd been so happy—or so I'd believed."

He'd thought that having popped into bed first— refreshing their memories, in a manner of speaking, with a taste of what they'd once had together—it would give them a kind of incentive to work out their differences. Ignore the difficult parts, at least for a while.

Lead with your strength. Any boxer in Britain could tell you that. Do what you're best at.

No question what *they'd* always been best at.

Too bad it hadn't worked out that way. For he loathed apologies and had hoped to avoid that part of it.

"I *couldn't* touch you that time," he said. "Well, you know why. I'd got a disease.... Couldn't touch anybody. I expect I should have explained it to you more carefully, the details, you know. But it made me shy, talking about that sort of thing to a lady...."

She'd sat down at the dressing table, her neck rising from the folds of the shawl. The back of a woman's neck, he thought, a few bright chestnut curls nestled in the declivity at its center, was every bit as provocative as the parts people made more of a fuss about.

For a mad moment he imagined himself dragging her from the chair, tossing her onto the bed—solving their problems the easy way, by exercise of force. The thought rather repulsed him. Not that they hadn't played at such things—and of course he knew plenty of men who felt it their right to impose themselves on a woman, as though to protect the public order. But no matter how infuriating she could be, he wasn't one of those men. Nor would he be playing, if he tried to take her right now.

He peered over her shoulder, at her white face glaring up at him from the mirror.

"Yes, and when you *did* heal—isn't it odd, Kit, how you were too shy to tell this lady *that* crucial detail, that you were quite well and ... functioning again. *He's at White's,* I'd tell myself—*or at the fives court watching the pugilists. He's doing one of his gentlemen's things that he suddenly needs to keep secret from me, these nights he stays out so late.*"

When she spoke again her words fell heavy and dull as lead. "And so I had to find out for myself about that . . . actress, as I believe she called herself . . . hearing the news at Gunter's, of all places, over my favorite . . . pistachio ice, from some ladies who didn't think I was listening."

The timbre of her voice grew stronger, burnished by irony now. "Let me amend that—from some ladies who must have known full well that I was listening."

※※※

For she'd already borne some animosity from that particular set, whinnying like overbred mares in a paddock at whatever stupid joke had been making the rounds at White's Club.

Better concentrate her fury on his slut of an actress. About whom, it seemed, he had the grace to evince a hint of discomfiture.

Or was that a trick of the light from the fire? He stood in front of it now, his hands (gracefully, elegantly—amazing that she could find them so at this moment) spread out to warm himself.

You don't need the fire. Touch me instead. Here, where I'm so very warm. Her thighs trembled; she'd parted her legs without realizing it. She clamped them shut. Damn those absurd stray thoughts (if thoughts they could be called), tripping her up amid the worst of their arguments, disarming her before his next round of attack.

"That actress meant nothing, dammit, and you know it. And *you* were out too, quite often, in the afternoons, when I'd be, um, waking up. Gadding about with that swine Morrice . . ."

"He wanted to meet Sir Francis Burdett, who'd been Papa's friend, and I was happy to do him the favor of presenting him to a circle of intelligent people. He'd had enough—as I expect I had too—of the imbecility that passes for talk in Mayfair and St. James. He was interested in learning. . . ."

※※※

"About what mush-minded Jacobins thought? About what *you* thought?"

Politics again. Was there any more deadly combination, he wondered, than eros and politics?

"Please, Mary, the only thing Richard Morrice was interested in learning was what was under your skirts."

❧

She blinked at a sudden loud crash. Thunder and lightning: an unanticipated storm must have blown in from the Atlantic.

Nice to imagine so. Nice to delay acknowledging, for even an instant, that she'd hurled the bottle of Calvados at him.

Invigorating in its way.

She supposed it was relief she was feeling for not having hurt him. He'd leaped out of the way; the bottle had shattered against the mantel. Brandy was dripping down to the hearth, raising blue flames as though from a plum pudding and causing a ridiculously festive round of popping.

Well, he shouldn't have said that about Richard. Though of course she and Richard shouldn't have given him cause to say it. Not that they ever *would* have, if . . .

They were shouting at each other now.

It appeared that a part of her had wandered off into a corner of the room to witness their verbal sparring. Quite as though she were a spectator at a match between a pair of boxers.

A good, experienced couple of pugilists, each of them leading with a classic gambit.

"But he was my closest friend, Mary!"

"Rubbish! You'd begun ignoring him, quite as you were ignoring me!"

Feinting, parrying, now; dancing on their feet, catching their breath while exchanging stupid, babyish insults. She'd never minded that he wasn't much above medium height, but *he* minded terribly—he left her the opening; she took it. It was as easy a jab as ever. And *he* could always get to her about certain inadequacies in her toilette—damn him anyway, for making fun of the state of her undergarments.

Ah yes, and now the new moves they'd picked up during their years apart. The political vocabulary: *Tory* and *radical. Habeas corpus. Treason.*

"Danger in the countryside," he said. "Sedition, even if your friends are too blind and naïve to see it."

"Nonsense," she snapped. "Just because your family has always and entirely opposed any extension of rights to the general populace doesn't mean . . ."

They circled the ring, taking the time to repeat some of their earlier gambits. The actress . . . but I wouldn't have *looked* at her, he was shouting, if *you'd* ever listened when . . . no, of course I didn't try to explain it to *her,* why should I, *she* wasn't my bloody damn wi—

"*Nor would* I *be at this moment, if we lived in a civilized nation.* If the law didn't insist on considering the two of us one person—and you know very well which bloody one of us they mean. But I shall manage. I've managed thus far to live a quite reasonable and satisfying·life; I shall continue to do so, and you can like it or . . . or lump it. England isn't so small a country that we can't both reside in it."

But she must be running out of energy. She imagined a boxer staggering against the ropes. *One final offensive,* she thought—against him and against her own ambivalence.

"While as for being your wife—perhaps I shall give you cause to put an end to that."

Had she scored a knockout blow?

The pity was that it never felt quite as good as you thought it would.

"Suit yourself, Mary," he was saying. "I wish you well with your *reasonable* life. Of course, you never really did have the dash, the ton . . ."

Bits of glass crackled below the soles of his boots as he made his way to the door.

✣

Had she meant to speak of the possibility of divorce?

Until this moment, it had remained only that—a distant and rather abstract possibility.

Not so distant now. She'd opened a Pandora's box; the room seemed to swarm with nasty little winged things, with names like *alienation of affections, bring suit, criminal conversation, Parliamentary divorce*.

A legal nightmare and a public ordeal.

But at the end of it, she'd be free to marry a man she wouldn't want to pitch things at.

She found that she was pacing again, between the fire and the window. *I freeze, I fry,* the old poets liked to say. . . . Simple, not inaccurate, and not entirely unpleasant.

Her hands were icy, her breasts were warm. . . . Dear Lord, her nipples were hard and erect as cherry stones, through the fabric, between her fingers.

She'd have to watch where she stepped, with all that glass on the floor. Too bad; she'd wanted to taste the brandy straight. They'd have drunk it by now. She'd have had his boots off by now. His boots, and probably more than that.

She ached from her thighs to her belly. And didn't exactly mind it.

There hadn't been a great many lovers in his absence. But those there had been, she'd chosen with great care, both for their attractions and their inability to upset her life's precarious balance. Capable, intelligent, and always profoundly self-involved men: a painter, a married physician from Edinburgh, a Milanese patriot smarting under restored Hapsburg rule—each of them secure in his busy, substantial life, with his own passions, commitments, and obligations. The affairs had been discreet, satisfying, meticulously planned and administered. No point deceiving oneself that a liaison could be kept entirely secret; the important thing was to maintain a certain public esteem for social convention. In each case it had been she who'd ended the connection, and there'd never been bitterness or recrimination.

An impressive thing to have kept up over the years, and an exhausting one. Which was why, when Matthew Bakewell had announced that he wanted more from her, she'd been disposed to take him and his importunities seriously. And why it wasn't a comfortable thing to find that her troublesome and entirely unmanageable husband could still make her feel so riotous and disorderly, so dazed, addled, lost, and distressingly exhilarated.

Too disordered to think any further about divorce; she'd wait until morning for that. Meanwhile, there was laudanum, put aside for strong megrims, and who could cause her a worse headache than Kit? No wonder Peggy had left the corked brown bottle so visible, with a glass of water right beside it.

Four careful drops, so distinct she could almost hear the tiny splashes they made: she watched the little dark clots of liquid spread, swirl, and attenuate, like feathery tiny clouds, before disappearing into the clear water.

She swallowed it down, threw off the rest of her clothes, slipped naked below the quilt, and—quickly and coldly, skillfully and purposefully—touched herself until she cried out. Until the aching became a burning, a hard white light easing to a warm orange glow, until the trembling stopped and the candle guttered and died and the visions faded, of blazing eyes and strong tapering hands, of pain and anger, disillusionment and rivalry—oh, and other visions, memories from youth, of things they'd done and things they hadn't dared to try. The smell of lemon oil, warm, smooth cherrywood surface of a desktop, her face and breasts crushed against it. All subsiding now to a dull dark red, as though dimly painted upon the velvet insides of her eyelids. Ebbing, waning, flickering. Until she slept.

Chapter Five

It isn't easy, even with the sunlight pouring through the window, for a maid to rouse her mistress from a heavy drugged sleep. Especially a maid who's moving a bit slowly herself, and who can't help rubbing her own red and swollen eyes as she assesses the disorder about her.

I should want to give me a good shaking, Mary chided herself, *if I were in her place.*

The night before was still a bit of a blur. The visions—best, she suspected, that they remain a thrilling, rather wicked blur. But the memory of what they'd said last night would come back, probably sooner than she wanted. Her limbs were heavy; she forced herself to be passive, to move where Peggy prodded her, to keep gentle and limp beneath the towel washing the smell of brandy off her, the strong little hands buttoning her into her clothes.

"You should eat something, my lady." The girl mumbled the words—or something like them—through pins stuck in her mouth.

She spoke more clearly now that she'd gotten Mary's fichu tucked and tacked inside the neckline of her dress. "The eggs is very fresh here. Me and Tom, we were, uh, hungry. . . . Well, you should try some eggs. And one o' them crescent roll things too."

So it was Tom, *now*—me *and* Tom. Lucky pair, Mary thought, to have spent . . . well, it probably wasn't accurate to say they'd spent an uneventful night, but she expected it had been less wearing on the emotions than her own. The girl's face was flushed and rather puffy, her mouth soft and babyish as she turned from her neatly dressed mistress to the bedchamber that smelled (and rather looked) like a public house after a rough brawl.

"Yes, thank you. Perhaps I shall try to eat, Peggy"—turning, waving a vaguely apologetic hand at the detritus and setting off down to the dining room.

The impertinent serving girl from last night's supper was nowhere to be seen. Which would be no surprise, Mary thought, if Kit's old patterns had run true. Her drugged sleep shed a protective haze about her; on the other side of it doubtless lay some low, unworthy sentiments. Too bad she wanted the coffee; emotional clarity wouldn't be pleasant. She accepted a cup from the plainer girl who offered it, and opened the book she'd brought down with her.

"Plus de café, madame?"

"Non, merci." It must be time to depart. How long, she wondered, had she been scowling from behind her spectacles at the novel in her hand?

But the more important question was how long *he'd* been staring down at her from just a few feet away. Face livid and unshaven above barely respectable linen, hair wet and combed back from his forehead—he'd been washed down like a racehorse. His valet hovered somewhere behind his elbow, lest he pitch over, as he looked alarmingly likely to do.

What a nice little barrier a pair of spectacles made between oneself and the world. Sliding them just an inch farther down her nose, she gazed at him from above the thin gold wire at the lenses' upper rims.

"You look ghastly," she said. "Why aren't you asleep or . . . or still with that girl? I'm disappointed; it's not like you, Kit. I should surely have thought that she . . ."

"Disappeared quite early," he told her, "after I'd
drunk myself into a state making indecent toasts to you,
just before collapsing . . ."

She could feel the ends of her mouth quivering. He
winked; she suppressed a fledgling smile. *Don't press
your luck, darling.*

"Wait, no—I didn't collapse on the floor. Almost
did, yes, right. But she's stronger than she looks, a real
peasant—propped me up on her shoulder and walked
me to the bed, where I rather drifted off, just this side
of stupefied and almost enjoying the sensation of being
parted from all the coins in my pocket."

He patted himself around the waistcoat (which looked
even more disreputable with its bottom button missing)
and croaked out a short attempt at laughter. "Pocket
watch too. A gift from you quite possibly. Engraved, as I
remember—most charmin' obscure poetic stuff."

Had he still been carrying it last night?

"She must have found it rather a humiliation," he
added, "that a nation of such buffoons could have de-
feated *l'empéreur* Napoléon." He shook his head.
"Clever fingers on her. Too bad . . ."

"And so you made your shambling way down here to
tell me about it?" Pretending it was a matter of indiffer-
ence that all he'd given the girl was the contents of his
pockets.

"I shambled down here to inform you that I'm coming back to London today. I shall be staying at my
mother's house in Park Lane."

He swayed rather alarmingly on his feet as he spoke,
and winced as the valet put out an arm to steady him.
"Well, later today," he said, "an early afternoon boat,
perhaps. I should have liked to accompany you, but
Belcher here"—he nodded in the direction of the
valet—"is of the opinion I'm not quite up to a choppy
voyage across the Channel this morning. Unless you'd
like to wait, to accompany *me*."

"Back to England today!" She pushed the spectacles
back over the bridge of her nose. "But you said . . ."

"I lied. Well, no, I didn't, not exactly. I exaggerated—rearranged a few points. There *were* a great many details to attend to, official ones, rather. . . . Letters of introduction—oh, but I told you that part, didn't I? Anyway, I got them done quickly. The position I'm after . . ."

She wouldn't allow him to draw her into another argument. "Yes. Well. I'm sure we'll manage to pursue our separate courses in town. Your confreres at White's, the girls at Mrs. Goadley's, will all be delighted, I'm sure, to welcome you. . . ."

"The position at the Home Office . . ." His voice was firm, though his gaze flickered for a moment—defiant, even if half-abashed at his evident need to emphasize it.

"You already told me. You fancy a minor position in one of Lord Liverpool's government's smaller ministries."

"You find it unlikely?" he asked.

"Well, if someone were to ask me who the most *ungoverned* personage I'd ever met was, I shouldn't have to think awfully hard about it. Shallow, callow . . ."

"I've been nine years at war, Mary. Give me credit for having learned a little organizational ability, a few things about power and administration and the flow of intelligence. . . ."

"You can barely stand up, and you've clearly spent the last few hours with your head over a basin."

"Fortunately, she was kind enough to leave me with one in reach. Whereas you, Lady Christopher . . ."

"I slept quite well, thanks."

"You slept unaided?"

"I took something for headache."

"My point exactly."

She'd let him have that one. Still, "You thought you needed only to stride back into view for me to put aside a perfectly well-regulated, carefully constructed, and really quite satisfying . . ."

"Yes, you keep telling me how satisfying . . ."

"Must you interrupt me? An *extremely* satisfying life—as though it would have been a simple business

for me these last years, for *any* woman whose husband
left her so suddenly and scandalously . . ."

"I didn't think. . . ."

"No, you didn't."

He opened his mouth and then closed it without having said anything.

"While in the matter of the Home Office, Kit, you
obviously don't understand . . ."

"You made it clear enough last night, the veritable
encyclopedia of things I don't understand. No, please,
don't pout. You've already proved yourself a woman of
action. Look at all the heavy kitchen pottery on that
dresser. Here, I'll get you a pitcher to toss at me."

She shouldn't have begun ragging him on about politics. Especially, she thought, after her decorous little
speech about their *separate courses*.

"I must go. The packet boat will be leaving soon. I've
got quite a bit of traveling before I'm home again in
Derbyshire."

He shrugged. "Dismal place. Just as well that I'll be
too busy to come down. Difficult to avoid each other in
such a small, close neighborhood.

"And anyway," he continued, "we shouldn't be seen
together any longer. Not if you want me to bring suit
against your friend Mr. Bakewell. The divorce courts
don't look kindly on collusion."

So he knew about Matthew.

She tried to push her spectacles higher on her nose,
but they were already quite as close to her eyes as they
could be. She could see him most clearly as he explained
what bringing suit for a divorce would entail.

He should have to sue the man for alienating her affection, then bring suit against her for adultery in eccle-
siastical court, and only then petition Parliament for
their Act of Divorce.

"*If* I can afford to do so. It costs about a thousand,
you know."

Again, he stressed the necessity that they not be seen
together upon their return to England. If it appeared

that he and she had planned this, the government would reject his petition for divorce.

An exceedingly lucid presentation, especially coming from someone who'd spent the night with his head over a basin. His eyes were red, his posture increasingly unsteady, and (when he leaned forward to make a particular fine distinction), the smell of his breath was really quite dreadful.

"Of course, you and your Manchester manufacturer must become *demonstrably* adulterous. And I shall have to hire spies, you know, to catch you at it."

Your Manchester manufacturer—reeking and disreputable, he'd still managed a most fastidious, Stansell-like curl of the lip.

She ignored it.

"Spy away," she said. "He wants us to be able to marry, and he's willing to bear the scandal. We both are. He'll be returning to England for Midsummer Eve. Just don't set your spy on us at Beechwood Knolls, I beg you. I shall be leaving soon after midsummer. Wait and keep my family out of the business."

"Your servant." His bow was less than graceful. "My congratulations. He sounds a splendid fellow. Too bad I shall only make his acquaintance indirectly, through the legal process."

"Yes, it is too bad. But then, you won't be crossing paths with us very often. You'll doubtless marry again as well, to a lady of great dash and ton. Who will admire you. *And* your position in the government."

But here, mercifully, was Thomas in his newly brushed mulberry Rowen velvet. For the coach was ready, the lady's things were all packed up (yes, and a very good morning to *you*, Lord Christopher), and they must, indeed, depart directly.

Which (thank you, Thomas) the lady was altogether eager to do, wishing as she did to put the width of the Channel between herself and his lordship—who had, in any case, already turned away, all shaky, aggrieved, crapulous dignity, and allowed his valet to lead him back upstairs.

Chapter Six

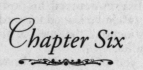

"I'm hardly surprised." Richard Raddiford Morrice's northern voice made a soft rumble against the cluttered room's bookshelves, paneling, and purple drapery at the windows.

"For the two of you *would* wait until the last possible moment," he continued, "to build up the suspense, set the level of histrionics as impossibly high as you could manage. Your final night on the continent—quite banal, really, Mary." His steel pen glinted in the lamplight above a sheaf of papers, held with a slightly unsteady hand.

Mary groaned from the depths of a plush armchair in the room's far corner. "You've been writing your newspaper's theater criticism of late, Richard."

"To my shame. But for the next issue I'll be taking on a new chap to do it. Young and eager, far better educated at his dissenting academy than Kit and I at Oxford—got more learning in him, for that matter, than Kit, I, and a goodly percentage of the House of Lords taken together . . ."

"But in the main," she continued, "you're quite correct. We were worse than histrionic. We were stupid, impatient, and less tolerant of one another than ever. Without even our youth to excuse us."

For a few minutes, the only sound in the dimly lit room was the low fire's crackle.

"Still, it's the only thing." Richard's response seemed to come from a distance away. "Divorce, I mean. Both of you starting your lives afresh—it's what you need. Though I must confess that I'd rather hoped otherwise."

"You're very forgiving," Mary said.

"I'd like Kit to forgive me as well," Richard replied.

She'd made Richard's acquaintance soon after her marriage. Kit had sometimes spoken of a friend and protector at Eton. But their paths had diverged at university, Richard passing his examinations in the undistinguished fashion befitting his station while Kit got sent down for dueling and riotous behavior. Bumping into each other in London, however—Richard setting up at the Albany just when Kit and Mary had taken the house in Curzon Street—the two had enthusiastically resumed their friendship and Kit had invited Richard to dine with them at home.

She hadn't been eager to have a guest before they'd gotten the furniture in proper order (though in truth, they never really got the furniture in order). But Richard professed to find it refreshingly informal. He brought a Meissen clock for the mantelpiece, played with their dog, praised the turtle soup, and in all ways made them feel quite the clever pair for having run away together.

He'd shared his reminiscences as well. Lord Kit had gathered a certain notoriety at school, Richard said, for never crying when he was caned—and given how many times he'd been caned . . . well, he must have set some sort of record, for the lower forms anyway. And so I was obliged to make him my fag, send him on errands and so forth, just to keep him out of the way of fighting and mischief.

Kit had bowed modestly, and Richard had winked. He's good at errands, he said; don't hesitate to set him fetching and carrying, Mary. And who would have expected—he raised his glass, sentimental or perhaps just tipsy—that such a skinny, scrappy little chap would go get himself such a trump of a wife.

After which the three of them were often seen in town together. A bit timid with members of the opposite sex, Richard hadn't seemed to mind when Mary and Kit would begin making eyes at each other around three in the morning, to disappear soon after. Anyway, he'd soon be going home to Yorkshire, to become squire and magistrate, master of the hunt, and husband to the nice enough young woman everyone expected him to marry.

It hadn't worked out that way. Aimlessly at first, he'd begun a course of reading, his lodgings cluttered and later choked with pamphlets and periodicals from obscure bookshops, broadsheets picked up along the street.

Well, one can't play and carouse all the time, can one? he'd asked.

One can try, Kit had said, drawing Mary closer to him. She laughed and kissed his cheek, and Richard had laughed too.

No, really, Kit had insisted. Better to carouse than bury one's nose in poisonous screeds that wish you and me and our families dead or at least starving.

Why not?

In his modest way, Richard had been remarkably logical-minded. If you were going to frequent dangerous neighborhoods in the hours before dawn, he asked, why not also entertain some dangerous ideas? As for reading, best to try something that would shake you up a bit, make you think about your place in the world and how others saw you.

Which is all very well for Richard, Kit had commented to Mary later that evening. Because Richard's never felt a moment's real doubt about anything.

How somber he'd looked. When just a moment before he'd been so charming, pulling off her stocking with his teeth and running his tongue from her knee to her instep; it was all she could do not to nudge his head back downward.

But no matter how seductively she kissed, stroked, and nuzzled at him, her senses heightened but also befuddled by the opium they'd been eating—it seemed that he would talk, about the things nobody talked about.

He'd stared into space. Richard, he said, has never had to wonder about himself or his origins, or . . . anything.

His place in the world, he'd added, in a very low voice.

It doesn't matter, she might have replied.

She might have winced, with the guilty knowledge that marrying her hadn't done much for his place in the world. Or perhaps she'd laughed. Isn't the world agreeable enough? You've got the Stansell name, there's plenty of money settled on us, and you've got me wanting you, at this very moment, more than I can fairly stand.

But most likely she'd made a small moue of impatient desire.

The opium set a strict order to one's wants. And uppermost among hers right then had been the absolute necessity that he remove her other stocking, the pink silk being so constricting against her skin and the color so . . . well, so jarring and out of place against the more subtle and gorgeous hues of his and her naked flesh in the lamplight, the stocking being the only item of clothing either of them was wearing at the moment.

Please, darling?

And so he'd shrugged, dipped his head downward, and proceeded with the serious business of making elegant, complicated love to his very demanding wife.

Even as Richard continued scandalizing his fellows at White's with dangerous ideas. Pamphlets gave way to slender and then thicker books; he allowed his club membership to lapse at the time (as he confessed much later) he'd come to fancy himself in love with Mary.

Which also had been when Kit had almost stopped coming home at night, and Mary became quite frantic and in need of all the attention and affection she could get.

What a relief, she'd thought, to have Richard to pour out her rages and fears to. What a comfort to confide in someone who knew Kit as well as she did.

And what a pleasure that there was someone who obviously still found her pretty. For she was only twenty-one and she *was* still pretty, even if her bloody damn husband preferred to spend his nights with garishly painted doxies and had got a nasty inflammation for his troubles.

Could it really be taking such a long time to heal?

She'd wept and wailed, drenching her handkerchief and quite ruining Richard's coat, her head against his shoulder and the rest of her body shuddering in his arms.

Until her sobs subsided, and he and she drew back to opposite ends of the settee, each staring at the other as they smoothed hair and straightened disordered garments.

Richard didn't call for the week after that. *Good,* she thought, for she wouldn't be inviting him. Even better if she took a holiday. She'd go to Glasgow as soon as her nephews got over whatever illness Julia had written was keeping them bedridden and wrapped in flannel this time.

She congratulated herself upon these excellent resolutions until the day when Kit didn't come home at all. Half past one in the afternoon: she'd been weeping and wringing her hands since shortly after midnight.

No use continuing to agonize over his safety. He was probably passed out in a gutter somewhere—or sleeping off his inebriation in the arms of . . . but even thinking the name of his *soi-disant* actress felt like grasping a fistful of nettles.

Kit deserved to feel as miserable as she did. Not that he actually *would* be hurt; well, how could he be? He was never home anymore. And not that she'd *want* to hurt him—but if he *did* saunter in, well, she'd like to see the look on his face when he saw what *she* was capable of, in her own bed and with someone who admired and appreciated her.

Though of course she hadn't liked it at all when, in the way of a folk tale's wishes coming horribly, literally true, he'd strolled upstairs with torn coat, dirty, grinning face, and scuffed boots. She could remember all too well his words in the hall as he'd approached, "And so I says, 'Please, sir . . .' " doubtless the beginning of a wickedly entertaining tale of fisticuffs and night wardens, just before he reached the bedroom door and did, indeed, get his eyeful of what she was capable of.

Even now, she could hardly bear the memory of how his words and grin had melted away, mouth fallen open, unshaven cheeks caved in and red-rimmed eyes like ice, before he stumbled backward and disappeared from her sight, and she began pushing at Richard and screaming and pleading for Kit to come back.

She could summon up Richard's image with equal clarity; how young, how pale and frightened he'd looked without his shirt and neckcloth. But they'd all been young, at least until that moment. It rather robs you of your first youth, to comprehend how cruel it is to use someone you don't love, to take revenge on someone you do.

They'd also been too young—or at least Kit and Richard had been—to grasp the absurdity of dueling over it. Too proud of what they'd called their honor, too stupidly enamored of their reputations; it still sickened her to know that one of them might have killed the other out on Hampstead Heath, while she sobbed and hiccupped, and Jessica patted and hugged her and gave her doses to make her sleep.

And when Kit did come home again—the only time she'd seen him until Calais—they'd been too furiously incoherent to do anything but hurl invectives and some rather good porcelain at each other. The Meissen clock had been reduced to shards, powder, and a few crazily spinning gearwheels beneath their feet, while their little dog yelped piteously from behind the fire screen.

Richard's right hand still trembled from where Kit's bullet had torn the nerves in his forearm. He was clumsy at attaching his papers together, and many of the pins had fallen onto the Turkey carpet.

"We all wronged one another," she said now. "But you must cease hoping. Kit will gather evidence on me, prepare a case, sue Matthew for 'alienating my affections,' and then we'll finally be free of each other. As though my affections were anyone's to alienate but my own . . ."

Their laughter gave way to the rustle of the fire and the scratching of pen on paper, many sheets of it strewn about, some held together with pins that winked under the lamps. A few pages were splashed with tea, Richard having coughed and spluttered in dismay at Mary's announcement that Kit wanted to work for the Home Office.

No matter, he'd told her—the pages were just early proofs. He'd been making his first corrections for the next issue of *Everyman's Review* while Mary replied to the letters she'd found waiting for her at his house in Lincoln's Inn Fields.

She hadn't provided a great deal of detail about Calais. But Richard wouldn't have needed much, knowing Kit as he did, and continuing to love him—though a gentleman might not have expressed it that way.

Bless him for remaining such a good friend to her. And bless his wife, Anna, for having become her friend as well.

The three of them had enjoyed a gay supper upon her arrival last night. Finishing off several bottles of good claret, they'd laughed, gossiped, and interrupted one another for hours, speaking of art and history, Mary's travels and the affairs of the nation. A satisfying, wide-ranging conversation, and yet constructed with some art to exclude any reminder of long-ago events at Curzon Street.

Astonishing how meticulous we can be, Mary reflected, *who profess our shared contempt for petty social convention.* But Anna was the true artist among them.

The offhand announcement, over this morning's muffins and marmalade, of a shopping expedition in Bond Street, and would Mary care to accompany her?

The bright nod in Mary's direction, coffee cup clinking against gold-rimmed saucer for emphasis.

The significant pause: chin raised, cornflower-blue eyes so coolly communicative of their owner's wishes that Mary had no choice but to plead exhaustion and the necessity of catching up on her correspondence.

"Yes, of course. How foolish of me. Well, I'll leave you to Richard. You two can shut yourselves up in his dreary study with your papers and some strong tea. Just finish it up quickly, will you, so we all can go for a drive later."

Brava, Anna. And bravo to Richard for finding himself such a perfect mate.

"Please do come in," he called now, in response to Anna's rap on the door, precisely two hours after he and Mary had closeted themselves in his study.

Mama and Papa had sometimes arranged their affairs in this manner ("I shall disturb you and your guest in an hour, Joshua." "An hour and a half would be better, my dear."). Watching a smiling Anna make her way to the table and begin repinning the papers, Mary allowed herself an instant's pure envy.

But only one, she reminded herself. *You're entitled to only one such moment for every visit with these good friends,* so snugly and smugly sure of each other, their beliefs, and their roles in the universe's scheme for humanity's betterment. Anna doubtless spent part of every day in this "dreary study," helping Richard keep his work in order so he could produce the twice-monthly newspaper he was so proud of.

But Mary's spite had already given way to bemused affection for a good friend's more than good opinion of himself.

Richard's political convictions had outlasted his infatuation. By now he was a familiar presence in drawing rooms where the furniture was worn but the ideas glittered like fresh-minted coins. He'd first encountered Matthew Bakewell at one of these venues last year, and presented him to Mary soon after.

And when he'd come into his fortune, he'd simply poured it into the *Review,* publishing the opinions of everyone he admired, treating his moral and artistic heroes to good food and excellent drink, and occasionally providing more substantial help as well. Even Mary had once contributed an essay, a rather dry thing on the Corn Laws under the name of Edward Elyot (she'd only shrugged this morning when Richard had wondered if Mr. Elyot might like to try something else).

His life with Anna was amiable and exceedingly comfortable, his kitchen and wine cellar superb. His opinions were bracingly radical, but (Mary had to allow) in certain particulars comfortably static as well. Although Kit had professed to have no political sense whatsoever, he'd been most prescient when he'd told her years ago that historical events wouldn't ever cause Richard to alter his hero worship of Bonaparte, the Scourge of Tyrants.

(And yes, she thought now, some of the rulers Napoleon had deposed *were* tyrants. And no, some of them were not. It would be a neater world if one could have it all one way or the other. But then, it would be a neater world if she weren't plagued with all these thoughts and memories.)

"Would anyone care for some luncheon?"

She blinked; Anna had opened the drapes to let in some midday sunshine.

"Yes, thanks," she heard herself saying. "I'm quite ravenous. And then what about that ride in the park you promised us?"

❧

Park Lane stretched away to the right of the Morrices' barouche; Hyde Park lay in front of them. Mary kept her eyes straight ahead until their carriage entered the park.

No, she told Anna and Richard, she wouldn't be able to stay an extra day. "Thanks so much for inviting me, you darlings, but Jessica needs me; I shall have to depart quite early tomorrow."

Not that her sister wasn't an excellent manager. "There was the period when her steward took advantage of her grief to rob her, but she's got a good new man helping her now. Still, she needs companionship—of someone more her age than her daughter. Julia's been there, and now it's my turn to help her prepare for the Midsummer's Eve party. There wasn't one last year, of course, while she was mourning for Arthur, and also because things were so bad in the neighborhood. At least things are a little better now; nobody's breaking any more knitting frames."

Richard cleared his throat. "Very little machine breaking these days. The actions of the last few years were actually quite successful; the men got better wages out of it. Good that they were so scrupulous about only disabling the frames that belonged to cheating owners—*and* that produced inferior stockings. Luddite machine breakers weren't stupid; they weren't out to destroy their own livelihoods."

He paused. "Though of late the recession in the textile industry has caused new hardships. Together with the bad harvest and worse weather."

Jessica had written about whole families living on oatmeal, and not much of that.

"But I hear good things as well," he continued. "Hampden clubs, Parliamentary reform societies springing up in the countryside. Luddite victories seem to have made the men confident of themselves and curious about what else can be changed, speaking more broadly. They've taken to reading Paine, Cobbett. . . ." He paused.

Mary took her cue. "They're even reading *Everyman's Review,* I expect. And perhaps a few women are reading it as well."

He nodded. "Bit of a rise in circulation; an honor to contribute to the spread of ideas. For there's a sentiment growing, you see, that government should represent more than those that own the land. Shocking, ain't it, that Manchester has not one MP to represent it, with all that industry? Of course, if our esteemed government chooses to label such thinking as anarchy . . . if they make it illegal to discuss these things in public meetings and then suspend habeas corpus so as to more easily arrest those who *do* speak out . . . and then last January, to ignore the men who petitioned for the reform of Parliament . . ."

"Appalling to treat them that way," Anna said. "Although one could also wish that someone would petition for Mary's and my right to vote."

Richard shrugged. "You should read the report, written by a bunch of Parliamentary blowhards who call themselves the Committee of Secrecy—pompous asses equating free discussion with the 'total overthrow of all our institutions,' hyenas howling that the reformers are 'undermining the people's habits of decent and regular subordination.' "

The report that Kit had found so alarming. In case Mary needed any further proof of how unsuited he and she were to each other.

She sighed. "Perhaps I will try another essay," she said, "about the hardships poverty-stricken wives and mothers are suffering in the country at a time like this. Poor things, to be so bereft in a place of such beauty."

"You'll be happy to get back there," Anna said.

"I expect that I shall. I couldn't live there all the time; I'm too fond of theater and lectures and painting exhibitions—not to speak of the brilliant society of people like you. Life does rather creep by in the country."

Though at least one wouldn't have to wonder whom one might catch sight of, as one did driving past Park Lane.

"But while I'm home—yes, I guess it *is* my home,

really—I enjoy helping the Friendly Society, and Cathy Williams's school for girls. I take tea with the vicar, accompany Jessica on her charitable errands, go on long, solitary tramps through the meadows. And then there's my niece. I like being a favorite aunt and having her confidence. Betts will be eighteen now." She paused. "No, not Betts. I'm told she wants to be called Elizabeth now."

"I envy her, whatever she calls herself," Anna said. "For I should have loved to have you for an aunt when *I* was at that dreadful age—one day so fearful of growing up, the next so eager and impatient for it. Of course, you'll be awfully busy helping your sister—with the estate, the charities, *and* the midsummer preparations. We look forward to seeing your entire family—and dear Matthew Bakewell as well—when we come down for the festivities. It'll be an especial treat for us, you know, because we'll be coming after a week spent dozing by the fire with Richard's Yorkshire aunts." Her tone was soothing. As was Richard's, when he hastened to add that Mary must not forget the essay she'd promised him.

Had she appeared to need so much soothing?
Of course she hadn't.

She'd be busy and contented at Beechwood Knolls. Kit wouldn't be a bother; he never came down to the country. The Calais encounter was already receding in her memory; the divorce proceedings, when they came, could mainly be left in the hands of the solicitors. And though she hadn't quite known how to finish her letter to Matthew this morning, she was sure to think of just the right words by tomorrow.

Chapter Seven

✦✦✦✦✦✦

The lamplight in the library of the Park Lane house was too bright and the fire needed stirring.

I could ring for assistance, Kit thought. But the real problem was the clamor of accusatory voices ringing in his ear. *A late-night seduction at a remote inn—indeed and indubitably the worst strategy ever chosen for a lovers' reunion, and what the devil could I have been thinking anyway?*

He pulled a plush pillow from beneath his head, tumbling it down over his eyes to screen out the glaring light. Too bad he couldn't similarly muffle the cacophony in his head. But then, he was used to being hectored, lectured, and otherwise belittled, having grown up under the tutelage of the old Eighth Marquess of Rowen.

Which didn't mean that *she* should have sneered at him from behind spectacles that should have looked spinsterish but that he'd found oddly fetching. Needn't have proclaimed herself so bloody certain that he was still the boy she'd run off with. The old, *shallow, callow* Kit, *most ungoverned personage* she'd ever met.

He'd caught a pleasanter sound now, of someone stirring the fire. The light seeping under the pillow had grown mellower as well.

The room set swiftly to rights, the butler suggested a light supper.

"Thanks, no. My stomach . . . rather in a knot from traveling all day. A cup of tea, though—send Belcher in with it, won't you? He can pull off my boots while he's here."

The dowager marchioness wouldn't think kindly of how he and his boots had been treating the settee he'd flung himself onto. And of course she'd soon know (for Thomas would tell her, Kit thought) about how he'd failed with Mary. . . .

Well, he hadn't failed in *all* ways.

If only they hadn't fallen into argumentation. Had he really needed to regale her with all his most cherished plans when he'd barely got his buttons open?

Such a promising beginning. When he'd lain on top of her, when he'd entered her. And afterward, her voice in its throaty lower register. *I want you again. Soon.*

Then you bloody well shouldn't have started in on lecturing me.

The Channel had been choppy, his hours on the packet boat anything but soothing. He'd had a bad night in Dover and his bones ached from being banged about in the post chaise up to town. The words of their last confrontation still rang in his head, in nagging counterpoint to the recurrent cadence of hooves, traces, and springs.

How many times between Dover and London?

"I didn't"—clippity—*"think . . ."*

"No"—squeak and jingle—*"you didn't."*

Unfair. He'd thought of nothing *but* her since several weeks ago, when he'd glimpsed her at the theater in Paris. In truth, he'd thought about her for all the nine years of their separation. Not every minute; he'd had orders to follow, duties to attend to. But her image, her voice . . .

En route to Spain, he'd entertained himself far into the nights by imagining how awful and guilt stricken she'd feel when he met his heroic death in battle.

And when he'd left off thinking about death—when he'd begun instead to live in the service of responsibility and obligation—he'd taken to wondering what she might think of the man he'd become.

People sometimes spoke admiringly of him. Might she have heard any of that?

Because *he'd* heard about *her*. Englishmen abroad knew each other's business. Impressive, how she'd managed to please herself and still maintain a margin of respectability. All but the narrowest people seemed to accept her.

All very well for *them*. The bargain Kit had finally struck with himself was to rage against her infidelities (as he called them—*his* affairs of course being only affairs) on Mondays, Wednesdays, and Fridays, while reserving the majority of the week (four days *was* the majority, was it not?) for a measure of toleration, and to congratulate himself on his liberality in this, late at night, with the baroness curled against his flank in satisfied slumber.

A game. An abstraction. He hadn't actually seen her yet, even while they'd both been resident in Paris. His duties had taken most of his attention, his responsibilities shifting to what one might call intelligence (though *she'd* likely call it delivering secret messages to Britain's despotic allies). Call it what you would; it had been his job to help keep the information flowing. He'd enjoyed it, even while planning for his future.

Military discipline had done him good, but he'd had enough of it and he wanted to come home. Obtaining the letter of introduction to Lord Sidmouth had been a good first step.

And then he did see her.

In the course of his work, as it happened, in the lobby of the Théâtre des Variétés. He'd been in evening dress, fading into the crowd, ready to retrieve a message from the bewhiskered gentleman, and—as invisibly as possible and at exactly eleven minutes after nine—to brush against the blond dandy in the black moire neckcloth, passing the folded piece of paper along to him.

After which his time would be his own. The baroness was at home in the Faubourg St-Germain.

The crowd in the lobby was beginning to thin. He'd already completed the first part of his assignment; it would be more difficult to do the second part discreetly.

Or so he'd been thinking when *she* appeared. He'd almost taken her for an illusion, an apparition stirred into being by fleeting memory. If an apparition could be breathless and distracted, an illusion so patently annoyed at itself for being late.

There'd been nothing apparitional about her hurried steps across the marble floor. The rose pink evening cape fluttering over pale ivory silk, pink-and-green-striped bandeau holding a sprig of lily of the valley in her hair, had all been wonderfully matter-of-fact and palpable. A light drizzle was falling outside; tiny drops of moisture clung to her curls like scattered sequins.

Under their dusting of rouge and powder, her cheeks were less plump than he remembered; he thought he might have discerned a touch of weariness. But her peremptoriness was exactly what he would have expected. He'd found it hard to keep from smiling, harder still to wrest his eyes from the swirling cape, stop himself from trying to ascertain the changes time had wrought upon the body beneath it. He couldn't see very much; he found he didn't care. She was Mary still and Mary completely.

Odd that it had happened in the line of duty. Though you could argue that it was only on duty that he hadn't been free to avoid the theaters, restaurants, and parks that were always so irritatingly thronged with British tourists.

She'd entered the lobby at eight minutes past nine and disappeared by the time he'd handed over his message. She must have run upstairs to join her companions. A few white blossoms, too small to shed their scent, lay scattered on the stairway carpet.

He'd wanted to scoop them up in his fingers. Alas,

he'd been obliged to maintain his invisibility. Which it seemed he'd done quite adequately. Well, *she* hadn't seen him, had she? Which was just as well for the discharging of his duty. Shocking, to think of the disruption any display of recognition would have effected in the flow of critical information between England and the other forces of order and legitimacy in Europe.

He'd continued to follow his orders. To leave the theater and to make a tour of some of Paris's darkest and most circuitous alleys until absolutely certain he hadn't been followed.

After which he'd proceeded to the baroness's apartments, to explain that he wouldn't be visiting her anymore because he'd fallen back in love with his wife. She'd laughed, cried, slapped him, and informed him he was no gentleman to invent so crude and fantastical a story. If he'd tired of her, well, *c'est la vie.* But he shouldn't insult her by telling fairy tales.

Following her advice, he said very little when he resigned his commission the next day. Keeping the fairy tales to himself, it seemed, in the service of a bloody stupid romantic scenario of instant reconciliation at a remote country inn.

Just see what *that* got you.

His tea was cold. The fire had burnt down in the grate. His irritating, peremptory, irresistible wife wanted nothing to do with him, and could still spout radical claptrap like a Jacobin. Doubtless she thought him as inflexible and autocratic as the old Eighth Marquess, not to speak of wild and stupid. . . . *The most ungoverned personage* . . .

Which was neither true nor to the point.

He blinked, pleasantly surprised to hear himself think that. Nice to know that his thoughts weren't *all* self-belittling ones. That he had a few things to be proud of, chief among them having earned the respect of the common soldiers under his command. Not immediately, sad to say—but he wouldn't think about *that* right now.

Still, he'd been a good soldier, and now he'd like to be a good civilian. Work for the good of the public order, for *everyone's* good, including hers. Was that really so terrible?

Amazing, even now, how much he cared about her good opinion. Not that it would make much difference, when she had a lover who was willing to be sued as an adulterer, so keen was the man on releasing her from their marriage. She must be pretty keen on Bakewell herself.

And it seems I've agreed to set the divorce engine in motion. Set informants on her, as a magistrate might upon the rebellious men in his district.

Damn her for goading him into agreeing to it.

For he could hardly have admitted to a measure of affection that *she* manifestly didn't feel.

Even if they *could* still make each other laugh. Finish each other's sentences. Make each other respond in other wonderful ways as well. One time only. Damn.

He ducked his head back under the pillow, hearing once more the sighs—hell, the screams—he'd drawn from her. Remembering what he'd intended they'd be doing next. Imagining things they'd never done that they might have tried . . .

Instead of sniping at and insulting one another for an hour. Raking up old memories. Morrice. That half-wit of an actress. Apology evidently not a possibility; where would one even begin?

Leave it alone. What did it matter? If they'd managed to apologize, they would have found themselves butting heads on . . . oh, trivial matters, like the proper way to govern the English nation.

One's thoughts did seem to go around in circles when the lady in question had a brain as well as a body to be reckoned with.

When the lady . . . but he could remember further back, to an implacable young girl in pigtails and pinafore who'd caused a certain angry thirteen-year-old boy to boast and to puff himself up most absurdly.

Much (to his shame) as he had when he'd shambled down the stairs to remind her that he had a letter of introduction from Wellington. To insist that she hear the part he'd memorized and most wanted to repeat, informing Lord Sidmouth that the Home Office could do a lot worse than to take on Major Lord Christopher Stansell.

Any woman in Britain (except the one he was still married to and still wanted to do . . . well, *all sorts of things* to) might find it a bit of an honor.

Forget her. Get past this muddle of past and present, aching memory and sharp-fanged desire. He had work to do. *No, Mary,* not *ceremonial puffery, but real work in the service of the domestic order*—if, in fact, the Home Office agreed to take him on.

He should move his aching bones and get himself upstairs to sleep.

❧

He should . . . but he didn't.

He sank back into the vortex of memory. Voices, glances exchanged . . .

Quite the dandy . . .

The French . . . expect an English gentleman . . .

And you, you kept your hair short . . .

❧

He'd cut it himself, the first time, with a pair of little silver scissors he'd found on her dressing table in Curzon Street. He could remember the coal fire popping in the grate, even while the slender bones and muscles had trembled beneath her skin.

The scissors were shaped like a hummingbird, with fine steel blades for a beak. He'd barely breathed as he snipped and clipped, the blades so close to her bent nape, her spine like a string of pearls, his bare arms and torso held carefully away from her body. If he touched anything but her hair, he'd be certain to lose all control of himself.

Her shift hiked up around her naked hips, she'd sat backward in a little gilt chair; the chestnut curls, falling to the parquet floor of her dressing room, piled up around her bare feet.

Glancing at herself in the mirror, nodding with satisfaction. "There, you see, I'll make a perfect boy."

He'd had to laugh.

"No, really, Kit. In one of your coats and a cut-down pair of your breeches. And a neckcloth, a big bright one, like the ones those ridiculous coaching bucks wear."

Squinting at her, trying to imagine her in disguise.

She'd responded by squaring her shoulders and twisting her facial expression into a sly simulacrum of his when freshly shaved and prepared to meet a new day.

"I've been studying you," she whispered.

He'd had to work to keep his countenance. "I expect we could pull it off." Shrugging in an offhand manner. "A beardless youth in ill-fitting, rumpled clothing—yes, it's just possible. I'll call you Ned, introduce you as a distant cousin just up from the country; all you'll have to do is nod and gawp at the wonders of the metropolis. And Morrice can help us. If anyone tries to engage you in conversation, he'll just barge right in with a stream of his endless claptrap."

Oh yes, Morrice had been a very big help indeed.

"And so you'll take me to a boxing exhibition? And a gaming hell too?"

"The pugilists first: everybody's attention will be fixed on what's happening in the ring. Yes, all right. We'll try it."

Surprisingly circumspect at routs and assemblies, she'd been brazen and curious about his gentlemen's pursuits, demanding so strenuously to see for herself that he'd finally agreed to take her, show her everything he found thrilling and fascinating.

Not only because she'd been so adorable behind her crimson neckcloth, but because it allowed him to see everything twice, first in his own way and then through her brave, clear eyes. Wonderful to have her beside him, out in the exciting world beyond Mayfair and St. James, Rowen and Beechwood Knolls—to show off for her, present the raffish companions he'd made during earlier forays.

As though he'd known anything, really, about the world—except that he cherished a taste for risk and danger, for chance, change, and harsh, shocking contrast. And that (mostly thanks to Joshua Penley) he could afford to pursue his tastes in a leisured, gentlemanly fashion. No demands upon his time except pleasure . . . nor, for that matter, on her time either.

In Calais, he might have asked her if she hadn't sometimes found herself bored during that aimless first year of marriage. Impossible to confide such a thing back then—any admission of imperfection was as bad as a betrayal when you were young; better to go out and betray each other instead.

Which was exactly what he and his wife had *done.*

So young, so stupid. At twenty-one and -two it had felt a queer thing even to *have* a wife. He'd repeat the word to himself, whisper it silently: *wife,* or (even more strangely) *my wife.* Waking up at night, he'd wrap his lips about the reedy little syllable and shake his head in private astonishment—that his *wife* was sleeping beside him, close by and yet secreted away, tiny movements so familiar and dreams so unknowable, her body curled as in a nest of voluptuous murmurings and smells.

If he wanted, he'd think, he could simply wake, touch, enter her. But no matter if he did or didn't, she'd still be there in the morning.

At which point in his meditations he usually *would* wake her, to lose his confused self within her.

It hadn't been true, of course, that she'd always be there. He and she—and both their families' solicitors— had found a way around that.

It was years since he'd let himself feel these things. Well, you couldn't when you were responsible for people besides yourself. Anger—like anarchy—needed to be kept in check.

Yes, right. A word or two from *her,* and the angry boy he'd been had emerged from hiding like a fox poking his head out of a hole after the hunters had gone by.

Even as he'd wanted to show her the new, responsible Kit, who'd won his men's respect, who wanted a real career, and who'd even rather enjoyed exchanging letters with his dullish brother—the old Kit had stomped out the door of her bedchamber, given it a thumping loud slam behind him, and to hell with any lodger who'd still be trying for a little sleep. To summon the little serving girl Mary had glared at in the dining room—*Good,* he'd thought, *give her something to glare about.*

One woman as good as another for certain things— or so he'd been instructed, long ago, by a group of gentlemen at White's. The French girl would have been perfectly good at what the Old Kit had wanted. Except for one problem. The New Kit hadn't wanted *her.* Hadn't wanted anyone (Lord, how his London cronies would have hooted at him) except the woman who no longer wanted to be his wife.

⁂

At this moment, however, in the library at Park Lane, both Kits had had enough of painful reminiscence—as well as of wondering where one Kit left off and the other began. *Pull yourself together, man.* Summoning his valet, he got himself neatly and cozily put to bed.

A book he liked lay on the nightstand. *Good for times like this.* But tonight he didn't require anything but a few easily summoned images. A curve of her lips, the slope of her nape, even (or perhaps especially) the angry flash of her eyes above that absurdly wonderful threadbare shift.

Reminding him, quite suddenly, of a night when Cousin Ned had rather misbehaved. A ragged shirt, perhaps, unbefitting even a country cousin.

"*You've been a bad boy, Ned.*"

"*Have I, sir?*"

Her eyes very round, dimple flickering into sight,

even as her hands crept toward the buttons of her breeches.

"*You need a bit of a punishment, my boy. Come here; it'll be the making of you. A touch of . . . discipline. Yes, bend over . . .*"

A challenging week lay ahead of him. Meet with Sidmouth, finally find out what the letter of introduction was worth. Apply himself and his abilities, one way or another, in the service of the public order. Duty, discipline . . .

Surely tonight he could allow himself a few small private pleasures.

"*That's right, Ned. You can rest your head on the desk.*"

Breeches around her ankles. Her legs parted, toes barely touching the floor. He'd raised the ragged shirt, pulled down the boy's drawers she wore beneath the breeches.

Indecent.

Hands on himself now, the tightening now, the pulling, the . . . ah, the release. From desire (at least for the moment), from responsibility, from duty and from his own ambitions as well.

And from the pull of memories so carefully suppressed for so long, and now, it seemed, so constantly, confusingly, and overwhelmingly present.

Chapter Eight

❦

The coaching inn yard was noisy, crowded, and quite fun this morning, Peggy Weightman thought. Say what you would (and Peggy felt herself eminently qualified to comment, what with all the places she and Lady Christopher had been), London was still the center of the civilized world: so many people to watch, all their clattering comings and goings. For herself, Peggy didn't mind in the slightest about the delay with the post chaise. In her line of work, there was always something that wanted fixing or mending.

But Lady Christopher was impatient to be gone, so Mr. Morrice had got her a seat in the stagecoach, with a place for Peggy on top. It would be a pretty day, dozing in the sunlight on the way to familiar places; they'd be reaching home late tonight. Peggy sipped the beer the waiter had brought her. Considerate of Lady Christopher to send him from the bar; she would have become quite parched out here, keeping an eye on their mountain of luggage.

Perhaps it was the beer that was making her sleepy—not forgetting that she hadn't had a good night's rest her entire last week in France.

Ah, well. There were better things than a good night's rest.

Too soon to worry about what else the sleepiness might betoken. Nor fret about whether Tom would mind if such a thing did come to pass. Her smile grew warmer, *Tom* being such a cozy name for such a big man. They'd been kissing in the pantry of Lady Rowen's apartments in Paris when she'd first called him it. He'd laughed, but she'd seen well enough that he liked it. And he *would* be coming down to the country soon enough, for the marchioness was already wanting to get back to Rowen. Peggy trusted him. Well, she had to, didn't she?

She wouldn't worry about anything, except to wish now that she hadn't bought all those pretty trifles in France; better to give her people at home the coins directly. Still, it would be fun to tell about her travels. Her cousins (not including Cathy, the schoolmistress) would admire how well she looked in the dresses Lady Christopher had passed down to her, and all the girls would want to hear about . . .

Everybody else called him *Thomas*. It suited how grave he looked; Lady Christopher had raised her eyebrows when Peggy slipped into using the little private name for him. Surprising the lady would have noticed, her clearly having troubles with *her* gentleman, medicine bottle still uncorked on the table, room reeking of brandy. It had been all anybody could do to scrub the smell off her and get her dressed.

But that was how she was. Surprising, inconsistent— one minute distracted or buried in her books, and the next quite sharp and noticing more than you wanted her to.

And when Peggy had her own little moment of sadness (waving from the deck while the packet boat pulled away and Tom's head and shoulders faded from view), Lady Christopher had turned and given Peggy her own handkerchief. Silent-like. Tactful, you might say.

Peggy found it interesting to be in service—even if Tom *would* protest that a footman weren't more than a large monkey, tricked out in velvet and trained to fetch and carry. And heaven only knew how Lady Christopher would manage without Peggy keeping her neat and pinned together.

The Penleys had been known as fair employers, and so were their daughters: Lady Christopher, Mrs. Grandin, and Mrs. MacNeill in Glasgow. A pity, people'd said last year, how that steward was cheating Mrs. Grandin, and so obvious about it too. And you could still hear the old story, repeated round a cottage hearth, of how Mr. Penley had saved a poacher's life.

Must have been a shock to him, his youngest daughter running off with one of the Stansell boys. People'd thought Lord Kit had got her in trouble, but that part wasn't true (proving that it didn't *always* have to be, if a person was lucky). Peggy had been quite young at the time, but even a little girl could find it exciting, a bit mysterious, all the talk about whether he really *were* the marquess's son—and if not, who *was* his dad anyway?

The more serious workingmen at Grefford, who read the pamphlets and argued over the newspapers and went to the night meetings, would quell such gossip—and so would Peggy's cousin Cathy.

"Don't you have better things to chatter about," Cathy'd say, "than the gentry and what they do in their beds? Aren't life's real problems enough for you?"

But real-life problems were dull and intractable, especially these hard days. Peggy didn't see why you *shouldn't* get a little amusement from people whose lives remained cozy and comfortable no matter how bad the harvest, who wore fine clothes and rode in carriages even after a marriage's scandalous separation or a night spent throwing things at each other.

Why *not* get some entertainment from the gentry and especially the aristocrats, she'd asked Cathy; don't they owe us that much anyway? And Cathy, she could see, didn't have a good answer, except to sniff that she was sure she'd done right getting Peggy a job as a rich lady's maid. Which she hadn't meant as a compliment, even if it *were* Mrs. Penley who'd paid to educate her as a schoolmistress.

But Cathy hadn't seen Paris or Constantinople or the Alps or antiquities like Peggy had. Travel made you wise, and that was a fact.

I've seen the world, Peggy repeated to herself. *I have a fine, tall man who loves me and is surely coming back for me.*

It was a pretty day, and she was wearing a neat drab poplin that Lady Christopher had grown tired of. Smiling up at the waiter who'd come for her glass, she could feel how well the skirt hung since she'd taken a needle to it. She could even feel a bit sorry for her employer, who appeared in rather a state of disconsolation, like there were someone in the crowd she'd hoped to see.

And if men want to flirt with me, Peggy thought (for she'd caught a glimpse of a brown coat with bright buttons moving in her direction), *I'm sure it isn't my fault.*

A decent-looking man, though she herself didn't care for whiskers. Nearly as tall as Tom, if a bit on the corpulent side. Just off the night mail from Derby, ruddy-faced, like he'd gotten a good sleep on the journey. He had a bold expression on him, the sort of man you'd say could sell coals to Newcastle.

Wouldn't hurt just to talk. If he wanted more than talk, he could just take himself off to Soho for it.

Though at the end of ten or so minutes, when his friends came for him, he left in a great hubbub of self-importance, which she *didn't* like, nor that he hadn't presented her to them, even after he'd seemed so interested in what she'd had to say about her travels and the people back home at Grefford.

The stagecoach was boarding. She turned to make sure that their bags and trunks and boxes weren't tossed about too roughly. And here was Lady Christopher looking about her one last time before Mr. Morrice handed her into the coach, where it would be stuffier, more crowded, and a lot less fun, Peggy thought, than on top, even if the top of a stagecoach wasn't no place for a lady.

Mary supposed that it could have been worse. A relief, in any case, finally to be under way. She squeezed herself into her backward-facing seat, tried not to sneeze at the dust rising from the worn cushions, nodded to her fellow voyagers, and held herself steady as they clattered off.

At least she was sitting by a window, the better to watch London slip away. Its farthest suburbs gone, she dozed, woke to finish the novel she had with her, dozed again, woke for a bad luncheon, dozed some more, and by late afternoon had drifted into a haze of reminiscence of a much earlier ride along this same route, on just such a bright day and also in the backward-facing seat—though of a far more comfortable vehicle.

She'd been ten, a spoiled, demanding, too energetic and impatient ten, alternately indulged and savaged by her older sisters, who always got to sit facing forward in the Penleys' second carriage. Typically, neither Jessica nor Julia had as much as peeked out the windows; they'd ignored the landscape as completely as they'd ignored Mary, their thoughts and conversation quite entirely occupied by the young gentlemen they were engaged to marry.

Mary could smile affectionately now at how different each of the two courtships had been, and how characteristic of each sister. Jessie's love story unfolding in a leisurely and classically correct sequence: Arthur Grandin had asked for two dances on the night of her come-out, paid a charming and attentive call the day after, sent a large bouquet and then a series of witty little gifts, and in due time made a proper offer of his blond, smiling, baronet's-younger-son of a self.

While Julia's amours had been conducted more briskly. More economically too, if you didn't count the price of postage. An introduction to Mr. Jeremy Mac-Neill during a family trip to Glasgow, a daily exchange of letters after their return home, and a visit a month later from young Mr. MacNeill himself, proposing within the week and saving the Penleys the expense of a second come-out.

Still (and unlike another pairing Mary could think of), it had been an entirely suitable match. Jeremy's father did business with Papa; the MacNeills were clever, industrious, rich, and growing richer, while—as Julia still took pains to point out—figuring prominently among Glasgow's patrons of the arts and learned societies.

Both her sisters' marriages had worked out as splendidly as anyone would have predicted, and until Arthur's death two years ago, as happily as everyone had wished. Well, everyone except a certain badly behaved ten-year-old.

Ninnies, she'd thought. Idiots, with their sighs and giggles. *Id-jits,* she repeated silently to herself (much preferring the way the servants pronounced the word). But at least her sisters would be obliged to pay her a little attention when they discovered that . . .

"You're in for it now, Mary! Miss Archer, the vile little wretch has tied our bonnet strings together."

"And got them all sticky with lemon drops too! Just wait, imp, until I get my hands on you."

She'd stuck out her tongue—it must have been a nasty bright, sugary yellow—from the safety of the far corner of the carriage.

"I want a story," she'd declared. "I've been crying for one ever since we came through Leicester. And all *you* big, stupid things want to talk about is the silly oafs you're going to marry."

Mama always had stories for long journeys. Mary had begged to ride with Mama and Papa in the other carriage, or failing that, in one of the wagons following behind, the servants perched atop trunks of clothing and crates of household goods. But she couldn't be allowed to travel like a gypsy. And her incessant fussing would have been a bother to Mama, who was very delicate these days.

Something wasn't quite right about the baby due to be

born this fall; the doctor had advised Mama and Papa to repair to the country for the remainder of the pregnancy. Mary imagined the selfish little thing thrashing about instead of lying quiet and curled up like the babies in the illustrated volume she'd found in Papa's library. Impatient with its own too-long journey, the creature was probably fidgeting as uncontrollably as she was. Well, too bad for it. Too bad for *him*, as everyone wished it to be.

He'd occasioned too much inconvenience already, just because of the hope of his being a boy. It was Mama's last chance to give Papa a son to inherit the brewery, and Papa was beside himself with anxiety, having never entirely recovered from the death of the boy twins who'd preceded Mary into the world.

Not that anyone had actually told her any of this. She'd pieced together what she knew from every clue she could find—and probably from a few made-up details as well. From servants' gossip, the expressions on big people's faces and what they said when they thought she wasn't listening. The same way Kit had learned that the marquess wasn't really his father. There are always ways for a too-inquisitive child to find out more than he or she is meant to know.

How old had she been when he'd told her about the mystery of his origins?

Fourteen? Fifteen?

Had he kissed her yet? No, of course not, because it had been she *who'd first kissed* him. *Not directly after he'd said it. The next day, rather—she'd stayed up all night planning it, tossing about in an agony of delicious anticipation. How exciting it must be to know oneself the secret issue of illicit desire; how thrilling to feel such a desire oneself.*

Or was she already feeling it?

Was desire what she felt for Kit?

After she'd kissed him, she'd known that it was—the knowledge only serving to make her life more perplexing during the year that followed, especially when she'd sneak out to meet him, during his school holidays.

At night, she'd scribble certain words with a drawing crayon, on the final pages of the journal that she'd kept in a locked box under her bed, along with a book of obscure sonnets. Words like carnality, concupiscence, greed, heat, fervor, wantonness, weakness, longing, thirst, *and finally and most frighteningly,* lust.

Tearing out the pages and burning them, the morning after she'd written that last word. But it was no help, for she'd already, involuntarily, committed the list to memory.

Sundays, she'd screw her eyes shut rather than peek at him in the Rowen pew across the aisle, lest the vicar catch a glimpse of her and divine her culpable state.

His holidays ended and him safely returned to school, she'd haunt their secret places, trying to puzzle it out.

But none of what she'd felt had really made sense to her until they'd finally gone to bed together.

And since Calais it made less sense than ever.

The coach lurched to a stop, as though to punctuate her thoughts and illustrate their futility.

Esslynne. A passenger took his leave from the top of the coach, and some fellows hauled a stout lady up to take his place.

Mary rubbed her eyes and straightened her traveling cloak. Esslynne had traditionally marked the last leg of the Penleys' journeys between London and Beechwood Knolls. In an hour or so they'd enter the vast extent of the marquess's lands, and in another hour the verges of their own much smaller property would slip into view.

But at ten years of age, the advent of Esslynne had only proved to her that the journey would never end. And would only grow more unendurable, for their governess had pronounced Mary too old to be told stories.

"You're an extremely capable reader. Here, I've brought your copy of *Original Stories from Real Life.* And if that doesn't interest you, remember that there's your Latin exercise still to be done today."

On a traveling day? But she wouldn't dare stick out

her tongue at Miss Archer. Definitely no Latin, though, at least for as long as she could put it off. Sullenly, she opened the book she'd been handed, a set of moral tales about two insipid sisters who liked nothing better than to distribute their pocket money among the poor.

Even her own sisters were more interesting than *that*, whinge as they might about the vexations of being the second family in the neighborhood and never invited to a ball at Rowen. Of course, they agreed, Papa had been in the right about the poaching incident. But couldn't he even try to make it up with the marquess? For almost a decade had passed. And it would be such fun to know the dowager marchioness, who was as beautiful as Mama but much more fascinating.

"Her new muslins are the latest thing, more elegant than what most of Mayfair is wearing but so simple and comfortable, one could wear the lightest stays . . ."

At which point Julia had whispered something to Jessica, and Jessica had gasped and giggled in response.

Id-jits.

Mary had turned back to her book with renewed disgust for her sisters, pride in Papa's strength of character, and a child's fierce hatred for the cruel and murderous Stansells.

Everyone in the neighborhood knew about the disputed estate boundary, and how Mr. Penley's claim had quite bollixed the marquess's case against a man accused of poaching game. The grouse having been bagged upon the contested tract of land, the poacher went free—causing the marquess to rage that his neighbor was a traitorous Jacobin, and to forbid his wife and children to speak to any of the Penleys.

Indecent that a brewer should be so rich, he'd shouted. Disgusting that the ancient laws of property had fallen into such disrespect. No wonder the country was going to the devil.

Mary had been a baby at the time, and Kit a very little boy. But it had made a strong impression on him. *Helpless with fury, his lordship was,* he'd told Mary after they'd become friends. *Unbearable to be bested by a man of lesser station, you see.*

She did see, now that it was too late for it to matter anymore. She gazed aimlessly out the window, at the misty-moist green fields bordered by thorn and hornbeam, elms and giant beeches casting long late-afternoon shadows as the coach swayed against the bends in the road.

The coach was stifling, the motion of the coach more jolting as the roads became more primitive and rural. She closed her eyes to ward off dizziness, and woke with a start at Grefford, to Jessica's fair, pretty face smiling in at her through the coach window.

The prettiness grown a bit faded: widowhood was difficult for her sister. Jessie looked tired and a bit dazed, as though still not believing that her charming, buoyant husband had succumbed to the influenza. For (leaving aside the episode of the kitchen maid) Arthur Grandin had continued kindhearted, good-natured, and as delighted to have fallen in love with a brewer's educated daughter as with a duchess. Jessica's marriage portion was just what he'd needed to complement his own sparse income and excellent pedigree; he'd accepted his happy fortune as his due, and so had everyone who knew him.

Of course, there'd been no question of a baronet's son managing a brewery. Jeremy MacNeill would have done splendidly, but Jeremy had inherited far too many business interests of his own. So Papa had sold out his shares, invested the proceeds in superbly reliable securities for his daughters, and retired into his gardens, his library, and a lingering melancholy after that last baby (it *had* been a boy) was born dead, sometime around Mary's eleventh birthday, which had slipped by with very little notice.

Enough memories. Among hugs and kisses, laughter, and a few tears, she and her sister passed arm in arm out of the inn yard to the little High Street, deeply rutted and perhaps a bit shabbier than when last she'd seen it. Probably from the long, wet winter they'd had, or was it simply the effect of the shadows, the deepening violet sky?

A haggard, rather frantic-looking workman pitched himself by her and Jessica, nearly jamming into them, quite as though he hadn't noticed them walking toward the Grandin carriage.

Now that's *a rude mechanical*—the joke had barely taken shape in her mind when her eye became distracted by a most exquisite creature making her slouched, languid way toward them—willowy and graceful, pitiless and perfect, with huge, brilliant eyes rolling in exasperation and—ah yes, Mary was beginning to understand, utter mortification at the sound of every entirely commonplace word Jessica uttered.

Betts? She swallowed the name back. Jessie had been right—the girl had become a beauty. Mary felt herself unwillingly and unaccountably intimidated, awed as though in the presence of royalty.

"E-Elizabeth?"

Did royalty suffer itself to be hugged? Just barely, it seemed.

"Hullo, Aunt Mary." Pulling away and making for the carriage, where Peggy, a footman, and Jessica's coachman were loading Mary's things.

"Another quarrel this morning," Jessica whispered, quite as though the girl weren't watching, her narrowed eyes sending blue-diamond sparks in their direction. "About her new gown for Midsummer Night. I'll tell you about it later."

As they set off, Mary just had time to wave to Cathy Williams, briskly leading the stout lady down the High Street. *The Grandin carriage would be turning in the opposite direction, through the market square. . . .*

"She must be the school's new cook," Jessica said. "Which is a blessing, for Cathy's been doing it herself these weeks, and the word about the village is that her scholars aren't enjoying it."

I'll turn away from the window, Mary thought, *shut*

*my eyes if necessary, when we pass the spot where he'd
swung himself up on his horse. . . .*

A local boy had been holding both horses' reins,
young Lord Christopher and his older brother Lord
William having ridden together into the village. The
village boy's face was a study in sullen confusion: annoyed to be pulled from an ongoing game to mind the
marquess's sons' horses, yet proud despite himself to
have been the one asked to do it.

Kit would have been thirteen; by then Mary would
have had a proper twelfth-birthday party, to make up
for her lonely, unsatisfactory eleventh. Mama would
have been doing charitable errands, leaving Mary to
distribute her leftover birthday sweetmeats among the
girls and boys playing in the square.

He hadn't noticed her, though she'd been standing
quite close by. Well, why should he? After an hour with
the village children, she'd be as dusty and unkempt as
they were. And anyway, the Stansells and the Penleys
were enemies.

Head high, reins held carelessly in a long, strong
hand (not a boy's hand at all, she remembered thinking), Kit had ridden away with a haughty expression on
his face, even as the village boy had begun salving his
self-respect by muttering curses. Too softly spoken to
be heard by the young gentlemen on horseback, they
were nonetheless quite awful and entertaining curses,
about parentage and bad women—far worse and much
more fascinating than anything Mary or her sisters
would dare to say.

She'd gasped and giggled at the clods of earth (and
worse) that he and his mates were throwing, now that
Kit and his brother had gotten far enough away not to
see. *Good,* she'd thought, *that conceited Stansell boy
deserves it.*

"Good," she'd called out, along with a few of the other
children. "Good," and "Throw 'em another, Peter.
Throw 'em a good 'un!"

Her mother had come to fetch her just then; she had

to wave good-bye to the children, sad to leave their play and oddly conscience-stricken, as though she'd witnessed—or even participated in—something she shouldn't. Which had been a new sort of experience for her, because until then she'd liked nothing better than to learn something forbidden and mysterious, depending as she did upon just such surreptitiously gathered knowledge for her understanding of the world.

⋘⋙

"... To add to the disarray," Jessica was saying, "there's a new laundry maid and I'm not sure she understood how I wanted her to iron the petticoats." Putting her head out the window, she called to the coachman, "Can you go a bit faster, Mr. Dodge?"

Another fit of eye rolling on Elizabeth's part.

"He can't, Mama. Not until he gets that wheel fixed—don't you remember?"

"She's right." Jessie smiled apologetically at Mary, conciliatingly at her daughter. "We're still a bit at sixes and sevens with our vehicles, I'm afraid. It was one of the ways my old steward used to cheat me. He and the coachman were in league; repairs were shoddy, parts weren't replaced."

⋘⋙

"And as you can see," she told Mary over a late supper in her little parlor, "it's not as though our Miss Elizabeth doesn't know the details of managing things. She knows better than I do, as she demonstrates every day, just civilly enough that one can't quite accuse her of pertness. It's her particular pleasure to point out how much better a job, *of everything,* they do at Rowen. But to lift a finger to help . . ."

"She didn't seem awfully pleased to see *me.* I confess it's made me a bit peevish."

"Well, she's rather divided the world into friends and enemies. And any friend of *mine* . . ."

The laundry had been done satisfactorily. Jessica

liked to mend the most delicate pieces herself; they brought a sweet green smell into the chamber. Mary took a deep, happy breath.

"I never have such clean linen as when I'm here."

Jessica laughed. "Wasn't that Brummell's first principle? That no one could be a gentleman without plenty of country washing?"

"Or a lady, I expect," Mary said, "though Brummell didn't seem to think there was any art to being a lady."

"It hasn't been so easy, even to do a good laundry, with all the rain we've had. Still, today was lovely and it's good luck you came when everything's so fresh. You'll sleep well tonight on the sheets we've put on your bed. . . . Mary?"

"Yes, sorry . . . I must have drifted off for a moment."

Her sister only nodded, it being clear that both of them were remembering the time when Jessica, who'd been home for a visit with Arthur and the children, had helped Mary tell a lie about the sheet she'd stolen.

"But I've forgotten the news," Jessica said now, "that has set the countryside on its ear."

"Not more machine breaking? Angry meetings?"

Jessica shook her head.

But if Richard were right, the government's repression had driven the men to meet in secret. Better not to bring up that *possibility,* Mary thought. *Not just yet anyway.*

"Even so," her sister continued, "there's a good deal of grumbling, even rudeness, as you saw—well, what would one expect when there's not enough employment? We'll be improving things a little bit anyway, by hiring some of the young people as occasional help for our house party.

"But the *news* is that Kit's brother the Ninth Marquess has had a second fit of apoplexy, just day before yesterday. It seems he'll live; he speaks very little, though they're hopeful of him getting some of that back—they've got him in an invalid chair. His son Gerald is on the continent; I should think they've summoned him.

"I shall have to call, of course. Not quite yet, though; let the young marchioness recover from the initial shock of it. Still, it's awkward while you're here. Not that anyone will mention your presence—the Stansells are quite masterful at not mentioning things, and even I shall hold my tongue in the matter of your visit. But you won't mind too much if I go, will you, Mary?"

"Oh, dear. Yes. No. I mean, of course you should call."

For a moment, she wondered if Kit would be coming down. Surely not; he'd want to be in London. And anyway, he knew that *she* was here.

Her face had given her away.

"You've seen him. And you haven't told me." Jessica's gaze was as insistent, her voice as implacable, as about a stolen bedsheet a great many years ago.

"Tomorrow. After we meet with your nice new steward, and then the man who'll be assessing the state of the water closets. I quite tremble at the possibilities, don't you? Oh, and you didn't finish your story about Fred and his school prank. Well, at least you've got *one* steady, dependable child out of your three. Julia writes that Joshua has taken wonderfully to business—Papa would have been proud of his namesake. And I've quite forgotten to go see Mrs. Ottinger down in the kitchen—do you think she'll forgive me if I wait until tomorrow? Such a long day, I must go to bed . . . the coach . . . the ride . . ."

"Tell me now. Tell me everything."

But she didn't. Not really, and certainly not everything.

"We had a glass of wine," she said, which was true in its way.

"We spoke a bit," she added. "He didn't apologize. He was the same arrogant, irresponsible boy we all remember. And then he went away and got himself quite horribly drunk over it." None of which was a lie—more a matter of judicious elision.

"Poor Mary," Jessica said. "But I must say, I'm a bit surprised. One would have thought that after such a successful military career . . . his brother the marquess spoke so proudly of him—quite a new thing from *him,* as you can imagine—which led me rather to hope . . ."

Everyone, it seemed, was hoping for something.

Well, everybody could stop right now.

"Drunk," she said, "and debauched. Took himself off with the serving maid."

"No."

Well, *that* had had the desired effect. She nodded. "He hasn't changed in the slightest, except that he's added an overlay of Tory priggishness. He fancies a political career, you see. In the Home Office, of all places."

"I expect I still feel guilty, for my . . . ah, contribution to his courtship, you know."

Mary sighed. "I don't know if it could rightly have been called a courtship—more like two wild young things hurling themselves at one another. And I was such an innocent. If you hadn't showed me how to protect myself, heaven knows what would have happened."

They were silent for a while.

"But the Calais meeting turned out all to the good," Mary concluded, "because Kit knows about Matthew now, and he knows that Matthew is willing to go through the awfulness of a divorce scandal. He was actually quite reasonable about that part; it seems that he's quite willing to bring suit. Well, it'd be better for him too. He could marry someone younger."

"And sillier," Jessica added.

"Perhaps."

"You've written to Matthew about all of this, I trust."

Mary shook her head. "Not yet. I shall finish my letter tomorrow. Let's walk outside for a bit, shall we? The stars are out; I want to smell Papa's gardens."

The roses and lilac, violets and lemon verbena shed their fragrance more intensely after dark, the sweet air of the English country night seeming to glimmer with benign spirits. Mary could feel her parents' presence; it seemed to her that Arthur Grandin had added the warm light of his memory. There were a few more restless shades abroad as well: she shook her head at the one who stuck a sugary yellow tongue out at her. When she was sure that Jessica was looking the other way, she stuck her own tongue back at the little imp—who giggled silently and flickered off toward the forest.

"It will be fun to have you home again, Mary."

"In some ways, it's as though I'd never left."

The sisters kissed good night.

Chapter Nine

Kit couldn't decide whether his week in town had crawled or flown by. Time seemed to have lost its shape; he could better account for the past nine years than these few days. *Let's see,* he thought, *I've ridden in the park, purchased a new pocket watch, dined with my sister and her family in Upper Brook Street....* The rest, it seemed, was a fog of uncertainty about his career and worry about his sick brother (and what a time for poor old Wat to be struck down too, with the countryside so rife with dissension).

And then there were the distracting reveries he kept drifting into. Sometimes angry, sometimes penitent. Distressingly real and on occasion dizzyingly physical—like the sudden torrent of feeling that had nearly immobilized him the afternoon he'd allowed himself to walk down Curzon Street.

Peering up at the window of what had been his bedchamber ... the bedposts, looped with scarlet silk cord ... first time they'd tried *that* ... her back arched, breasts lifted against the pull at her wrists—legs splayed, ah yes, her ankles too. What artful knots he'd tied; he'd practiced while she'd been visiting her sister. He'd computed the length of cord he'd need, with diligence and rare thrift as well.

He'd visited the draper's himself. The shop man was barely able to contain his amusement: evidently Kit wasn't the only gentleman who'd ever bought a length of drapery cord, though he might have been the youngest and most serious about it.

Worth it, though, worth everything—her eyes so wide, body thrashing about (good to leave a little play in the cords), mouth loosened in such a wobbly, woozy smile afterward. The best times had always been when he'd been able to surprise, to amaze her.

Yes, and dashed painful to hobble home under the assault of *that* particular memory. He'd never walk down *that* street again, rankle though it might that there should be places in England that were off-limits to him.

Not that her presence at Beechwood Knolls was keeping him from going down to see Wat. Not at all. His sister-in-law had written that he needn't bother; silly to travel all that way and then back again when he had imminent business in town. Wat must have told her about his Home Office aspirations; Susanna had been most definite that her husband wouldn't want Kit to change plans on his account.

You see, Mary? As though any of it would have made a difference to her, given her stiff-necked, Penley-ish view of all the Stansells except the dowager marchioness.

Only one more day of this limbo to get through. He'd be dining with the Home Office secretary tomorrow; his head felt clearer already in anticipation. This morning he'd visit Shumway in the City, see how his money was faring. Tonight he'd stay home, reread some documents, try to sound like he knew what he was talking about, for when he met Lord Sidmouth.

Only the afternoon to dispose of.

Lovely weather. The sun shone through the skylight; his boots quite glistened as he stepped downstairs.

The house's marble-walled foyer was set with a row of mirrors. Happily, the Old Kit couldn't be seen in any of them.

On the contrary. Retired army officer done up in excellent linen, good French waistcoat and well-brushed blue coat snug about a torso and shoulders he'd never thought he'd have when he'd been such a stick of a boy. Even his nose didn't look so bashed up this morning; its blunted, broken shape might possibly pass for *Roman* (well, that's what *she'd* always called it). No point wishing for more height, of course, though he'd doubtless continue to do so for as long as he stood on his legs. He mussed his hair a bit; his valet had made it too pretty.

Nothing in the newspaper about a disturbance in the Midlands.

But there wouldn't be one yet. Not according to his eldest brother's last letter anyway.

Kit had been surprised about a year ago when Wat had begun sending him regular and detailed communications. The two of them had never been congenial; Will had been the brother everyone got along with, his death on the march to Corunna a blow even to the Eighth Marquess, and probably hastening the old man's death.

Perhaps Wat had felt isolated in the country, especially after his first bout of apoplexy. Very likely he regretted not having his own chance for military glory. At home in placid Derbyshire, the Ninth Marquess must have wanted to show the family's scapegrace-turned-war-hero that he too was doing his part for England.

As—rather surprisingly—it had come to seem he *was.* Kit had replied to the letters, at first out of a kind of shamed sympathy *(poor, dull, stay-at-home Wat),* later from guilty curiosity *(but should English magistrates be setting spies upon the people of their districts?),* most recently with some genuine alarm *(well, perhaps they should, if the situation were really so dangerous).*

Lord Sidmouth would know about the extent of the danger. Kit would ask him when they dined tomorrow.

"No," he told the butler at Park Lane, "don't bother ordering the carriage. I've plenty of time to get to the

City. Interesting to walk about and see how things have changed. Besides, I can see how hard you're all working."

The house being turned upside down—maids beating carpets, workmen regilding the moldings—in preparation for the marchioness's imminent return from the continent.

"It's coming splendidly. No, truly, I'm glad to walk."

South and east on St. James Street. Sunshine bounced off the bow window at White's Club and rendered it opaque. He wondered who sat there nowadays, in the deep armchairs. Probably the same overbearing ninnies as before, telling the same overwrought jokes and dispensing equally bad advice. Growing gray in those chairs, running to fat or shriveling to leather.

Still, he might drop by. Pay the fees that had piled up in his absence. Have a drink, play a hand or two, hear all the gossip, of clothes and horses, fortunes married or gambled away. He had time to waste this afternoon. Why else had institutions like White's been invented, except to help you waste your time?

Stumbling on an uneven length of paving, he caught his balance and righted himself. New construction made crossing treacherous; the route he'd chosen had almost been swallowed up in a confusion of building and demolition. The air rang with the cries of workmen, quivered with the anxieties of populations relocated, houses and shops destroyed or soon to be so.

He was approaching Whitehall Palace now, with the Thames nearby. A crowd swarmed at the entrance to the government offices—returning soldiers, most likely, who hadn't gotten their pay yet. The wind off the river reeked of fish and food, tar and timber, the strong sweat of boatmen, and odors whose provenance was better left unknown. The fellow pulling his oars so evenly would make an excellent boxer; how long, Kit wondered, since he'd seen a pair of good British pugilists demonstrate their sweet science?

The capital was larger, louder, busier, but not so awe-inspiring anymore, now that he was older and had spilled his blood for it. Better that way. Dearer. England. Home. His and (even if she *would* make her disapproving observations about the Lord Liverpool's government) Mary's home as well. He wanted to protect it.

⁂

"Everything in good order, my lord, especially since I took the liberty of investing a thousand in Mr. Bakewell's new manufactory. Lady Christopher has done very well to direct her, ah, separate funds in that direction, and I didn't think you'd find it amiss to profit from it as well." Shumway's plump face glistened pink behind silver-rimmed spectacles, his surprisingly slender fingers precise as he traced the history of Kit and Mary's still-linked finances, trapped in clear rows and columns of pounds, shillings, and pence.

He'll be taking care of your money, the old marquess had said, after Kit and Mary had returned from Gretna.

"My solicitors met with Penley's," his lordship had continued. "We've settled some money on you. Cleared up some other long-overdue business too. Penley conceded his risible claim about the estate boundary. In return, he took the opportunity to stipulate some clever ways to keep some funds apart for her in trust—just so you don't suppose, Christopher, that your new father-in-law"—he'd fairly spat out the word—"is any happier about this, um, misbegotten alliance than I am—or more sanguine about its chances for success."

The money in trust had its own column in Shumway's ledger, next to her settlement from the separation. And yes, Kit was definitely rich enough to pay for the Act of Parliament necessary to obtain a divorce.

"Nothing amiss, Mr. Shumway, so long as I'm benefiting from it. Rather what I pay you for, I expect—perhaps you should invest another thousand if Mr. Bakewell's prospects are really so good. And the man so capable, so . . . trustworthy."

Indeed, quite so, the money man agreed. Excellent prospects, and very forward-looking too: the earlier, smaller manufactory a model of efficient yet humane employment of labor. "He conducts tours of it, you know, for investors and charitable sorts. The ladies quite enjoy it, him being such a well-spoken gentleman, quite tall and well-looking too, Mrs. Shumway says. . . ."

Kit glanced carelessly at his fine new pocket watch, "My word . . . the time. I must scamper. Thanks, as always, for your excellent . . . ah, and well wishes to the very discerning Mrs. Shumway . . ."

⟡

More pleasant, the welcome he got at White's. Toasted as a hero, stood to an excellent dinner. He settled back to lose a little at whist, win it back at piquet. Placed a few bets on the most trivial items he could find: the Earl of Derby's favorite fighting cock, the cost of the Duke of Ennisbourgh's divorce, and whether Mr. Smythe-Cochrane could down three bottles of port every day for a fortnight. And learned that bets had recently been laid on *him*.

"With your eldest brother's illness, and then there's only that nephew, the viscount, standing between you and the marquisate. Reckless boy, broke his arm last year hunting . . ."

"But of course Kit must have his own bets laid on his fortunes." Henry Claringworth was a particularly unpleasant specimen of the genus *Nobilus Britannicus*. Kit could remember him flirting, languidly and patronizingly, with Mary one night. (*I'd like to kick him,* she'd said.)

The talk made its inevitable way to women; his memory turned to a particular earlier conversation in this high-ceilinged room. Thin, bored voices echoed over the chasms of the years.

But you can't only *be making love to your* wife, *Stansell.*

Why? Well, because it's indecent, *that's why.*

No question that she's very pretty and all that. But you wouldn't always get your champagne from the same vintner, would you?

Though not champagne, I expect. In her case it would rather be ale, wouldn't it?

A laugh all around. Claringworth had laughed the hardest.

No matter. Penley brews the best ale in Britain. Surely his daughter should be made milady for that. Must have set you up with lots of blunt, Kit. Well done.

Following it up, soon enough, with a challenge. *What, never had two girls together—really?*

Shamefaced at twenty-two, he'd had to admit he hadn't. Not until that night. But often after that.

To find out what they all found so thrilling.

To turn his darker passions to the sort of women who were paid to tolerate it—for he'd begun to fear that it wasn't right to implicate Mary in so much playacting. She *seemed* to like it as well as he did—but could a lady really?

Most importantly perhaps, to demonstrate to all and sundry that though it might look like a rich old brewer had bought his daughter a Stansell for a husband, Lord Kit was under no obligation to anyone, and was free to do whatever he liked.

As *now* he most indubitably was.

For all she (and her tall, well-spoken Mr. Bakewell) might care.

⁂

Hell, he'd lost count of his cards.

Looking up into Claringworth's wide, guileless eyes, he affected a careless smile as his opponent played his trump and took him for two hundred pounds.

"He'll need it," Raikes murmured, "to support that mistress of his. And that pair of . . . grays for his phaeton."

Claringworth laughed and put down his cards, and sauntered off. "Think I'll be going, to make use of my winnings. My woman needs to be coaxed, my wife to be consoled, rather."

Hope you kicked him bloody hard, darling. Kit followed Claringworth out of the room.

❧

Back at Park Lane, he had a cold supper brought into the library. Time to prepare for tomorrow's dinner conversation.

The Parliamentary Committee's report had been published in *Gentleman's Magazine* the prior February. First time he'd read it, he'd been put off by its inflated, rather fatuous language. Rather like some of the dreadful diplomatic prose spun out at Vienna. Still, he'd mastered diplomatic communication—just as (with a little help) he'd mastered Latin. Soon, he promised himself, he'd be reading reports like this one with ease.

He gave a short bark of embarrassed laughter, remembering something foolish he'd once said. It had taken a decade to learn he *couldn't* play and carouse all the time. His afternoon at White's had rather driven the lesson home.

Upon second reading, however, the important words of the Committee of Secrecy's report rather leaped out at one.

. . . The widely diffused ramification of a system of clubs associated professedly for the purpose of Parliamentary Reform . . . to include every village in the kingdom . . .

. . . Whatever may be the real object of these clubs in general, your Committee have no hesitation in stating . . . particularly in those which are established in the . . . districts of Lancashire, Leicestershire, Nottinghamshire, and Derbyshire, and . . . composed of the lower sorts of artisans, nothing short of a revolution is the object expected and avowed.

Was it true? Was there evidence to back it up?

The committee couldn't reveal the sources of their information. Which meant that it came from infor-

mants. Unpleasant, the notion of Englishmen spying on
their fellows. What was worse than unpleasant was what
he'd learned from military intelligence: information so
gathered wasn't necessarily reliable.

Which would put one in rather a sticky situation, if
one had to use force against fellow Englishmen, based
solely on such information.

But what *would* one do, if the informers were telling
the truth? If, having *been taught to look to . . . London
as a signal for their operations . . .* the revolutionists had
agreed that *a day, at no very great distance, is appointed
for a general rising . . .*

Again, no corroborating evidence.

Except if you counted the fact that Wat had been
hearing the same thing. From *his* informant. In the
years Kit had been away, had half of England taken to
informing on the other half?

For a moment, he forgot to be nervous about his dinner with Lord Sidmouth. For a moment, he was simply
curious about what was really occurring.

Which was probably why the dinner went as smoothly
as it did. One always makes a better impression when
one is sincerely interested in the conversation. And
Lord Sidmouth knew how to make it interesting, even
compelling.

He put his case modestly, dispassionately.

"Regrettable, Lord Christopher, about having to get
our information as we do. But what's our alternative?
Are we to accept no intelligence but from persons of
the purest virtue? Or, given what's at stake, do we employ the means that offer themselves?

"For surely we Britons have something worth holding on to, wouldn't you say, from your time spent in less
happy nations?"

Kit could hardly deny it.

"There's been a certain diffusion of knowledge,
these past years—by our press, in particular—spreading

unchecked among the uneducated. Apt to instill an unwonted self-confidence among angry and distressed elements of the population who lack the advantages of tradition, culture, leisure—the broad view of things."

Easier to accept if you didn't picture Henry Claringworth as someone taking the broad view. Still, Kit knew what it had felt like to be angry and distressed. And no, it didn't encourage wise decision-making.

"When the radicals turn the people on the soldiery, there will be violence. In an intellectual sense, there is already violence. Fortunately, *we* are in a position to influence the course of these events."

Violence inevitable; only its outcome at issue.

The young assistant drinking sherry with them had nodded gravely before taking his leave.

Lord Sidmouth smiled after him. "A pity he couldn't stay for dinner. He'd have given you a sense of the nature of our work—from the bottom up, you know. Merely the volume of correspondence is overwhelming: details, details. Still, there'll be time. . . ."

All very encouraging, Kit thought, as the Home Secretary led him in to dinner. For in his letter, the general had particularly praised Major Stansell's skill with details.

They worked through that same letter of introduction over a delicate pea and lobster soup, discussed the peace negotiated at Vienna during the dory and salmon on a bed of pickled cucumber, touched upon a famous battle or two during a lime sherbet, and reviewed Kit's school and family connections over a fine haunch of venison served with jelly.

Kit kept his face still, as though over a hand of whist. A footman was serving around a splendid pineapple with port and Sauternes.

A pity, though, the Secretary said now, about the Ninth Marquess's very recent illness. For they absolutely needed their magistrates to be pulling together at this time, with the danger so pressing.

In fact, Lord Sidmouth recommended that Lord

Christopher go down to Derbyshire, at least for a month
or so.

"Your brother was wise to apprise you of his activities; puts you in a good way to take the reins. Anyone
can collect his rents, but what's important is order in
the countryside, when the London radicals urge a rising
in your district and others nearby."

So Wat's story *was* more than a stay-at-home brother's self-regarding fancy. It would be very agreeable to
help, of course. Go back home as . . . the New Kit. With
his military intelligence experience to guide him.

"I've enjoyed our conversation, Stansell," Lord Sidmouth told him. "And you're much the sort of person
we need."

Kit let out a very long breath, which it now seemed
he'd been holding for a week at least.

"But not now, when your brother needs you so much
more. Go down to the country; keep watch over the
situation. We're depending on you lads to call out the
troops. . . . Coordination, clarity . . . in light of the present danger . . . and then come back and talk to us and
we'll find a place for you at Whitehall."

❧

He'd go tomorrow if they could get the traveling coach
ready. He'd interview Wat's informant and report back
to London, talk to the men of the militia, make sure
they had the arms they required. A pity if there had to
be bloodshed on English soil. Still, the secretary had
been sure of the plot and of the necessity of protecting
the people in the countryside against the poison spreading among them (even those of them, like a certain lady,
who were too deluded to understand the danger).

He'd keep busy (which in itself would be a relief),
fighting anger and rebelliousness as best he could. As
he'd done since Spain. Quelling his own anger and rebelliousness had saved him; he was happy to put the experience in the service of his nation.

And as for the deluded lady in question—well, they'd

simply have to keep out of each other's way, or she out of *his* way, to be more precise. For her own good, after all.

And afterward, when she saw what important work he'd done. Afterward, perhaps . . .

※

He celebrated his plans that night at a pugilistic exhibition and won a thousand into the bargain. Great sport, boxing. He waved to the young Home Office assistant from across the large room.

Or perhaps it wasn't the assistant, for he didn't wave back, and seemed deep in conversation with a tall, bewhiskered fellow in a flash brown coat. Not the sort of companion Kit would have imagined for a member of the Home Office, but then, sport made Britons equals as few things did.

No matter either way. England was beginning to feel like home again. He shouldered his way up to the table to collect his winnings.

Chapter Ten

If the village of Grefford were any different from a hundred others along the coach route, it wouldn't be apparent to a stranger upon first arrival. There were the usual shops—butcher, baker, post office, apothecary, and well-stocked dry goods establishment among them. The church was at the end of High Street, the coaching inn just off the market square. The neighborhood's less prosperous residents lived farther out from the village center and so were less visible than they might be—except for a few men who spent their spare hours arguing the issues of the day with Mr. Williams, the shoemaker.

Village life being of a comforting daily sameness, a coach's arrival could be depended upon to precipitate some interest—or even excitement, if the approaching vehicle weren't part of the regular service between London and Chesterfield.

Peggy was the first to hear it from inside Mrs. Roberts's shop, where she'd been making orders according to the list Lady Christopher had made her go around home to fetch. For they needed heaps of things quite suddenly, some Grandin family members having taken it into their heads to arrive sooner than expected—as though there weren't enough work already, in preparation for the house party.

Not to speak of all the disputation about Miss Grandin's new gowns, which had thrown the young lady into a fit of the sullens and her mother and aunt even worse. Not that any of it should have given Lady Christopher the right to be so sharp with Peggy this morning—blaming her for the shopping list her ladyship had forgotten herself, and then making her go back to fetch it in the tiring midday heat.

All because of a length of lace trimming along the neckline of a gown. As though an inch of skin at a young lady's bosom could mean . . .

But Peggy knew full well what it could mean. So when she'd heard the coach (for Tom had explained to her the particular kind of jingling a superior set of springs would make, and now she knew how to listen for it), she'd become very still and alert, though the vehicle was still a bit off in the distance.

It would be the dowager marchioness, and Tom with her.

She ran out the door, standing entranced in front of the casks and kegs and rushes for brooms, to wait for the coach to come into view. Enjoying her anticipation of what he'd look like up there on the box next to Mr. Frayne, sun lighting his face and shoulders—it was like she could already see him leaping off in his graceful way, legs flashing in their breeches and white stockings, when he'd arrive at the Dower House at Rowen, to help the marchioness out the door.

She'd call out, catch his eye, wave to him and Mr. Frayne as they drove by. . . .

Except that it wasn't Mr. Frayne driving the coach. Nor was the big noodle of a footman sitting up there anything like Tom.

Oh, it was one of the Rowen coaches—for hadn't Tom told her there was more than one? It had the crest on its door. But it wasn't the one the marchioness had lent them in France, nor was it the marchioness riding inside. The passenger's handsome boots preceded the rest of him out of the coach. Peggy wasn't the only person on the street who watched the whole of him stroll over to the shoemaker's shop while the coach continued on its way. Toward Rowen, she supposed.

But she found that she didn't care where he *or* the coach was going. Nor was it *her* job to go inform anyone of this new arrival. In fact, it was no concern whatsoever of Peggy Weightman's if Lady Christopher found out quite for herself, in full view of everyone in the square, the surprising news of who'd arrived in Grefford just now. For her employer would be finishing her call upon Cathy Williams (Peggy smiled, just a bit wickedly), and very soon indeed.

❧

"It'll be better, Lady Christopher," Cathy Williams said, "for Miss Grandin to have her brother and cousin to occupy her these days than you and her mother."

Mary suspected that the schoolmistress was right. After all, she did know young people. Too bad she couldn't have taken on Elizabeth's education.

And yes, it would be worth anything to get the girl off their hands—even four unexpected early guests due to arrive while the water closets were undergoing renovation.

No matter, Mary thought, *we'll put them in the older wing of the house, where there are no improvements to worry about.* At any rate, it would be a felicitous combination of guests: Jessie's son was bringing a friend, and Fannie Grandin was traveling with a chaperone. The chaperone was a distinct advantage; she could shepherd the four young people through picnics and tours of the countryside, leaving Mary and Jessie free to plan two weeks of menus, to see to the linen and silver. . . . *And* to begin considering the project Cathy had proposed to Mary this morning.

"Because it's such a splendid project, Cathy, that we shall want to begin as soon as possible." Mary shook the schoolmistress's hand and picked up her basket, emptied now of the apple tarts she'd brought when she'd walked out to the village this morning.

Trust Cathy to think of building a cistern in the village, so the local women could get their water close to home and not have to trudge all the way downhill to the spring. The school was prospering too, the girls actually learning their French and history rather than parroting it back as rote nonsense. Her call here this morning had entirely raised her spirits.

There'd have to be a committee, to raise funds. Jessica would probably preside if Mary promised to take charge of the accounts, at least temporarily, before she left with Matthew. Perhaps they could hold an assembly, sell tickets as the people of Cauthorn did for their medical clinic.

The tiny girl who'd escorted her through the garden held the gate open and curtsied. As Mary bent to kiss the child's cheek, she found herself thinking about the forgotten shopping list—which, if truth be told, hadn't been Peggy's fault in the slightest.

She'd apologize directly after she posted her letter. And Matthew would also be a great help, both with money and expertise; no doubt he understood how things like wells and cisterns actually worked. Together he and she could do a lot of good in the world. A few months, a year perhaps, of unpleasantness during the divorce proceedings, and her life would finally take a reasonable shape.

She smiled and bowed to the vicar's wife as they passed one another in the street. The village remained a comfort in its imperviousness to fashion, soothing monotony of conversation, the friendly, respectful faces she'd known all her life, stately pace of calls made and compliments exchanged.

While at Beechwood Knolls . . . absurd, the tumult over Elizabeth's gowns. Impressive in its way, the girl's instinct for what would most infuriate her mother.

"We shall be going to call at Rowen in two hours," Jessica had told her, as the maid folded the fabric. "And don't be late."

"Of course I won't. I *like* the Marchioness Susanna, even if you don't."

Mildly funny now, the mirror expressions of exasperation on their fair faces. Less funny this morning. All Mary had wanted was to escape to the village. And so she'd rushed away, forgetting all about the shopping list and then insisting that it had been Peggy's responsibility to bring it.

Still, Peggy looked less aggrieved than Mary would have expected, idly examining the assortment of goods displayed in Mrs. Roberts's front window, and now raising her head to gaze down across the square to the street that led you to the shoemaker and the post office (yes, and Mary must not forget to post the letter). Ah, a gentleman was coming from that direction. Well, that would explain it.

Hmmm, and he was looking rather well turned out in a neat blue coat too, and—damn and double damn, as she recognized him—he was quite evidently the cause for Peggy's wicked good cheer.

⁂

The shoemaker had promised to fix the boot heel in a week. It seemed to Kit an excessive wait, but Williams had gestured at the unimpressive assemblage of footwear on his shelves. *I've got all these to attend to first, you see, my lord*—spoken to emphasize that Kit wasn't *his* lord, not really. While the hardened, blackened hand indicated that every shabby boot and patten was equally deserving of his attention as a Stansell's unevenly worn-down heel.

Hardly surprising, Kit thought—even if one hadn't read Wat's letters. The Grefford people (and their children too) had always prided themselves on their independence, one might say their superiority, to their counterparts who lived and worked on the Rowen estate.

"As you will." He'd send the boot with his man tomorrow.

Williams had returned a summary nod, and Kit stepped outside and around the corner to the sunny village square, where a very long time ago, Joshua Penley's daughter had stared up at him from amid a ragged gang of children—and he'd done his best not to appear to notice her.

He remembered mounting his horse and turning away as though deaf to the faint jeers at his back. Directing their horses back toward Rowen, he and Will had ridden past a lovely-looking woman he thought must be Mrs. Penley. Her walk had a sort of floating quality, even as she made her brisk way toward the square, carrying a large basket on her arm. She'd appeared to be gazing sympathetically at him, her concern as irksome to him as her grubby little daughter's hostility.

Or perhaps he'd simply been envious of the daughter and her place in the game of hare and hounds. As a boy he'd done a lot of things to make the old marquess angry, but playing with the village children would have been unthinkable. Even supposing they'd wanted to play with *him*.

For a confused moment, he thought he saw Mrs. Penley again, in a white dress with tiny black dots printed over it, black shawl, and a deep straw bonnet. Floating toward him with a basket on her arm.

But Mrs. Penley had died a number of years ago.

Odd, the tricks the mind played; Mary didn't resemble her mother very much at all. Jessica, he recalled, was the tall, blond sister, while Julia was shorter, dark like Mr. Penley (he'd rather admired how Mary's mother had never slouched in a misguided effort to make her barrel-shaped husband appear taller). Pink-cheeked, brown-eyed Mary was somewhere in the middle, a bit like each parent but generally like neither—a changeling, he'd once called her, stolen from her cradle by fairies; she'd giggled, they'd kissed and then they'd kissed again (kissing, at the time, being something they were confident of, while other kinds of touching were still new, strange, and a bit frightening).

She a changeling, and he (as he'd once overheard a

nursery maid call him) *a little dark secret.* Neither of them belonging to anyone but the other. Or so they'd vowed and so they'd believed—before life and other people and their own frailties and foolishness had gotten between them and shown them what all of *that* was worth.

Surprising, then, to observe how she'd grown into her mother's grace, her impatient stride and gestures moderated, at least in this familiar setting, by an air of being at ease and at home.

Dammit, it was *his* home too.

After which observation he had to wonder how long he'd been standing with his mouth agape while people passed by him on either side. He couldn't swear to it, but she appeared to have paused in her steps as well.

The church clock struck a quarter past noon.

She started forward and so did he. The dusty haze of midday sunshine glared off the shop windows. He squinted to get his bearings.

The footpath to Rowen Park was over to the left. He could remember it quite clearly. It was the direct way to go; the more picturesque path took you on a meandering stroll through the forest and connected you to some more obscure little byways.

But he'd already lingered too long. At Rowen, the coachman would have informed them of his arrival by now; Susanna would have had time to get Wat ready to see him. Which was why he'd stopped in the village in the first place—to give them a little time to prepare. Well, *wasn't* that why he'd stopped in the village?

He and she were only a few feet apart. He paused long enough to bow. More of a nod, he expected. She nodded back and swept impatiently around the corner to the post office. He shrugged and turned away toward Rowen.

⁂

How many people had there been in the square? Quite a few, Mary thought, by the number of curious gazes she could feel prickling her skin.

No matter. He and she hadn't spoken. Their legal separation was still in evidence. Everything was coldly proper.

Nor was there a need to apologize to Peggy—at least not in so many words. Sufficient for Mary to nod (as a concession of defeat) and then to shrug her shoulders to signal that she wouldn't be making unfair accusations anytime soon.

⁂

And yes, as her sister and niece were good enough to report at dinner, they *had* seen him at Rowen. He'd arrived just as they'd been taking their leave.

Which was too bad, for Mary had hoped to discuss the cistern project. Or Fred's and Fannie's impending visits. Or anything else in the world. Algebra, perhaps.

Mercifully, Elizabeth kept herself relatively quiet, as though occupied with thoughts too interesting to share with her mother and aunt. While Jessica, on the other hand, seemed to feel it incumbent to observe that *she,* for one, had "found him much improved when we encountered him today at Rowen, Mary. Even if *you* might not agree.

"Oh, and by the way," she added, "he'll be reading the lesson at church tomorrow, in his brother's place."

It seemed that his sister-in-law had insisted upon it. She'd be speaking to the vicar about it. And his brother had looked very pleased at the notion.

Which meant that if she wanted to avoid stares and unpleasantness, Mary would have to remain at home.

She responded with a snort of disbelief at the thought of Kit peering sternly down over the lectern as the old marquess had done. Absurd, sanctimonious.

And was she to be shut up at Beechwood Knolls while *he* had the run of the neighborhood?

"It's as though he believes himself some personification of order and rectitude these days. He'll enjoy walking about Grefford, people gazing respectfully at him, when in his heart he's really the same unruly . . ."

"Odd," Jessica said, "I've heard you say quite similar things about yourself on your visits home. And after all, he is a war hero now."

Perhaps. If a bit ungenerous of Jessie to point it out.

"As well," Elizabeth added, "as seeming quite the orderly, polite, respectable gentleman." Shrugging her slender shoulders. "At least to *me*."

But that surely was a bit much to swallow. Mary narrowed her eyes at her niece. "Yes," she said, "and *you* like the young marchioness as well."

Traitors. The wretched girl and her mother both.

Jessica burst into peals of sudden laughter. The three women looked curiously at each other, none of them quite sure for the moment just where her own loyalty lay.

Chapter Eleven

〰️⚜️〰️

Just as well, Kit thought, that she hadn't been at church. The scriptural passage was very fine and he'd done a reasonable job of reading it aloud. But he might not have been able to carry it off if he'd had to avoid catching her gaze. Yes, he could just imagine it. *You, reading the lesson?* Her eyes mocking him from the Penley family pew.

In truth, he'd rather enjoyed booming out the biblical sonorities. Even pausing to glare for an instant at a little boy who'd been whispering to his mate.

Why not, Mary? Why should you be the only one to find your simple, serious, respectable self in the country?

How pretty she'd looked, passing through the village square with a basket over her arm. White gown with black dots. But they weren't dots, they were very tiny flowers—he'd only realized it during the instant when she'd swept past him so haughtily. Lovely flowing stuff the gown was made of, especially lovely to think of her wearing that particularly disreputable shift under it. A length of scarlet cord around her wrist—no, that had been merely a trick of his imagination, set aflame by, of all things, her ladylike village propriety.

After church, he'd enjoyed the well wishes and congratulations from people in the neighborhood. Good to meet Colonel Halsey, who led the militia; they'd be speaking next week. And everyone had chuckled when he'd shaken the hand of the child he'd terrorized from behind the lectern. Of course, Mrs. Grandin and that pretty daughter had come up to greet him. Too bad: he'd wanted a few more words with Halsey. But Susanna had been anxious about Wat. He'd hastened to take her back to Rowen.

"He'll be very happy when I tell him how beautifully you read it." Kit handed her into the carriage a bit charily.

Still, she wasn't such a bad sort. Fearful of unconventionality, in the past she'd stayed as far as she could from him—odd now to be thrown together, to have to make halting conversation.

Growing up in the glow cast by a brilliant, beautiful mother, Kit had always assumed Wat had married Susanna because he'd been told to. Certainly he couldn't have *wanted* to marry this small, timid, rusty-haired woman, with her pursed mouth and jutting chin.

But today he found himself admiring the patient slowness with which she spooned beef jelly between his brother's tremulous lips, heedless, as she wiped it from his shirtfront, of the bit that stained the lace cuff of her gray gown.

"It must be awkward for you," she told him after Wat had been put to bed for a rest, "with Lady Christopher in the neighborhood. Still, now that you're here, perhaps she'll return to London."

He suppressed a smile. Whatever her newly revealed strengths, Susanna clearly didn't know Lady Christopher.

"I hadn't realized you received her family nowadays," he said.

"Times change," she said. "The estate boundaries are settled, which was the main thing. Mrs. Grandin is more liberal in her opinions than I like, but she does her best. And Mr. Grandin was quite what he should be."

How strange to be having this conversation, as

though *he* were also what he should be. Perhaps he was now. Part of him enjoyed it—the same part that had once delivered messages across enemy lines—while part of him expected to be arrested any minute as a foreign agent.

"And then, of course, I quite dote upon *Miss* Grandin," his sister-in-law was saying. "She sometimes comes to call of her own accord, and I daresay I've had a hand in improving her. She's not at all the forward, hoydenish, bluestocking sort of creature one might have supposed her to turn out, given her mother's family. . . ." She stopped, blushed. "I beg your pardon, Christopher."

"Not at all." He wouldn't have expected anything else.

Though what *was* unexpected was his sadness, that the estate borders were no longer ambiguous, social intercourse more amiable and better regulated between the two families. There'd been something magical about sharing a secret friendship in the place where the boundaries ran together.

"But you'll want to get back to the magistrate's papers," she was saying now, leading him out of the dining room and down a corridor.

Rather a dreary little office. They'd moved the papers down from the tower room, Susanna had told him, so that Wat might be able to work with Kit on them when he recovered a bit more. She'd made a very small pause before articulating the word *when*.

Still, he was glad not to be working in the tower. The old marquess would summon you up there to pronounce judgment on you. He'd sit at his writing desk and you'd stand in front of it like a supplicant.

He wouldn't exactly get angry. You'd have to be worth a lot more than you were, his manner implied, to make him angry. Mostly he'd be bored, mildly amused, and visibly hankering to be out riding or fishing. As when Kit had been sent down from school. Or when he and Mary had returned from Gretna.

Handing over the marriage papers, to be registered in

the parish and then tucked away in the family files for the solicitors and genealogists.

"*Mary* Artemis? *Couldn't give the girl a decent* English *name, eh? Quite the sort of thing one would expect of the Penleys.*"

"*Yes, your lordship. Here's where we signed.*"

"*I can see that.*"

"*And* I *think her name is beautiful. Your lordship.*"

After reaching a certain age, Kit had always called him *your lordship.* The old man didn't seem to mind. He certainly never asked to be called anything else, which Kit supposed made sense under the circumstances.

He'd gotten a scowl out of him anyway, with that comment about her name being beautiful. A small victory in those days.

Surprising how vividly he could remember it. Physical proximity, he expected, a sense of place. Smell of the air, rustle of weeds and hedges, weight of looming skies.

Walking the footpath from Grefford, it had been as though she'd been by his side. As though he could still make out their younger shapes, pressed into the grass, molded into the heavy air that meant a storm was on the way.

But she's not at your side. And doesn't want to be.

Time to get on with business.

The downstairs office contained a safe, which held instructions on how to communicate with Traynor, the informant. Messages in a hollow tree. He'd walk out later, leave a note telling the man that he'd be receiving the reports from now on. Paying for them, too.

Interesting stuff. He'd read some of it last night; finishing it up now, he felt something of the excitement one felt decoding a military communication—disparate elements suddenly cohering into a story. In truth, rather a frightening story. It vindicated everything Wat had been writing to him and matched exactly what the Committee of Secrecy had been saying.

*To the Right Honorable Magistrate &c &c &c with
the Compliments of his Most Loyal Servant in the Matter of . . .*

Traynor was clearly no professional. His wordy reports on the doings of the local Parliamentary Reform
Club were written in neat if wobbly writing, but one had
rather to hack through an overgrowth of irrelevancies
to get to the point.

*The meeting took place in the Wheel. . . . There were
twenty-three persons present. . . .*

Though, in fact, the local malcontents were meeting
less frequently at taverns these days and more often in
barns, as new laws against seditious meetings were
handed down from London. But on an occasion when
they still came together at a place that served food and
drink, Mr. Traynor seemed to feel it incumbent to begin with a description of the various members' suppers—
who'd had chops and who'd had ale, and whether they
had to borrow the money to pay for it. The first pages of
certain reports would thus be bathed in a glow of fel-
lowship, the warmth of a public hearth. Reading them,
Kit felt sometimes as though he were back in uniform,
drinking and joking with his men.

Until one got to the real stuff: *In Lancashire and
Nottingham they were all ready. . . . Sheffield Bar-
racks to be attacked and the guards and soldiers made
prisoners . . .*

In one of Wat's last communications to Kit in Paris,
he'd written that Sir Charles Benedict, over near Nottingham, had been receiving extremely similar reports
from *his* informant.

Write to Benedict. Find out more.

He gazed out the window across the velvety lawn at
Susanna wheeling his brother's invalid chair in front of
a stand of rhododendron. All calm and domestic peace,
or so one might think.

Even as late as last February, Kit had doubted the
existence of a conspiracy.

The letters Wat sent him last year had been singularly

unimpressive. There'd been just as many meetings for
Traynor to report on—more of them, perhaps, after the
harvest had turned out so miserable. Snow on the ground
as late as June; hunger and anger—though at least they'd
been spared the food riots some districts had endured.
Invective had flowed from the spy's reports like small
beer at a village festival: the sort of extravagant, furious,
gaseous oratory Kit imagined a poor man might glory in
when he'd had some drink in him.

Which was exactly why he *hadn't* been disturbed by
it. Kit had spent enough of his own life annoyed, an-
tagonized, insulted, or incensed, to have a certain familiarity with anger's themes and variations. In the
army, moreover, he'd heard plenty of talk that flattered
itself on its audacity but left off short of mutiny.

Whereas in these more recent reports . . . suddenly
one could discern a different order of reality, of confidence, of resolution, of detailed planning and disci-
plined organization. And although it seemed entirely
ridiculous for the several dozen members of Grefford's
little local Parliamentary Reform Society to think they
could take London, the disturbing part was that they
weren't planning on doing it themselves.

Sheffield would be sending ten thousand men; Bir-
mingham a great many more than that. The speaker
had it from a Mr. Oliver, whom he'd met at Derby.
"He'll be here with us next week, and *then* you'll hear
some speechifying. A fine man, imposing in his brown
coat and Wellingtons.

"For the lads from *Derby* will be marching, you can
bet. The London Committee expects to raise fifty thousand." Evidently, the Oliver fellow had been delegated
by his London confreres to come and speak up north.
And so the weavers and stockingers, joiners and car-
penters, puddlers and bellows makers—all manner of
laborers from Grefford—were swilling down mental
poison bottled in the metropolis.

Another London delegate, named Hollis, had spoken at Manchester, according to a man who had a

brother-in-law there. Told the Manchester crowd that the Leicester-Derby-Nottingham area would be sending thirty thousand.

How had the Committee of Secrecy put it? *A system of clubs . . . to include every village in the kingdom.*

And all taking their orders from London—the level of coordination and discipline most impressive indeed.

He wrote his note to Traynor to tell him he'd be acting in behalf of the marquess for the next while. Yes, continue sending your correspondence; you'll be receiving your pay and orders from me now.

It would be more important than first he'd thought to talk to Benedict in Nottingham, share information with a fellow magistrate. Which meant another letter explaining his newly assumed position and asking if he might hope to find him at home on Tuesday.

Folding the letters, sealing them—the one to Traynor to be deposited in its hiding place; too bad he'd have to pay to post the one to Benedict. But it would be worse to risk finding out if Wat could sign his name well enough to frank the letter.

All right, let's see now. Once he was started on a task, he liked to keep going. He'd organized the filing system, the correspondence neatly divided into separate portfolios—to and from Traynor, to and from the Home Office—and sorted by date. He lined the portfolios against the edge of the desk and drummed his fingers alongside them.

But absent a next communication from Traynor, or additional information from Benedict, there was nothing to do but wait.

Or take a walk in the forest. See the old places. Why not?

Chapter Twelve

(FROM THE JOURNAL OF LADY CHRISTOPHER STANSELL)

Sunday Evening, May 25

Upon her return from church, Elizabeth announced that she might add an inch of the Belgian lace I brought her to the neckline of the gown she'd be wearing to the Cauthorn assembly. It would be much more proper, didn't Mama and Aunt Mary think so?

After Jessie and I have talked ourselves silly for a week, trying to convince her of precisely the same thing. But now it seems there's a very proper gentleman next door, who might disapprove of anything too forward or Penley-ish—or so she's convinced herself.

Provoking, but Jessica was pleased with the result—enough so to promise to preside over the cistern committee. Too bad I didn't need anything else—with her son Fred due to arrive so soon, she'd have promised away a kingdom.

Still, once he did arrive, I could see why. How like Arthur he is—easy smile, comfortable manners, knack for making everyone seem likeable.

*Whereas his friend, the tall and polished Lord
Ayres, is a bit of a walking cloak rack, though perhaps that's just the effect of the startling number of
capes his greatcoat boasts.*

*Handsome, in a rather killingly Byronic way,
with large, damp violet eyes and enough carefully waved hair to make up for the smallish size
of his head. Offered a low bow and a studiously
deep gaze to each of us ladies, each gaze calibrated to a different vibration on the spectrum of
sensibility.*

*Elizabeth standoffish with him, her imagina-
tion monopolized by our neighbor, I expect.*

⚜

**(FROM LORD CHRISTOPHER STANSELL'S PORTFOLIO,
IN THE MATTER OF POTENTIAL DISTURBANCES)**

Monday, May 26
   *Wrote to Halsey: Confirm drilling the Militia,
next week, June 4, Rowen's fallow fields, north.*
[They could go over the details, at the Cauthorn
assembly next week.]
   More from Traynor (received this morning):
   "*The Leicester chaps are to retreat upon Nottingham, there to await the Yorkshire men, & when a
junction is formed, they are to march to London. At
stated places in the road the Lancashire and Derbyshire men are to join them. At London to contend
for a change in the government.*" [Whew. So there
you had it.]

⚜

LADY CHRISTOPHER'S JOURNAL

Monday, May 26
   *Fannie Grandin and Miss Kimball arrived af-
ter breakfast. Fannie's a delightful-looking girl—
rich auburn hair and knowing hazel eyes; Miss K.*

a nonentity whom Fannie's mama was doubtless sick of having about her.

Jessie predicted they'd send Fannie to us, and I can see why. If I had a plain older daughter making her come-out, I'd pack this one off to the country too. Not so heart-stoppingly lovely as Elizabeth, but that's as it should be. Fannie's papa is a baronet; sometimes providence plays fair with its gifts. She received Lord Ayres's attentions with good grace and much sense of entitlement, but was mostly happy to see Elizabeth. Lifelong friends, much hugging and squealing—giggling too, and whispering, some of it obviously about me. Which is to say, of course, about Kit . . . I overheard the words Rowen, divorce, Cauthorn, and so elegant.

I expect one could say that about him nowadays. Indeed, with the military bearing he's picked up, he'll do very well at Almack's.

The young ladies and Miss K. called on our neighbors this afternoon, while Fred and Lord A. did some shooting. Lady Grandin would want her daughter to dance attendance upon the young marchioness. And if Lord Christopher happens to be there too, well, what of it?

Jessie and I stayed home to welcome an entirely different group of young people into our house— the village boys and girls who'll be helping us prepare for the house party. A chance for us, of course, to reduce unemployment in the district, and fill some of their bellies as well. And a day's work for us, the butler, and the housekeeper too, to get them settled in.

Though I did wonder about that striking-looking boy—Nicholas Merton—odd, he almost reminds me of Kit at around sixteen, but it's probably the standoffish look. We were told during a charity visit that Nicholas's father has disappeared, for fear of being arrested for sedition. So we could hardly refuse to hire the poor boy—it's not his fault, after all,

*and he's Cathy Williams's nephew into the bargain;
I'll ask Peggy to look after him.*

*So much to do; Fannie and Elizabeth home
much too soon from their calls. We could hardly
attend to their girls' mournful report that Lord
Christopher was off somewhere on business.*

*Kit? Business? No, they must have got that
wrong.*

❦

LORD CHRISTOPHER'S MEMORANDA

Tuesday, May 27 (late)

*Rode to Nottingham. Rec'd handsomely by
Benedict—luncheon, access to files, his informant's reports. Notes:*

*Their local Reform Society met last Friday, great
excitement, London delegate Hollis expected when
next they convene—ah, that'll be tonight; I must get
a further report. . . . discussion of pistols, places to
be obtained; informant speculates a cache of pikes
is buried.*

Rising set for June 9.

B. to send me copies of tonight's report.

*Rode home through sunset . . . tomorrow bids
fine . . . hermit's hut.*

[The last words had been crossed out, for he liked
to keep his files—and his thoughts—rigidly divided
between business and whatever other claptrap might
be running through his head.]

Chapter Thirteen

⸺⬥⸻⬥⸺

I t was certainly none of *her* concern, Peggy Weightman thought, to make judgments on the way Lady
Christopher was acting once she were ready to go to
bed these nights.

Cheerful, busy all day, when the bedchamber door
closed behind her, she became like one of them traveling balloons come down to land when they let the air
all out. Pale, passive—well, it was easy to get her tucked
into bed anyway, give her a tiny dose to make her sleep,
though Peggy doubted she got to sleep so soon, which
were *definitely* none of the business of a chambermaid,
even if you couldn't help but suspect ... especially
since, as the lady's eyes got heavier, she got more
eager—sometimes angrily so—to be left alone.

Peggy knotted a length of thread—how in the world
had the lady torn that pocket anyway? Of course, Lady
Christopher *might* want to be alone with her thoughts
of that very kind and pleasant Mr. Bakewell, but Peggy
wouldn't lay money on it. For she did know a bit about a
certain particular kind of thing, though in truth Lord
Christopher couldn't hold a candle to her own Tom,
neither for countenance nor, of course, for stature.

If so a person could still call him *her own Tom*. Were
he and his employer ever to come to England again?

And when he did finally come home, what would he think? For her predicament was becoming more probable every day, and she'd begun to mull over using a solution of tansy and pennyroyal—or (worse perhaps) to give some consideration to the man up in Ripley that her father wanted her to marry.

Perhaps, after all, she didn't know as much as she thought she did. Perhaps Tom hadn't cared for her after all. Or never had—not really, not like he'd said, and certainly not as she needed him to. *Perhaps,* Peggy thought, *I've been wrong all this time.*

And then this morning to have to put up with Nick Merton's teasing—about the airs she gave herself, according to him, just because she liked to wear pretty clothes. Like she imagined herself some kind of lady, he'd said, instead of proud of where she come from— the *true* England, he'd said.

The true England, is it, she'd replied, smart enough, and who's giving himself airs *now?*

Still, she'd been glad to go the village to get more thread for Miss Grandin's everlasting gowns.

Only to meet up with the man with the whiskers and brown coat. He'd been in Nottingham, he told her. . . . After asking all those questions again, about everyone around the neighborhood . . . and then inviting her to go walking with him.

Like *walking* was what he really meant. Like she were some light kind of creature . . . though these days sometimes she felt like one. Well, what *was* to become of her? And she *hated* the Ripley man her father was so taken with. . . .

✦

Mary had found her sobbing, collapsed in a heap in the corner of her dressing room, the pelisse, with its torn pocket, abandoned on the parquet floor.

"But what *is* it?" *Well, that sounds stupid enough,* she told herself. For what else could it possibly be?

"Oh, don't cry, he'll come. After all, he must wait for

Lady Rowen; she'd be lost without him, you know. He's a fine, responsible man, Peggy. He'll come. Lady Rowen is simply taking more time than had been expected."

But time isn't really the issue, is it? Or perhaps time is always the issue *to a confused girl who fears herself pregnant. Though of course she wouldn't admit it to her sharp-tongued and demanding employer.*

Who was trying her clumsy best, at the moment, to be a comfort. Mary put her arms around the small person on the floor and patted her back until the sobs subsided a bit and the words came clearer.

"Ah, at the coaching inn. You don't know his name? And he said what? He treated you in which way? But that's dreadful."

Even more dreadful—infuriating, really—was the way the man had continued to ask Peggy for information—about a great many things, including her employer. Which could only mean that Kit was paying him to spy on Mary—in the service of the divorce, of course. Except that he'd promised not to do so until after she'd left Beechwood Knolls.

Perhaps he thought his promise didn't count anymore.

"Leave the pelisse and get a little rest," she said. "And don't worry. The man won't be bothering you again."

⚜

Not if I *have anything to say about it, Lord Christopher.* Her angry thoughts seemed louder than the bracken crashing under the soles of her walking boots.

She'd confront him at Rowen. In front of his sister-in-law, if need be. He didn't own the district, any more than the old Eighth Marquess.

He'd made a promise. And she'd see that he stuck to it.

She could have taken the curricle, she supposed, but it felt good to walk. And if you were walking, this path along the stream would get you to Rowen as fast as any other—though it mightn't seem so if you didn't understand the design of the grounds, which had been laid out to appear "naturally" meandering, on the way to the hermit's hut.

⁂

The path, at the outskirts of the Rowens' park, near Beechwood Knolls, had always been dark, mysterious, and overgrown, for what would be the point of a hermit if he were too easily approached? You got to the hut by climbing over a cunningly constructed stile that appeared to be broken. A little way farther, you'd find a well-built cottage, which boasted a good fireplace, a reasonably comfortable bed, glass in the front windows, and a writing table. It needed to; a good estate hermit would have his comforts.

"We advertised in the newspaper." The marchioness had told the story one long afternoon, when Kit was in Spain and Mary had needed distracting.

"It was Mr. Brown's idea—a hermit's hut was just the thing, back in the last century, to add a certain *je ne sais quoi* to an improved estate. I, of course, was charged with choosing the hermit. You should have seen me, pouring tea for a series of wild-eyed, long-haired gentlemen, doing my lady-of-the-manor best to discern which of them was the most picturesque and poetical."

Several had been tried and found wanting.

"I must not have had the knack of choosing," Lady Rowen continued. "Or perhaps we were simply unlucky. The first man we hired didn't like the food we brought him, another was discovered to be in league with a band of poachers, and the third couldn't keep himself away from the girls in the village."

Even going so far, she added, as to wash his hair, in order to ingratiate himself with his particular lady love. "At which point we had to let him go, and after which I prevailed upon his lordship to stop this silliness and have Mr. Brown build the set of ruins you now see on

Rook Hill, if we must have something picturesque about the place."

The plan had been to take down the hut, the marchioness had concluded, but somehow they'd never gotten around to it. Which of course, Mary already knew, having discovered the place for herself one day. Though there'd been no need to tell Lady Rowen any of that.

Today it looked more picturesque than ever. Vines festooned the windows; the silvery stone walls were spattered with lichen and chinked with moss. She could hear loud cooing from the family of doves that had nested somewhere under the eaves.

Or perhaps they were roosting in the chimney, which meant that one wouldn't be able to build a fire on the hearth anymore, as Kit had once done with such care. Neither he nor Mary had known how such a thing was done—it of course being servants' work. She'd been fascinated by how well he'd managed it, and delighted that they could take off their clothes without first diving under the ragged quilt for shelter from the chill, dank air.

She'd covered her quim with her hands that first time. He'd prised them away. She'd clasped them behind her back, to show that she wasn't afraid.

But that had been much later.

For they'd only been children when she'd first happened upon the cottage.

She'd been wandering on the far side of her family's land. Distracted by some pretend fancy, she'd strayed past the disputed borders and even farther, to what she should have recognized as the clear beginnings of the Rowen property. Crashing through bracken, singing or reciting to herself—she might have been twelve, she thought now.

Yes, it couldn't have been too long after that time she'd spied him in Grefford. She'd been out of breath, her heart pounding—not from the thought of *him,* of course; she hadn't been thinking of him at all. She'd been running, skimming along and barely keeping her footing. Paying no attention to a darkening sky and threatening wind, or even then to the raindrops making ripples in the brook that ran beside the path, until it had gotten much too late for her to get herself home, before the rain began in earnest.

The pretty cottage had seemed to her like something out of an old tale of sprites and elves. What great good fortune to find it—although at twelve, and still half immersed in whatever she'd been pretending, finding shelter from the rain (and just in the nick of time too) hadn't seemed a particularly magical occurrence.

The cottage didn't appear to be occupied—well, who'd live out here in the forest anyway? But she'd knocked politely, preparing a smile and a curtsy as she did.

Good, no answer. She turned the knob, pulled open the door, and took a step inside—only to find *him* planted firmly in her way, fairly pushing her outside into the wet again, before she'd even gotten over the threshold.

"Damn and double damn." She didn't usually say such things out loud. But she wasn't about to be shoved—and certainly (now that she recognized him) not by that conceited Rowen boy.

"That's nice language," he'd said, "from a girl."

"I beg your pardon," she'd muttered.

He'd only shaken his head.

"Beg pardon, *Lord Christopher.*" But her voice had come out too petulant. And she'd rather get herself soaked than curtsy to a nasty boy who wasn't much bigger than she was—even if he seemed awfully strong, not budging an inch when she'd tried to push him aside.

"It's my family's property," he'd said.

"Isn't," she replied, according to the rules of childhood confrontation, though, in fact, she knew it was.

"*Is.* You don't know what you're talking about."

Not only was he right about the property, she'd thought; he probably remembered her from the day she'd been playing with the village children.

"Get out," he said.

"Isn't," she repeated a bit dispiritedly. "And anyway," she added with more energy (and a bit of logic as well), "I *can't* get out when I'm barely in."

Would he push a girl out into the storm? It seemed he might. He'd raised his hands to put them against her shoulders. She'd stood up as straight as she could. *Just let him try.* But he'd drawn back, too polite or proper, finally, to attempt physical combat with her.

Polite was better than impolite, but the fact remained that the wet was beating down—more intensely now— on her back and bum and calves.

"But it's raining," she wailed. "I'm getting wet already and my governess is evil and will beat me with a stick for it. I'll be tied up and chained, punished and starved and fed bread and water for a week."

Which was an odd thing to say, since neither Mr. or Mrs. Penley believed in using any sort of corporal force, even on the least tractable of children. Much as her governess might have been tempted, Mary had never been physically punished in her life.

Still, she liked the sound of it—it was exciting to imagine herself in such a helpless and piteous situation. And it did get the boy's attention.

"Really?"

"Truly. It'll be your fault if I'm punished and beaten, and I bet you'll be glad of it."

He'd laughed, but he'd backed up and let her in.

After which there didn't seem to be much to say, so they stood side by side at a broken window and watched the storm without further comment. It turned out to be a brief downpour, tumultuous while it lasted but traveling quickly south and leaving her enough time to run home before the next clouds blew in.

Not the most auspicious way to begin a friendship. Nor a love affair either. And certainly not a marriage. But they'd both come back the next day, which was mild and sunny, and she'd had an apple in her pocket, stolen from the sideboard.

"My governess isn't really cruel," she told him. "And actually," she added, "she's not allowed to strike me."

"Of course. I knew that. I never believed you." He'd laughed, though, in fact, he'd seemed a bit relieved—after all, who knew what he'd been taught to think of the Penleys?

"But someone struck *you*," she said.

The bandage on his nose and the black marks around his eyes were a great deal more visible than they'd been the day before, when the cottage had been so dark from the storm outside.

"A fight. Pugilism. Broke my nose."

All of which she found far more impressive than her silly imaginings about a cruel storybook governess.

"It must have hurt."

He shrugged, took a casual bite of the apple she'd offered, and passed it back to her.

"Did you win?"

He shrugged again, but she could tell that he *had* won, by the grin, spreading proudly, widely, and no doubt painfully over his bruised face.

"Sent home from school until it heals. Have to keep up with my studies, though."

"Let me see."

Spread out on the writing table under the window.

"Latin," he said carelessly. "Very complicated. Difficult. Only for gentlemen."

She took a peek.

"Poo," she said. "You're only in *Caesar*?"

❧

"It must be a very absorbing memory." He stood in the doorway with his arms crossed, and she jumped a bit at the suddenness of seeing him.

"How long have you been watching me?"

"Long enough to see a smile flit across your face before you sighed, rather ruefully."

She'd smiled, had she? Well, enough of *that*.

She took a deep breath and squared her shoulders.

"*Why* did you set that spy on me? After you said you wouldn't. I trusted you, you know. It's cruel to me, Kit, and unfair to Peggy and my family too. Isn't it enough that you've got me a prisoner at Beechwood Knolls? And that you've pulled the wool over the eyes of everyone in Grefford as to your . . . character. But to *spy* on me. I won't stand for it, and I . . ."

He raised his hands. "Wait. Halt. Desist or in any case explain. This could be serious. There's some *spy* set upon you?"

"Don't pretend not to know. She's seen him twice now—the red-bearded man, tall, brown coat, I think she said. . . ."

His eyes widened. "*Him,* really? *Peggy* saw him?"

"There, you see, I knew you were behind it. He's approached her twice now, bold as brass. It's just not fair, Kit, not gentlemanly, and you promised . . ."

"Which way did he go?"

"What, you want *me* to be keeping track of *your* spy . . . ?"

"Mary, stop, he's not my spy. Hell, if only she'd told you which way he . . . wait." He'd taken a folded piece of paper from his pocket. "He says . . . damn, on his way to Sheffield. What time does the Chesterfield coach . . . ? No, by the time I get to the village he'll be gone. Nothing to be done about it now." He stepped the rest of the way into the cottage.

❦

Now that they were both all the way inside of it, the room seemed smaller than she remembered it. He dragged a broken-down chair from next to the bed to nearer the writing table. "I seem to remember that the writing desk chair is the better one. Take it, won't you?"

She shook her head. "I'll be going as soon as you explain to me who the man in the brown coat is, and why he isn't spying on me. No, that's not what I meant. But you know what I meant and you know who he is. He's working for you. . . ."

"Indeed he is not."

"He's in the employ of someone . . . you owe money to?"

"No again. In fact, between my winnings at the fives court last week and the money your Mr. Bakewell has made for me, I've never been richer. But this is interesting. Try again, Mary. What other crimes would you like to indict me for? A vile seduction?"

"No, that's not your style." *Whoring, rather,* she was about to say. Except that she'd said it all already in Calais. She'd said everything bad about him that she could think of—and a few more things into the bargain. "Are you acting as magistrate these days? Oh, Lord, don't tell me you want to arrest him for poaching."

The heartiness of his laughter was proof—if she'd needed any—of the silliness of *that* guess. She dropped into the chair he'd offered, and he took the more rickety one, leaning it back against the wall in that way that men enjoyed doing for the way it rather foregrounded their legs and other, proximate parts of their bodies.

While as for the man in the brown coat. It could be only one thing, then. "You're after him for a revolutionist."

"I'm not at liberty to say."

❧

Then he was. Some vile government business she was bound to disapprove of. No point staying any longer.

She sat a bit straighter. Actually, she thought, if she were to sit any straighter in this small, uncomfortable chair, her bum would slip off the front end of it.

"I thought you'd be in London, working for the Home Office."

"I hope to be. They said to come back when Wat's better."

"Well, that's . . . good, then."

"*They* didn't find me ungovernable."

"I'm sorry I said that."

"You were angry. We were both angry. It's all right, Mary."

She felt herself trembling a bit, like she lately had been doing at bedtime. "I must go."

He shrugged. "I expect so. Ah, but wait a moment. You said I was holding you prisoner at Beechwood Knolls. Which sounds bloody unfair of me. Rather provocative, but unfair still. For I shouldn't want to keep you from walking to the village, especially as you look so fetching with a basket over your arm. We need a schedule, as to when you can be seen in the neighborhood and when I can. Maximum freedom, minimum fodder for the gossips."

"That *would* be most helpful."

"I'm good at that sort of thing. Let's see . . ."

He was right. In very little time he'd sketched out an orderly, even a fair arrangement.

❦

He'd kept her there *this* long, he thought. But they seemed to be approaching some sort of threshold. For she was standing now.

"But how did you think to find me here?" he asked.

"I didn't. I was so furious I was going to confront you at Rowen. I just came through here in case . . ."

"Yes, I came here just in case as well. I've come by every day, in fact, since I've been home."

"A coincidence, then."

"If you like."

It wouldn't be easy, he thought, for her to get by him, the way he'd situated himself in the doorway. Odd. Once upon a time he hadn't wanted to let her in.

"Mary?"

"I'd like to go."

"I know you would, but, Mary?"

"Yes, what is it?"

"Just allow me to say it. You needn't even answer. Mary, I'll be here every day, at one in the afternoon. Waiting for you. Wanting you. It won't *mean* anything,

I swear it—it doesn't change anything we've discussed up until now. No one will know, and at the end of it you'll still have your freedom from me."

She'd opened her mouth to speak. He waited a moment and then continued.

"No, it's not right or good or kind or moral. It's simply what it is and what I want. I shan't beg or apologize or ask again, so you needn't . . ."

He hadn't blocked her way. He'd let her slip out the door as once he'd let her slip in. Wordlessly, running down the path as quickly as she'd come so many years ago.

Chapter Fourteen

It was an awful lot of work, when the chances of her coming were so small. Probably nonexistent, Kit thought. Still, once he'd written a report and some recommendations to Lord Sidmouth, he couldn't think of much else to do. Anyway, he didn't mind the labor of carrying firewood over to the cottage. Rather like in Spain, during some moments when officers had had to help with various duties around camp. More difficult, though, to do it so that no one noticed the marquess's brother hauling firewood.

Luckily, Mr. Greenlee hadn't evinced any curiosity about it when Kit had wandered down to his workshop. In fact, the estate carpenter had appeared to think it the most natural thing in the world, that Lord Christopher might want a fire in the old hermit's cottage in order to be alone there with his . . . thoughts. And that, wanting to be private, he was willing to do the physical labor himself.

Help yourself, my lord, there's plenty of scrap wood, ash and oak; it will burn quite well—and here, take these smaller bits and shavings. You do remember, don't you, that you'll need kindling? Kit assured him that he did still indeed remember how to build a wood fire in a grate, and he was obliged to Mr. Greenlee for having taught him how, more than a decade ago. . . .'Pon my honor, how the time flies by, don't it?

After which—Mr. Greenlee having packed up the wood in strong canvas sacking—they'd spent a pleasant hour smoking clay pipes and whittling away at some nicely shaped bits of ash wood, saying very little once Kit had expressed his condolences about the recent lingering death of Mrs. Greenlee. His mother had told him about it in France, where it seemed she maintained her knowledge of domestic matters back at Rowen. Mrs. Greenlee had always been sickly; too bad the couple hadn't had any children.

And her ladyship, your mother, the carpenter had asked, I've heard she's expected back in England. I trust she enjoyed her tour abroad.

Enjoyed it famously, even gathered a bit of a salon around herself in Paris. Kit had laughed. But you know how she is. *She* doesn't change.

No, Mr. Greenlee had agreed. My lady doesn't change.

Nice old fellow. Quiet, unprepossessing, but at hand when you needed him—even to answer a few very confusing questions, in a straightforward but comforting way, when Kit had been six years old and very seriously attending to the activities of the breeding stallions in the paddocks.

※

The other task he'd set himself to was to find a sheet and perhaps some blankets. She'd brought the sheet the first time, but since she hadn't committed to anything, he thought he should now. Anyway, he knew where to find it. For he'd had hiding places all over the house when he'd been little, and some of the best of them had been wardrobes.

※

One of them in the nursery wing, where some serving maids were taking care of baby Georgy. Kit had just had his sixth birthday, and he'd thought that one of the serving girls was awfully pretty. Her name was pretty, too—Jemima; he liked the long *I* sound of it. It sometimes gave him a funny feeling in his belly—sort of like when he was hungry, only much better—to breathe her name while he watched her, especially when she loosened her gown and, ah yes, her stays, as the nursery maids sometimes did while they were working. For it had been an especially warm and sunny July, the year his youngest brother Georgy was born.

And since the wardrobe had a rather large keyhole in its door, and since he'd been the sort of child who could fit himself into the smallest spaces, it had been rather wonderful, and quite enlightening too, to see Jemima going about her work, and even better when she took a rest now and again.

Were all little boys so curious about these things?

But at the time he'd been curious about everything, though none of the answers he found ever seemed any good. Probably because he hadn't known what he was looking for—and hadn't recognized it that particular day, even when it had hit him on the head and knocked him down.

He'd hardly been listening to what she and the other maid had been saying, so intent had he been on Jemima's outstretched legs and the way her dress hung. But then he had picked up a few words. What, he wondered, could they be saying about the king?

Wait, no—he'd got that wrong—not the king, after all. King George was called *His Majesty*. . . . He thought of the engravings on the wall of the schoolroom he shared with Belle. He knew that Jemima and the other one didn't mean King George because they'd said *His Highness,* not *His Majesty,* and *His Highness* was the Prince of Wales—who was also George, of course; so many Georges, including the big red-faced baby who was his newest brother. She was holding up the infant in front of her now; his fat little legs dangled, and she kissed him a loud smack on the cheek.

"Just look at 'im, as like to 'is Highness as like can be, ain't yer, little Georgy?"

They'd both laughed at that, and the other maid, the one who didn't give him funny feelings, had replied, "Oh, but she's a sly one, my lady Rowen is. . . . With little Belle and Kit so like her that you couldn't know *who* their dads are—if you didn't see the Viscount Bevington so taken with the little girl when he comes every year for the hunt. Quite spoils 'er with ribbons and candy."

They'd laughed even louder at that, and then went about their work for a time, their laughter so wild and so loud—so frightening, in a way—that he probably wouldn't have bothered to try to decipher what they were saying. Except that he could hardly help attending to what—well, *who*—Jemima was talking about now.

"But as to the little dark imp, her brother just out of petticoats, all stick arms and legs and angel face on 'im, if you can find it below the mop of hair that always needs brushing . . . well, *he's* my lady's secret, and a dark secret too, I reckon. . . . But no one much cares these days to unriddle it, everybody so interested about the dad she found for the next one."

He might have found out a bit more about it if the housekeeper hadn't shooed the girls away and swept Georgy up to be dressed in a fresh lace gown and taken to his mother's bedchamber, where she sat up against the embroidered pillows and showed him off to company.

The queer thing, as he'd told Mary, was that he hadn't been bothered very much by it at the moment it happened.

(How old had he been when he'd told her about it? Almost fifteen, probably. He'd been doing Ovid that school term; by that time she'd made something of a Latinist out of him.)

But it wasn't school right then. It was summer and he'd been on the long holiday. They'd been out in the forest together. The warm air was still and almost too sweet. Little brown butterflies were making themselves drunk on honeysuckle. The brook was high and flowing quickly.

At first, he confided, he felt rather gratified by what he'd overheard. For hadn't the pretty maid said he had an angel face? And then he'd felt a bit insulted—because he *wasn't* "just out of petticoats."

"I was *six*, after all. Hadn't worn petticoats for a year at least." He and Mary had both laughed at that.

He'd thought a lot about what he'd heard. Though it took him a while to figure it out.

"Well, I'd still thought the marquess was my father then, you see. I mean, I *called* him Papa—what else could he be? Never occurred to me that there was more to being somebody's father than a name."

She giggled nervously, and he wondered whether it was wise—or even decent—to continue telling her such things. Too late to stop, though.

"I went out to the farmyard, and then to the paddocks where the horses, the stallions . . . well, you know."

Her eyes had gotten very large and her mouth very round.

"I . . . I found it pretty frightening. Lucky for me that Mr. Greenlee happened by, to answer my questions."

Had *she* ever had such questions, he'd wondered? Did girls worry about things like that? Well, it would be easier for them, wouldn't it? Just lie back . . .

Was it wicked to be talking about it with a girl? Or *thinking* about it, even . . .

Easier to turn his mind to something he could control.

"And if anybody tries to insult me over it," he told her, "or my mother either, they know they'll get a good pounding for their trouble, like the time my nose got broken, and the other boy got much worse. But I never thought that maid was very pretty after that."

Nor got that funny feeling again until just recently, spending so much time out in the forest. Of course, he knew what it was *now;* it was just that he preferred to have it in private, where he'd be more in control of things.

They were by the side of the stream when he'd told her all that. Their boots were muddy, from rambling about; they'd been trying to clean them with leaves. But one of her boots had a hole in the sole, and the mud had leaked in.

"Dash the nursery maid," she said suddenly. "I hate that nursery maid," she added.

She was staring at him; he couldn't do anything but stare back; it would have been rude to look anywhere else. Though he'd wanted to, because she was unbuttoning her boots. From the corner of his eye, he could see her pulling off her black stockings. Stretching her legs as wantonly as the nursery maid he'd spied upon, she plunged her feet into the stream to wash them.

He watched helplessly while she dried her feet with her handkerchief, letting them dry for a while in the sun, and then putting back on her stockings and boots.

"A pity to have to put them on while they're still muddy," she said softly. "But it'll be worse if I try to walk home without them."

And when they met the next day, it was as though he'd dreamed it. For surely she'd never have shown him her bare feet and ankles.

Except that he hadn't dreamed it; he couldn't have, because he'd been up all night, fevered, trembling, and less in control of . . . things than ever before in his life, his mind's eye all amazed by images of white feet and black stockings, rainbows glancing off icy, quickly moving water.

He yawned (angry at himself—could she see that she'd kept him up all night?). She yawned as well (for she hadn't slept either, which she'd only confessed much later), and then she kissed him.

And now—a marriage, a separation, and a war later—he spied her waiting for him, framed in the doorway of the cottage, next to the brook at the no-longer-disputed edge of the property of the Marquess of Rowen.

Chapter Fifteen

"I agree with you," she said. "It's neither right nor good nor moral. But here I am anyway." She laughed nervously. "It probably won't take very long. No doubt we'll begin squabbling soon enough."

"Why did you come?" he asked her.

"Why did you ask me to?"

"That's not an answer," he told her.

"Because I wanted to," she said. "Is that an answer?"

Well, is it?

Is desire an answer or a question?

Luckily, when you're in its toils, you find you're not awfully concerned with the fine points.

Better to concentrate on practical matters: the bed in want of a sheet, grate of a fire; the gown and stays, coat and waistcoat that must come off as quickly as possible. All were dispatched with brisk, wordless, and rather solemn efficiency so that it was soon enough that Mary stood in the middle of the room in her shift, shoes, and stockings and Kit sat at the edge of the neatly made-up bed, his shiny new pocket watch on the rickety table next to it.

The room was small enough that their hands would have met if they'd extended them forward.

Mary's shift stirred softly in a draft of warm air. Her

pale pink stockings had elaborate clocks down their sides, disappearing into fragile black slippers.

The light in the room was dappled green from the vines at the windows.

Her voice seemed louder than it was, when it broke the watery silence. "And if we hadn't argued at Calais? If we'd drunk our Calvados and exchanged our compliments? What do you expect we would have done next?"

He reached to pull her shift over her head.

"Please," he said.

She smiled. They both knew perfectly well what they would have done next. But it was pleasant, all the same, to be asked.

She knelt between his legs. He held her shoulders between his doeskin-clad thighs, hugged her hips with his boots. She could smell the oil his valet had rubbed into the leather to make it flexible. Clasping him around the waist, her face rubbing against the linen of his shirt, breasts crushed against the rising tautness between his legs—she could smell all his smells now, sweat and skin and the mysterious humors of masculine arousal, through the clean, cared-for, and supposedly impervious materials that separated him from her. Doeskin and leather—it piqued the imagination, a gentleman enveloped in skins besides his own. She shuddered; he stroked and played with her hair. She breathed the dark smells; the tremors inside her rose, crested, and subsided.

"Unbutton me." His voice was hoarse.

"Yes." Hers was ragged, distant. *Yes, yes, of course.*

Her fingers felt swollen, clumsy. *Damn.* The buttonholes were tight. "Bloody hell and double damn," she muttered.

Still, finesse wasn't everything—not, at least, in the matter of buttons. *Now,* however, that she'd finally gotten to him . . . but now she was home free. She kissed the head of his cock, bent her head to lick it along the length of the shaft, lightly stroking the underside with her fingers. Kissing, nibbling . . . she sighed a deep, long sigh, arched her neck and softened her throat, heedful, alert— aroused once again (and so soon too) by the weight of his hand on her nape, his fingers grasping her curls.

❧

There was always a moment, he thought—at least there'd always *been* a moment; yes, there it was—where she'd stop to lick her lips and wet her mouth. No propriety or pretense of being taken unawares—for even if she sometimes fumbled with the buttons, in the main she was proud of her skill, open and unaffected about wanting to do a good, capable job where it mattered most. Softening her jaw, she'd make herself all moist velvet down to her throat before allowing him to guide her down over himself. He'd been waiting for this moment since . . . Calais? Merciful heaven, since *long* before Calais.

His hand at her head, her lips around him now. Faster, sweetheart, yes, that's right, that's good—the liquid insides of her cheeks, the nimble, clever tongue. Her motions growing eager, greedy—he allowed himself a growl of contentment. A sigh of selfish delight, to have all that attention, will, and intelligence in his thrall.

He tugged again at the curls at her nape: he wanted it slower now, deeper—yes, just like that, oh, very good indeed. No need any longer to show her. He dropped his hand, letting himself fall back onto his elbows. To watch.

The shadows of her eyelashes on her flushed cheeks.

Her lips, curved and supple, careful and attentive.

The more he lengthened, thickened, hardened, the more devoted she'd become. Taking him. As a challenge. Well, he *hoped* she still found him a challenge.

Yes, he could tell. Good, she was having to put a bit of work into it. Her shoulders quivered *(wings, poised to take flight);* he tightened the muscles of his thighs to hold her clasped between them. *Stay here. Captive. At home on earth. With me.*

❧

Her knees ached and her jaw had grown a bit tired—for there was rather a lot of him to take. Had she forgotten? No, not really and not ever. Still, the naughty books never told you just how stiff and tired a pair of knees could get; you had to learn that part for yourself, surprising yourself each time. Thank heaven for the threadbare and slightly mildewed rug on the floor at the side of the bed.

She stretched her back and shoulders as he hugged his feet and legs more tightly around her. Naked against his boots, thrilled and yet at ease. For when you knew someone so well, when you were so familiar with what he wanted now and would want next . . . when it was new and old at the same time . . . when you were making scandalous, challenging love to someone you very possibly knew better than yourself . . .

Because with all the tricks and goads, the embellishments and elaborations, it was as though they'd made these movements yesterday, or last night, or (as once they might have) every afternoon for a month at least.

He'd begun thrusting more quickly now—forceful, demanding, joyfully exuberant—well, there really wasn't any word you could substitute, could you, for *joy*? She clasped her arms around his waist, crushed her breasts against the side of the bed, arched her back, pressed her flanks hard against his legs. Parting her knees, to plant herself more squarely upon them— savoring the moans she'd wrought from him, tremors at the root of his cock.

He wanted her throat now; she could feel coarse hairs pressed against her lips. Breathing deeply through her nose, his darkest, mossiest smells. She could smell— no, she could *taste*—the salt of his sweat and (ranker, saltier) the semen coursing up from him; it would overwhelm her, spill out from her lips. . . .

No it wouldn't. For *she* was taking *him*. Take him, drink him, breathe him, swallow him, have him, drown in him. Wash up to shore now, in his lap.

❧

She heard his contented and very self-satisfied sigh just
as she'd begun to think she'd really be a great deal more
comfortable next to him on the bed, rather than collapsed all on the floor between his legs, on that not-so-
nice little rug.

"Come up here." He stretched out a hand. They arranged themselves somewhat charily, for he still had his
boots on, and there wouldn't be any servants to change
the linen.

"You've got *many* too many clothes on." Her voice
came out a bit muffled, for she'd whispered it into his
shirt, where his neck met his shoulder. She raised her
head. "Well, it's not very fair to me, is it?"

"Are we playing fair?" One of his hands was cupped
over her quim, the tips of his fingers moving slowly over
the place where the lips met, and sometimes straying
down over her thighs.

"*You* aren't," she told him. "Not at this moment.
Not . . . oh, my word, Kit." For there are moments when
the smallest, simplest fingertip touch—from a lover who
knows just where—is all that's needed. She nestled into
his side. *How lovely,* she thought—in some last moment
when it was still possible to think. She spread her legs,
stretched her back and arms, and took up all the room
she could. To enjoy it completely.

❧

"I should apologize," he said sometime later, "for how
things went in Calais. It wasn't the right way to meet
each other after so long."

"I expect you should," she replied. "Are you? Apologizing, I mean."

"More like saying I should."

"That's like you. Are you going to tell me about what
you've been doing since you arrived here? Oh yes, and
who *was* the man that Peggy saw anyway? Will you tell
me any of that?"

"Do you want me to?"

"Yes, I think so. Sometime. Not right now." She raised her head. "Because right now it's time to get you out of your clothes," she told him. "Sit up."

She straddled his legs. He kept his face cool and noncommittal as she unknotted his neckcloth, unbuttoned his shirt, and rose on her knees to pull it over his head.

Hesitating now, for in truth she was fearful of what she'd find. And it did come as a shock, how long and livid the scar was, the stretched and puckered flesh snaked from shoulder to collarbone and almost to his neck.

She tried to hide her dismay, to keep her voice light and her expression unconcerned. "Well, I expect we're both a bit worse for wear."

Too late for her to offer comfort.

He shrugged. "Worse for not knowing how to stay out of harm's way, one's first real time in battle."

Nor would he offer any comfort to her.

She slid back and off the bed, standing on the floor in front of him again. Chin tilted and hands on hips. "And about them boots, Major Stansell? I'm good with boots, you know, sir."

Coyness and posturing didn't suit her, but it was the best she could do at the moment.

He shrugged, almost grimaced, and managed a smile instead. "Yes, I do know. You'd have made a good batman. Well, come on, then, be quick about it. There's a good fellow."

Even when he hadn't cared much about clothes, he'd liked a good pair of boots. And so she'd *gotten* good at boots, in order to have them off him quickly.

She knelt at his feet while he braced himself against the bed. Gripping the toe of his right boot with her left hand and the heel with her right, she gave a light tug, being sure to pay close attention to the angle of her hands and his foot. The boot slid off easily, and she grinned up at him.

"Nothing simpler. The left boot now, if it please my lord major."

But the left, in the inevitable way of an intractable world, refused to budge. She shouldn't have been so cocky over her first success. Nor allowed herself a dizzying breath of the leather's oily perfume, darker and more redolent as her palms grew hotter and more slippery.

For that matter, she shouldn't have stolen that little glance up at him, his eyes so calmly fixed upon her breasts, which *would* continue their stupid fleshy jiggling, the harder she tugged at the damn, bloody, sodding left boot.

When had she begun muttering to herself?

"Now, now," he chided her. "Can't allow my batman such indecent vocabulary. Filthiest language I've heard since I poked my head in on the Penley sisters having their tea."

She snorted. "Don't make me laugh, Kit, or I'll never get this damn thing off you."

There was nothing for it, finally, but for her to straddle his outstretched left leg with her derriere indecorously turned toward his face. She sighed and he laughed at her. *Let's just get this over with,* she thought.

She held tight to the infuriating left boot.

He'd pulled the stocking from his bootless right foot. "Less slipping about this way," he explained, as he propped the sole of the warm and lively foot against her bum.

He wriggled his toes a bit. "Now, when I count *three . . .*"

She and the boot would both have gone flying across the room if he hadn't caught her around the middle—hands squeezing her breasts; mouth against her neck; cock hard and impatient once more.

She might lose every remaining shred of dignity if she were to continue rubbing back against him so crudely. She dropped the boot onto the floor and he loosened his hands from around her.

"Let's do this properly," he said.

He made short work of pantaloons, drawers, and his

other stocking. Gloriously naked at last, he took the briefest of moments to preen for her before sweeping back the quilt with an extravagant flourish that made her giggle, and putting out his hand.

She took it. "Dance for me," he said.

Nodding silently, moving slowly, while the years swirled and dissolved around them.

He propped his head against the pillows and put a hand on each of her hips. His broad chest, coarse whorls of black hair interrupted by the vicious scar, rose and fell with his breath as he prodded her to straddle him, to open herself and grasp and envelop him. Not that much prodding was necessary—his hands, her hips, the pulse in his throat and the flesh rising and stiffening at the apex of her vulva, were all caught suspended in an aching sweetness of shared movement and slow time.

Rising, she almost lifted herself off him. He shuddered, whistled through his teeth. She lowered herself as slowly as she could, coming back to rest against him, her arse against his hips and belly.

More quickly now: she arched and curled her back, stroking herself against the length of his cock and molding herself around its thickness. Gasping, she watched the lines his features took, mirroring what her own must look like, eyes black and opaque, pupils distended as though drugged, mouth loose and slightly open. Thoughtful, almost meditative.

He moved slowly beneath her, just the smallest arching of his hips keeping time with hers.

Dance for me.

In Constantinople, she'd watched a pasha being entertained by a suave-hipped dancing girl. Behind the curve of smoke from his hookah, he'd seemed almost bored by the painted eyes, veiled face, exquisite bare feet below ankle cuffs tinkling with tiny silver bells. But Mary had caught a slantwise view of his hand—the one not holding the hookah—compulsively opening and closing upon itself, in perfect rhythm with the drums.

She'd pled a megrim and hurried back to her hotel.

*Her companions had supposed her offended by the
spectacle, and Matthew Bakewell had begged her pardon the next morning, for exposing her to it.*

Kit would have known better than to beg her pardon.

She raised her arms, stared down as though over a
gossamer face veil, wiggled her shoulder blades, and
felt her breasts raise and bounce in rhythm. He couldn't
look completely serious; well, it *was* a bit ridiculous that
he and she could take such delight in their shared,
crude, dancing girl fancy—ridiculous and absurd, childish and really rather marvelous.

He touched her nipples with cold fingertips. She
gasped, moaned, and would have made a botch of the
rhythm if he hadn't taken it up for her, moving his hips
and thrusting his cock up higher within her, with vehe-
mence and perhaps a little more heat.

But suddenly, there wasn't a rhythm anymore. Nor a
dance. There was only flesh and breath, muscle and
movement and blood coursing beneath the skin. The
oriental fancy had dissolved. There were only—*they*
were simply—Mary and Kit once more. The notion that
they could have imagined themselves anyone else was
quaint and utterly nonsensical.

*Nothing more than what it was, and everything quite
good enough.* His hands, his mouth on her breasts:
stroke and squeeze, tease and tongue and pull and
suckle. His arms around her now, drawing her downward to grasp and hold him, beneath and within her,
drenched and clinging, no music but their ragged
breath.

Chapter Sixteen

S he didn't want to get out of bed.

"Once I do," she whispered, "I *shall* begin making troublesome inquiries about what you've been doing and whether it's something I should approve of."

"By what right," he asked, "will you be inquiring?" He said it curiously, rather lazily, his arms still tight around her.

"None," she said, "except I find I can't separate out what you do in bed from what you do the rest of the time. Well, perhaps I can today. Make today a special, privileged day."

"I'm glad," he said.

"But next time . . ."

"Do you want there to be a next time?" he asked.

How odd, to be measuring time so stingily. In Curzon Street, they'd had nothing *but* time.

She kissed him.

"Yes, tomorrow afternoon. For in the morning Jessie and I will be writing out invitations to some local ladies, to discuss a cistern for the village."

"Cistern?"

"There, you see, you're curious about what I do as well. It's natural for a couple . . ."

Except that they weren't one anymore. They drew their clothes on silently.

"We dine at half past four today," she said. "The young people will be returning from the ruins on Rook Hill. I must hurry."

He tied her stays just a bit too tightly for perfect comfort. She found that she didn't mind. The pressure would be rather like an extension of his touch.

She turned her neck to kiss him.

He helped her pull the dress down over her head and did up the buttons.

"Saturday, then. And we'll tell each other a few things then. Unless I can contrive to make you forget what you want to know."

She laughed. "By all means, contrive away. I shan't forget. Do your contriving first, though, won't you. If we argue later, we'll still be ahead of the game."

⚜

Stopping to dip her hands in clear rushing water, she drank deeply before hurrying away from the cottage. Climbing over the stile that pretended to be broken, hurrying down a footpath, leaving the outskirts of Rowen and entering the precincts of Beechwood Knolls, she felt her other selves joining with her.

Aunt Mary.

Provisional Treasurer of the newly organized Grefford Village Ladies' Cistern Committee.

Matthew Bakewell's mistress (*however did you manage it, Mary, to be unfaithful to your lover, with your husband of all people?* Too complicated. She wouldn't think of that particular self right now).

The path had turned away from the river; the woods had thinned. The hill was a bit steep, but she managed it all right. Stepping over another stile, she made her way across the meadow to encounter a lonely Lord Ayres gazing poetically out toward the vista, his horse cropping the grass behind him.

"Ah, good afternoon, your lordship," she said. "I didn't expect to see *you* here."

And not even very annoyed, on this privileged day, by his callow, violet-eyed presence. It was time, after all, to be Aunt Mary again. Even with her hair in elf locks and sleeves sopping water from the brook. While he was—as she'd come to expect him—all foppish elegance.

"And the expedition? I trust you were properly moved by the spectacle of the Rook Hill ruins?"

He shrugged—trying not to show the boyish pouts and sulks beneath his carefully cultivated demeanor. "The young ladies made very accomplished sketches. When they weren't surveying the horizon for chance intruders, Miss Elizabeth Grandin in particular."

Too bad, she thought, that the girls were so pretty—it must make him feel awfully rejected. And she could guess whom Elizabeth had been scanning the horizon for—to show off to Fannie, as a marvel of the neighborhood, and a much better one than a stupid set of fake ruins.

Poor boy, she wanted to be generous to him. "It must have been a bore for you," she said—adult to adult, which seemed to cheer him a bit.

"A walk in the forest like you've had," he said now, "a simple, contemplative ramble, among the bluebells and butterflies, nightingales, dog roses, and wood anemones, would have suited me far better, and rested my unquiet spirit, don't you know."

She might not have been able to keep from laughing were it not for the double infelicity of his phrasing—his own peevishness elevated to *unquiet spirit* rather canceling out the absurdity of her afternoon recast as a *simple, contemplative ramble*.

The problem was what she might possibly offer in reply, if *Unquiet spirit, my arse* was forbidden to her. A simple nod was best, a wistful, respectful softening of her eyes, in deference to his *unquiet spirit* and the demands it made upon him.

Yes, he liked that. "My father has a similar set of ruins at home," he told her, "not far from the Chinese bridge the landscape gardener erected when I was a boy."

She laughed (for he really wasn't so bad in his way), and he smiled his eagerness to share his contempt for his father's boorishness. For it seemed he'd decided she was a kindred spirit, or at least a sympathetic one—especially after a wearing day of being ignored by two pretty girls.

"But there's nothing in our homely British Isles like the Colosseum at twilight. In Rome, you know."

"Yes, I imagined you must mean the Colosseum in Rome."

"When I was there," he told her, "I caught a glimpse of Lord Byron, silhouetted against the pillars. I recognized him immediately, even from a distance, and hurried to pay him my regards and to invite him to dine with me. Very decent he was too, very apologetic that he'd be leaving in just two hours."

As Byron often did when confronted with eager young devotees. Unless, of course, he was particularly strapped for pocket cash, and in need of a good dinner.

"A pity he couldn't stay," she murmured.

"I'd wanted his opinion on some little scribbles of my own."

Even if penniless and ravenous, Byron would be off when the devotee was a would-be poet.

"Still, he thought we might well bump into one another again. And more than once—after that . . . do you know, Lady Christopher, that we *almost* did bump into each other again? Several times, at some particularly poetical venue, I'd arrive to find that he'd just departed—well, the demands upon his time, you know, the exacting standards that genius must answer to . . ."

The important thing at this moment was how to turn the conversation, or she'd be in for a look at those scribbles herself. Luckily, her bootlace had come loose. She bent, with a tiny sigh, to tie it.

"But you're tired from your ramble. Would you like to ride up to the house? I could lead you back."

Which *was* generous and even rather charming of him, if a bit excessively picturesque. And if Elizabeth's antiquated relative were to show a bit too much ankle, perched up on his saddle, she couldn't imagine any harm in it.

"Yes, thank you," she told him. And he led her back to what turned out to be an excellent dinner—a fine sensible English version, in fact, of the marinated capon dish.

After which she was happy to retire early.

To hum carelessly, as Peggy wrestled unhappily with her stays—for the knot Kit had tied could evidently have held down the rigging of a warship.

And, "No, nothing tonight. I think I'll sleep quite well without it."

❧

He'd stayed behind to watch her walk down the footpath. And then to fiddle with his neckcloth, straining to catch his reflection in a windowpane.

She was right. Delicious as the day had been, they wouldn't be able to continue in this way. Yes, they still enjoyed pretend fancies—and he'd already had some thoughts about the "contrivance" he'd be working up for their next time together.

But he also very much wanted to tell and ask her things. Real things. Trivial things. Cisterns. In the army, he'd known a chap who was an engineer. Interesting to try to explain it to her, though; all quite new.

Was that what happened when you grew up, made a place in the world for yourself?

Years ago when there'd been no other place for them, they'd found each other here in the cottage, away from the world's gossip, petty rivalries, minor and not so minor injustices. Curious and alert, ignorant and volatile, they'd made a place for themselves where no one knew where to find them. Running, rambling, wrestling—touching, kissing, making love—fleet and changeable as the woodland creatures in the myths.

What, who, were they now?

He shrugged. Time to be getting back; he patted at his waistcoat pockets to make sure he hadn't left anything behind.

His watch. No longer on the table where he'd left it. Must have gotten knocked off, rolled behind the book that had been peeking out from under the bed. He retrieved the watch and the book too. All the creatures of myth and legend, bound up in a witty, powerful, and thoughtful volume.

Mildewed almost to a brick. But when he did get it open, it opened to the very page.

They'd gotten quite proficient at kissing by that time. Kissing, and in truth, some other things as well. They weren't children anymore.

Weren't adults yet either. He needed to make something happen, and so he'd come here early, set the book out on the table.

"Hullo," she'd said. "Been busy?"

He'd shrugged. "Rather. Bit of a problem with my Latin."

"Let me see."

The Tiresius story begins, as Ovid begins so many of his stories, with the gods at celebration. Jupiter is rather in his cups, jesting with his wife, Juno, as to whether . . .

"But you can construe this perfectly well, Kit. You know that what he's asking is whether a man or woman gets more pleasure . . ." Her voice had trailed off.

"You were saying?"

"Voluptus . . . from making love."

He'd tricked her into saying it.

"We shouldn't be talking of such things," she'd said, even while she'd allowed her wrist to be caught and immobilized.

They'd shared a level, if frightened, stare.

"Yes," he'd said. "We should. We need to. And to do more than talk. About such things."

And now, today, it seemed they'd come full circle. Now it was time to talk of everything else.

Chapter Seventeen

Her plan had been to get to the cottage before him. To have a calm, uninterrupted time while she made her indispensable preparations (indispensable, at least, to an "eddicated lady" who wasn't about to risk a pregnancy).

But first she'd needed to run down to the kitchen—and on the way she'd overheard a conversation that she'd have to consider at her leisure. After which Jessica wanted her opinion on a few additional candidates for the cistern committee, and Lord Ayres needed a book from her father's library. And, of course, neither of them would have found it very convincing that she must hurry off immediately on a ramble in the forest.

And so she made her preparations in her dressing room at home—sponge doused in the vinegar solution and pushed up inside her as Jessica had taught her so many years ago. She was always careful about this (though she couldn't deny that she'd also been very lucky). *Important, indispensable,* she repeated to herself, as she hurried through the little ritual.

No surprise, then, that she got to the cottage ten minutes late, and a not a little out of breath.

"Kit?"

A nervous quiver started up in her belly. Couldn't he

have waited? Or hadn't he come at all? Perhaps he'd simply decided to give the whole thing up. Well, he had every right. . . . She should check to see if there was a note on the table. . . .

No doubt it was her nervousness—if not the fact that she was still trying to catch her breath—that had prevented her from considering if he might be holding himself still behind the door she'd opened. Nor had she heard a squeak of hinges or an intake of breath as he tiptoed out to grasp her from behind.

Shouting *OH-HOH*.

Or *what-ho* or *ahoy*.

Or *some* ridiculous thing a child might imagine that sailors or pirates were wont to cry out—he sang it out into her ear as he caught hold of her arms and bent them behind her waist.

Binding her wrists together—quickly, deftly, taking advantage of her surprise.

She laughed out loud at the broad, crude silliness of it. Though in truth, he hadn't tied her so crudely as all that, her hands were immobilized. He'd used his neck-cloth. The linen chafed against her wrists. Her only feeble recourse was to kick her feet when he picked her up and carried her the few steps to the bed. Oh, and to bite at his neck where the shirt was open, before he dropped her onto the mattress and climbed onto the bed to straddle her.

Rubbing the spot where she'd bitten him, he grinned down at her. He still wore his pantaloons and boots— she felt herself squeezed tight by his thighs pressed hard into her sides. She contented herself with what wriggling, kicking, and thrashing about she was able to do, while he lifted her skirts and tossed them over her head. Leaving her sputtering in a sea of white ruffles, he moved downward to dive between her legs.

"A pirate treasure," he declared while he rubbed his rough, unshaven cheeks against her belly. Kissing, nibbling, sniffing at her—practically drooling like a hunting dog. She bounced about from the hips, arching her back, shrieking in mock terror.

"Villain, monster! Unhand me, you vile knave!"

By now he would have known (having caught a faint whiff of vinegar) that it was all right to proceed as he might. "Never! I'll have my treasure, and the very enlightened lady too," *enlightened lady* pronounced with a wry twist of a London workingman's accent—she'd become familiar with the intonations when he'd taken her out adventuring all those years ago.

She tried to close her legs against him and found that she couldn't. He'd always been strong, but he was a lot stronger than she remembered. *All that loading of muskets,* she mused; she couldn't have fought him off if she'd wanted to.

The light of midday shone gauzily through the white cotton of her petticoat. Nice to picture the muscles in his arms, held taut as he forced her legs open. Her thighs trembled. His face was scratchy against her skin. How long since he'd shaved? Had he scandalized his sister-in-law by appearing that way at breakfast? He kissed her thighs, slowly moving his head upward now.

"Rogue, swine, how dare you!" *And whatever you do, don't stop*—but she knew he wouldn't. On the contrary, he was using his tongue to bring her off quickly. She arched, crested, lay panting while he raised himself back up, brushing the skirts and petticoat away from her face to kiss her mouth, her neck, her breasts. . . . Voraciously, with just a hint of her own smell on him.

There'd been a fichu about her neck and shoulders when she'd set out today. Gone. Lost in the sea of bedding. If there'd been pins, they'd long since been pulled out. At least he hadn't torn her clothing. She was lucky that the tartan gown she wore had a wide neckline.

Lucky? Or had she given it a bit of offhand thought this morning when she'd pointed to it hanging in the wardrobe. . . . *A bit old, Peggy, but surely good enough for a ramble in the forest.* And had she just imagined the wry, knowing stare Peggy had returned? *Yes, my lady, good enough for* that.

He had one of her nipples between his lips. She whimpered, writhed underneath him—tossing her head back, thrusting out her chin in a simulacrum of aggrieved hauteur. She hoped he was enjoying her playacting—she was doing her best to make it as broad, as ridiculous as his.

Ah, but she'd also let out a deep groan, at the feel of his large warm hands, so tight around the cheeks of her arse. Lovely to be held so firmly. To be spread, opened, *handled* . . .

He chuckled. "But what's this?" he exclaimed. "Another way into the treasure chest?"

Rolling her over, one of his hands tracing the curve of her rump, slapping her now, murmuring that the enlightened lady was far too bold and needed a little pirate discipline.

She felt herself bouncing beneath his palm. Her skin must be growing quite pink, she thought, and she found herself suddenly, humiliatingly, wishing that there were a mirror close at hand so she could see it.

He must be reaching with his other hand to undo his buttons.

With her wrists bound as they were, she wouldn't be able to balance on hands and knees. Shoulders and knees it would have to be, then—breathless, with her face buried in the bedding beneath her. No matter— he'd manage the angles; she wasn't sure how, but the nice thing about his uncouth lady-and-the-pirate game was that she didn't have to know quite how he'd . . . *take her,* the words inescapable, if crude and beneath her dignity.

He'd manage it. Yes, he was managing splendidly. For he'd entered her now and she heard herself calling out with surprised pleasure, to feel the parts of her quim that usually went quite untouched when one did it from other positions. She squeezed back against him— one wouldn't want to be *entirely* passive (would one?)

while being (but how might his enlightened lady prisoner put it?) *ravished, taken?* . . . And with such profound, cheerful, and energetic disrespect.

He'd reached a hand now under her belly, his finger touching her flesh where it became hard and knotted. "Pearl," he whispered. *Pearl in the oyster.* His tongue traced the whorls of her ear; his finger continued to thrum against her while he made his last thrusts and even as he gushed into her. She screamed against the thrumming and then against the suddenness of his release and the intensity of her own. Until her scream became a gasp of astonishment, for her cries had frightened the doves in the eaves, who now took flight in a great cacophonous flapping of wings.

⁂

Difficult to pull himself off her, he thought. He'd like to stay just as he was—mouth against her nape, cock and belly against her arse. But he could feel her shoulders growing stiff; she needed to have her hands freed.

The knot he made was quite a bit tighter than necessary; the linen of his neckcloth would never be the same. It had been years since he'd had to make excuses to his valet for this sort of thing. Still, he wouldn't have wanted to go to the village shop for drapery cord.

He used his teeth to loosen it.

"Ahhh, much, much better." She rolled into his arms, laughing softly, kissing his throat, his ears, even his shoulder where the scar was.

"Your arms aren't too terribly stiff?"

She laughed. "The left one has gone quite numb, but I don't mind. All in all, you managed to get things quite . . . correct."

He laughed too, and reached out to massage the poor arm. Agreeable to have succeeded so well, delightful to be appreciated. Interesting to remember her youthful fancies about a cruel governess. Even then she'd needed an occasional holiday from her willfulness, her intelligence, her everlasting fastidiousness of mind.

Too bad he hadn't understood this better, back when it would have counted. Might have saved him some boring nights with paid companions who only pretended to enjoy it.

Her eyelids had grown heavy. He kissed them. He thought she'd sleep.

Certainly she wouldn't remember what she'd proposed yesterday, about telling her his business in the district. He drew her closer to him.

She rolled over on her front, eyes wide and clear as though she'd slept ten hours, chin propped on her hands.

"Now," she said, "tell me what you've been doing in the countryside."

Oh, Lord.

⁂

"You're not going to like it."

"Tell me anyway."

He was right. She didn't like it at all.

By the end of their rather brief conversation, they'd moved to separate sides of the bed.

"I liked you a great deal better as a pretend pirate than I do as a pretend magistrate."

Damn that everlasting fastidiousness of mind. She had an answer for everything.

The letters from Traynor? ("But of course an informant would lie and exaggerate," she said. "Keeps him in business, after all.")

Secret meetings? ("Well yes. If the government insists upon making it illegal to meet in public. Not to speak of disseminating and discussing certain literature.")

Caches of weapons? ("Has anyone ever really seen them? For Lord knows, men *always* like to talk and boast and exaggerate about weapons." And in truth, he'd never gotten Traynor to point to any proof here.)

The way Traynor's reports seemed to match up with the Nottingham magistrate's informer's communications, not to speak of the Parliamentary Committee's report. *(What a pity how many poor men needed to sell themselves, to tattle on their fellows.)*

"And if their lives were better, Kit? If their petitions hadn't been refused and they themselves had been treated with some respect when they'd delivered the petition last winter?"

He'd found himself occasionally wondering the same thing.

"But it's too late now. They're going to march to London, Mary. I think there will be violent disorder on a scale we're not accustomed to in Britain. The London delegate told them the time for parliamentary redress was past, and it seems they believe that. I wrote to Lord Sidmouth, recommending that they be arrested. Perhaps that'll be our only chance to stop this thing."

"London delegate?"

"Ah yes, the man who was bothering Peggy was one of them. Name of Oliver. Sent from the London Committees, to spread their poison. You can see why I was so exercised, thinking I might get to see him. Traynor sent me a report of the meeting. Williams the shoemaker, his son Merton the stockinger, and his grandson—three generations of revolutionists, all there. Oliver gave a stirring speech—called it 'The Mother's Last Admonition to Her Children.' Said the London Committee could rally seventy thousand men and that the men of the countryside must stand up in support. Very successful, according to Traynor."

She knit her brow, but didn't say anything.

"Well?" he asked.

"I don't know, Kit."

"At least you didn't throw anything."

"I didn't tell you everything I think either."

"Would you read the correspondence if I brought it tomorrow? Then you'll know everything I know."

"Why would you show it to me?"

"Because you, of all people, know I like to get things . . . correct. I have a reputation to uphold with you.

Because I think I can convince you of my position. Because I know you can be fair-minded when you want to be. Because you're my wife and I . . . trust you."

He was silent for a while. And when he did speak, it was only to ask if she might help him tie his hopelessly spoiled neckcloth.

⚜

She'd keep his secret, then. At least for a while. After all, she was keeping her own secret, wasn't she, about what she'd overheard Nicholas Merton saying this morning, in a pantry just off the kitchen? He'd slipped away soon after, but she'd recognized him even in the dark corridor.

There'll be guns. You can be sure of it. They know what they're about in London.

She should tell someone. Perhaps she would have already if the boy's father hadn't been forced to run off in fear of the same stupid laws she'd just been arguing about. And then there was the ridiculous fact that he still reminded her of how Kit had once looked.

The boy's family had had enough troubles. And anyway, he'd probably simply been boasting to impress his mate. Just as Traynor was probably making up the business of the weapons to impress his employer—and to keep him paying for information. If *she* were a paid informer, she'd certainly exaggerate the evidence in order to keep her employer interested. And men were so unfailingly fascinated—dazzled, really—by talk of weapons, weren't they?

Which didn't, however, mean that there wasn't *some* plot afoot. Much as she hated to own it, Nicholas had been talking about *something;* after all, he had been to the meeting—it said so in the damned informer's letter.

Difficult, painful to think of it happening in *her* village. *Other* reform clubs might be plotting violence, but not here, where her mother had done so much charity. Where she and Jessica had recently gone about distributing food and blankets. Where the women were so grateful for a little packet of tea . . .

Would she *be grateful for a little packet of tea?*

The truth was that *she'd* be ruddy furious if a pair of well-intentioned gentlewomen were to descend upon her home with food, smiles, and a blanket—and then disappear back into their pretty, comfortable lives until next time her children took ill or hungry. *She'd* be proud, prickly, disrespectful, a veritable Nick Merton. Maybe it wasn't only Kit the boy reminded her of.

She wasn't sure where any of this led—except to mortal confusion, a possible megrim, and a strong desire to forget all about it. Even as she needed to become Aunt Mary again at dinner, and to try not to drift off into delicious memories of the moment when the doves had taken flight.

Chapter Eighteen

"He's not at all like that," Elizabeth Grandin told her cousin Fannie, and rather crossly too. "And *must* you continue to refer to him as my uncle?"

Fannie instantly regretted whatever silly babble she'd evidently let slip from her lips. She'd spoken lightly, and now she couldn't even recall the words she'd uttered— some nonsense, she expected, about Lord Christopher's "Byronic" looks, or was it his manners? But *Byronic* was only a convenience among Fannie and her erstwhile schoolmates, the poet's name a cipher, regularly employed in reference to all things masculine, attractive, and forbidden.

Not that Elizabeth, poor dear, could be expected to understand such things. No wonder, Fannie thought, that her country mouse of a cousin had responded so warmly, scowled so roundly, and still sat glaring in the front seat of the dogcart, all prickly and proprietary, about the interesting *tendre* she'd conceived. She felt a surge of protective affection: Elizabeth was acting as any girl of spirit should, in the defense of the first gentleman to arouse a fluttering of excitement in her breast—rather like Fannie and her set at the Misses Duxbury's Athenaeum for Young Ladies two years earlier.

By now, of course, Fannie's London schoolmates had learned a measure of worldliness. Still, Fannie was amused, sympathetic, and rather relieved that her cousin was finally beginning to act as she should. Eighteen was awfully old to begin exercising one's tender feelings toward the male sex, but everyone had to start somewhere, didn't they?

She smiled her melting smile and dropped a soft, conciliatory kiss onto Elizabeth's delicately sculpted cheek.

"I didn't mean to suggest that his manners aren't entirely proper. It's only that he *does* give one rather a frisson, doesn't he, with those eyes, and that air he has, of being so exceedingly, physically, alive?

"But there's still no denying that he *is* your uncle—and will remain so, in any case, until he and your aunt Mary actually divorce. Which will be fascinating in itself, don't you think? I've never met anyone who's been divorced. We encounter Lady Holland in the park quite regularly, but Mama always insists we avert our eyes."

The girls were driving back from Rowen through midday air so heavy and moist that they'd loosed the strings and allowed their bonnets to slide to the backs of their necks. The sky was overcast; a rainstorm was on the way. With the sun so well hidden, they'd agreed there could be no risk of their becoming brown or freckled. Unfortunately, there was no one to correct them in this misapprehension. Miss Kimball had jammed herself behind them in the cart, along with the album of Mr. Brown's original landscaping plans that Fannie had borrowed from the marchioness; her loud snore rose from the seat where Aunt Jessica was given to piling up her charity baskets.

The morning's expedition had proven at least a partial success, not counting the loan of the fascinating drawings. They hadn't discovered when Viscount Sherwynne was expected to return from his tour, but Lord Christopher had stopped into the young marchioness's sitting room, which event was far more interesting to

Elizabeth—and even to Fannie, as evidence of her cousin's precarious emotional condition, and (she couldn't help affording) it had constituted an agreeable encounter in itself.

Congratulating them on how merry they made a dull morning, he'd beamed with pleasure to see his brother the marquess smiling and even attempting to pronounce a few halting phrases. "You have my deepest gratitude, ladies," he'd told them, "for sharing your presence and your *esprit* with us."

"But it's no more than the family at Rowen should expect," Elizabeth had responded. "For we *are* your nearest neighbors, after all," she'd added, in an indignation so purely sincere, Fannie thought, that no one could accuse her of putting herself forward. Well, perhaps just a little, but in the main the effect had been extremely pretty.

Lord Christopher had laughed and said that at *his* advanced age, one could remember when relations between the families had been otherwise. Sadly, though, he must beg to be excused from the young ladies' company; he'd been occupied all morning and had a busy afternoon ahead of him.

He'd moved quickly to the doorway, but halted there in response to a remark of his sister-in-law's. Glancing back over his shoulder—"Ah yes," he'd exclaimed, "I'd quite forgotten." With his eyes glittering so green, Fannie thought, and his smile curving so provocatively that one might even forgive him his mediocre stature.

Of course. For he and the Marchioness Susanna would be seeing their nearest neighbors, he'd told the girls—*and* their neighbors' charming guest, he'd added—quite soon again. In just two days, wasn't it, at the upcoming assembly at Cauthorn?

"We'll be stopping very briefly," the young marchioness had interjected with her characteristic caution. "Just to bid the company good evening."

"Perhaps for an hour or so," Lord Christopher had agreed. He'd nodded at his sister-in-law. "Just to afford this good lady a dance or two, a change of scene and a brief respite from the ceaseless and splendid attention she'd been paying her husband."

Whereupon the girls had fairly twittered their approbation for her ladyship's devotion, their sad disappointment that they were to lose Lord Christopher to his business this morning, and their delight at the advent of the upcoming assembly—only in two nights, just fancy.

What sort of business can he have, Fannie wondered, *when he's so recently arrived from the continent?* For charming and attractive as he'd been, Fannie couldn't help thinking that he'd looked pleased enough to get to whatever he was obliged to be doing and to go wherever he was going.

He hadn't mentioned his destination. The omission had troubled Elizabeth as well. "He walks out every afternoon," she said now. Her cheeks were pink, and Fannie wondered whether it had been such a good idea after all to take off their bonnets.

She hated to be the one to suggest putting them back on again. Well, what was the point of being young if one had to set curbs on one's own freedoms? But there *was* the upcoming assembly to consider; reluctantly, she covered her head and nodded for her cousin to do the same. Provoking how remiss in her duties Miss Kimball was; the least the old bat could do was keep a lookout for their complexions, leaving Fannie at liberty to attend to her cousin's interesting and volatile emotions.

Astonishing that no one else had noticed the flutter Betts was in. *I'll have to take charge of her myself,* Fannie thought. For *someone* had to.

Anyway, it was always instructive to watch someone fall in love, particularly because Fannie didn't intend to do it herself. Well, perhaps in a number of years, after she'd safely and successfully discharged her obligations to herself and her profession.

For like a dutiful son directed toward the army or the church, Helen Francesca Grandin had had her career charted out for her almost since birth. Or at least since the inspiring moment when she'd smiled her deeply dimpled smile, fluttered her long lashes, and executed a wobbly but promising fourth position, a three-year-old prodigy of Mayfair femininity at her first dance lesson.

Fannie's profession was to come out brilliantly and marry splendidly; any suitor below the rank of viscount would be turned away at the Grecian portico of Sir Edward Grandin's house in Cavendish Square. But this long-cherished project (Lady Grandin's life work, if truth be told) must be put by until a reasonably acceptable husband was found for Philamela, the eldest of the family's two daughters. The younger wouldn't be out until next season at the earliest, which would have been a boring and provoking situation for anyone—even a young lady as good-humored and interested in the world around her as Fannie was.

How foolish of her parents, she thought, to exile her from London, merely because Lieutenant Birney had tried to kiss her while dear, timid Phila was upstairs retying her sash for the eleventh time.

At least that was the official story; in actuality the lieutenant had tried and succeeded quite brilliantly (in his own estimation, at any rate), the week before in the Grandin library. For her part, Fannie reserved some doubts, along with a firm conviction that her family should have been grateful for the assistance she'd rendered them. Well, how else, she'd argued, should they weed out suitors of questionable character?

Her mama hadn't been swayed by her logic. And so Fannie had been banished—under the tutelage of one of those pokey relatives a wealthy family collects like scraps and patches from worn-out gowns—to rusticate and romp and giggle at Beechwood Knolls with her cousin Betts-become-Elizabeth.

She'd been sorry to be interrupted in her researches. And her sister, Philamela (who was as deeply in love with the curate in their country neighborhood in Buckinghamshire as the curate was with Philamela), was equally sorry to see Fannie go.

"Without you around, to remind her how much fun she *could* be having, dressing you up and setting you pirouetting across a dance floor, she'll simply redouble her efforts to find me someone who's more the thing than Adam."

Fannie afforded that she'd been careless—not to speak of ungenerous—to have given way to girlish curiosity, especially in the company of a gentleman with such a pronounced overbite.

"It *is* awkward," she agreed. Surely there was more to this kissing business, but sadly, all that would have to wait for a more propitious time and a less toothy partner.

"Don't worry. I'll write every other day from Derbyshire, lacing and spangling the prose of my letters with illustrious names and titles, to remind Mama that I haven't forgotten my purpose in life.

"After all, we shall be calling upon the Stansells at Rowen; surely *they're* splendid enough—perhaps if I'm very lucky, the Viscount Sherwynne will have returned from his tour. Lord Ayres is moderately acceptable as well—and who knows, it could turn out that Aunt Jessica has invited someone else Mama would approve of. That Penley family Uncle Arthur married into has such quaint, random notions of who's worth knowing, a few peers must occasionally creep into their circle of acquaintance, if only by statistical probability."

Sta-TIS-ti-cal. She smiled as she clicked her tongue over the word she'd recently learned. Such a piquant way to look at the world, she thought: gentlemen and ladies bowing and smiling, marrying, conceiving heirs, and going to war—an entire population moving as though in a dance, through the figures of bloodless mathematics. She'd picked up a text that explained it all quite clearly—reading it absentmindedly, as she read most things, while she stood in a bookshop, waiting to purchase her own copy of *Debrett's.* For it had been her plan to sprinkle a few additional names and titles through the correspondence she'd be sending home. Wisely, Phila had cautioned prudence; their mama (who was as quick-witted as Fannie, but more single-minded) maintained her own inner calendar of the comings and goings of at least nine of the nation's upper ten thousand. Fannie had nodded soberly and promised to be careful.

"While all *I* can fairly promise," the elder sister told the younger, "is to bore her to tears in your absence."

"Yes," the younger replied, "boredom is best. Spectacular failure at Almack's would be a sad miscalculation—she'd only take it as a challenge. Mediocrity is what you want, Phil; you must dance with cousins whenever possible, or with debt-ridden nobodies. A pity Fred had got into his scrape when I got into mine; *he'd* have queued 'em up for you. Still, I'll insist he write to his least impressive schoolfellows and solicit their help in the service of true devotion. If they intend to dance with *me* next season, they'll do as they're told for the remainder of this one."

For Fannie was of that happy race of mortals who enjoy arranging matters in the simultaneous interest of as many people as possible. She was rather like her universally lamented uncle Arthur in this, but blessed with superior initiative and originality. Loving her sister dearly, she sincerely hoped to marry her to Adam Evans as soon as could be managed—both in the service of true devotion and in her own self-interest, being impatient to get on with the career she'd been prepared for. It was a pity, Fannie Grandin sometimes thought, that she hadn't been born a boy; she might have liked to be a bishop, a diplomat at the Congress of Vienna, or perhaps (given her secret penchant for figures and equations) Chancellor of the Exchequer.

But in the meantime (and like her uncle Arthur as well), she continued to find herself entertained by the family he'd connected the Grandins to. How oddly passionate they all were, even Betts. Just see, at this moment, her erstwhile hoyden of a cousin becoming so lost in her romantic imaginings that she was making the horse skittish. Fanny took the reins from her.

"He goes in the direction of their farms, and I keep hoping that I'll encounter him when I ride through the meadows near there." Elizabeth's eyes were soft and clear as early morning skies reflecting back the dew on the grass. "I'll be cantering by, with my hair untied. It's rather a bother when one's riding, but I think it looks best that way, don't you? And there he'll be, striding across the land like Mr. Knightley in the book Aunt Mary lent me."

How passionate and how annoyingly like a novel reader.

Still, Elizabeth did look best with her hair untied.

While Fannie's hair was beginning to frizzle in the heavy air. Impatiently, she pushed an auburn tress back from her moist forehead. When they returned to Beechwood Knolls, she'd have her maid rinse it with rosemary water, of which they'd brought a large supply from London. Enough for Elizabeth too, if she wanted—not that those loose ripples of pale spun gold ever seemed to need extra attention.

How amazingly pretty her cousin had become these past months. Which might have grown irksome, if Fannie hadn't already assigned Elizabeth a part in a strategy she was planning: next year, when they came out, the two of them would join forces with the Honorable Mariah Plummer, a redoubtable raven-haired beauty from the Misses Duxbury's. Three was a good number: comparisons to the Graces inevitable, if boring; their various colorings a point of fascination; together, the little battalion of them would be unstoppable.

Strategizing kept one busy and cheerful; what was more difficult was maintaining patience with Elizabeth's nattering on about the book she was so taken with, about a country gentleman who'd spent a good portion of his adult life ogling the little girl next door. Fannie, who preferred books with facts in them, could nonetheless understand why Elizabeth might find that particular novel so apposite to her fancies.

I should be more sympathetic, she chided herself, *to*

someone who hasn't had my advantages. Because al-though Fannie and the other girls from the Misses Dux-bury's had recovered from their own cases of novel reading and other literary hero worship by the age of sixteen or so, poor Betts had spent that particular year of her life grieving over Uncle Arthur's death. No won-der her cousin was having such trouble making her way to young womanhood—and now that she had, no won-der she'd chosen a handsome older neighbor to focus her feelings on.

Simple enough to construe—but then, Fannie had always enjoyed so many advantages over Elizabeth.

Or had she? Fannie still wasn't sure of how to resolve the conundrum of the tender solicitude and violent envy she bore her adored childhood friend.

Rather as though one life wasn't enough for a young woman; the more you appreciated and enjoyed what you had, the more tempting you found the things you lacked. When they'd been younger and Fannie the unri-valed beauty of the pair, she used to wish for Betts's freedoms to romp, ride, and run about the estate, to speak her mind at a dinner table whose conversation was a fascinating jumble of books, poetry, food, fash-ion, and even politics—often with the ladies' opinions taking precedence.

Mama and Papa used to shake their heads in dis-tressed amazement in the carriage on the way home from the midsummer festivities at Beechwood Knolls, review-ing the proceedings and concluding that Arthur's wife and her sisters had as little propriety as guinea hens, and less ton. Of course, Mama was sure to concede that Mrs. MacNeill was extraordinarily well dressed. But *Glas-gow* . . . now, really. While as for Lady Christopher, her scandalous separation from her husband, her raffish, radical friends . . .

How delightful to have such an aunt, Fannie would think—usually at the inevitable moment when Lady Grandin would nudge her husband, put a finger to her lips, and nod at the two girls in the backward-facing seat, eyes glued to their embroidery while they pretended not to listen.

She laughed now at the memory, loudly enough to jolt Elizabeth from her reverie. "I was just thinking how dreamy and bookish you sound. A veritable Penley after all—and how surprised your mama would be, to hear anyone call you that."

Elizabeth frowned. "Don't tell her, please. I can't abide it when she gets so taken with her own cleverness—she and her sisters too. You can't imagine how tiresome it gets, their self-regard when it comes to their precious educations, their self-congratulation for not being like *most* silly women, and their insistence that I be grateful for being included in their little sisterhood."

None of which sounded so awful to Fannie.

"Your aunt Mary's all right, I think. And she's still even rather pretty—for her age anyway. Lord Ayres is quite excessively smitten with her, or has decided to be, since *you* pay him no attention. Of course, you haven't noticed this, but it's clear as day. A pity she won't be going to the assembly; it would be fascinating to watch him pine after her in a public venue. And it gets other gentlemen's attention as well, you know, but I believe I've already explained that to you. Still, I gather your aunt only cares for her man of business Mr. Bakewell. Do you know, if I were a man, I might find business and manufacturing quite fascinating. . . ."

Elizabeth shrugged.

"And your mama's quite correct," Fannie continued, "about most women being silly. Most women *are,* and so are most men, especially in exclusive society. Perhaps you'll be permitted to come spend Christmas with us in Buckinghamshire, and you'll see for yourself."

※

There had been a time, little more than a week ago, when Elizabeth's heart would have leaped with delight at just such an invitation. What perfect happiness, she would have thought, to spend time in a family where outrageous demands weren't always being made on one, and where being pretty, well dressed, and otherwise quite *ordinary* was to be quite as one should. To dress, to dance, to meet new people, to think of nothing but looking one's best, and to let one's precious interior life go to the devil if it chose to—all quite splendid, she would have thought.

But now . . . "I don't know. If he's still stopping at Rowen, perhaps I'd better remain at home. Even if it becomes awkward while they're divorcing, I could nod good morning at church, and give him a little smile to show him that *I,* at least, don't bear him any ill will for wanting to remove himself from his marriage. A modest, subtle smile of . . . admiration. Good cheer. And . . . encouragement, I was rather thinking."

Her cousin's eyes had grown very wide, their clear hazel lit by sudden disapproving surprise.

But I don't care, Elizabeth told herself. *She may* think *she understands a great deal, and I suppose in some ways she does. But it's different when one is in love. One becomes more mature, more . . . womanly, I expect.*

"I've begun to wonder," she continued, "whether I should come out next year after all. I might just remain at home while they get this divorce over with. Perhaps he'll continue helping his brother—apoplexy is awfully difficult to recover from, isn't it? And if *I* wait another year . . . well, in any case, I needn't hurry as I'd planned to, to be out."

⁂

Fannie had never seriously considered how one went about marrying a gentleman who'd been divorced—or even if you legally *could,* in case of a divorced uncle. The situation was so rare, the laws governing property and consanguinity so much more difficult and correspondingly less logical than the laws of statistics. Of course, the complexities of the thing *could* be understood; from time to time she'd thought it might also have been interesting to become a barrister or a parliamentarian. She'd puzzle out the law in her papa's library, when next she had a moment free.

But none of that was really the point.

Not, at that moment, that she was exactly sure of what the point was. Something about envy—of a girl who'd recently become so beautiful as to think that anything was possible (if you could call it *thinking*—well, then to *believe* it, which was all the worse). Suddenly, Fannie felt an awful pang—of loss to herself and bitterness toward Elizabeth. Suddenly, she found herself wanting a passionate devotion as well, while just yesterday she'd thought such things were only consolations—for the plain, like Philamela, or the odd and quaint, like the Penleys.

Was she simply envious of how Elizabeth looked these days? Not just the physicality, but the power, the *magic* of it. When a girl looked like Elizabeth, she might be able to set her own rules—of conduct, and who knew what else?

Or perhaps . . . but no, she couldn't credit it, for he was a younger son and—well, one had heard the speculations about his mother. Still . . . after all, he *had* (had he not?) expressly mentioned that he'd be seeing their *charming* guest as well. Yes, she was sure of it—Lord Christopher had said that Fannie was charming and hadn't said a thing about Elizabeth. And one *could* even make the case that it was at *that* moment that his lips had curved so provocatively and his eyes had—could one say they'd flashed? Well, if eyes of such a moody, fascinating hue could flash, his had. The color made one feel—well, the first word that came to mind was *womanly*. But she rejected it—her mama was womanly; everybody's mama was womanly. *Womanly* wasn't what she wanted.

The truth was that Fannie didn't know if English had a word for what she wanted. Not proper English anyway, and not the French they'd parroted at the Misses Duxbury's either. It was all a bit disorienting.

But even with her mind on a tear and her emotions

on a wild, unaccustomed ramble, Fannie's hands had remained firm and quiet. The horse trotted through the gate and up to the house; she climbed down and handed the reins to the groom waiting to take them from her— while a certain flare of light seemed to make her very dizzy.

The sun might be poking its head out from a cloud; Miss Kimball might be making her nasty little dormouselike sounds of waking; Fred and Lord Ayres might be strolling by—she might have heard them say something about the wondrous fireworks display they were planning for Midsummer Night.

Elizabeth might be staring at her in some confusion.

Fannie wasn't sure of any of this. Nor did any of it matter, except, of course, for her astonishing latest thoughts.

· "Fannie?" Elizabeth asked.

"Miss Grandin?" Lord Ayres had his hat in his hand.

"Cuz?" Fred reached out his hand to assist her. She shook him off.

Smiling vaguely at the company, she heard herself apologizing, protesting a certain sudden exhaustion. "From the heat," she added faintly, "the oppressive humidity."

She must go, she told them. She needed rest and solitude—perhaps it would comfort her to take a look at the pictures in the album she'd borrowed (yes, thanks, Miss Kimball, I can manage it). Grasping the large book in both hands, she hurried down the gravel path to the house, leaving them all quite bewildered, she expected, for she'd never been known to be ill or even faint for a moment in her life.

Nor was she now, except for wanting the rosemary water rinsed through her hair.

And—on sober reconsideration—there certainly wasn't enough of it to share with Elizabeth. Nor was there room in the little alcove off the bedchamber where Fannie was staying for two girls to get their hair washed and their heads cooled. Which was just as well, because Fannie needed all the space she could get, to think through the remarkable thing that had just happened to her—and to see if she could figure out how those confusing footpaths at Rowen really connected one to the other.

Chapter Nineteen

"We should have done the reading first." Mary adjusted the gold wire of her spectacles down over the bridge of her nose.

"Indeed we should've," Kit agreed. "I've never made love to a lady in spectacles, and I'm findin' it deuced difficult, Lady Christopher, to restrain myself. . . ."

Allowing herself a final giggle or two, she picked up the portfolio of spy correspondence from the bedside table.

". . . from grabbing the papers out of your hand and ravishing you in your current fetching state.

"Ravishing you once again," he added.

"I need to concentrate," she told him. "Go stir the fire. Oh, and after we finish, I've a document to show you as well."

She drew the quilt up over her naked breasts. He watched until they were quite hidden, then shrugged his shoulders and slid out of bed. Just as well to turn his thoughts away from her and whatever she'd make of the papers she was reading—not to speak of whatever document she'd mentioned. Anyway, the room could do with a bit more heat. For even on a warm day like this one, the cottage tended toward dankness, situated as it was in so overgrown a part of the forest.

But the fire could wait until he dealt with the room's rather distressing state of disarray. Though he couldn't suppress a small, rueful smile at the mess they'd made, hurling themselves at one another, tugging and peeling at their clothing in a frenzy not to waste precious time.

He'd learned to tidy up after himself a bit while living in primitive conditions in Spain. Not that he liked doing it; he doubted that anybody *liked* doing it. And Mary, it was clear, had never for a moment considered applying herself to the matter of physical order. But now that he'd managed to assemble the rest of what he'd been wearing, *where* the bloody hell was his other stocking?

Of course, where else should it be? Strewn over the book on the table, as though marking some phantom reader's place, the book still open to the eternal question of whether a man or a woman got more pleasure from lovemaking. Damned if *he* knew the answer: probably it came out about equal if you played fair. At least he hoped so (not that he was complaining), though Ovid had it that the female sex was privileged in this area. But a poet wouldn't know more than the next man. Idly, Kit wondered whether every man cherished a secret unspoken fear that his lady was getting the better end of the bargain.

The floorboards nearest the cottage door were caked with mud they'd tracked in. He or she might try sweeping it, he supposed. With a broom—the slightly decayed specimen standing in the corner would answer for it. And damn, his stocking was stained with mildew from the old book he couldn't bear to throw away.

For though it might *seem* a romantic idyll, their meeting secretly in such a picturesque setting *(gurgle of swift rushing water, doves cooing against the rustle of wind in the trees),* and though at one time this cottage had actually *been* a sort of paradise for them *(being the first bed and the first roof they'd shared),* the truth was that *these* days *(well, at his advanced age, at any rate)* the arrangement left something to be desired.

Come live with me and be my love—an old lyric she'd liked to sing, words and cadence coming echoing back now from behind his thoughts. Pastoral, a shepherd's love song: giddy swain wooing his lady with promises of beds of roses, food served al fresco on silver plates, and absolutely no messes to worry about. Poetry, in a word.

While reality was quite a different matter, especially if you were accustomed to having servants clean up after you. Astonishing, Kit thought, how smelly a linen sheet could become and in how short a time, at least when subjected to such excellent usage as this one had been getting. The odor had been piquant at first; at this moment one might call it earthy. Give him and Mary an additional sweaty day or so of pounding each other so delightfully, and the only thing one could honestly call it would be stinking.

> *Come live with me and be my love*
> *And we will all the pleasures prove*
> *On stinking sheet in chilly air . . .*

It scanned well enough, warbled softly (so as not to disturb her) in his middling tenor while he sprinkled wood shavings around the boards he'd placed in the fireplace. Perhaps she'd be able to think of a clever last line. Later, after they'd settled the affairs of the nation.

Squatting naked at the hearthside, he fanned the low flames up toward the kindling. Too bad he hadn't brought that second quilt with him today, not to speak of the sheet he'd cadged, just before the girls from Beechwood Knolls had come calling. Very kind of them, he thought, to show such solicitude for Wat and Susanna. But they were young and inquisitive and would naturally have wondered at his carrying a bulky package of linen under his arm; as things stood, he'd had to chart a complicated journey for himself among connecting footpaths to give the impression of heading in the direction of farm rather than forest.

He shivered, blowing on the fire and on his hands too. Sneaking a look at her over his shoulder—why was she rearranging his neatly sorted papers? She looked thoughtful: picking up various of them, spreading them out in her lap and comparing them. Anyway, he needn't be so circumspect with his glances; she was so clearly intent on what she was doing as to have no attention whatsoever left for him. Using up the whole damn bed too. And what was taking her so long?

Warm orange glow, pleasing whoosh of air and soft, low roar of flame: the last of the ash wood he'd brought from Mr. Greenlee's workshop finally caught fire. Kit basked in his moment of pride and primitive wonder (passionate shepherd, noble savage cozy and contented in his hut with his woman). Of course, he'd need to fetch more wood if they were to spend any additional time here. Which would rather depend upon whatever she was making of those papers he'd shared with her. Noble savage's quiet, compliant helpmate, bed partner, and skilled gatherer of acorns (for they'd have to eat something, wouldn't they?). He grinned at how singularly inapt his fancy was when applied to the lady with gold spectacles, brow knit in concentration, and beautiful round breasts once again visible as the quilt slipped down around her.

He spread out his hands in front of the flames. First things first: his hands weren't the part of him that most needed warming. He rose and turned to face her, sighing and arching his back for the pleasure of toasting his arse against the excellent little blaze he'd brought forth (and perhaps, he thought, for the pleasure of showing himself to her, scars and all). She looked up, smiled in a rather abstracted manner (the fire's glare bounced off her spectacles; he wasn't sure she'd seen him at all), and turned her head back downward again.

To hell with it—he was coming back to bed. Surely she couldn't need *all* that space just for a few pieces of paper. Anyway, it wouldn't kill her to finish reading while he curled up beside her—even if she *would* groan and complain about his feet being cold, and his hands too, if he clasped them around her waist.

Yes, much better, with his hands around her middle, thighs pressed up against her leg, belly curved around her bum, and his cock—happy to be somewhere soft and warm—briskly waking up from its hibernation. Not—it seemed—that *she* was taking much notice, intent as she was on whatever specious argument she was doubtless preparing to toss in his face.

Nonsense. There was absolutely no need to worry. The truth was all on his side. Facts were facts, Traynor's accounts confirmed by Benedict's.

But it seemed she was finally finishing up. High time too: she was gathering up the papers, sorting them back into the order he kept them in. She laid the portfolios down on the rickety bedstand now and turned onto her side to face him. He let his hands slide around to the small of her back; she sighed and snuggled closer, drawing the quilt tightly about them and grazing her breasts against his chest.

"Gracious," she murmured, "it's quite a different thing, seeing you close up with my spectacles on. It seems I've been missing quite a bit . . ."

He'd have none of her blandishments. Fascinating as it might be to wonder what aspects of his face or body she could see through those lenses that she hadn't seen before . . .

He lifted his head onto his elbow.

"The letters." His voice a bit strident now, even to his own ears. *Come on, Mary. I need—I deserve—to know what you think.* Even if it wasn't the most prideful way to ask it of her.

"Yes, well . . ."

"Well, *tell* me, dammit. I'm correct, am I not? And I've *been* correct too. I've been right all along to be attending to the seriousness of this situation."

She nodded, slowly and a bit abstractedly. "Yes," she whispered, "you have." She bit the corner of her lip.

He wouldn't crow over it; it was enough of a victory

to have her coming around to his way of seeing things. And (who could say?) as events unfolded, perhaps even Morrice might be brought around to understand. . . .

"Of course," she continued—softly, so that he had to lean forward to make out what she was saying, "there's no evidence that they're gathering large stores of weapons. A pistol here and there, I shouldn't wonder . . ."

"But there's no evidence that they *aren't*."

"Yes, I expect you're right about that as well."

As well—she might have proclaimed him Prime Minister and Archbishop of Canterbury. *You're right as well*—perhaps he could get her to put her signature to it; never before had she capitulated so readily in an argument. He relaxed his head onto the pillow and drew her closer. A celebration was in order.

"Though surely"—her voice was muffled and yet insistent—"you've realized that there's only *one* London delegate and not two. Rather odd, it seems to me, even if I can't see how to assign any significance to it. . . ."

"What do you mean?"

Her eyes shone, very large and keen, behind the ovals of her spectacles.

"You mean you didn't see that this Hollis and this Oliver are clearly the same man? Ah, I should have kept the relevant papers out to show you, but I thought for certain that you'd notice for yourself . . ."

Bloody little know-it-all of a bluestocking, even without the pigtails and pinafore. Yes, now that he'd sat up and had a look for himself—yes, she was quite correct. And no, he'd completely missed the singularity of it. For if you compared the informers' descriptions of the two rabble-rousers from London, they readily coalesced into one tall, well-spoken, red-bearded man in Wellingtons and a brown coat. Same one who'd flirted with Peggy, and same one whom Kit had begun to imagine he knew personally.

"You see"—she pointed to certain passages in the documents—"the meetings are set for different nights, here and in Nottingham."

Except for the last set of meetings, when Hollis (or should one call him Oliver?) had made a brief but rousing speech at midnight in Nottingham and then hurried on to Grefford to deliver the same set of remarks to Williams and company, down the lane beyond the foundry, in the dimly lit and dangerous hours before dawn.

"It would take him just about that long, don't you agree, to walk from Nottingham to Grefford, though chances are he would have begged a ride on a wagon or cart."

Kit shrugged. "I expect you're right. He does seem very much the itinerant."

"Both occasions when Peggy encountered him," Mary said, "he had just disembarked from some public coach or another. And it's rather striking, don't you think," she continued, her eyes wide and thoughtful, "that he doesn't appear to be afraid to travel in broad daylight."

What is she suggesting? But he knew her well enough to know that she was merely speculating on the possibilities. Unluckily for him, she didn't seem to have any agenda at all.

Wait, why *unlucky?* It would only be unlucky—her knowing so much of his business—if he were to persist in seeing her as an adversary and not (why, he wondered, did he find this so bloody damn difficult?) as an aide—an associate, a confederate.

A colleague? Well, *colleague* might be taking it a bit far.

"An interesting point," he told her. "But not, as you say, one that yields much significance. Except perhaps to show that your . . . um, I mean *the* London Committees are thrifty, and have sent only one representative to this part of the Midlands. Perhaps he's simply the best man they've got, and in excessively high demand."

"He's continuing on toward Manchester, it seems."

"Nonetheless. The fact remains that he represents the London Committees—who are busy preparing for an insurrection."

She nodded, winced a bit. "Yes, except . . ."

❧

Just let it go, she thought. *Allow him to get on with things for once, can't you?*

For it *did* seem clear that *something* was going to transpire. The reports, the words she'd overheard from Nick Merton . . . everything seemed to point to some sort of conspiracy.

Stupid to rehearse the feeble truth—that the thing simply didn't feel right to her. Stupid, useless . . . especially when his arm around her felt so exactly and precisely right, clasped tight about her waist, his body so firm against hers, in their cozy cocoon of warm, if slightly ripe-smelling, air. A part of him rather *more* than firm, in truth—especially after she'd afforded that he'd been right about a few things.

Couldn't she let the trivial demurrals go? What was she trying to prove anyway?

"It feels . . . inaccurate to me. I don't understand what's happening, but there's something else—something rather singular."

An anticlimax. Their limbs disentangling, cold air rushing into the widening gap between them. Neither of them even had the heart to throw anything at the other.

She expected that it was a lucky thing that he'd tidied up—made it easier, at any rate, to find her clothing.

"It's all right." His voice was leaden. "I'll lace you. You needn't go home to dinner looking like something out of a naughty engraving."

Neither of them, she thought dully, had ever found much amusement in naughtiness, their shared sensibility running more to the conundrums of power and the mysteries of intimacy than to silly cartoons of portly people with their huge breasts and arses hanging out. For all the good, finally, that sensibility had done them. And not that it mattered anymore.

Except that it *did* matter. It mattered terribly.

❧

And so, he thought, *that's the end of it.* For if she were to persist in maintaining her illusions, her stupid, radical, bloody *pastoral* faith in the stout, simple, loyal workingmen of quaint, unchanging, picturesque Grefford . . . if she couldn't trust him enough . . . if she weren't willing to face reality with him at his side . . .

But what was she canting about now? Probably complaining that he was pulling the laces too tightly. As no doubt he was (he gave an extra, spiteful little tug, but she didn't seem to notice).

"You do understand, don't you," she was saying, "that I fully accept the Grefford part of the evidence. I think there *will* be men marching in the direction of Nottingham. It's the London part I'm having difficulty with."

Oh, Lord, she wasn't going to suggest . . . ?

"Is this really necessary, Mary? You've already said your piece. Thanks for your . . . attention, but . . ."

⁂

In for a penny, in for a pound, she told herself.

She turned to face him.

"No, listen to me. I would have said it more readily, but I knew how you'd respond—and I was a bit . . . intimidated, I expect. The London Committees—well, Richard told me . . ."

His mouth was contorted, eyes distended. For a moment she imagined that she'd be turned to stone if she continued to stare back at him while he was so angry.

She chose a spot on the wall and trained her gaze upon it.

". . . that he ceased attending his London Hampden Club meetings because the entire reform society apparatus had become so distressingly defunct. Just a few nice old gentlemen in attendance, and they all think it's still 1789. They have *no* connections with the workingmen in the country; most times they get together, they nod off to sleep over their port, reading Thomas Paine to one another. Of course, they might *dream* of summoning seventy thousand men, just as well as they might dream of *seven* men actually showing up for one of their suppers."

His voice was flat. "Well, one way or another, and even without the assistance of one R. R. Morrice, your old gentlemen have managed to connect themselves to an awful lot of workingmen throughout the country-side. Or would you deny that, Mary, on the basis of the evidence I've shown you?"

"I didn't say there aren't a lot of angry workingmen."

"Then what *are* you trying to say?"

"I'm not sure. I'd rather want to ask Richard's opinion on the matter."

Well, she hadn't turned to stone, and she'd said what she'd needed to. She congratulated herself that she'd stayed calm. And would continue so, even if she did feel herself a bit fearful of the way his hands had clenched and his jaw trembled. But although *she'd* slapped *him* once or twice over the years, he'd never struck her and she knew he never would.

"I don't want you to tell Morrice about this," he said quietly.

"Of course I shan't. I wasn't proposing to do so. I think *you* should tell him. Find out what he thinks. Listen, Kit. He's the only person you or I know who can shed some light on this business of the London Committees. And he's nearby, in Wakefield, staying with his aunts."

"How do you know he's not in favor of this insurrection?"

"Because he believes in reform, which is quite a different thing. Yes, he has a few romantic fancies. But you haven't seen him in a decade. He lives a comfortable life with a good wine cellar. He . . ."

"No. Absolutely not. I'm charged with obeying orders. I shouldn't have told you any of this."

It was a very solidly built cottage (as one would expect, it being constructed according to the designs of the great Capability Brown). And so nothing broke or shattered or was even knocked from its place, when he quit the room and gave the door a great thundering slam behind him.

⚶

Nothing to do, she thought, but take the path home to Beechwood Knolls.

Odd, how calm she felt, to be parting like this. Or maybe it wasn't odd at all; maybe it made perfect sense. After all, they weren't parting. Well, that was her problem, wasn't it, to keep forgetting that they were *already* parted—separated and soon to be more than that; this just-ended interlude merely a long final farewell, an indulgence, a very long kiss good-bye.

Nothing had changed between them. The letter brought along with her could be sent without her having to show it to him.

If it weren't that she were also *right,* dammit. There was something singular about the elusive Mr. Oliver, about the whole unfolding situation. Surely, when he thought more soberly on it—tomorrow, perhaps . . .

Not a chance. Tomorrow he'd be just as unwilling to talk to Richard as he was today. A pity that the only person they knew who might be able to explicate the situation was the person Kit would be least able to face.

It wasn't her concern any longer. She'd done what she could to help him. She was tired of the whole affair. And certainly of plots and informers.

Listen to the birds, she told herself. *Fill your head with the rustle of trees.* Or with someone else's words—stray phrases from a play she loved, about lovers and madmen, their "seething brains . . . shaping fantasies that apprehend more than cool reason ever comprehends."

A comfort to take distraction from such wit and beauty in words.

Or so it might have been, if she hadn't just now caught sight of Lord Ayres waving delightedly at her as she made her way over the stile.

Had he really chosen this most inopportune of moments for a poetic tête-à-tête?

Worse, it seemed. He'd chosen exactly this moment, on this oppressive afternoon, to protest that he adored her, that he'd never met such a woman as she, that she was driving him mad with passionate desire.

But, but . . . this is so unexpected, sir. Her voice was faint, though he wouldn't notice that. The words were right, anyway; *so unexpected* was just the sort of flirtatious, encouraging banality he would have been hoping for.

Ah yes, he burbled, precisely so—he couldn't have said it better himself; how unexpected, how astonishing and delightful. How magical in a word, wouldn't she agree—that notwithstanding the disparities in their ages *(she couldn't help noting that his passion was not so great as to ignore this disparity)* their spirits had come together as from a higher etc., etc., etc. *(but she always lost track of a man's words when his spirit entered into the proceedings).*

"And to learn, my dearest, beautiful Mary, that you ·can feel it too . . ." *(If she remained so distressingly tongue-tied, she thought, she might simply have to slap him.)* He seemed to have grasped both her hands during that last effusively delivered phrase of his as he began pouring out his longings and sufferings of the past few days, when his extraordinary respect for her had caused him to refrain *(thank heaven for small favors anyway)* from following her into the forest.

But certainly *(he cleared his throat here),* she wouldn't take it amiss if he were to visit her late tonight.

❧

Which, she realized—upon blessedly solitary reconsideration later in her bedchamber—would have been the perfect moment for her to slap him in a fit of outraged propriety.

Instead of continuing to blink in stunned disbelief at

this poor sprig with his violet eyes, hyacinthine curls, and dreadful ear for language.

If she had her wits about her, she would have realized that a slap was exactly what he wanted. At least in lieu of the kiss he wasn't going to get, a slap would have been rather a mark of honor for this ardent ninny of a would-be lover, all grasping hands and raging *amourpropre*. But she *hadn't* had her wits about her, and so she'd done something infinitely worse.

She'd laughed at him.

Well, not merely at *him*, though of course he wouldn't be able to see that. She'd laughed at him and herself and even at Kit, in all their tragically vulnerable pride and absurd comic egoism. She'd laughed helplessly and rather hysterically, her eyes first brimming and then overflowing with tears, nose and cheeks growing red and raw as she wrested her hands from his to cast about for the handkerchief that, needless to say, was nowhere to be found. Things tended to get so *moist* between her and Kit—her handkerchief was doubtless somewhere among the tumbled bed linen at the cottage.

She'd laughed so long and hard that poor Lord Ayres must have wondered if he'd driven her to a lunatic, apoplectic, or even an epileptic fit. But as she got hold of herself, sighing and dabbing at her eyes with the handkerchief he'd finally thought to lend her, she could see his growing assurance that she was perfectly and regrettably all right. Though considerably less attractive, with her red eyes and roughened, tearstained cheeks, than he'd imagined she might be in a state of heightened emotion—the disparity between their ages was considerably harder to ignore than he'd previously supposed.

And so he'd scowled, turned away, swung into his saddle, and spurred his horse toward Beechwood Knolls—no chance, she thought, of an offer today, to lead her homeward on horseback.

He'd appeared quite calm at dinner, however, and paid Elizabeth such modest and agreeable compliments that the girl couldn't help but respond—rather to Mary's surprise. But all in all it was an unusually quiet meal, except for Fred's chatter about the fireworks he'd bought. Even Fannie Grandin seemed lacking in vivacity and oddly drained and abstracted, causing Mary to wonder if she too were suffering from the disagreeable effects of the day's humidity.

Chapter Twenty

❦

It was settled, then; their forest trysts were over. It had been fun, Kit told himself, or even more than fun. His eyes softened here, perhaps at some memory, caught in his mind like a silvery fish in a net. But he had his duties to uphold—to nation, family, public order, and the man he'd been struggling to become.

And anyway, she'd be learning the truth soon enough. Too late for regrets or apologies—the crisis would be averted, everyone (including her and Morrice) would understand the danger the nation's magistrates had faced down.

(And if *he* had any doubts about the rebellion—if he'd once wondered about those London Committees, or questioned the Home Office's certainties—well, he didn't any longer; he hadn't the time or energy for it. One couldn't know everything. The truth would unfold as it would.)

After which he'd return to London. His family didn't need him anymore: yesterday Wat had taken a few unsteady steps with a cane in each hand. The dowager marchioness would be back when the spirit moved her. Even that rapscallion Gerry ought to be showing his face eventually.

A tedious Sunday, for according to the schedule he'd

worked out, it was her turn to make an appearance at church. Too bad. There were those parish records he'd been wanting to have a look at. Tomorrow, then; he could ride over to church in the morning and satisfy his curiosity.

He'd go over the plans for drilling the militia with Colonel Halsey tomorrow night, at the Cauthorn assembly, after dancing a turn or two with Susanna.

※

"Do you suppose the girls have had a falling-out?" Jessica spoke in a whisper, though she and Mary were quite private in her sitting room.

Mary shrugged. "Perhaps they're simply too busy primping and preparing for the assembly tomorrow night. Or they've confided everything they possibly can confide to one another and need a bit of a respite. I know I should, if I'd been chattering so incessantly."

"I expect so," Jessie said. "Well, I hope they enjoy the dancing. We'll have just enough time to ask them about it and they'll be off to spend a few days at the Halseys'. So good of Colonel Halsey's daughter to think of them, and to invite Fred and Lord Ayres as well."

"It'll be nice to get some quiet," Mary murmured rather absently.

"Well, you've had a lot of quiet already, I should think, walking about as you have in the forest." Jessica's eyes shone with unasked questions.

But Mary had armed herself for such a moment. "Miss Halsey seems a pleasant girl," she observed. "Do you suppose she's setting her cap for Fred?"

The tactic worked as well as it needed to. For Fred, in Jessie's estimation, was in no position to tie himself down with any young lady until he got his degree, and if he imagined that he was, well, then he was in dire need of some maternal counsel; she'd be sure to speak to him before the lot of them set out tomorrow for Cauthorn.

Forgive me, Fred, Mary thought. *And forgive me,*

Jessie, for keeping the truth from you. Not that it mattered very much, when so many things had come around to their natural conclusions.

"We have enough ham and game in the meat larder," she said now. "I think it's time to be planning for the pies and puddings, the syllabubs and trifles. Mrs. Ottinger has suggested a few variations. And I believe we may finally breathe easy about the plumbing.

"Oh, and by the way," she added, "have you checked on the local young people we've engaged to help? I mean, are they working out as they should? No problems there, I trust."

Jessica hadn't been apprised of any.

❧

Elizabeth's reflection returned a sweetly wistful smile, floating as though out of darkness between the tall tapers on either side of her dressing room mirror. The little coronet of braids her maid had done up looked quite well, she thought, with the rest of her hair sweeping back over her shoulders. Better for when she went riding anyway.

And Lord Ayres really wasn't so bad either. Rather gallant, and a bit melancholy looking, which was agreeable in its way. She hadn't really noticed his good qualities before Fannie had pointed them out. Or perhaps she'd simply been a bit abashed to have a young gentleman flirting with her. It seemed one could get used to it, though, and (she scanned her silvery reflection thoughtfully) could it really be that she'd become as pretty as people seemed to think?

How strange that she hadn't noticed the changes. Hadn't noticed much of anything, it seemed to her, during these last months spent riding, escaping the house to chatter with the young marchioness, mourning her papa and feeling so furious at her mama—for such a long list of transgressions that sometimes Elizabeth wasn't sure what she was actually so furious about.

But surely Fannie was wrong about Lord Ayres liking Aunt Mary.

And what was wrong with Fannie anyway, that she'd suddenly become so closemouthed?

Not, Elizabeth hastened to assure herself, that Lord Ayres could compare to Lord Christopher. Still, it *was* agreeable to be paid compliments. And perhaps tomorrow night at Cauthorn, well, it couldn't *hurt* to have him gazing so steadfastly at her as he had at dinner; hadn't Fannie explained that one gentleman's attention tended to gather and concentrate a roomful of other gentlemen's glances? Fannie's example had been taken from optics or astronomy; Elizabeth had lost the thread of the argument, but the general idea was clear enough.

Just as long as she were asked to dance. Of course she wanted Lord Christopher to ask her, but in truth she was more worried that no one might. She thought she might die if that happened, though she also worried that she wasn't as graceful a dancer as Fannie, whose mama (unlike Elizabeth's) had been wise enough to employ the best teacher in London.

⟡

"Yes, Miss Kimball, I am aware that my bronze-hued sarcenet was intended for the Midsummer Night ball." Fannie hadn't meant to be so sharp with the poor old thing, but it was irksome to have one's thoughts so consistently interrupted.

"Well, I hope," she continued, "that I may be permitted occasionally to change my mind. We'll save the lilac muslin for midsummer—no one here at Beechwood Knolls really cares what one looks like. . . ."

She smiled and shrugged in an effort to share an ironic pleasantry with the tedious millstone of a chaperone her mama had tied around her neck.

"But I'm quite determined to wear the bronze gown tomorrow night." It was by far the most expensive thing she owned, its brilliant color and simple cut making a vivid contrast to Elizabeth's sweet but rather girlish and flouncy pale blue lawn.

But she must be fair to Miss Kimball—for whatever

her deficiencies, she hadn't really proven an encumbrance. The pathetic old thing must be horribly poor, to judge by all the pleasure she derived from the meals provided for her; Miss Kimball was so intent on simple comforts that Fannie guessed her life hadn't included a lot of them.

I should be kinder, she resolved. *Half-blind and rather deaf as she is, she's absolutely the ideal chaperone, and I shan't want to lose her. Thank heaven Mama had been so distracted by Phila and her awkward season so as not to pay closer attention to the old lady's limitations.* In a newly sweet voice, Fannie called out her thanks.

But Miss Kimball had already stumped off to relay the changed plans to Fannie's maid, that the bronze gown must be aired and a tiny stain seen to, not to speak of getting up the matching ribbons and slippers and amber necklace, leaving Fannie free to turn her attention back to the great Capability Brown's sketches for the landscape at Rowen.

What clever designs, she thought, *and particularly the quaint arrangement of footpaths that lead in all sorts of unexpected directions. Fascinating,* Fannie thought, *the contrivances that go into improving an estate. What a splendid vocation, to be a landscape gardener.*

Ignoring the lateness of the hour, she continued her perusal, all the while twisting a lock of her hair over her forehead in a pretty, absentminded way that might have led some people to believe she wasn't extracting every possible atom of information from the pages spread out in front of her.

❦

"Will he ever come?"

The servants' rooms upstairs were particularly airless tonight, and Peggy had thrown off her coverlet in despair of getting to sleep at all. If only the rain would come and make things fresh again.

She had an extra candle. Perhaps she could pass the

time by doing some sewing. It might make her sleepy; the cloak Lady Christopher had told her she could have would need to be shortened, though Peggy was grateful that it was cut so full in the front.

The only problem was that she'd forgotten to bring it upstairs with her. Still, Lady Christopher often stayed up to read or write in her journal. Peggy would be able to tell from the seam of light below the lady's door. If she were still up, Peggy doubted her employer would mind the interruption. For even in the midst of her own complicated comings and goings these past days, Lady Christopher had been most unusually kind and understanding. Lighting a candle, wrapping a shawl around her shoulders, Peggy padded out the door of her room to the staircase.

⚬⚬⚬

Only a week to wait.

The stairs Peggy had taken were particularly squeaky ones. But Nick Merton, a flight up in the attic, had hardly taken any notice of the noise. Nor was he bothered by the stale, still air he and the other local temporary boys had to breathe, cooped up as they were at the very top of the house. The straw pallet he lay on was quite comfortable—newer and rather larger, if truth be told, than the one Nick shared with his youngest brother at home. In any case, Nick's own thoughts were far too interesting to admit distraction from stray late-night household rumbles, creaks, and clatterings.

A week and a day, to be more precise.

Nice to have such a full belly. The food was good here too, besides being plentiful. He stretched out his long legs and arms and grinned in the darkness, imagining himself on a raft, buoyed on waves of the breathing (some quiet, some raspier) of the boys asleep on every side of him, floating out somewhere in the middle of the ocean he'd never seen.

A week and a day had a nice round sound to it—oratorical, almost a scriptural ring to it. Nick no longer read the Bible—there were so many other stirring things to read—but when he thought about something really important, he liked to put a ringing cadence to it. Like that excellent speech Mr. Oliver had delivered.

Good man, and there'd be others like him in London, who knew how to *act,* to call out large numbers of men in a noble cause. Nor was a week and a day really so long to wait—for the moment when everything would change. When the last should finally be first and Albion's real rulers rise up to claim what was theirs, and when Nick's dad wouldn't have to sneak about like a criminal for having spoke his mind, and his mum might get a rest now and then from weaving *and* the hungry babies still at home.

Not a long wait at all, even if it seemed that way. Because sixteen-year-old Nicholas Merton felt he'd been waiting all his young life for the New World the London delegate had promised him.

***

My Dear Matthew,
It is with the deepest regret and not a little chagrin that I write to inform you of my changed intentions. . . .

She'd made a fair copy from the original she'd written the night before. Same words, though—which was rather a wonder, given the difference in her state of mind today.

All or nothing; post or burn it. More prudent to burn it, forget whatever fancy had caused her to write it in the first place. Matthew would be a good husband; they'd have exactly the sort of serene, satisfying life she wanted.

Burn it instead of blotting and folding it, as she seemed to be doing, and now sealing and addressing it. She corked the ink bottle and stared up at nothing in particular from over the writing desk resting on the coverlet atop her bent knees. And then, as though searching within herself for anything left unsaid, she closed her eyes and leaned back for a moment against the pillows heaped behind her on the bed.

She opened them again. Nothing to add or emend. She'd post it tomorrow.

Would Matthew be surprised? In truth, he'd probably always suspected how hard it would be for her to break her connection with the husband she couldn't agree with on anything. He'd probably be less surprised than angry, or perhaps disappointed that she'd known herself so little. No doubt upon reflection he'd decide himself pleased to be well out of it.

A pity. It had been such an agreeable notion to throw her lot in with a man who offered so many solutions to so many of her problems. It simply wasn't the *right* notion—especially when you respected the man so heartily. Respected him enough to believe he deserved a wife who wanted him in her bed quite as wildly and passionately as Mary had recently rediscovered it was possible to want someone.

Would Kit be very angry that he wouldn't be able to look for a new wife as soon as he'd hoped to? Ah, well, at thirty-two, a man's time was still cheap. While for a woman of thirty-one? (For in retrospect she didn't know whether to feel regretful or wildly amused at the horrified look on Lord Ayres's face while she'd sniffled, wiped her eyes, and tried to keep from guffawing at his importunities.)

Still, she had a few more good years in her.

Sorry, Kit. You'll simply have to wait a little longer to be free of me. Not that long. There'd be another lover sooner or later, an affair of her more typically pleasant, practical, well-managed sort.

She turned her head in the direction of her door. Now that she thought of it, the soft rapping had probably been going on for some time while her distracted mind rejected it as one might slap away a gnat. She called out her apologies and bade her visitor come in.

"It's only me, your ladyship." Peggy dipped into a

brief curtsy. "Come to see if I might take the russet cloak you promised, for to . . . to turn up the hem, you know. Beg pardon for the lateness of the hour, but I can't sleep, you see, ma'am."

"Nor can I. Of course, when one is waiting . . . for a rainstorm, sometimes . . ."

"Yes, my lady."

"Well, the cloak's in the press. Of course you may take it."

But instead, at the sound of the explosion outside, Peggy had thrown herself into Mary's arms, the two of them huddled together for what had felt like a very long and noisy moment.

Thank heaven she'd corked the ink bottle.

Which of us screamed? Shamefaced, Mary rather suspected it had been herself.

Was that sudden loud popping and cracking noise a fusillade of pistols or muskets?

It wouldn't be a cannon. No, of course they wouldn't have a cannon. But what *was* that flash?

Her stomach clenched with the sudden suspicion that she'd been terribly wrong not to tell Kit about what Nick Merton had said about weapons.

The local revolutionists . . . she'd been a fool . . . and if anyone got hurt, it would be her fault . . .

"What did you say, Peggy?"

"I asked if you supposed it might be fireworks, Lady Christopher. It give me a start at first, but then I remembered what we seen in Rome—do you remember?—and the sound was very like."

The girl had drawn herself away from Mary and was smoothing out the papers. "Here, my lady, lucky nothing you been writing got too wrinkled. But what's odd is that there was just a few sounds here, and fireworks, you know, they go on forever—it's the fun of 'em. Could such a thing be, ma'am?"

Of course it could. In clear fact, it was nothing else.

She'd been too abstracted to attend to Fred's dinner-table chatter, but she could recall now that he'd wondered whether it would be worth doing fireworks on a night like this one. For they'd had so few clear nights lately. . . . What if Midsummer Night were cloudy and overcast? "Well, then we'll simply have to go without," Elizabeth had answered, and the other young people had agreed with her. But Fred, always the optimist, had thought it might be worth a try, just to see what *would* happen. . . .

For all Mary had been attending, he and Lord Ayres might well have agreed to try it tonight. It might be only she, among the household, who'd been taken by surprise.

Which was apt, she supposed, since it was only she, among the family and their guests, who knew about the danger of insurrection.

And only she who'd overheard Nick Merton. And who *was,* in truth, more concerned about the dangers Kit had warned her about than she'd liked to admit to herself until now.

"Lady Christopher?" Peggy's timid voice seemed to be coming from a long way off. "Lady Christopher, are you quite all right?"

"I beg your pardon, Peggy. I'm fine. And yes, you're absolutely correct. It's fireworks. Mr. Fred Grandin and Lord Ayres performing a late-night experiment. I . . . I completely forgot about their project. You don't suppose I woke the household, with my silly screaming?"

Peggy peeked outside the door to the hallway where the family had their bedchambers. No one seemed to have been disturbed, and Peggy hastened to assure her mistress that she hadn't screamed so awfully loudly— more like a squeak, you know, or perhaps a yelp, as though she'd had a bad dream.

"Would you like a glass of water, my lady, or me to go down to the kitchen and make you some tea? Or, um, something else, to help you sleep?"

"Water, thanks. Don't bother with the tea. And no . . ." She laughed, rather dryly at first and then with a bit of pleasure. "Just water; I won't be dosing myself tonight. Because listen, Peggy, the wind's blowing in the trees, and I think those are raindrops."

The girl laughed too as she poured water into a glass. She handed it to Mary, straightened the coverlet and—at Mary's nod—took away the writing desk, implements, and papers, putting them neatly in their places.

"Yes, well. The russet cloak is in the press—please take it. And take this letter, to post tomorrow, and those coins to pay for it. But perhaps you needn't begin turning up the hem tonight." Mary waved her hand at the windowpane, where fat raindrops were beginning to make their quick paths down the surface of the glass. "Perhaps you'll be able to get a good sleep now, and even to have some happy dreams.

"Yes, leave the window open—I shall want air, even if it makes a bit of a puddle. Yes, thank you, I think I shall also sleep well."

And with a clearer conscience, at least about Matthew. Even if happy dreams might be a bit too much to ask for.

Chapter Twenty-one

A good thing, Kit thought, that Wat had gotten a few additional words back this morning—enough vocabulary to inform Susanna that he'd had quite enough b-b-b . . . well, he couldn't quite manage *bloody,* though Kit applauded him for trying. But he'd had enough gruel, and wanted an egg.

"Why not?" Susanna had replied. "Yes, why not indeed, love? An egg soft-boiled, Stephen, as quickly as you can. Tell Cook the marquess wants an egg soft-boiled." Turning her head to speak to the footman, so quickly, almost girlishly, that Kit wasn't sure whether he'd seen or only imagined a gleam of moisture sliding down her cheek from the corner of her eye.

Nice to have someone who'd stand by you during the difficult times.

In any case, he was grateful to find his brother and sister-in-law so distracted by the matter of breakfast—and by the weather, for although the rain had thinned to a fine mist, the freshened air was rather chilly, leading Susanna to wonder aloud if Wat ought to be kept inside this morning, and Wat to scowl in response.

There was still a bit of a wind blowing, though with nothing of the fierceness of last night: leaves and branches were strewn about the lawn out the window; the rhododendrons were nearly denuded of their blossoms. Kit watched the gardener cleaning them up, boots and wheelbarrow sinking into the sparkling, very wet and bright green grass.

The gardener disappeared behind the hedge. Kit's eyes remained fixed upon the pristine vista the man had left behind him. He would have liked to lose his thoughts in that wide, blank green expanse. But Lord Sidmouth's letter lay before him on the table, and would continue to lie there, until Kit decided what to do, or at least what to make of it.

He had to believe that it was good luck, the London mail coach coming so promptly through last night's storm. Always best to receive a vexing communication as soon as possible; capable Major Stansell never procrastinated in the face of the inevitable. Urgencies existed to be managed, surprises and reversals a part of the life of the world.

Not that he'd necessarily expected the Home Secretary to agree to Kit's suggestion that they try to arrest the London delegate, in the interest of squelching whatever dissension was brewing among the people.

But he'd expected rather more of an answer than a curt demand that *I should wish that no Persons should be arrested at present. . . .* With no explanation whatsoever, followed by a request that *you continue to procure all the Information in your Power, & that you will transmit it to me at this Office without Delay, under a Cover marked "Private."*

In response to which, one could only whisper *b-b-bloody hell,* and then turn one's eyes back downward to the letter, perusing it yet again, in an attempt to extract the redeeming scrap of meaning that one had surely missed during the first nineteen readings.

"You were saying, Kit . . ." Susanna turned to him.

"No, nothing at all . . ."

"Ah and here's the egg—just see, Wat, how nicely they've set it into one of those pretty silver eggcups, and snipped off the top exactly as you like them to. . . . Yes, thank you, Stephen, a perfectly boiled egg. Yes, very good indeed, and all our thanks to Cook for her promptness . . ." Smiling at Kit, inviting him to share her joy at Wat's evident pleasure in eating something he'd asked for by himself. And then turning her attention quickly to her husband and his breakfast.

Violence was certain if no one moved to arrest the London troublemakers. Couldn't Sidmouth see that the situation would only build and worsen?

Kit needed to discuss it with someone.

Colonel Halsey? But after so many years of drilling, the militia commander would be thrilled by the prospect of real engagement. Which would hardly make him a dispassionate confidant. And not Sir Charles Benedict either. For Benedict *enjoyed* being told what to do, the less thought demanded of him the better, the sad fact of the matter being that Benedict wasn't terribly bright.

At least when compared to . . . the only person he *did* trust to parse the logic of events and help him put his thoughts in order.

Which made it rather too bad, didn't it, that he'd made such a hash of his chances of speaking to her about it? Or about anything at all.

Still, there was no point continuing to stare at the remains of his breakfast.

Nor was he improving matters by pacing around the room with the crumpled letter in his hand.

"I'm going to ride out to Grefford," he called to his brother and sister-in-law, from the doorway where he seemed to have found himself. Good to get some air. He'd go down to the church, have a look at those records he'd been wanting to see. Cool his head. Maybe—who knew?—an idea would come to him about what to do next.

"And do take him outside, Susanna; the air will do him good," he added, winking at the crooked but indisputable smile of appreciation the marquess summoned up in response.

❧❧❧

The parish records told him pretty much what he thought they would. Lots of the names were familiar to him; he'd read them enough times in Traynor's reports. Which confused his feelings even more thoroughly. Still, it was good to know. No illusions anyway.

A nice-looking round-faced girl was curtsying to him from the porch of the post office. Absently, he nodded in response and urged his horse along the street.

No. Wait. He wheeled the horse around.

"Peggy," he called. "Peggy, I need to speak to you."

He'd wait. The worst she could do was not show up.

❧❧❧

"He didn't say where to meet him, your ladyship. Like you'd know, I expect. And I didn't like to ask." *The maid's announcement coolly and demurely put.*

"Yes, thank you, Peggy. Thank you, ah, very much indeed." *The mistress's response rather less so.*

"Oh, and Lady Christopher?" The girl had pursed her lips at the thought of the gentry and their inexplicable outlandish tastes. "His lordship said to be sure to bring your spectacles."

❧❧❧

An unbearably long luncheon, the young people unusually talkative. Fred had a thousand ideas about last night's pyrotechnic experiments; Elizabeth was nearly as voluble about a new pair of earrings in moonstone and aquamarine. Each of them seemed to have an interminable list of things needing Mary's or Jessica's assistance in preparation for the assembly tonight. (And why, she wondered, was Fannie gazing at her so thoughtfully, her fine wide brow so deeply furrowed above those keen hazel eyes?)

When she finally did get out, the day had turned chilly, the sun, still fairly high in the sky, sporadically obscured by clouds that were still blowing in. Her cloak billowed about her in the brisk, wet wind.

The forest was quiet, muffled by wind and water. A few birds were calling, but one mostly heard dripping and rustling, the branches and undergrowth being too wet to crackle under someone's feet as he approached.

For it seemed that she wasn't late after all. They'd reached the stream at nearly the same time. She'd arrived a bit sooner; he was approaching briskly, appearing and disappearing behind tree trunks, his head bobbing up from behind wet tangles of blackberry, his hand carelessly batting branches and vines out of his way as he came.

Be careful what you wish for.

Had she wished for this?

He looked angry. Absurdly, his hat was in his hand rather than on his head, where it might have done him some good. His thick black hair was mussed, tightened into curls, and quite soaked in the misty air. She remembered—across how many years?—how he'd mimicked Jemima the gossipy nursery maid. *Angel face on 'im below the mop of hair . . . mother's dark secret . . .*

And she remembered not only what she'd said to him, but what she'd been thinking, which was a good deal worse: *Bitch. Cow. I hope you die, Jemima. For making Kit like you.*

I'm not quite *that bad now,* she thought. She'd made some progress from the wild little pagan she'd been at fourteen. Thank heaven for small favors anyway.

Why was his face contorted by such anxiety? Had he also heard last night's fireworks? Had he thought they might betoken violence? Was he—rather as she deserved—blaming her from keeping important and dangerous information from him?

Lovely. First she'd confess to Kit that she hadn't reported the dangerous things Nick Merton had said. Then follow it up by telling him that he was still encumbered with her, there no longer being a lover waiting to take her off his hands.

Her mouth was dry. She couldn't seem to speak now that he was here.

Which might have been just as well, because he'd begun speaking as soon as he'd broken through to the clearing where she stood.

"I must tell you something." His voice was hoarse; his breath came sporadically. "And you must listen very carefully."

Well, at least no one had been hurt last night. "Yes, of course I'll listen," she whispered. "And I'm so sorry," she added.

But why was he staring? Was it really so inconceivable, she wondered, that she might apologize for something?

Her eyes were so limpid, he thought, her half-opened mouth so eager to help, the whole of her expression and posture so troubled and uncharacteristically sympathetic. But how could she possibly know about the letter he'd received?

No, she must be thinking of something else. Well, whatever it was, it could wait—and anyway, it was too wet and windy to speak seriously out here.

"I'll tell you in the cottage," he said.

"Of course."

He led her by the hand, only vaguely aware that she was nearly running to keep up with his steps.

"Bloody hell."

She gasped and he whistled at the damage last night's storm had wrought. Of course, no roof lasts forever; but it's still a shock to see one caved in, especially when you've taken such pleasure beneath it. There was no roof at all above the bed—which was soaked through and strewn with leaves and thatch. One wouldn't want to use it for anything, perhaps ever again.

Ah yes, and they'd used up the firewood when last they'd met.

"It'll be a brisk discussion," she said. He didn't laugh.

One of the chairs was reasonably dry. She mopped at it with the moist quilt, wrapped herself in her cloak, and sat down.

He remained standing. "I've had a letter."

She looked relieved, and he wasn't sure why. No matter: he hadn't the energy to spare. Just let her be willing to help.

"First I'll read it aloud," he said, "and then you can look it over for yourself." She nodded, her eyes very wide from inside her hood.

"Tell me what I'm not understanding in this message from Lord Sidmouth," he said. "Help me see what I'm missing."

Please, Mary, he almost added, before clearing his throat and beginning to read.

※

After he'd finished—and after she'd read it again for herself—they discussed it quietly.

Briskly, yes, and briefly too. For she couldn't discern much more than he could. She could construe a complicated text, but there was little anyone could do with such a terse one.

"It's almost as though the Home Office *wishes* there to be violence. . . ." she began.

His eyes narrowed; she turned her face away.

They were silent. There were things one couldn't speak of.

※

His neck and jaw were stiffening—in an effort, she thought, to think of an explanation other than the one his eyes had warned her not to give voice to.

"Perhaps he wants someone else to make the arrests," he said, "for some important reason of his own."

"Well," she said, "he has a week in which to do it. The longer he waits, the more dangerous the situation will become. The people have pinned their hopes upon the London Committees."

Kit raised his eyebrows.

"Yes," she said, "I'm as concerned as you are about possible violence. I don't want it breaking out in Grefford or in London either. I'm frightened for the people—well, I'm simply frightened."

Odd, how difficult it was to admit that.

"I overheard a young man talking about it," she said. "He's been working in our house—temporarily, for the midsummer party. Nick Merton, the shoemaker's grandson . . . yes, I should have told you about it before, I suppose, but one doesn't like . . ."

". . . To spy," he said.

Was it a good or a bad thing that they could still finish each other's sentences?

She shrugged before continuing. "I only heard a few words, but I caught his enthusiasm, and his strong belief that when he gets to London there will be someone there to tell him what to do next."

He awarded her a curt nod.

"But if, as Richard says, the London Committees are truly moribund and powerless," she continued, "if perhaps they have only sent one very energetic delegate down here—well, why would they promise the people so much more than they are capable of providing?"

He raised his hand to cut her off. "Yes, you like to ride this hobbyhorse."

"And I shall continue to do so," she replied, "until you explain to me why you won't ask Richard Morrice for advice. Richard used to *belong* to the London Hampden Club, for mercy's sake."

"And why would I give away secret information, to a man who used to belong to a London Hampden Club?"

"Why would he be willing to tell *you* what he knows?" But she replied to her own question. "He'll tell you what he's willing to tell you, just as you'll say what you're willing to divulge. In the interest of the commonweal—because both of you are decent, fair-minded gentlemen, who don't want to spill innocent blood."

She sighed. "Forget about mercy, Kit. You should do it for the sake of duty. And . . . and honor."

He turned his head away, as though he were addressing someone on the other side of the broken window.

"And so you think I should speak to the man who . . ."

She took up his words only when the silence had lasted long enough to make it evident that he wouldn't be saying anything further. "The man who did something unspeakable, and who was punished for it, or perhaps you don't know that his wounded arm and hand have never worked correctly since then. And yes, I do understand that you were also wounded, Kit, in . . . other ways—and I'm dreadfully sorry for it, and always have been. But Richard's heartily sorry as well," she concluded, "and you must believe me that he's never stopped loving you either."

"Honor, you said." His voice was hoarse and very low. "In such a matter as this. When he cuckolded me. He has the advantage of me. He took my wife to bed. He's probably still laughing at me."

⁂

It must be very difficult to be a man, she thought.

"Yes, well," she said, "that was clearly expressed, if badly reasoned. But I can't say anything more about it. If you want to understand the situation among the radicals in London—if you want to understand more perhaps than the Home Office intends you to understand—you know whom to ask. And he's only about fifty miles north of here, in Wakefield."

She shrugged her shoulders, as though none of it was of much importance. "But you will have to be setting off soon enough for the assembly tonight. Your sister-in-law will be wondering where you are."

"Cauthorn." He grimaced. "Where Colonel Halsey will be wanting to discuss militia practice."

She was surprised at how amusing she found this. "It's a dance party, for Lord's sake, not a postprandial hour with the gentlemen over port. Avoid the colonel. Dance with the ladies—dance with our young ladies from Beechwood Knolls; they're quite wild to dance with *you*. Are you still as good a dancer as you once were?"

They hadn't actually danced together a great many times, for they'd always seemed to gravitate to wilder diversions. Which seemed to her a very great shame now, there being something so pretty about the relatively innocent entertainment of country dancing. Moving down the line with your posture so straight and your shoulders well back (wonderful how visible you'd be, and how well you'd look doing the steps, as long as you had a good memory for what had gone before and a quick instinct for what would come next, and she did, she always had. Would she still?). Bowing, smiling, touching hands, and then (your smile deepening and your eyes warming), ending up with your original partner at the close of the figure.

Unfortunately, the pretty image called to mind what she'd originally planned to tell him this morning—that in order to divorce her, he'd have to wait until such time as she took another lover.

He was businesslike enough about it anyway. "You must do what you need to," he told her. "I shan't advise you."

"No, I expect not. We must make our own decisions about these things."

⁂

After which things became more formal as well as ambiguous. The air in the cottage felt fraught and unsettled, even if less dank, due to the large holes in the roof.

She straightened her cloak while he wandered about, idly inspecting the damage.

Perhaps, she thought, she needn't have been so quick to urge him to dance with Fannie and Elizabeth.

But in truth it didn't matter whom he danced with. In truth, she thought, what mattered was that she'd liked him today, in a new, different, and rather amazing way. He could still seem a bit stiffnecked and priggish about the government (whereas she, at least, was willing to countenance some more daring, even frightening, suppositions about the current situation). But she found she didn't mind any of that—would gladly accept it, in fact, as an element of his stubborn refusal to take things for granted, his unwillingness to employ force unless force had reason and justice behind it. It was a quality, she thought, that one would want in a person one trusted to govern and to defend.

Which was a surprising thing to discover about someone you knew so well. Or *thought* you knew ... *most ungoverned personage.* Oh, dear.

"You should go," she said. "The young marchioness will be wondering where you are." She put out her hand. "And I wish you luck in discharging your responsibilities. The district is lucky to have you."

His eyes widened (rather, she thought, as though he feared he was leading troops into an ambush). After which he laughed and took her hand, shook it, and then seemed to forget to let it go.

"I shouldn't have to give Morrice a very great deal of information," he told her, "in order to find out a few things. One learned, at Vienna, what one might say, in such an encounter...."

She nodded.

"Well, I may make the journey to Wakefield," he said finally. "I'll think about it."

"Good," she said, "I'm very glad."

He dropped his hand. "Well. As you say. Susanna will be wondering where I am."

"Yes."

He remained standing where he was.

"Mary, if I go to Wakefield . . . I mean, I'm not saying I *shall*; I've got to think about it. But if I *do* go to talk to Morrice . . ."

"Yes, Kit."

"Mary, will you go there with me?"

Chapter Twenty-two

It was one of Fannie's great delights to dance at a country assembly. How fortunate, she thought, that a young lady not yet out to society could do so, and what a pleasure to share the Cauthorn festivity with Elizabeth, who'd missed the last two of these events while her family had been in mourning.

Fannie suspected she'd always prefer this sort of party, even when able at last to attend the fashionable ones in town. Dancing at Almack's and in private London ballrooms next year would be work. Challenging work, to be sure—work that tested her skills and mettle as war or politics might do for a gentleman—but work just the same. Whereas a country assembly, to benefit the district's medical clinic and attended by anyone who could afford a ticket, served as a respite from all that, as well as a sort of ritual of fancy and condescension; the spectacle of a baronet's daughter dancing with a farmer's son allowed everyone to imagine their community an unspoiled Albion of toleration and fellow feeling, at least for an evening's duration.

It had been at a series of parties like this one, down in Buckinghamshire last year, that Adam Evans had silently and fervently wooed Philamela. Fannie could remember how the young curate's solemn gaze had remained fixed upon her sister's face while Phil, Fannie, and Lady Grandin floated like the Graces through the figures of the set and down the rows of dancers. Nodding and smiling at everyone, Fannie and her mama and sister had shown themselves delighted to dance with anything in a waistcoat.

Of course, they'd been obliged to do so, to maintain Papa's popularity in the district and Fannie's brother Edward's candidacy in the upcoming election. But Fannie's delight had been quite unfeigned, both for the vigor of the dancing and the fascination of watching her sister fall in love. Not to speak of the sly pleasure of witnessing something quite invisible to her mama. In the midst of all that energetic capering, Phila and Mr. Evans had been so shy, so solemn, so decorous and dutiful that Lady Grandin missed the entire thing, even as it unfolded under her very nose.

And although at the time she'd found the yearning in the lovers' eyes a bit sentimental for her taste, during these past few days Fannie had found herself reliving it, humming snatches of dance music to herself as though it had been she who'd been courted so ardently and not her less fortunate sister.

Which led her to see tonight's festivity through a particularly rosy glow of anticipation, as she and the rest of the party from Beechwood Knolls passed through the large double doors of the Cauthorn assembly room. In its own way, Fannie thought, a country assembly was a very romantic thing, and anything might happen while one was in attendance.

"Come on, Fannie." Elizabeth tugged at her arm. "You'll get us trampled. My word, what a lot of people there are. I didn't know there'd be so many. But you do think, don't you, Fannie, that we'll be asked to dance?"

Absurd, her cousin's attack of nerves. But it would soon fade to nothing, Fannie thought, when Elizabeth began to feel the effect her looks were having—even now, among the crush of people at the door.

And what a lovely, variegated crush of people, so

colorful and picturesque against the assembly room's excellent proportions. Fannie smiled up at Fred.

"Come on," she told him, "I want to dance this reel."

They'd gotten here rather earlier than intended, accompanied by Lord Ayres and Miss Kimball. The Grandin carriage had arrived at eight, spilling them out into the midst of the crowd of merchants, small tradespeople, and their families, who liked to get as much dancing as they could for the price of their tickets.

Fannie suspected that Elizabeth's mama and aunt had coveted a peaceful evening and had thus conspired to pack them off so adroitly. Of course, Miss Kimball might have objected to the lack of ton implicit in an early arrival. Fannie was grateful she hadn't—and even Fannie's mama would have afforded that promptitude was a venal, rather than a mortal, sin against gentility (unlike gluttony, Miss K. having immediately and promptly disappeared among the refreshment tables). And so Fannie found herself unreservedly happy to dance for the pure pleasure of it—before another interesting party made its entrance and the important events of the evening unfolded (if, in fact, they *were* to unfold; she crossed her fingers for an uncharacteristically superstitious moment, before opening them to take hold of her partner's arm).

The reel having drawn to a merry close, she set Fred free to prowl about in wait for the Halseys. Of course, neither she nor Elizabeth lacked for partners, and the more recherché, Fannie thought, the better. She entirely enjoyed being guided about the floor by a most agreeable young blacksmith, a Mr. Smith as it happened, and why shouldn't he be so named?—well built, with coal-black eyes glowing over a rather alarming yellow cravat.

Mr. Smith yielded to a baker, Mr. Bunns (no, it must have been Barnes); Mr. Barnes to Mr. Wills, whose father owned the local drapery establishment. Laughing and curtsying, rosy and breathless, Fannie caught Elizabeth's arm and bade farewell to the two young men squabbling over which of them was to bring her a glass of lemonade.

"It's delightful, isn't it?" she whispered to her cousin. "Much more fun than Almack's, I should think. And— oh, good, I'm parched—here's Lord Ayres with our refreshments." Country dance or not, he wouldn't miss a chance to fetch a drink and a biscuit for the two prettiest young ladies in the room.

"More fun than *Almack's?*" Elizabeth, who'd also had a picturesque series of partners, giggled with pleasure, sighed with evident relief, and gaped in utter astonishment at what Fannie had just told her.

She looked like she'd been out riding—pale gold hair just a bit disordered, cheeks like dark damask roses. It was her cousin's best face, Fannie thought, but the face had been prettier before her cousin had come to know it her best.

"Oh, but Almack's must be so much lovelier," Elizabeth was protesting, "though I do like the decorations here. See how they've looped up the streamers with red and white paper roses, Fannie. Or do you think they're silk?"

"Almack's isn't lovely at all," Fannie replied, "at least not from Philamela's description of it. Whereas *this* is an unusually well-proportioned room. Though I'll grant that a private ball in a great London house *is* something to see. . . ." Fannie's mama had spoken approvingly of a particularly lavish event in Grosvenor Square, the walls of the party-giver's high-ceilinged ballroom entirely lined with fresh-picked rosebuds.

"A ballroom lined with rosebuds? It can't be. You're teasing—you're . . . you're *funning.*" Elizabeth's beautifully curved lips had shaped themselves into something Fannie might be tempted to call a simper. "You're making it up, Fannie, to taunt a poor country girl who hasn't had your advantages."

It took a bit of work on Fannie's part to keep her

eyes from widening into an unseemly stare. *Wherever had Betts learned how to be so coy?*

"Don't *you* think so, Lord Ayres?" Elizabeth continued.

The simper had become a pout, the entire thing, it seemed, staged for Lord Ayres's benefit. Elizabeth gazed up at him from beneath her lashes. "She must be teasing, mustn't she, my lord, for surely no one, not even the Prince Regent, could afford *that* sort of expense."

And when, Fannie wondered, had her cousin learned to tilt her head that way, the pretty moonstone earrings twinkling so brightly in the candlelight that when you looked at them you'd have to look into her eyes as well? *I think I may have taught her that one,* she decided. *But upon my word, she's a quick study, a perfect little automaton of my own creating.*

The proof was in the pudding: Lord Ayres was gazing into Elizabeth's blue eyes as Narcissus might at his own reflection, beaming and smiling away as he informed Miss Elizabeth Grandin that she'd simply have to wait and see for herself, when she came out next year and graced all the most splendid parties in Mayfair.

"But if I'm not invited, sir?"

"If *you're* not invited, no one will be. Next season no one will give a ball worthy of the name without Miss Grandin in attendance." He raised his eyes for a moment. "*And* Miss Fannie Grandin, of course."

Which might have stung, Fannie thought, *rather like the bite of a gnat, if I still cared to receive compliments from just* anyone.

Absurd to lose her equanimity upon finding herself relegated to the category of an afterthought by a young gentleman with a hyacinthine haircut, a lavender waistcoat, and a handkerchief perfumed to match.

She didn't care a jot. Or in any event, the woman she'd recently felt herself to have become didn't care. *That* woman (a *woman,* she reminded herself, and not simply a young lady) would care for nothing but keeping watch over the entryway of the Cauthorn assembly hall, for the arrival of . . .

She'd spilled what was left of her lemonade. Fred, who'd had the misfortune to tear himself away from Miss Halsey just a few moments before, was being very dear about it, laughing and turning the whole thing into a joke as he blotted up his lap—thank goodness the lemonade had splashed him and not her, at exactly the moment she'd glimpsed the party from Rowen, just entered the foyer, on the other side of the tall double doors.

He and his sister-in-law seemed to have brought two younger gentlemen along with them. But she hadn't enough attention for the others, so intently was her gaze trained upon *him*. He was helping the young marchioness off with an evening wrap of an odd salmon color. Not quite the thing with her ladyship's rusty hair, but thrilling as a momentary splash of color against the severe black-and-white of his evening clothes.

Arm in arm, he and his sister-in-law moved to congratulate the members of the assembly committee, who were standing in a self-satisfied little knot, quite close to where Fannie, Elizabeth, Fred, and Lord Ayres had their chairs.

✥

"But how extremely lovely you young ladies look."

And how sweet of the young marchioness to say so, Elizabeth thought, as she and her party rose to greet their estimable neighbors. Her ladyship was looking very well this evening. Less pinched than usual; it was good for her to get a little recreation—Lord Christopher had been quite correct on that score. Odd, how upon first espying him tonight she'd thought him a bit overshadowed by the tall young man with the austere features and interesting aquiline nose. It must be Viscount Sherwynne, finally returned from the continent, while of course the last gentleman of the party could be no one but Lord George.

"And have you all been dancing?" Her ladyship asked, and then laughed, for of course they evidently all had—even after their lemonade (inside and out) they still rather glowed with the exertion.

"It's been wonderful," Elizabeth said. "I didn't know it would be so agreeable—well, it's my first dance party, you know, except among my family."

Too bad Mama didn't come this evening.

The guilty thought surprised her. *I might have suggested it,* she told herself, *if I'd been more generous. If I'd been willing to share the pleasure of my first assembly with her. Well, if I hadn't been so terrified of this evening that I couldn't have borne having her here to see me if I'd been a wallflower.*

But she hadn't been a wallflower. Parties weren't dreadful after all. Well, anyway, Mama would enjoy hearing about it later tonight. And even Aunt Mary, if she liked—she hoped they'd still be up, so she could tell them.

She smiled at her uncle Lord Christopher. Hmmm, now that she was paying better attention, he wasn't so awfully much taller than she was. Which might be worrisome, if it weren't that there were quite a lot of tall men in the world once you kept an eye out for them; most of the Stansells were quite tall, actually. She extended her smile to include Lord Christopher's nephew and younger brother, who were just sauntering up to join their circle and who'd be at Rowen, no doubt, next time she visited there.

Interesting, she thought, how all those years she'd been growing up she'd never really paid much attention to the viscount. In fact, it seemed to her now that she'd been shamefully ignoring most of the male sex, which was awfully silly, since of late each new gentleman she met had something interesting about him. Viscount Sherwynne, poor thing, must have had another riding accident, for he had his arm slung up in a large kerchief of purple silk. She'd never considered it before now, how a wound—well, a modest and temporary one anyway—rather added to a gentleman's allure. She widened her eyes to indicate compassion for the viscount's suffering, and then, just to be cordial, extended her glance to his youngest uncle.

Of course, everyone in the neighborhood knew Lord George Stansell; the difficulty here was ignoring his pronounced resemblance to the Prince of Wales—or willing oneself to believe it didn't signify anything. She would have warned Fannie if she'd known he'd be here tonight. But surely Fannie was a cool enough presence and had probably already heard the gossip.

And indeed (now that she'd sneaked a glimpse in her direction), her cousin appeared a regular ice maiden of rectitude and self-possession, dipping into a perfectly calibrated curtsy when Lord Christopher presented her to his brother and nephew, bestowing a calm and very adult smile on all the company *(how does she do that? Elizabeth wondered. I shall have to try it at home in front of the mirror),* and now murmuring her well-bred delight and astonishment at the welcome surprise of their presence.

"My grandmama insisted we both were to come home with her," the viscount replied, "but when she discovered I wasn't well enough to travel, she decided not to bother Mama with the details of all that, and then"—he seemed to be attempting not to smile, and *Yes,* Elizabeth thought, *he's glancing at me as he speaks; he wants me to share the joke*—"Uncle Georgy had some, ah, *business* to finish up in Paris."

She wanted very much to giggle, the joke being that Lord George resembled the Prince of Wales in more than just his looks. But giggling wouldn't be the thing at all—and Fannie needn't be sending her that warning look either. *I know my manners perfectly well,* she thought, *even if it* is *my first dance party outside the family.*

"In any case"—the marchioness seemed almost beside herself for happiness, and willing, at least this once, to let her son's innuendo pass without censure—"with the marquess's condition improving so rapidly, and having the viscount home with us again . . ."

Everyone murmured the appropriate felicitations. And Fannie even remembered to ask after the dowager marchioness.

"And so you've arrived only today?" Elizabeth asked the viscount. "You must be terribly exhausted. How extremely good of you and your uncle to come this evening, to our little country dance."

※

It was an entertainment, Kit thought, *to watch a beautiful young woman emerge like a butterfly from a cocoon.* And, as in nature, Elizabeth was emerging from her girlhood with more than a little awkwardness, her postures and expressions far too obvious in their flirtatiousness. But one could forgive so lovely a creature a great many things, for the simple pleasure of watching her spread her wings, or even of watching her discover she had them.

A simple, disinterested, even an *avuncular* sort of pleasure—it was with a certain abashed relief that Kit afforded this to himself. He hadn't wanted to mention it to Mary this morning when she'd suggested he dance with the girls. But, in fact, he'd been a bit troubled by the suspicion that Elizabeth might have conceived an attachment to himself—not to speak of chagrined, that he found himself rather enjoying it.

No need to concern himself any longer with *that* business. At this particular moment, the blazing candlepower from Miss Grandin's blue eyes was turned directly in Gerry's direction. As were some inky black scowls from the puppy in the lavender waistcoat, poor fellow.

No doubt he'd simply imagined her interest, out of petty vanity or fear of leaving his youth behind. Or perhaps in truth he *had* flirted, even postured a bit for her benefit, while all in a muddle and confusion about his reconciliation with Mary.

And then there'd been the fact that the girl had made herself so constantly visible the last week or so—she and the red-haired one as well. It had seemed to him they were always underfoot—rather like Snug, the little dog from Curzon Street, now grown fat and somnolent, living a contented old age at Rowen with Mr. Greenlee seeing to him when he needed it. Kit wondered if Mary ever gave a thought to what had become of Snug.

In any case, no harm had come of his flirting and posturing, and Mary needn't know it had ever transpired. Though the muddle and confusion still remained, as to whether he and Mary *were,* in fact, reconciled.

How do we manage to get ourselves into these scrapes? And moreover, to intertwine their own future with that of the English nation? And if they really did make the journey to Wakefield tomorrow, they'd be dragging Morrice into it as well.

And whom, he wondered, did he suppose he was deceiving? *If they made the journey* . . . he and Mary would be setting off for Wakefield as surely as the night follows the day, if for no other reason than for the prospect of the day's drive up there, just the two of them in the carriage. Make no mistake: he and she would be in one of the formidable Rowen traveling coaches tomorrow morning even if it meant he'd have to face ten Morrices at the end of their journey.

Good to get *that* settled anyway. He hoped he hadn't been too rude to those around him, letting his thoughts drift off like that. No, they all seemed quite cordial: no impatient stares at him or scowls at his lapse of manners. He smiled apologetically at the person directly across from him—the red-haired young lady, and very pretty as well in her bright gown. Nice to see a young lady wearing something so simple, so little fuss and frill about her. Though one was supposed to say auburn-haired, wasn't one? She'd returned his smile; so far as he could see she wasn't at all put out by his woolgathering. Very sweet-looking, actually.

The musicians were striking up a quadrille. Damn,

he'd forgotten. For there was Colonel Halsey, making his way over to this corner of the room, armored, if you liked, with that unmistakable look and bearing a certain sort of gentleman always wore at an occasion like this one—of wanting to be anywhere but in the midst of a knot of dancing ninnies, and couldn't one speak of something sensible, like troops, weapons, or munitions?

Kit's original plan in this eventuality was to dance with Susanna. But he'd been slow to move, abstracted by his thoughts; Georgy had already led her out to the dance floor. And although Gerry wouldn't be able to dance, he'd evidently claimed blond Miss Grandin's company for a promenade about the room's perimeter, while the lavender fellow—Ayres, was it?—appeared about to turn to Miss Fannie Grandin.

Sorry, Ayres, Kit thought. *It's a military matter. I need to dance. For England's sake.*

And indeed, she rather reminded him of Mary at her age—that gleam of good sense in her eye anyway. If he had to dance—if he couldn't just drift homeward to meditate upon his situation (or rather dream about the two of them being jolted about, with Mary in his lap, all the long day's drive up to Wakefield) . . .

Colonel Halsey was advancing like a crack cavalry regiment.

"Should you like to dance, Miss Fannie?"

⁂

She'd been quite absolutely correct. There was nothing so romantic as a country assembly. He danced very well indeed; he was charming, circumspect, graceful, and polite.

And it did seem as though he liked her a little.

While she found herself entirely captivated by the dreamy, almost magical look in his eye. It seemed to promise something; she was fascinated by the secret knowledge she felt he must be carrying about with him. It was this . . . well, this *aura* one might say, that she

liked about him, besides the fact that he clearly wouldn't
be hers for the taking. Fannie always liked a challenge,
and here was one entirely worth the attempt.

And he was intelligent; he knew things. He'd been at
the Congress of Vienna; he understood how Europe
was being disposed of and what might happen in the
next decade. She'd picked up a bit of understanding
from Papa's newspapers—not a great deal, of course,
but she tried to follow the careers of Lord Castlereagh
and the brilliant Prince Metternich.

He'd been happy to answer her questions at supper,
before the Stansell party made their early farewells.
The young marchioness wanted to get back to her husband. And then, of course, there was the dowager, Lady
Rowen, who wouldn't leave her oldest son's bedside until they returned.

And being as intelligent as he was, and so adult—
well, surely he must have noticed that she found him
appealing. Not that she'd flirted in such an obvious way
as Elizabeth had. But sometimes she'd gotten the sense
that he knew something. And certainly wouldn't object
to speaking to her once again.

Fannie sank into a chair, as though any physical exertion at all might disturb the fervid motion of her
imagination. For now that she understood Mr. Brown's
design of the confusing footpaths at Rowen . . .

Of course, she, Elizabeth, and the young men—and
Miss Kimball as well—would be going to the Halseys'
tomorrow for a few days. But they wouldn't be leaving
so early as all that.

Some faceless gentleman seemed to have material-
ized in front of her. Bowing now, putting out a neatly
gloved hand, asking for the pleasure of the next dance.

Pray excuse me, sir, she murmured. Ah yes. Bit overwrought. Lovely party. To attempt the next cotillion.

Nice simply to watch Elizabeth instead. Dear Elizabeth, how young, how charming she was. And so very
much cleverer than of late—more like the old Betts,
who wouldn't have paid the slightest attention to a gen-

tleman who everyone could see was very much too old for her, and her uncle besides.

Fannie smiled to watch her cousin curtsy to Lord Ayres and then turn to bestow a mirror-image curtsy upon Mr. Smith (who remained, to be quite honest, the handsomest man in the room despite his yellow cravat).

She stifled a yawn. Best to rest a while, and then to get a good night's sleep. And to wake up early, for a bracing early morning walk upon the fascinating footpaths at Rowen.

Chapter Twenty-three

B ut he'd phrased it so absurdly, Mary thought.
If I go to Wakefield, will you go with me? As
though she could turn around all her plans on a whim—
and a whim, moreover, entirely his.

As though it would be a small matter for Peggy to
pack her things for the journey—without even knowing
how long they'd be gone—and yes, as usual, the day before laundry day.

Not to speak of having to drop everything she was
doing, party and cistern committee—*just* on the slender possibility that he *might* decide to go down to
Wakefield.

Absurd. Inconsiderate. Thoughtless and really rather
childish.

And yet, when he'd asked her, she hadn't hesitated
an instant. "Yes, of course I'll go with you. You know I
will, Kit. You can tell me on Tuesday morning, and I'll
be ready."

He'd tell her his decision when they met at the large oak
tree, at the beginning of the woods, past the broken stile.

At least Jessie wouldn't be alone for too many days,
for the MacNeills would be arriving on Friday.

The important question was whether Kit would be
willing to face Richard Morrice after all these years.

Well, in truth the important questions concerned the incipient rebellion and the Home Office's perplexing response to it. But the personal aspect of a situation always trumped the more general, didn't it? And if that made her a silly, trivial person . . . and she expected it did make her exactly that . . . well, then so be it.

Ah yes, and then there would be the little matter of the long coach ride to Wakefield.

The newspaper didn't mention rain coming from the north. The weather would be mild—perfectly fine for a maid to ride outside, with Kit's valet.

❧

"I think you should pack enough for three days, Peggy, and then, of course, there's a day of travel on either side of it. I'm not sure how long we'll be staying." Or even where—she knew very little about the inns in Wakefield. "I think I'll wear the green chambray to travel." *(It's very pretty on you.)* "But you can pack the white muslin with the black dots. . . . Yes, and the pink is very lovely too, and that one too. . . . What excellent choices you're making for me. . . ." Peggy had a far better eye for clothing than she herself did. Though the girl seemed a bit down—but that was probably due to the condition that she didn't feel ready to own.

"You're not feeling . . . ill, are you, Peggy? Ah, good, I'm happy to hear it. But remember that if you *do* take bad, with a . . . a cold or with anything at all, well, you needn't be a martyr. I and my family will help."

But Peggy was quite well, thank you, Lady Christopher, for your consideration. And what time did her ladyship think they'd be leaving tomorrow?

"I'm . . . not quite sure yet, dear, but best to be ready early. I'll have a little walk in the forest right after breakfast, and then we'll see."

❧

Explaining it to Jessica was a bit more complicated.

"So you're going to be seen in public with him? But

won't that appear as though you two are back together. . . . And interfere with things when it comes to Matthew Bakewell?"

"It would indeed, if I hadn't already broken off my connection with Matthew."

Jessica's silence was as eloquent as her raised eyebrows.

"Since yesterday," Mary said. "Well, in a letter I posted yesterday. It . . . I decided, given the state of my affections, that it wouldn't be fair to Matthew."

"Hmmm. It took you long enough."

Mary returned her sister's gaze. "Yes, I expect it did."

"And as for Kit?"

"You'd have to ask Kit. I don't know how any of this will end. Not necessarily well, I should think. But at least I'm not deceiving myself any longer."

She was happy to be enfolded in a long, silent, and equally eloquent hug.

Pulling herself away finally, to share a smile with her sister, she continued, "Now let's go over the list of what we were supposed to accomplish in the next few days, and figure out what tasks we can assign to Julia. *If* he and I do actually go."

Which passed the evening quite entertainingly, until Mary found herself yawning and gaping over the voluminous list they'd compiled—for Julia liked to have her responsibilities made most explicit.

But even with every chore painstakingly noted, Jessica *would* insist upon lighting another set of candles, in wait for the carriage from Cauthorn.

"Well, it's her first real dance party, and even if, as is more than likely, she'll simply curl her lip and roll her eyes when I dare ask how it went . . ."

"Of course," Mary replied, "but you won't mind, will you, if I go on up to bed?"

Jessie shook her head, and the sisters kissed good night, the younger one rather in awe at how one could still love so ungrateful a wretch as a daughter, and a beautiful one at that, whom Kit may or may not have danced with this evening, not, of course, that it mattered one way or another.

·⁂·

The Dowager Lady Rowen was still asleep, Thomas told Kit, when he'd stopped at the dower house the next morning.

Well, it was still awfully early. Kit hadn't waited to be shaved nor to eat breakfast. His head was still swirling with a night of dreams. Spicy, sugared ones, and some odd, confusing ones as well—the London delegate had even appeared in one of them.

But the impeccable Thomas looked a bit less composed than usual as well, his words still polite but a bit uncharacteristically short. Not only that: Kit could have sworn that the footman had quickly stuck a pamphlet into a pocket of his mulberry velvet coat.

Et tu, Thomas? Certainly *you're* not also planning sedition.

One never knew. Still, he hated to feel himself suspicious of so loyal a servant. Thomas had retrieved a few items that Kit had left behind in Calais; his mother had given them to him yesterday when she'd arrived.

"Ah, well, tell her ladyship that I'm off to Wakefield for a few days, on magistrate's business," he replied. "Oh yes, and here," he added, "this is for you, with all my thanks." Whatever swill he might be poisoning his thoughts with, Thomas deserved a reward for finding what had been lost. "No, please, it's the least I can do."

He turned away and started down the path, stopping suddenly, to call back a final piece of information.

"Wait, Thomas. I didn't word my message quite correctly. You can tell her, if you please, that *Lady Christopher and I* are off to Wakefield."

Why not?

·⁂·

And, for that matter (for there she was, waiting by the oak tree), why not sweep her into his arms for a happy morning kiss? His dreams of her had been of a more exotic genre, but she looked so pretty and natural there in the clearing in her green dress, that it was randy pleasure enough just to peer into her sunlit face, just to draw her to him, curve his hand around her arse, and then to imagine . . .

Drawers? No, I don't.

Of course not. Drawers would be an absurdity in a carriage, not to speak of an assault upon common sense. While without them . . . delightful to think how little it would take—just a few buttons of his pantaloon . . . with the moist green fields slipping by on either side of them outside the windows.

"I expect"—she was pressing her belly and thighs against his quite shamelessly—"that you want to go to Wakefield this morning."

He laughed and buried his mouth in the curve of her throat.

But what was that crackling? Over there on the path, behind that stand of pines?

So absorbed had they been in each other, it took them a moment to absorb the fact that they'd been spied upon, the interloper running quickly and lightly away toward the east, where the low morning sunbeams glared through the trees, obscuring their vision.

"Not that it matters, I expect," Mary said. "I've already told Jessie about our journey, and didn't insist that she keep it a secret either."

He laughed. "The only person I told was my mother."

"She's back?"

"With Gerry and Georgy. The delay was all their fault. The poor lady was hard-pressed to gather up the pair of irresponsible rapscallions. . . ."

"Just listen to the very serious and solemn Lord Christopher. . . ."

"Better keep your hands to yourself, my lady, if you

expect him to do his serious and solemn best later today. . . ."

"Why do I expect that he'll manage quite splendidly no matter *where* I put my hands at this moment? But of course," she added, "you're right that I shouldn't be pawing you as I am in this venue. We've gotten over-confident, when we're really quite public here—well, our intruder of just a few moments ago proves *that*. I expect it was Lord Ayres, making his long-threatened poetic ramble through the forest. . . ."

"You haven't been flirting with that pomaded ninny. . . ."

Her face changed; she stopped him short as a new thought struck her. "But if the dowager marchioness has returned home, that must mean that Thomas . . . Kit, you should have told me sooner. I must go . . . yes, come get me in an hour and a half. That will be perfect."

❧

For although she hadn't always been the most patient of employers—nor by any means the easiest to keep neat and well-dressed or to clean up after—there were certain basic demands of human decency and loyalty to her sex.

She'd gotten a stitch in her side, walking so quickly and sometimes breaking into a run on the way back to Beechwood Knolls—on the same path that once she'd skimmed so lightly, not even noticing the first raindrops.

I must look a fright, she thought, waving hastily to the group just starting out for the Halseys'. Lord Ayres ignored her completely, his eyes trained upon a flirtatious Miss Fannie Grandin, looking very pretty and composed with her hands on the reins of the dogcart. Yes, it must have been the pomaded ninny who'd stumbled into the forest, perhaps to prepare himself for this morning's conquest. . . . Well, at least he'd had the tact to run away rather than show himself.

It didn't matter. "Have a lovely, lovely time," she called out to them, and to Fred, conferring with the groom about the horse who'd be pulling the curricle, and Elizabeth, hugging Jessica good-bye at the side of the carriage.

She threw open the door to the house. "Peggy," she called, as she thundered up the stairs.

"Peggy, where are you?"

Panting on the landing now. But wait. This needs to be done with some tact.

Well, as best I can anyway.

The girl had just finished strapping the trunk shut. She looked up now from where she was kneeling beside it. Pale, anxious.

She knows he's returned. And she hasn't seen him yet.

"Peggy, I've been thinking. Well, you know, it's rather selfish of me, going off so suddenly like this to Wakefield with . . . um, Lord Christopher, though in fact, he, well, we are rather obliged to . . . ah . . . but with all the preparations for the midsummer party, and leaving Mrs. Grandin alone here, and you know how imperious Mrs. MacNeill can be, not that she isn't very dear and good in her own way . . .

"Well, in any case, Peggy, I've rather been thinking that perhaps I should leave you behind these few days, here, you know, at Beechwood Knolls, well, in the *neighborhood,* I mean. . . . So as to . . . um, to be of *assistance* to my sisters . . ."

Mama would have done it with genuine tact and grace. But the slow, serious, anxious, but also resolute smile taking form on Peggy's wan face was proof enough that Mary had succeeded well enough.

⁂

Her little trunk was packed; her portable writing desk sat on top of it, next to her folded dark red traveling cloak. A miscellany of necessaries—lavender water, her all-important drawstring bag, even her spectacles—were knotted up in a large India shawl.

She sat alone on a bench built round a large beech tree near the front door. To wait. For half an hour? Half a year? The better part of a decade? Or merely an instant. She couldn't tell if time were rushing by or stopped forever. How odd, when her pocket watch was ticking so evenly and objectively. She tried to set her breath to it.

But at least she needn't be alone. For here was Jessica, carrying a covered wicker basket.

"The inns between here and Wakefield won't give you an edible luncheon, and so I thought . . . well, there's a bottle of wine, another of cold springwater, some pretty good Stilton, sliced cold meat, bread, and—careful, they're delicate—a few strawberries from the kitchen garden, wrapped in cheesecloth."

Arthur Grandin had particularly loved the strawberries that grew at Beechwood Knolls. Mary took her sister's hand, and together they listened for the jingle of traces, the crunch of wheels. The path from the main road was screened by dense hedges, ancient elms and beeches. They'd hear the Rowen coach before either she or Jessica caught actual sight of it making its stately way over the gravel.

Chapter Twenty-four

Their meeting in the forest—her very unladylike hands, not to speak of the guilty frisson of being spied upon—had inflamed his imagination again.

He grinned, quite forgetting that he was being shaved at the moment.

"Careful, my lord." Good luck that his valet hadn't been holding the razor a quarter inch nearer his cheek, or Kit would finally have something like the dueling scar he'd once coveted, when he was too young and stupid to know better.

"Sorry, Belcher. My fault entirely."

Neat and decent at last, dressed and shaved for a day's travel. A pity, he thought, to disturb the excellent knot in his cravat—or to crease his linen or possibly to tear a button from his waistcoat. A pity, and the sooner the better too.

He was still grinning while he helped himself to a quick breakfast and bade good-bye to the family group around the table.

But in the unwieldy, inevitable way of these things, his mood took a precipitous shift in direction during the minutes it took him to quit the house. And now that he stood poised to step up into the traveling coach, his thoughts were a muddle of obscure anxieties and simple annoyance.

Must they have that grinning idiot Frayne up there on the box? Alas, it seemed that they did. Kit had requested the other, politer coachman, but the man had gotten a cold.

Frayne would have to do.

"We shall be taking the north road to Wakefield," Kit told him. Blandly, patiently. "But first we shall be stopping at Beechwood Knolls."

A gleam stole into the coachman's eye.

No need to speak a warning—just to *look* one was quite good enough; Kit had learned that much, at least, from the old Eighth Marquess of Rowen. Gratifying to watch the coachman shrink down into his multiple capes, shivering in the chill of Lord Christopher's glance, even as his brow grew moist in the morning sunlight. Sometimes one needed to manage one's coachman, rather as one's coachman managed the horses.

And as one wished one could manage one's dreams.

For the quaint yet oddly disturbing dream he'd had last night had come back to haunt him. He'd found himself in a large, crowded room—or was it a street?—surrounded by Britons of all sort. Somehow, he knew that there were seventy thousand men present, most of whom appeared to be bleeding. (*There's violence already—Lord Sidmouth had suddenly appeared, whispered this to him, and disappeared back into the crowd.*) But even as they bled, it seemed that all seventy thousand men were pointing, whispering, and laughing at Lord Kit, while Mr. Oliver stood on a podium and delivered a Latin oration.

Absurd. Meaningless.

But if one *must* dream . . .

For he'd also had some very pleasant ones last night. *Think of those.* Ah yes, as he slid onto the padded and tufted blue velvet upholstery. Dreams and memories too of past carriage journeys, the more recherché positions one could assume, as they *had* assumed during some well-remembered rides. (Times during the first year of their marriage, when the Curzon Street furniture had become too tame for them.) The positions worked better, though, with the help of extra carriage robes and cushions, particularly for tired knees on the jolting floor of the coach.

Good, excellent—Belcher had already laid the cushions and neatly folded blankets on the backward-facing seat.

Yes, let's go, tell Frayne I'm ready. The valet nodded. Kit leaned back; Belcher climbed up to take his seat next to Frayne. The carriage jolted slightly and started down the avenue.

But he still wasn't quite at his ease. Because they hadn't undertaken this journey merely for its erotic possibilities. The aim of this journey was a serious one.

To find out more about the dangers threatening his nation—from a man he'd sworn never to speak to again.

Still, Mary was right. He owed it to himself to speak to Morrice. Could the London radicals really call out such large numbers of men?

And if Morrice appeared to be lying, if he really was as vile and low a person as Kit had been trying to convince himself he was for the last nine years . . .

Well, nothing would be lost, would it?

Except, perhaps, a sneaking hidden hope he'd barely admitted to himself of a possible reconciliation. Ah, well, if such a thing were impossible, better to know now.

Just get all the information. Understand the situation. Easier that way to follow orders. No doubt in the end he'd do exactly as he'd been told. Wait until the moment arose, then call out the militia, suppress the rebellion, arrest the Williamses and the Mertons, the Turners and the Watsons and the Weightmans (no surprise how well he knew their names by now).

Difficult but necessary. Banal, ordinary, clear, and inescapable as the day. Duty wasn't a problem.

It was honor that presented more of a challenge. Honor and its Janus face, betrayal.

He'd promised Mary that he'd confront the man who'd betrayed him.

They passed through the gates of the park at Rowen. The gamekeeper saluted him from the side of his lodge.

He'd promised her. . . . Not in so many words—but wasn't that the curse and the blessing of loving an intelligent woman? He knew, and she knew, and she also knew that he knew that she knew. . . . *Yes, all right, enough of that*—each and both of them knew perfectly well what he'd promised her.

Which was to confront all the betrayers in the case. Including the betraying little wretch that had been his younger self.

. . . Cheating and lying, whoring and not touching me for weeks . . . ignoring Richard just as you'd been ignoring me . . .

Yes, quite possibly one could count some of that as a betrayal of those one loved. A betrayal of oneself too, not to speak of the friend he'd . . . oh, all right, he *had* loved his friend Richard, even if it wasn't so easy to use the word about a boyhood companion.

Betrayals all round. How cruel their younger selves had been.

Perhaps, he thought, *we owe a debt of honor to our poor, flawed, frightened and deluded younger selves, to become the people we should have been, if only we could have.*

The carriage had entered the gates at Beechwood Knolls.

Stupid name, the old marquess had sometimes muttered, *Beechwood* bloody *Knolls*. Even if it *were* merely a brewer's holiday villa, purchased a scant three generations ago, one ought give it a more venerable name.

Never mind (as Kit had been astonished to learn, when Mary had taken him to be introduced to her parents) that they liked it just as it was.

"Well, it's not exactly a country house." Mrs. Penley

had had an enchanting smile, and an intimate, confiding way of taking the arm Kit offered, even while he'd felt her husband glowering at his back when they went in to dinner. "Even with the wings and ells we've added onto it, it's really only a house in the country, you see."

He'd been charmed, but not convinced.

What a humorless young dunce I was, Kit thought: serious, ponderous, proud, and yet absurdly impatient, and about all the wrong things. Though hardly alone in that—damn it, Mary hadn't had the patience either to listen to him, nights he'd spent wondering who his real father was and simultaneously fearing it above all things. Which anxieties, he supposed, hadn't helped him stand up to the idiots at White's.

The real wonder, it seemed to him now, was that they'd come as far as they had—that they'd be traveling together and stopping at an inn tonight, openly, as Lord and Lady Christopher. Still, given their past—and the unclarity of their present—he could only shudder at what the outcome of this journey might be.

The Rowen carriage had passed beyond the hedge. He could see the house in its entirety now—simple, rambling, inviting, and comforting as usual.

A comfort as well, her silhouette against the grayish bark of the giant tree as she rose to greet him. Looking far prettier (as the coach came nearer) than in last night's dreams, or even than she had this morning.

Or was that how love worked itself out over time? Did familiarity have its own charms? Or was he simply growing old, staid, and avuncular as the young people at the assembly last night had made him feel?

Not old at all. And he'd prove it too.

Which led him nearly to tumble out of the carriage in his haste to grab her up, hand her in, get away and onto the road as soon as they could.

❧

As though he could have cut short Mrs. Grandin's polite inquiries as to his family's comings and goings—

because of course Elizabeth had reported Gerry and Georgy's attendance at the assembly. And then one had to make all the happily optimistic responses (thank heaven he could speak them truly) to Mary's sister's well-meaning hopes for the present marquess's health.

Neighborly. Civilized. And in Kit's current state of confusion, nearly unbearable, until at long last her things were packed, she seated, their final good-byes made, he and she side by side, surrounded by all that padded and tufted velvet, Mary seeming every bit as befuddled as he.

Quite as though she hadn't pawed so deliciously at him this morning, she now appeared shy and oddly formal. The few inches of space between their bodies might have been the Channel at Dover.

Most distressingly, she was quite uncharacteristically tongue-tied. Which didn't do much for his own loquacity.

❧

"Your sister is looking well," he managed finally.

She nodded, evidently grateful that he'd thought of anything at all to say.

"You noticed, then. Yes, she's very happy—and I am too, for her. Her daughter, Elizabeth, had a wonderful time last night at Cauthorn, and, *mirabile dictu,* she wanted to tell Jessie about it. Jessie's been floating on air ever since."

"She's quite the little flirt, the pretty daughter."

Mary raised her eyebrows. "Really. Perhaps Jessica ought to have accompanied them. But we thought that with Miss Kimball there . . ."

"Oh, not a very bad sort of flirt. No need to worry; she kept it all within the bounds of propriety. A little giddy was all—a bit overwhelmed, having just learned the effect of her looks on a large number of young men simultaneously."

"Did you dance with her?"

"Once. She didn't dance much. Spent most of the time promenading about with Gerry."

"Which couldn't have pleased her ladyship your sister-in-law. I should imagine she has higher aims for him."

"Actually, Susanna confided to me that if the presence of so pretty a girl could keep him at home for a while, she'd have no objection to a possible attachment. She quite likes your niece, you know, having worked so hard to transform her into less of a Penley."

"I see."

"But in truth, I think it's your niece who'll object to a too-hasty disposition of her affections. It looks to me that she's set upon having a brilliant season next year and enjoying every minute of it. Though she does need to become a little more subtle in her flirting."

"Like her cousin Fannie."

"Really?" He shrugged, since for his own part he'd found Miss Fannie Grandin not at all a flirt, but on the contrary quite artless and sincere. Still, they'd fairly exhausted that conversational gambit. For how much could one say about a pair of green girls, pretty as they might be?

A bit of a relief, that, she thought. Silly, no doubt, to have worried about it.

Her turn now, to offer a topic of conversation.

"We've got a nice day, anyway, for our journey. There will be some more rain later in the week, they say, but . . ."

She heard her own voice fade in midsentence; the sudden dismayed realization on her face must have been all too patent. *Had they truly been reduced to discussing the weather?*

His laughter boomed out through the carriage.

"Do you remember how shy you were," he asked, "our first time after the marriage ceremony?"

She nodded, smiling despite herself. "Such as it

was—the ceremony, I mean. I don't think we vowed to anything except that we were 'joined in the heat of the moment.' But yes. I was seized by a terrible fear that now I should have to do it properly, like a married woman. Whatever a married woman actually did with her husband."

"Yes, it must have taken me . . . oh, a good twenty-five minutes to convince you that you were quite acceptable as you were."

"You're wrong. It took you an hour, at least."

"If you insist, but it's not true. I remember expressly." She shrugged her shoulders.

"Of course," he continued, "we have all day before we arrive at Wakefield."

"Yes, obviously."

"We could entertain ourselves by betting on it. Oh, just to pass the time. To see if Lord and Lady Christopher, public and peaceable as we are today, would take as long as an hour, to . . . well, to do it properly, or at least acceptably . . ."

"An hour, you say." She fumbled for her reticule, to retrieve the timepiece within it.

"I've got a better one."

"I noticed, a rather showy thing you must have bought to replace the one the girl pinched in Calais . . . oh, Kit."

For the watch he'd pulled from his fob wasn't at all the dreadful one of too-yellow gold that he'd used to check the time in the cottage.

This one was smaller, made of white gold and platinum and done in a quaint, old-fashioned design. She'd agonized for hours about which of the timepieces displayed upon black velvet would be the thing for his twenty-second birthday. And then felt even more of a goose after she'd chosen it. He'd had so many pocket watches stolen in the rough neighborhoods he frequented; this fearfully expensive one would probably be gone within the week. Anyway, she'd supposed it was silly to buy a gift mostly for the words she wanted engraved upon it.

I wonder, by my troth, what thou and I did, till we loved?

Unsigned, for she hadn't liked to put her own name where the poet's should be. (Her papa hadn't had the faintest idea how the obscure book of sonnets had gotten into his library. No doubt as part of some job lot, he'd surmised, to flesh out the collection—someday he must catalog what was on the shelves and clear out the rubbish too. She'd been lucky, she thought now, that he'd evidently never opened the volume; if he had known the cast of the poet's mind, he'd have snatched it out of her hands.)

Kit had laughed exultantly a decade ago when he'd read the inscription.

"It's a good-luck piece," he'd exclaimed, "I can feel it."

Not that his luck at the gaming tables had improved any. But there must have been some charm about the object, for its having eluded the fingers of so many pickpockets—until Calais, at any rate.

"Thomas," he told her now, "caught sight of a fellow selling it in the street—in Paris, of all places. He asked the dowager marchioness whether she might not like to buy it back for me. Odd, isn't it, the way fenced goods sometimes make their way to quite distant places?"

She nodded. And equally odd how lost things sometimes made their way home again.

She might have wept that morning at Calais when he'd told her the girl had taken it—or shed a few tears simply to learn that he'd kept it with him it during all the years intervening. She might have—if she hadn't been so determined not to allow him to provoke her.

And now that he had it back again . . . typical, she thought, to find herself quite without a handkerchief.

"But that's not at all the response I'd hoped for," he protested. "Here," he said, "use mine. If you *must* cry, Mary."

"It seems that I must." Barely able to speak for the superfluity of tears slipping down her cheeks.

The inches of space between their bodies had melted away. His arm tightened around her shoulder while she whimpered, wiped, and sniffled; sobbed, blotted, and wiped her face again, at last tossing away the handkerchief and drawing him toward her for a very long, moist kiss.

※

She turned away now to fumble with the knotted shawl on the backward-facing seat.

Fixing his eyes on the hills and meadows out the window, he tried to ignore the busy little noises issuing from her side of the coach. Rustle of fabric. Slosh of liquid. A cork prised from its bottle.

And now the familiar, piquant vinegar smell. He'd always been curious. Sometime (if there were to *be* a sometime in their future) he should ask her exactly what she used to douse her sponge with.

Or perhaps not. Women's business.

Of course, she'd been using it in the cottage too, quite as maddeningly insistent upon it as ever. But it felt particularly outré here in the carriage.

The smell wasn't exactly unpleasant. In truth, it rather provoked the imagination. Exciting in its way, a bit disturbing. Images wafted toward him on currents of air—pretty white fingers moving upward past her long white thighs.

Upward. Inside her. Ah.

Even if it did rather interrupt the moment's spontaneity.

She has every right, he reminded himself. Of course *she has.*

And if she hadn't known to do it back then? *Well, that would've put us in a pretty fix, the two of us being hardly more than children ourselves.*

What *would* they have done so long ago if they'd conceived a child?

He'd always wondered what it might have looked like.

Presentable enough, he supposed. While as to the matter of its character? Willful and demanding, without a doubt. Disobedient? Yes, without question.

Stubborn.

But hardly stupid or insipid.

A challenge, rather.

He jumped at the sudden sharp tapping on his shoulder. Her voice came throaty, amused, close to his ear. "Have you lost interest, darling?"

Woolgathering, while he should at least have been unbuttoning himself. He laughed and made short work of it now. "What do *you* think?"

He'd show her whether he'd lost interest. "Come here."

Rising, turning, and moving to straddle him—naturally, she'd chosen the very instant when the coach had begun to pitch about, tossing the both of them forward and bidding fair to bump the top of her head against the ceiling, which might be covered with padded velvet but which (as he knew from experience) could be bloody uncomfortable to crack one's pate against.

He held her tightly against that possibility, as she clambered atop him and both of them struggled to maintain their balance.

No, she hadn't bumped herself.

"Thanks," she whispered, and kissed him again, her hands clasped tight about the back of his neck.

No more pitching about, it seemed; at least for the moment the road below them had smoothed itself out. He slipped his hands under her gown, cradling her arse, caressing her with his fingertips—stroking one careful finger along the crevice and then between her legs where she was just beginning to moisten. She closed her eyes. And when she opened them, her gaze had softened.

"Thanks again." Her voice came more faintly now, rough, unsteady, her body swaying, trembling beneath his hands.

He touched her near the small of her back, just below where the stays were tied. Fascinating to feel the play of little muscles there as she lowered herself onto (no, he corrected himself, it was *around* him; no, *onto* him). Well it was both things, wasn't it? Even if she would insist on being so bloody slow about it.

❧

She liked to test herself, to see if she could reserve control—to *take* him at her own pace and as she would, inch by fraction of an inch, opening, softening, and then grasping, engulfing him. Well, almost engulfing him, for he'd continued to grow, to lengthen and thicken as she made her leisurely way downward.

Teasing him, ceasing to move for moments at a time, bracing herself on her knees, having her own subtle pleasures along the way. "Selfish," he whispered once. And "you'll pay for that later . . ." hissing at her, with knit brow and reddened face. She kissed him lightly. He caught her lower lip between his teeth; she could feel the pinch of it.

But it's his own fault, she thought, *for continuing to grow as he enters me. . . .*

Wasn't there a mathematics for this sort of thing? Perhaps if she found the right equation, moved with some precise degree of slowness, they could go on forever, never . . .

So much for mathematics. Damn the vile coachman anyway; they'd hit another bump in the road and were suddenly thrust hard against one another. Not even air between their flesh—their sweating bellies and thighs slipped and slapped against each other—Lord, she hadn't prepared herself to be filled so deep; *skewered,* she expected, was the ungraceful word she wanted. *In up to the hilt,* the sort of masculine metaphor that would doubtless appeal to him.

Indeed. For he was chuckling with pleasure, bouncing her on his knees with great gusto, thrusting up and into her and glorying, it seemed, in every bump and jolt, every rock—hell, every stone and pebble and rut in the road.

Wasn't this supposed to be a well-sprung coach?

Ah, well, subtlety wasn't everything. Finesse had its limits.

She giggled and gave him a few good bounces back.

❧

He'd buried his face in the spaces above her clavicle. Something pricked his face—an errant pin, he supposed, at the neckline of her dress. He moved his tongue upward now, along the sinews of her neck; he could hear the pulse in her throat, sense the tremors in her belly. Feel all the glorious clutchings inside of her, where she held him so tightly and warmly and suited her movements so sweetly to his.

Followed *his* movements—there, is that really so difficult, Mary?

She'd thrown her head back, spine taut as a bow-string (Mary Artemis, goddess of the hunt—*I think her name is beautiful, your lordship*), movements fast and fluid; he thought of silver sunlight on swiftly moving water, a few yellow leaves of autumn poplar swept dizzily along by the current. Lovely to watch her slip into her ecstasies, mouth loose and careless, loud cries and even a low laugh bubbling up from deep in her throat. Her face glowed; he licked the sweat from where it had pooled in the hollow below her plump lower lip.

But when had the brook become a rushing river? How did it come to exert such force, gathering him up, pulling him along? Her eyes keen, bright, happy, amused.

Catch me, Kit, take my hand. Too stubborn? Well, then I shall wait for you on the other side.

He swam, he leaped, shimmering like a brown trout in sunlight—his vision a rainbow of fragmented color, quick, bright, dazzled but safe at home within her, falling into her and out of consciousness for a moment, even as he clasped her into the circle of his arms and felt himself engirded by her thighs.   •

Thus intertwined, they must have slid down off the velvet seat cushions, almost to the wooden floor, jolted and tossed about by the wheels and the springs and the rocks and the road and . . .

⁂

"Kit, darling . . ."

"Ummmm . . ." There was a fierce cramp in his left leg, an ache somewhere below his left buttock, and some throbbing where his shoulder had been torn during battle.

"My love." Her whisper somewhere between amused and urgent. "Do you suppose we could get back on the seat? Your bum's very heavy on my fingers, and I'm quite bruised at my right hip. . . ."

⁂

No serious harm done, they decided, each and both of them breathing deeply, testing and trying limbs and digits, groaning about bumps and bruises to the trunk, the bum and hips, and each of the extremities. He rotated his shoulder—anxiously at first and then with greater calm as the throbbing began to subside.

No blood except a tiny drop of it, she told him, on his exquisitely shaved cheek. "Let me lick it off. No, it didn't stain your linen. But I do apologize, for being such a pincushion."

"Don't apologize. Quite fun in its way . . ."

"In its way, yes."

"Exciting. Challenging."

"An experience, one might call it."

"Hardly subtle, though."

A contemplative silence followed.

"There's a bottle of wine in the basket, if you'd like any."

"Thanks, not so early in the day."

"Springwater?"

"Yes, that might be nice."

Jessie had packed a couple of pewter plates and cups.

"You don't mind drinking it from the bottle, do you? I'm afraid I might spill it."

"The bottle's fine. Give it here."

They drained the bottle, moving closely and silently together on the seat while they watched the hills and fields and the bright blue sky with its fat clouds slip by, until very softly at first, they began to laugh.

More loudly now. Raucously. Helplessly.

"I can remember when it was *nothing* to us. . . ."

"Easiest thing in the world, step into a coach, slam the door behind, and go at it for hours . . . twisting and turning like gimlets . . . the longer the journey, the better."

"Yes, and the rougher the road as well. With you sometimes suspended in the most extraordinary attitude between the seats . . ."

"Before I got so bashed up, I'm afraid, in battle. And *you,* fairly somersaulting . . . or is that simply a latter-day fancy of mine? Did I dream it sometime during the time we were apart?"

"No, it really happened. I was quite balletic; I could do splits like an opera girl. Once . . ."

". . . upon a time."

Another silence.

A long, gentle kiss, eyes opened very wide, in a shared effort to see each other as they were now.

"But you won't object, will you," she whispered, "if we wait until we're in an actual bed tonight . . . ?"

"Actually, I was going to suggest a very similar course of action. Mary?"

"Ummm?"

"What else is in that basket? I'm excessively hungry right now."

Bread and meat, strawberries and Stilton, eaten from each other's fingers. The fields and meadows, grown greener since the recent rainstorms, slipped by outside the carriage window. Stone walls separated the fields; hawthorn grew in profusion alongside. The landscape growing hillier, more picturesque as they proceeded; limestone would give way to gritstone, meadow to moor, as they made their way north toward Wakefield, in Yorkshire.

Her head on his shoulder, they peered together out the window, at the blues and greens, browns and grays, ubiquitous creamy hawthorn and occasional brilliant sprinklings of late spring flowers.

" '. . . Till we loved.' " She murmured the words from the poem. " 'Were we not wean'd till then? But suck'd on country pleasures, childishly?' "

He stroked her hair.

" 'For love all love of other sights controls, And makes one little room an everywhere.' "

Even a room that jostled and jolted on its springs, rolling over a country road that (at least from the point of view of a pair of travelers forced to admit themselves indisputably past their first youth) could well do with a bit of improvement and repaving.

Chapter Twenty-five

The sun had long set by the time they'd driven into the main square at Wakefield. Two inns; they chose the George. The one across the square, where the coaches stopped, would be noisier.

Neither place was probably the best in town, but Richard's aunts the Misses Raddiford lived fairly close by. Anyway, they were convenient to the road home to Derbyshire, in case they wanted to leave in a hurry. . . . At least that's what Mary imagined Kit's thoughts to be, as he told Mr. Frayne to stop and Belcher to inquire about food and lodging.

A pity, they agreed, that they'd wasted a night squabbling and throwing things at each other at that splendid inn at Calais. Still, this place wasn't completely dreadful, and they were impatient to step down from the coach and stretch their unsteady legs. A comfort to have the landlord bustling about, in deference to the elegantly lacquered vehicle with the Stansell crest, griffon rampant, done in gold on the door.

And if they themselves could hardly measure up to the splendor of their conveyance—looking, well, exactly as they felt: a less-than-perfectly groomed couple who'd clearly spent an eventful day out on the road—it took only another extremely haughty glance from

Lord Christopher to keep Mr. Frayne respectful and obsequious.

"It's hypocritical of me, I expect," Mary whispered, "but I'm grateful to you, with me so disheveled and no maid to help sort me out."

Perhaps the Misses Raddiford might spare a girl to help, if tomorrow's encounter were not an absolute disaster. Kit had promised to send a message tonight, requesting to speak to Richard.

"I'd planned to wait until tomorrow to do it. But the sooner the better." Spoken in his firmest, most responsible Major Stansell tone of voice, though he'd kept his eyes trained on some distant point beyond Mary's shoulder when he'd said it.

Belcher reported that the bedchamber was small but adequate. The sheets were dry and it didn't appear that Lord or Lady Christopher would be sharing the sagging bed with anything that crawled about or bit at their ankles.

Ensconced atop the coverlet with Mary's writing desk on his lap, Kit scribbled away while Mary struggled to pin her gown into a semblance of order, pained groans and muttered imprecations issuing from their separate sides of the room.

"Well, that'll simply . . ."

". . . *have* to do."

"I shouldn't like to do it every day, but . . ."

". . . Please, oh, please, my lady, may we go down to *eat,* at long last?"

※

One might, if one were charitable—as well as ravenous after one's day's journey—characterize the pickled salmon and lamb chops served with grayish peas as "honest English food."

Good enough, in any case, to fill one's belly with, if one ate it slowly—well, one *had* to chew the lamb slowly—leaning across the yellowed linen, gazing into each other's eyes across the table.

At any rate, one didn't have to make excuses for the ale. Or the pudding, from early gooseberries. Topped with Devonshire cream the landlord had brought out when Mary asked, demurely and yet with a certain earnestness, if there might be a little of it in the kitchen.

"Traveling with you"—Kit's eyelids flickered dreamily in the candlelight—"one would at least be sure of getting whatever was best to eat that night."

Mary opened her mouth to reply and then closed it again.

"You were about to say, Lady Christopher?"

She smiled to make her single dimple show, but only shook her head.

"And are you quite finished down here?" he asked.

"Quite. Down here."

"Ah."

"I'll take the candle, Lord Christopher."

"I'll have to follow you very closely, then. The staircase is most narrow and uneven."

And so he did. With his eyes and even (it seemed to her) with his breath. One could become extremely self-aware, she thought, of the movement of one's own legs and thighs, hips and arse, as one climbed the rickety steps with someone following so close.

So aware of how one occupied the space around oneself that one couldn't help but sway and even wiggle a bit, in a less than seemly manner.

He caught her at the doorway to their room, arms about her waist, hips and thighs and belly and cock pressed through his clothes and through hers too, hard against her arse.

"We never . . ." he whispered. "I was afraid I might hurt you. . . ."

"I'm still a bit afraid," she whispered, "for all that I trust you . . ."

"Not tonight," he breathed rather than said it.

"No."

They'd let themselves into the shabby little bedchamber and closed the door behind them as she pronounced that *no*. Both of them, meanwhile, noting that some Rubicon had been crossed, and some future plans laid. Some other night, perhaps, if there was ever to be another night like this one.

He began immediately on the hooks at the back of her green chambray gown.

"While as for tonight," he told her, "I got the distinct impression that you wanted something else to put between your lips."

"Wherever did you get that impression?"

"Can't . . . imagine."

"And you, Lord Kit? Do *you* crave . . . anything?" The gown had fallen to her feet. After all his practice in the cottage, the light stays she wore would hardly present much of a challenge.

"Now that you mention it . . ." He'd tossed the stays onto a chair, and then did the same with her petticoat. Her shift followed. She pulled his neckcloth open while he wriggled out of his coat and waistcoat.

His boots now. She'd grown so skillful at it, he thought, that she could give Belcher a pointer or two. Slipped the left one off while he caressed her nipples, growing hard and dark under his fingers.

"Your . . . ah, cravings . . . Kit?"

"Well, the gooseberries were tasty enough, and the . . . cream as well . . ." She'd gotten his pantaloons all unbuttoned, and had taken his cock in one hand, stroking it while she nudged a slow finger up and down the middle of his scrotum.

He'd intended to tell her that he craved something less sweet than gooseberries. Something spicier.

But he'd lost the words for it, moaning softly under her hands, gasping now as she let go of him. He stared most intently at the picture she made lying spread-eagle on the lumpy, saggy, altogether pathetic bed, her eyes on his cock, lips parted, back rounded to tilt her hips upward toward him.

Spicier, saltier than gooseberries.

He climbed atop her, head between her legs, hips suspended over her face.

Her lips still parted—he thought he could feel the warmth of her breath as he lowered himself, her fingertips nudging him into her mouth.

The insides of her cheeks smoother, slipperier than Devonshire cream, she pulled and sucked and gobbled at him as though he were more delicious than berries or wine or even a good strong English Stilton.

Her hands on his arse now, to bring him closer.

Ah.

❧

She needed to breathe very slowly, she thought, and through her nose, to take in all his deepest, saltiest, sourest—his *ripest* smells as she moved her mouth and tongue and opened her throat to taste him.

While another part of her wanted to kick and buck and writhe under his mouth. Thank heaven he understood this, and thank heaven too for his hands cradling, soothing, holding her still below his lips and tongue— oh yes, for now she could feel the flicker of his tongue, bright wonder amidst dark labyrinth.

Confusion, befuddlement, sweet sea of swirling distraction: she couldn't tell (didn't know and obviously was in no position to say) whether she was moving or sensing, doing or done to, lover or beloved or both at once.

Was it possible to be both at once? Could one sort it out, separate the each from the both of them, find the beginning or skip ahead to the ending? While the snake swallowed its tail, beyond words or thought, where there was only the endless circle, the ring of pure light, the blank low sound of *ohhhhh,* words faded to humming, ecstatic spiral of sensation? After heroine and hero have pushed and pulled, teased and taunted, come and gone and come and come again, to this quick, bright, simultaneous and happy confusion, bonds loosed and boundaries no longer distinct? Where does one pick up the story again, the then and now, he and she, lover and beloved?

❧

In the homeliest things.

In Mary's slow realization, that time had passed and her feet were cold.

And moreover, that the bruise on her hip had begun to throb. More pleasantly, she knew that Kit was awake as well. For he was kissing her belly, in the places where she knew she'd never again be so lithe and taut as the girl who'd done splits like an opera dancer.

Awakened to time and sensation, and always, most humanly, to need, "Come here," she whispered, "up with me on the pillow. Come close so we can warm each other."

Drawing together beneath the covers, limbs entangled, torsos flush between threadbare, much-mended linen, he raised his head to blow out the candle while she drifted off on the happy knowledge that when she woke to find the story continuing, he'd be here to wish her good morrow.

Chapter Twenty-six

H̲e did wish her a good morrow, smiling down on her as she woke to the new day. Lovely to watch her open her eyes, so eager and happy that he could do no less than fall upon her in a long, passionate embrace.

Which soon enough revealed itself as a hearty and dutiful embrace, in truth with very little passion about it. He should have realized just how distracted his attention was by the looming prospect of meeting the person he'd been so angry at for so long. And by the dream of the seventy thousand men, only in last night's version it had been Morrice whispering to him, saying something he couldn't remember, and the men were bloodier, and Oliver had looked even taller up there on his podium.

None of which had done much for his performance in bed this morning. Too late to stop, though: his and then Mary's movements became clumsy and disjunct, the shame of it all quite palpable, the failure (*his* failure) a humiliation.

Should have known. Shouldn't have been misled by yesterday's easy pleasures—both times, and even before, during the morning meeting in the forest, her hands so mischievous, her whispered voice so randy. *I expect you'll manage quite splendidly.* . . . Hell. Forget about *England* expecting every man to do his duty; it was a woman who really put the pressure on, and a wife was quite the worst. Was it any surprise that he'd wanted to prove himself this morning—to her, to himself, did it matter which?

Nothing to be done about it now.

And nothing to be done either about the communication he'd dispatched to her friend Morrice. Disgusting, the swill that had leaked out from his pen—*wrongs on both sides,* spineless womanish twaddle. Dutiful little soldier he'd been, to send the bloody thing off to the Misses Raddiford's house before dinner, so he wouldn't be tempted to tear it up. Today there'd be no escaping the consequences. Morrice had assuredly read it by now; perhaps he'd even sent his answer.

On the whole, Kit thought, it might be a relief if the man simply refused to see him. A relief or an additional humiliation. He tried to steel himself for either eventuality, even as he found himself plagued by Mary's efforts at cheery reassurance. Salt in a wound; he scowled and grimaced until she grew equally glum and nasty over a late breakfast of watery coffee, bluish milk, and lumpy porridge, the glassware chipped and smudged in harsh, hazy daylight.

"Well, you needn't mope about it," she told him. "Nothing matters *that* much. To look at you, one would think the sun rose and set by it."

Thanks, just what I wanted to hear. What a hypocrite she could be: if there existed another woman to whom such things mattered more, he, for one, had yet to make her acquaintance.

At which affectionate juncture, the landlord came by to inquire about how they'd found the bedchamber.

Excellent. Very fine indeed, we slept wondrously well.

Delightful couple we make, Kit thought, *nodding and grinning like a pair of condescending monkeys.* Though he couldn't help thinking it a good thing, that acting the hypocrite to the landlord had stopped him from calling Mary a hypocrite to her face.

"Yes, it's our best." The landlord beamed and then patted the pocket of his coat. "Ah, but I'd almost forgot the message I've got for you, my lord. Brought by just now by the Misses Raddiford's footman."

Kit accepted it casually, waiting to open it until the man had taken his leave of them. He tried not to tear the paper while Mary made a noisy, unconcerned show of stirring sugar into her coffee.

"Well, don't you want to hear what he says?"

"Only if you choose to tell me."

He hadn't called her a hypocrite *yet* anyway. But then, it was still distressingly early in the day. Morrice wouldn't be coming round to call upon them until two.

Not a badly worded response. Or so it seemed upon his first hurried reading. Difficult to get all its meaning with Mary's eyes fixed upon him in that brimmingly sympathetic way.

"Perhaps I'll ride over to Campsall this morning," he said. "Talk to the man in charge of the militia. General Byng—I knew him in France."

She nodded too quickly. Bravely even, to demonstrate her understanding that he might want to be away from her for a bit. Lives of saints and martyrs. Until now he'd forgotten that aspect of the wedded state.

But was he sure, she asked now, that he could be back by two?

Of course he was; why the devil wouldn't he be?

Damn, the little pocket watch told him otherwise.

They dragged themselves up the steep stairs to their bedchamber.

He'd have a smoke instead, he told her; take a walk about the town.

"Oh, and by the way," he added, "Morrice is bringing his wife with him. Making a domestic affair of it, I guess."

She smiled, quite as though he'd meant that to be a *good* thing.

Still, it might be useful to have the other lady about. Give Mary someone to talk to while he and his erst-

while friend said or did whatever the hell two gentlemen were supposed to say or do when both parties had
been wrong and time had passed and it wasn't a question of revenge or reparation. His experience in war
and diplomacy didn't yield many useful examples. Make
it up as one went along, he expected.

And where the bloody hell were those cheroots
anyway?

She shrugged her shoulders and turned her back.

"Well, why *don't* you know?"

He escaped the bedchamber just before whatever it
was she'd chosen to toss at him came crashing against
the door he'd slammed behind him.

⁂

Jittery on tobacco, he marched purposefully about the
town, pausing at unpredictable intervals to stare at
nothing in particular, one time gazing blankly through
the window of a local bookshop until Mary raised her
head from whatever she'd been perusing and he had to
duck away.

He grew hungry. A pasty from a pork butcher helped
clear the foul taste of breakfast from his mouth. He
walked more aimlessly now. The time crawled by, only to
speed up calamitously around half past one when he lost
himself in a tangle of alleyways. Willing himself to get his
directions straight, he ran all the way back to the George.

No harm done. The clock tower in the square agreed
precisely with his pocket watch; the Morrices weren't
due for another five minutes. He smoothed his waistcoat, caught his breath, straightened his cravat, and
grinned at the knowledge that he'd outrun his anxiety.

The street he'd come from adjoined the coaching inn.
He'd entered the square across the way from the George.
Yes, there was Mary, seated on a bench some fifty yards
away from him. The pink of her dress made a pretty splash
of color in the dusty, bleached-out light of early afternoon.
Perhaps he *had* been needlessly savage with her.

She raised her head from whatever she was reading;

he thought he could see a glint of her spectacles, but it might have been his imagination. He waved and so did she. He had the impression she was smiling. The Morrices would be arriving any minute. Too late to be nervous. And anyway, Mary'd see him through it. Buoyed by this thought, he hurried forward to join her.

Only to find himself amidst a crush of hurrying people, bags and parcels and the bustle of travel.

Leeds, the coachman was calling, *the Leeds Charger, boarding here directly.* So intent had Kit been on his own affairs that he'd stumbled, first into a knot of disembarking travelers, and then the people clambering to take the vacated places aboard the coach.

"Sorry," he muttered to anyone who might hear him, perhaps the young man in a green coat, or the taller, stouter gentleman in brown . . .

Brown coat, reddish beard, Wellington boots bright under a hazy midday sun. Vital, energetic, somehow a bit bigger than life-sized, now at last that Kit was seeing him for himself.

The man who'd flirted with Peggy. The featured player in the theater of Kit's dreams.

But was this really the first time Kit had seen him in the flesh?

Nonchalantly biding his time until the last moment to board, Mr. Oliver had finally taken a seat by the window. He was looking out now, his eyes scanning the square.

I've seen him before. I'm sure of it. But where?

To hell with it. I'll confront the blackguard myself.

Unfortunately, that proved impossible. For at that moment, Mr. Oliver (or Hollis, or whatever the rabble-rousing London delegate's name might truly be) was attending on someone else.

A footman in livery had rushed forward to doff his hat to the red-bearded man, addressing him with what looked like great deference, while Kit (and several people around him as well) stared in uncomprehending wonder.

A footman in livery, so humbly respectful to a work-

ingman? Or at least to a man revered by workingmen all over the countryside. A man who'd spent the last fortnight orating and bullying, exhorting them to tear down the established order and take London as well. It was all too contrary. Kit lost a minute while he gaped and tried to puzzle it out; by the time he'd made his way forward, the coach was rolling in a cloud of dust onto the road to Leeds.

❧

The dust settled. And here was Mary, arm in arm with a small, neat lady in a quietly elegant gown, with a lanky, diffident-looking gentleman at her side.

Changed and yet unchanged: a decade ago Morrice had appeared uncomfortably older than his years; now he wore his shy seriousness with ease. Kit took the tremulous hand held out to him, the grasp not as tight as it had been. *I ought to be better able to hide my emotion,* he thought. No matter. The moment passed willy-nilly. He and Morrice got through the handshake and a mumbled greeting, even some clumsy, random touches on the arm and shoulder.

"Been so long, *too* long . . . Egad, just look at the both of us. Not boys any longer, eh?"

It would go all right. Well, it would have to, Kit told himself, now that he'd been presented to the lady with the blue eyes and decided chin. He knew a reasonable, formidable creature when he saw one; Mrs. Morrice would make sure it went all right.

But what in the world had Oliver been up to, and how would Kit find it out?

Unbearable, to have to go through all the motions of civility right now. A lucky thing that Mrs. Morrice was determined to take the lead. Well, someone had to.

Still, he needed to speak to someone—Mary, or perhaps even Richard—about what he'd just seen transpire at the coaching inn.

"Shall we all take some tea at the George," Mrs. Morrice was asking, "or go for a drive in the barouche?"

"A ride in the barouche, I think," Mary said, when it had become clear that Kit and Richard were each too absorbed in their separate thoughts to be able to answer Anna's question.

Regrettably, though, it would have to be tea in the George's parlor, at least for Kit and the ladies. For a fellow in what appeared to be a state of extreme agitation had just now approached Richard and expressed an urgent need to speak to him.

"You all won't mind, will you," Richard said, "if I have a word with Mr. Dickenson here for a moment before I join you inside?"

Dickenson, who appeared to be some sort of tradesman, nodded apologetically to the group. Anna Morrice returned his greeting with great cordiality.

"A moment only," Richard said.

"Of course."

❧

I need only follow Anna's lead, Mary thought, *to negotiate this fascinating reunion. What a marvel she is, getting Kit to talk of pugilism, of all things. Poor dear, he looks so distracted, so very emotional—I can't imagine how he'd be able to keep hold of himself if she hadn't chosen his favorite subject.*

It seems there's to be a mill tomorrow, somewhere out in the countryside; Richard's quite looking forward to it. And although Anna must confess to Lord Christopher that she herself has never seen the attraction of such sport, she affords herself willing to believe that, as Richard says, it's more scientific than brutal, and very much an exhibition of character.

And Kit is charmed. Richard is quite correct, he tells her; scientific *is precisely the word for it. He's charmed and he's clearly also hoping that Richard will invite him along tomorrow to see the fighting. Oh yes, he's telling Anna, it's a great national institution, pugilism, too easily misunderstood by foreigners and even by some ladies. But if one takes the time to read the principles of the sport, particularly as delineated by the great Mendoza...*

Allowing me to take the time to cajole our landlord into getting us a decent tea: cheese (sorry, my lady, no chutney) and sandwiches. I almost ordered scones (but caught a tiny warning signal from Anna; the scones must be dreadful here). So we've got sweet buns and (at the landlord's prompting) a bit more of his splendid Devonshire cream.

But here's Richard, looking as though he's been considering something, very seriously and in extremely short order. The same look of resolution Kit adopts from time to time, which usually means there's consternation ahead.

How intensely Kit is staring at him.

❦

"A most fascinating conversation I've been having," Richard began now. "With Dickenson. Known him for years, a Dewsbury linen draper and a faithful reader of the *Review*. And"—he paused for emphasis—"a longtime and stalwart friend of liberty."

Thank heaven, Kit thought, *that we're going to be speaking of something real.*

And don't worry, Mary, I shall be fine.

For Mary, and Mrs. Morrice as well, had clearly found Richard's opening words to be tactless at the very least—Mrs. Morrice showing her annoyance in the curtness with which she handed Richard his dish of tea. Richard shrugged as he took it from her.

"Yes, thanks. Ah, well, as I was saying. You see, Mr. Dickenson has just informed me that he's witnessed a most curious occurrence. A man extremely well known, and up until recently held in the highest esteem, by those involved in the great struggle . . ."

Though he could use a lighter hand, Kit thought, *with the rhetoric.*

"That same man," Richard continued, "within just this past half hour, has been unmasked as an agent of government repression, when Dickenson, and some others, saw General Byng's servant doffing his hat to him."

Still, it was good that things were finally making sense. No matter how shocking the facts of the matter seemed to be.

He turned to Richard. "And I take it there could be no mistake as to whose servant the man was?"

"None. Dickenson made sure of it."

"Or to the identity of the highly esteemed man?"

"None there either. Dickenson has already made Oliver's acquaintance, though he didn't like to tell me exactly how."

"It's all right," Kit said, "I can guess at that part. Wat's a magistrate, you know, and I've been doing his business for him during his illness. It's turned a bit complicated of late, though—difficult to get to the larger truths."

"And you have an interest in the larger truths after all."

"Rather, yes. And I've been lucky to see some interesting events. For I've seen Mr. Oliver before, in the company of a Home Office functionary—a man doing rather the sort of work I'd aspired to. Of course, I didn't know who Oliver was at the time. And then I promptly forgot about it until my recent charming conversation with Mrs. Morrice. They were together at the fives court in London, you see. Of course, it might have been quite innocent; the appeal of pugilism being so widespread among Britons, much as I was telling Mrs. Morrice."

He paused. "I have no proof of any connection between Oliver and the Home Office. All quite circumstantial. Still . . ."

The two men were silent for a long moment.

"Magistrate's business, eh? And Home Office business as well. Gives one quite a breadth of perspective," Richard said. "Well, I shouldn't want to ask you to betray any commitments you've made, no more than you'd inquire any further about my friend Mr. Dickenson.

"But as to Mr. Oliver's connections. Well, in fact, he did show up at some meetings last spring, in the company of a Mr. Mitchell, who was arrested soon afterward. People have been inquiring about such things, you see, because there have been more arrests, a number of them this week; just this morning General Byng and his militia broke up a meeting—took a number of men into custody, all but Oliver, don't you know, who somehow managed to escape. Dickenson knows some fellows who are in an uproar about it."

Kit nodded. "No doubt the London delegate, as he calls himself, has got another meeting to address tonight at Leeds. Couldn't have him missing it."

"It does seem that Byng was protecting him, perhaps under orders. Of course, we can only guess whom Byng is taking his orders from."

Kit nodded. "It's a knotty set of problems. Perhaps if either of us had been more of a scholar when we'd had the opportunity . . . well, why *should* the government be sending a man out to this part of the country, to try to foment revolution among its angry workingmen? For it is beginning to look that way."

"Or a certain part of the government. The Home Office perhaps?"

"If you like. Hypothetically speaking."

"Of course," Richard said, "hypothetically speaking. Well, you know it wouldn't be easy to ask Englishmen to give up certain liberties. Right of assembly, no imprisonment without due process of law. Unless there were a threat so large—well, it would have to be something more frightening than petitions for reform, or propertyless men passing Paine and Cobbett from hand to hand . . ."

"The threat of an uprising."

Richard shrugged. "A smallish one, I should think, called for a specific date, with soldiers waiting to make arrests. And since no one else was calling for such a thing, I expect it might have had to fall to the government to do so. Hypothetically speaking."

Kit chewed the last bite of his sandwich rather meditatively. "It would take a great deal of organization. A lot of magistrates to keep in line. Communications always a problem with this sort of thing—it's a small office, you see."

Richard laughed. "Well, it won't fly," he said. "Dickenson's on his way to speak to a newspaper editor. The *Leeds Mercury,* splendid little organ of reform in this part of the country—one might expect a public scandal. And then, of course, my own publication will take it up, from rather a longer focus. Need a good writer, of course, but that'll come.

"But even before it appears in print, every reform-minded man in the region will have heard the news—through the grapevine, you know, word of mouth. The provocateur is exposed already. The kingdom is safe, I believe, for the nonce."

"Ahem." Anna's voice rang clear and distinct across the tea cart.

"My dear?"

"Mrs. Morrice?"

"Is *anyone* going to enlighten me as to these wondrous happenings?"

"I shall," Mary said, "at least to the extent that I've followed the conversation. Quite remarkable . . ." Her voice trailed off, her gaze softening at the sight of Richard and Kit bound together in their endeavor to understand the truth of a matter that meant quite different things to each of them. And—as gentlemen—to keep the discussion all on the plane of the hypothetical.

But it was rather stretching things to ask them to rehearse the broad outlines of the story, when what they really wanted to do was to work away over the fine points, and not around a tea table.

"Go find a public house," Anna told them. "Hash it out over a couple of pints of ale. Mary will explain it to me in your absence. We shall be entirely capable of digesting the information and amusing ourselves in the bargain, until dinnertime at least.

"For you two will come to dinner, won't you? I believe you remember the Misses Raddiford, Kit. . . . I may call you Kit, mayn't I? Their cook sets a plain table, but a very good one. And the ladies have sorely missed Richard's friend all these long years. 'The bright-eyed little boy,' they called you this morning at breakfast, 'with the lovely manners when he remembered to use them.' "

Chapter Twenty-seven

Their tea had grown quite tepid when Mary had finished recounting what she knew of the Oliver affair.

"Remarkable." Anna sighed. "And not a little bit frightening, an official of Lord Liverpool's government sending a provocateur among the people. Well, that is what we're saying, isn't it? That Lord Sidmouth sent this man on a tour of the Midlands, to stir up insurrection?"

"It does seem to be the case," Mary said, "as with that other man earlier this year."

"Indeed, a Mr. Castle played a large role in instigating the riot at Spa Fields. Luckily, it all came out in court. But this could have been so much worse, implicating men from the whole region. Well, we're fortunate that Oliver was unmasked. And that now that the word is being circulated, no one will venture out and get hurt. But do you suppose that this Oliver fellow might have gone rather beyond what the Home Office expected of him?"

"It does seem possible," Mary said. "And I'd almost like to think so, having recently developed a certain tolerance for Kit and his . . . loyalties. Still, leaving aside all prejudice, the evidence does mount up, and not in

Lord Sidmouth's favor. The government does seem to want to stir up anger among the people, turn reformers into insurrectionists for the purpose of making the rest of us fearful."

The ladies were silent for a time until Anna spoke again. "He's well worth tolerating, Mary.

"And how fascinating finally to meet him," she continued. "After all these years he'd become a figure of legend to me, rather like the angel Lucifer, if not so tall as one imagines Lucifer to be. Richard didn't speak of him often, but occasionally he'd retreat into a horrid little melancholy over the rupture of their friendship."

"They were awfully close." Mary sighed, paused, and then smiled at a new thought. "And they may become so again, in the course of protecting each other from calamity out in the countryside tomorrow. Those outdoor bare-knuckle matches can get rather raucous. I used to beg to be taken along—disguised as a boy, you know—but Kit wouldn't hear of it."

"Is pugilism really so interesting?" Anna asked.

"Actually, it is—there's something to all that twaddle you were entertaining him with. For myself, I could dispense with the gentlemanly self-congratulation it inevitably evokes, about English pluck and bottom, our native honest virtues, and so forth. But the strategic elements are worth following. While as to the boxers themselves, the muscularity . . ."

"Ah, there is that. I wonder that more ladies don't . . ."

"We're allowed to watch the gloved exhibitions in London. There's a fives court near Leicester Square; one can sit in an enclosed area. Perhaps, when . . . well, perhaps *if* . . ."

She'd been drifting into a pretty fancy, about London, about the future, about Kit. *A fancy only,* she told herself sternly.

"Today's discoveries are a great confusion to him," she told Anna now. "He'd hoped for a position in the Home Office, you see."

"I do see," Anna said, and covered Mary's hand with her own.

❦

Nor had Anna been speaking twaddle about the Misses Raddiford. Kit *had* been a favorite, as Richard's aunts reminded him several times over an excellent dinner, the reminiscences of his eyes and manners being served up once more to accompany the dessert course.

Fortunately, it was necessary to make a brief night of it. Kit and Richard wanted to get an early start tomorrow morning, to join the throngs at the boxing match, while Anna would spend the day at the old ladies' hearthside. The oldest Miss Raddiford had bought a great many skeins of wool, very cheap for the quality, that needed to be rolled up and then to be worked into several dozen shawls for the parish poor for the winter months; of course, the work would go much faster if Lady Christopher would consider joining them.

"Most assuredly, Miss Raddiford. I shall be delighted."

Thank you. Anna shaped the words silently from across the table.

"I shall think of you," Kit said, "your hands quite immobilized, held captive by Miss Sophy Raddiford as she winds an endless ball of wool."

They'd come to the top of the narrow staircase at the inn.

"In fact"—he shut the bedchamber door behind them—"I'm thinking of you that way at this moment. And quite an appealing picture you make, too."

❦

They didn't speak of Mr. Oliver that night; in truth, they didn't speak very much at all until the following morning.

"Belcher," Mary said, "will be scandalized by the condition of that neckcloth."

"Yes, I expect so." His eyes had grown distant again,

even with his body so warm and his arms tight about her.

"Come on," she said. "Time to pull ourselves out of bed. You and Richard will want to be at the front of the crowd. And at least his aunts will give us a decent breakfast."

❧

In fact, they didn't speak at all of Oliver until two days later—and then very briefly, in the carriage, their arms about each other, watching the afternoon skies darken and the clouds pile up high above the moors and then the meadows. The air was cool and tremulous, the leaves quivering as though in nervous anticipation of the impending rain, as Mr. Frayne drove them south through Derbyshire again.

She expected that Kit had continued to discuss the Oliver business with Richard, before or after the boxing match (which, both gentlemen had agreed, was a splendid exhibition of native English pluck) or perhaps while walking on the moors the following day. They'd discussed a great many things, Kit said, in the course of rebuilding their friendship.

Which wasn't to ignore the fact that they disagreed rather more than they agreed, their only areas of pure accord being pugilism, a sense of fair play, and an affinity for strong-minded women. Still, he concluded, a friendship could go pretty far on those three.

Mary thought she discerned a hint of ruefulness, a knowledge that their affections could never be so pure as in boyhood. At least they'd never duel again, though—which might be saying the same thing in another way.

"His newspaper isn't bad, you know, even if it's far too enamored of its own rhetoric." Kit stared at the blue velvet ceiling, as though the words he needed were written on it. "Too clever, too . . . *fatuous* in its claims for progress and the future, even when it speaks the truth about present injustice."

"He showed you a few pages?"

"He pressed a few years' worth of pages upon me; Belcher has packed it up somewhere. I don't object to it, but there was only one of his scribblers who truly impressed me. A Mr. Elyot, in one of the older issues. Excellent treatment of the Corn Laws. Sober, not afraid to use facts."

He's jesting, of course. Richard must have told him that *she* was Edward Elyot; Elyot was her mother's family's name, though he might have forgotten that information. *No,* she thought, *he's teasing me.*

"I shall have to read this Mr. Elyot myself one of these days," she said, and kissed him to show that she was amused but hardly gulled by his joke.

There wouldn't be more than kisses, however, today in the bouncing carriage. One could lose one's taste for an old pleasure. No matter: they'd found some fascinating new ones last night, at an extremely comfortable inn at Matlock.

"I wonder what he'll do now," she said. "Mr. Oliver, I mean, now that he's been exposed. Well, he can't have any further career as a provocateur. . . ." Her voice had trailed off at the word *career*.

She began again. "In any event, it's a good thing that the workingmen of Grefford won't be embarking on his false crusade. It would have been tonight, you know, around midnight. I should hate to think of Nick and his grandfather, arrested by the militia, tried for sedition. . . ."

She thought she might be in for a little lecture on disorder and the need to contain it. But all he said was, "Of course, it rather leaves them where they'd begun, doesn't it? With nothing settled—the whole affair come to nothing.

"The odd thing," he continued, "is that the Home Office might have been able to pull it off, if they'd better coordinated what they told their magistrates, saw the whole thing more strategically."

"If they'd had *you* working for them?"

"Yes, in fact. Well, it wouldn't have been easy. . . ."

"You've been thinking how *you* might have managed it."

"The idea, you see, was to tell a great many people what they wanted to hear. Those in possession of power are likely to believe that any challenge, any change to how things have always been done, might *well* be an insurrection. In a certain sense I don't believe Sidmouth or the Committee of Secrecy was lying. Not by *their* lights anyway. Workingmen speaking their minds, manufacturers who want representation for their districts—it's all suspicious and frightening. And if the workingmen don't know how to organize their own insurrection, if they're waiting for London to tell them how . . . well, why *not* send a London delegate to do the job, even if he represents a rather different London from what they think they're getting? Get the whole thing done quickly and frighten everyone else into quiescence."

His voice was quiet. "Spies and informants are excellent at telling people what they want to hear. Pretty soon you've manufactured a truth as well as an insurrection. Of course, different people want to hear different truths, so things can get unruly. It's possible that Oliver told Sidmouth what *he* wanted to hear; the Home Office might have begun with something a great deal more modest in mind. But if they'd had a detail man like me to help them keep their truths straight . . ."

To which she had no reply, except to kiss him again, rather clumsily on the cheek. He didn't speak for a few minutes after that.

"You're very good, Mary, to tolerate me in this infernal, cynical mood. And of course, to have bullied and badgered me into getting my friend back. Not to speak of putting me in the way of seeing Oliver and Sidmouth exposed. I'm in your debt. Ah yes, and then there was last night. . . . Mary?"

"Yes?"

"We shall have to speak about all this—really talk. Very soon."

"I expect we shall." She hoped the words hadn't come out as doleful as she felt. *You're not in my debt,* she wanted to protest. *It's not some kind of commercial, legal agreement we have between us.*

She held her tongue instead, in most un-Penley-like fashion. For if (as was seeming increasingly likely) they each held a differing view of what had transpired on this journey—well, then, *her* view of it must be wrong.

A reunion with a friend. A reconsideration of his political position. And a delicious, scandalous night at an inn.

What more, really, had happened?

And how was it, when she could know so well what he was thinking when they were arguing or making love, that she knew so little of his mind right now?

They'd reached a bend in the road, where it forked between Grefford and Beechwood Knolls.

"Beechwood Knolls," he called out, in response to Mr. Frayne's inquiry.

"You'll want to greet your sister and her family, I expect. The one from Glasgow, I mean."

"Yes, I know which one you mean. Indeed, it'll be very agreeable to see them. . . ."

She wondered when this annoying intermittent rain had started falling. Better a whomping big storm than this polite drizzle.

⁂

A curricle was parked on the side of the road next to the hedge, just before the turn one took to get to the house at Beechwood Knolls.

"Hold on, Frayne," Kit called. "What's that? Do you suppose they need any help? They don't look like they've gone into a ditch."

"It's some of our young people, I think," Mary said, "returning from Colonel Halsey's."

Indeed, seated in the curricle were a mournful Fred and a furious Elizabeth.

And as for Lord Ayres and Fannie Grandin?

Mr. Frayne was peering down curiously from the box.

"Come into the coach," Mary said. "Both of you. Immediately. Mr. Frayne will wait here until we've finished speaking."

Her first fearful surmise proved correct. Fannie and Lord Ayres had run away together just today; Fred and Elizabeth had been parked here for an hour, arguing about who was to blame and how to tell Jessica the news. Of the two young people, Fred seemed the more capable of telling the story clearly.

"He'd bought a flash new phaeton and pair, you see, while we were at the Halseys'. Gave everyone a ride this afternoon, each in turn. Fannie was the last; he said he might as well take her home to Beechwood Knolls, as she thought she might be getting a cold. We followed about an hour later. . . ."

"More like two," Elizabeth interjected, "by the time *you'd* made your sweet farewells to Miss Halsey . . ."

"Make it an hour and a quarter." Fred shrugged. "We brought Miss Kimball in the backseat. . . ."

Mary glanced out the window, for fear that the old lady was still out there.

"You needn't worry about *her*." Elizabeth's lip curled. "She was having such vapors, we imposed upon good Miss Williams to let her stay the night in Grefford. When we discovered that they'd eloped . . ."

"Discovered by means of . . . ?"

"A note to me. I found it in the seat of the gig." The girl opened it and cleared her throat.

"Is that quite necessary?" Fred asked.

"*I* think it is."

I haven't the heart for a Season next year, Betts. The heart I thought I had is quite broken, I feel such a fool. . . . And so I think I'd better marry quickly—someone rich enough, anyway, and get the whole grim business done with. And if your uncle does chance to ask after me. . . .

"What the devil?" Kit exclaimed, at the same time as Mary demanded to know what in the world he'd done to cause this.

"Nothing. I swear it. Explained a bit about Metternich over supper at Cauthorn."

"Treated her like a rational creature." Mary sighed. "As though you didn't know how charming that can be, from a handsome man in evening dress. Oh, dear."

"And as though *you* didn't know"—Elizabeth turned an angry face to her aunt—"how infatuated Lord Ayres was with *you*."

"Don't speak so loudly," Mary said. "Mr. Frayne is a terrible scandalmonger."

"All very well," Kit said, "for *you* to say at this juncture."

"It was nothing. He'd be there mooning about in the forest, when I'd be returning from meeting you. . . ."

The intruder in the forest . . . Fannie getting her heart broken, coming to look for Kit.

"Well, it's disgusting, is all I can say," Elizabeth said, "the two of you at your age. . . ."

"What?" *It shouldn't matter,* Mary thought, *especially in the midst of the crisis like the present one.* Shouldn't, but it did. *At your age . . .* how dare the little chit? "Are the two of us so superannuated that we mayn't be allowed a little *married* pleasure?"

"Certainly, if you knew how to take it reasonably, like my mama and papa, when he was alive. Well, we could tell—couldn't we, Fred?—mornings when they'd be gazing foolishly at each other over the breakfast table, even if we were too young quite to understand . . ." She began to blush, as Fred had been doing for quite some time.

"Still, Betts is right." He put his arm about his sister's shoulder. "It was our good fortune to grow up in such a household."

"As it was mine," Mary said softly.

But Elizabeth (*Gracious, she's a Penley after all,*

Mary thought) evidently had a few more opinions on the subject.

"What's not all right is a couple of a certain age sneaking about and misleading those around them into thinking they're out of love and . . . available."

Kit gave a low whistle, of . . . agreement, Mary thought.

"Especially when one can't come near either of them for the contagion of a . . . well, an *erotic* sort of mood."

Fred groaned, but his sister wouldn't be dissuaded.

"Because Mama was right about you, Aunt Mary, a few months ago when she told Aunt Julia that you remained a spoiled baby, and simply had no idea . . . what it would *really* be like . . ."

The blue-diamond eyes had filled with tears, but Elizabeth sniffled them back.

". . . to, to lose someone who'd loved you as no one would ever love you again. *Really* to lose him and not simply to play at it . . . poor Mama."

⁂

Had Jessica really said that about her?

She took a long, deep breath.

"Well," she said, "I shouldn't have wished to hear it, but it was almost worth it for Elizabeth's pronouncing her mama right about *anything*."

"That's all very well," Fred said, "but Fannie and Lord Ayres shouldn't be running off to marry, just to teach someone a lesson."

"And Lady Grandin will never forgive a one of us."

"She won't need to," Mary replied. "Nor will she ever know any of this happened."

"Ah?" Kit raised his eyebrows. "How's that?"

"Because they won't marry. Because you and I shall go get them back."

Chapter Twenty-eight

꧁⸻꧂

"Well," Kit said, "your family's produced another one, haven't they? Despite all my sister-in-law's best efforts."

They'd taken the curricle, after sending Fred and Elizabeth home to tell Jessie that Fannie had a cold and would be remaining at the Halseys' for another day or two, with Miss Kimball to nurse her and Lord Ayres to bring them back when she was well again.

"Elizabeth was wise," Mary said, "to hide Miss Kimball, and Cathy was an excellent, discreet choice. Oh, dear, and now I truly must find a way to help raise funds for a village cistern. . . ."

"Cistern?"

Ah yes, she'd never explained about the cistern. Not too difficult to sum it up, though, for it seemed he'd learned a bit about engineering in the course of his military career.

"I'm no expert." He'd knit his brow, rather engagingly, she thought. "But I think I know what one would inquire of an expert, and how to frame the questions."

His face changed just then, in response to a traveler coming in their direction. "Ah, good evening, Mr. Greenlee," he called.

The carpenter was returning from Grefford astride a

small, neat cob, his long legs rather dangling down the horse's sides. She'd never paid the man much attention—well, why should she? So many people lived and worked on the Stansell estate—but now she remembered Kit's childhood story about the stallions in the paddock. Clearly a kind man, and rather nice-looking as well now that she noticed. Spare, sinewy, even at his age—she chided herself for the condescending tone of that.

Not a very inquisitive man, though. No bothersome questions about what they might be doing out here in the rain: he simply wished them a pleasant evening and hoped the weather might clear.

"Well, then, Lord Christopher and my lady, I'll be on my way. . . ." Putting his broad-brimmed hat back on his head, and taking the reins in a long, graceful hand with elegantly squared-off fingers. Callused, of course, from his work, but . . .

A great many things had come clear in a very short time.

Good night and Godspeed.

And the very same to yourself, Mr. Greenlee.

"Well," Mary said a few moments later, "if the wishes of our near and dear ones can count for anything . . ."

She stopped then, blushing for the strangeness of referring to the estate carpenter at Rowen as *near and dear*.

"It's all right," Kit said. "I know."

"How long have you known?"

"Not very. Only since I came home this time. No one told me; it simply was apparent, as it was to you just then. He's a very good man, you know, and he's helped me with little things whenever he's had the opportunity. One comes to know a certain sort of thing, it seems, when one is ready to know it. And I . . . I rather like knowing it's he, odd as it must sound."

She tried to get another look at the man from over her shoulder. But the road had curved away.

"Though I could have wished to get some of his height," Kit said now.

"He's on his way to Rowen. To the dower house, do you think?"

"I believe that's possible, yes."

They were silent then, for some time afterward, thinking of the past's hold on the present—their thoughts then turning to less pleasant future eventualities, if they weren't able to stop the young couple and turn them back.

They tried two inns just the other side of Grefford, but no one answering to the couple's description had been seen at either of them—though at the second inn, they did have the dubious pleasure of barging in on another eloping pair. Both times, Kit's aristocratic preening helped them secure the landlords' cooperation—thank heaven, Mary thought, even as she wondered what Mr. Greenlee would have thought to see it.

"Ayres won't drive all night," Kit said. "They have to be at an inn along the way."

Mary was less optimistic. "Unless they've taken a less direct route, to hinder us from finding them. Perhaps he has a friend he plans to stay with.

"If they do marry," she said more softly, "I shall never forgive us for having a hand in it."

"Not very good for us, then." His voice was equally soft, even as he urged the horse forward along a road that was becoming muddier.

"But at the very least you will have to forgive yourself," he told her some minutes later. "Not entirely, and never in the very small hours of the morning when you wake—but day by day, to get through it."

She was silent and so was he, for a time.

"A man died because of me." His voice betrayed no emotion. "In Spain. And another man lost his leg. Because of me and in some sense because of you too, me being so keen on dying grandly in battle, to prove . . . I don't know what anymore . . . to prove *something* to you about my greatness of spirit and how much you'd lost by not appreciating me more. To make you mourn me and hate yourself forever."

His first time actually fighting, he told her. Heedlessly bold in the face of an ambush.

"The time I got that extravagant wound. I never thought I'd be telling you . . ."

He did so in a very few words, against the dripping rain and rustling trees, how his younger self had charged into combat, stupidly, needlessly, like so many reckless young Englishmen, in duels or on the battlefield. Happened all the time.

Except it shouldn't happen when the gentleman was an officer, entrusted with responsibility for others. Too bad he'd learned this lesson so belatedly. Half-delirious from his own wound, helpless to stop his ears against the cries, the sawing of bone. He hadn't started out caring about anyone but himself, but when one heard a man scream like that . . .

She laid her hand on his forearm. "And afterward?"

"Not much to say," he told her. "Duty. The dull business of trying to make it right when you never really can. The man who died had four daughters. I've tried to help his widow; the hardest thing to bear is her gratitude. And I did try to be a better officer, to remember what's more important than glory. To get on with things, you know."

"Yes," she said, "to get on with things."

"The Portleigh Arms is up ahead," he said a while later. "Do you remember?"

An absurd question.

In any case they'd be able to change horses. The place had once had a good stable; it was the best of the local inns for some miles.

"They might have stopped the night here." Mary essayed to control the quaver in her voice. "Of course," she continued, "they'd ask for separate bedchambers."

"As we did," he said.

For all the separate bedchambers had signified.

❧

Telling her hadn't been so awful as he'd feared. Natural, somehow matter-of-fact. *She knows the worst of me now,* he thought. And in truth the telling seemed to have freed his mind, to drift among memories of another elopement.

Smiling at each other, downstairs in the bar of the Portleigh Arms. Drinking wine—it hadn't been good wine; not that they'd have known the difference. Hurrying up the stairs, retreating to their chaste separate bedchambers. Somehow he'd forgotten to bring a dressing gown. Tiptoeing barefoot in his shirt and drawers, down the corridor to her room. Knocking so softly—terrified of being found out, believing as he had that anyone would care.

She'd opened her door at the first rap of his knuckles. Equally terrified, she'd fairly pulled him inside.

They'd stared at each other, he in his shirt, she in a high-necked night rail. Pretty thing, almost nunnish, austere white folds from her shoulders to her very white bare toes curled against the cold of a painted wood floor. So far as he could recall, she'd only worn it that one time, as though—once the vows were pronounced and they were therefore adults—he wouldn't have found it provocative enough. He'd never asked about it; in future he'd be clearer about what he liked.

If there really were to be a future for them. If that vastly silly other elopement they'd helped set in motion could be stopped. If it truly were possible to get on with things. Together.

They'd reached the Portleigh Arms.

Cursing himself for having ever cast his eye upon the troublesome Miss Grandin, he helped his wife down from the box and kissed her cheek.

She smelled of wet wool. Her short upper lip trembled, and her hair fell into tighter curls than usual on her forehead.

"I'll see about getting a new horse," he said, "and then I'll follow you in."

She nodded.

"Courage," he whispered.

But she'd run across the yard and had already pushed the front door open.

Courage, he repeated silently.

✦

She loved coaching inns: a fire in a dim room, the variety of accent and countenance, paths crossing and destinies conjoining, if only for an exchange of compliments or a flirtatious glance over a glass of awful claret. In the mornings people were rushed and rather cross. But at night, especially if she had friends or a footman about, she loved to nod to interesting-looking strangers, wonder about their lives and fortunes, and (keeping a little silver knife tucked in her sleeve) act the woman of mystery.

Tonight, however, she wanted no mystery at all. No surprises, no adventures. Only an untouched Fannie Grandin.

The bar was mostly deserted. No one but a few men in their cups, one of them telling a long story to the young woman who was stifling a yawn and hoping there'd be something in it for her.

No Fannie, and no Lord Ayres either. She'd have to speak to the landlord. Turning quickly, she tripped over an uneven stone in the floor. Which caused her to bump her hip against a table, mutter an impolite word, and suddenly feel every eye in the room fixed upon her. No silver knife up her sleeve tonight—she backed away carefully, hoping that Kit would be along soon.

Wait. Every eye in the room *wasn't* fixed upon her. One head was turned away. The pillar to her left must have blocked her view at first. But just a few steps from where she stood, a head of luxuriant black hair shed its lavender scent and was turned resolutely toward the wall.

She'd eviscerate him.

Grasping each well-tailored shoulder, she found herself overwhelmed by the smell of raw beef commingled most unappetizingly with the lavender. She began to giggle even before quite comprehending what was so wondrously funny.

Lord Ayres turned languidly in his chair, to stare at her with one moist ·violet eye, the other hidden by bloodstained fingers grasping a large slab of meat, juices thinly trickling into a fold of his cravat.

"Well you might laugh," he muttered.

Kit had appeared at her elbow. "Raw potato is surprisingly effective," he told the young man (just a bit too solicitously, in Mary's opinion), "and rather easier on the linen."

"And Fannie?" she demanded. "Where's Fannie, you pomaded ninny?"

Ayres grimaced. "Sleepin', I daresay. Cool as a cucumber, that one is."

⁂

Kit waited downstairs while the landlord took Mary up to Fannie's room. They found her sprawled across her bed, seemingly quite absorbed in *Debrett's*.

"Thank God you're safe." Mary had hoped to hug or in some way to comfort her, but found herself constrained to do so.

"Of course I'm safe," the girl replied. "It's been years since I learned that move out of Mendoza's *Modern Art of Boxing,* but one doesn't forget."

A few tears glimmered on her eyelashes. "You'll think I'm an utter fool," she added more quietly.

"No, no. Oh, of course not."

Except for her book and a silver-handled hairbrush, it didn't seem she'd unpacked anything. The landlord picked up her valise, rather as though he were afraid of her.

"Is *he* here with you?" she asked while she buttoned her pelisse.

"Yes."

"Yes, I expect he would be."

They waited in silence while Kit brought the carriage around.

Mary unfurled an umbrella to give to Fannie, as the curricle's small backseat was open to the elements. And when Kit tried to help her in, the girl shook her head and climbed lightly in by herself.

❧

At least the drizzle had eased off a bit.

"I could exchange places with her if you'd like," Kit said. "She'd be drier up here, and you could comfort her. Of course, you'd have to drive, and I'd be a tight fit back there."

"I don't know as I'd be comforting her. She's chagrined by the strength of her own sentiments, not to speak of having exposed them, though I daresay it'll be the making of her. Which doesn't mean *we* haven't also acted awful fools. One can't sneak about as we have—or one shouldn't anyway, with younger people about. At a certain point, it seems, one needs to do rather better."

"I expect so," was all he said.

"I should like to drive, I think," she said now. "I'm not the most skillful person with the ribbons, but I can keep us on the road."

She rested her head on his shoulder for a moment before taking the reins from him.

The rain had become more intermittent, the wind tossing the clouds before it. They sang to pass the time, merry songs, sad songs, the heartbreaking one about the weaver who tried to shield his lover from the foggy dew, and the passionate shepherd's song as well. And gradually, disjointedly, they found themselves telling each other things, odd bits and scraps they'd picked up during their years apart.

"A woman can't be tested as a man is in battle," she said. "But while trying to negotiate between pleasure and scandal, one does a bit of self-examination, considers whose opinion is important and whom one is willing to send to the devil."

He nodded, the faces of a few London gentlemen flashing across his mind's eye.

"I expect that must have been a useful exercise," he said. "Well, I might have found it useful anyway, after being in such a confusion of intimidation by people who had certain advantages of unambiguous parentage. . . ."

"And I," she said, "of not knowing how to help you, and of . . . of fearing that you'd regretted marrying a brewer's daughter . . ."

"A most generous brewer," he reminded her, "who kept us in such fine style so that we had very little to do but confound our senses with exotic substances and lovemaking . . ."

She was silent for a moment. "Almost as though we could be alone in London, as we had been at the hermit's hut—in a private world, with no responsibilities or connections or frighteningly worldly people for me to face."

"Very romantic," he said.

"Very much *not* like a marriage," she said. "Though one wouldn't want a marriage to be dull or *too* responsible or socially connected or proper. I mean it wasn't *all* bad. . . ."

"The lovemaking, for example . . ."

"I think we can agree that the lovemaking . . ."

"But yes, it was a great befuddlement," he said, "that one didn't seem to know how to straighten out, as dearly as one wished to. One wanted to apologize, you know; one *does* apologize. No, what I mean to say is that *I* apologize, most heartily, Mary. It's just that one thing would get tangled up with the next. I mean, there wasn't any *one* thing, you know, any single slight or misunderstanding. . . ."

"I do know, Kit. I know exactly. And I'm sorry as well."

❧

"But let's sing some more," she said, after some silent minutes had passed. "Here, take the reins. I'm going to teach you a strange dark one Lord Byron wrote."

*And our days seem as swift, and our moments
    more sweet,*
With thee by my side than with worlds at our feet.

But they should have been approaching Grefford by
now. Or at least have seen some landmarks—the road
to Silverwye Farm, a familiar stand of giant beeches.
It was awfully dark; Oliver and the men of the reform
societies had chosen a moonless night for the insurrection that wasn't going to happen. And with the clouds
shifting so quickly, you couldn't depend on the stars to
guide you.

"Do you suppose," Mary asked, "it could have been
that road we passed, going over to the left about an
hour ago, when the wind was so blustery, and we were,
ah, rather clutching one another for warmth?"

Kit shrugged and flicked his whip over the horse's
left flank.

"But there's no point going any faster, is there," she
continued (rather reasonably, she thought), "if we don't
know where we're going?"

He glowered, and she decided that he must agree
that they were quite lost.

"And I suppose I don't dare suggest that you might
have asked that old gentleman in the dogcart, whom we
passed perhaps half an hour before we came to that
turn . . ."

He gave a low growl of warning.

"No, I thought not. Well, at least the rain has let up
for a while. . . ."

Her optimistic utterance (not surprisingly to anyone
who's ever been lost on a dark country road) worked
like a wizard's charm to illuminate the sky with a long,
forked flash of lightning, followed by an impressive roll
of thunder.

She shrugged her shoulders in apology and tried a
timid smile, before pulling her red wool hood around
her face as fat raindrops splashed down her cheeks.

Absurd to argue about it. Though she might have appreciated the slightest recognition on his part of how silly he'd been not to verify the direction.

Instead of that familiar I-know-I'm-wrong-and-don't-you-dare-tell-me-about-it glint lighting up his eye.

No use arguing. Surely she could rise above it.

The rain beat down harder.

"Would it truly have been such a humiliation merely to *ask* . . . ?"

But wait. Faint light through the trees. An inn? He turned a sheepish face to her and kissed her.

"Yes, I should have asked directions. But a gentleman doesn't like to, you know."

Chapter Twenty-nine

The Anvil Tavern was small, dim, smoky, and a bit hazy from the moisture drying off people's clothes. The room occupied perhaps a quarter of the area of the bar at the Portleigh Arms—no matter; it was infinitely warmer and drier than outside, and surprisingly crowded. The walls, which had once been whitewashed, seemed almost black near the fireplace, where some men were talking in excited voices. Another group was singing—though Mary couldn't make out the words. She, Kit, and Fannie crowded around a small table, Fannie with her eyes still turned away from Kit.

"I'll get us something hot to drink," he said, and pushed his way into the crush of people.

"I'm an idiot," Fannie said very softly, when he was out of earshot. "I've acted a complete fool. Listening to the two of you sing and squabble and make up . . ."

"Then you've heard," Mary told her, "what fools we can be as well, with all our years and experience behind us. But at least your aunt Jessica doesn't know—of your folly, and not even all of mine. Fred and Elizabeth have told her you're still at the Halseys' . . ."

There were sudden loud shouts from the crowded space between the bar and the fireplace.

"Liar!"

"Ye know nothin' about it! They're waiting for us in London, fifty, *seventy* thousand, of 'em tomorrow."

"But, man"—it was Kit's voice now—"haven't you heard about him being exposed at Wakefield? I thought all the groups had decided not to go."

Confused murmuring. She heard the words *arrest, meeting,* and *plot.*

Of course, Mary thought, *there was bound to be one contingent—or probably more than one, who hasn't heard about the change in Oliver's fortunes.*

Or perhaps just didn't want to believe it.

"Rumors, planted to keep us home. Lies. Think of it, boys. . . . A mighty force all together to face the mightiest government on God's earth. Nothing like it ever before, even at the Bastille. Don't lose heart, just at the word of . . ."

"And who're you anyway, to tell us to go or stay? Speak your name, will ye?"

"Christopher Stansell."

"He's the magistrate's ruddy brother, from Rowen, at Grefford. . . ."

"And he *would* be telling us to stay home, like women and children safe around the fire, 'cept we don't have the coal for fire. . . ."

"Don't have nothing after we finish paying for bread and our rent to your brother, damn 'is eyes, but it'll be different this time, the London delegate told us. . . ."

"The London delegate was a provocateur, by the name of Oliver or perhaps Hollis, in the employ of the Home Office. It's a trap. They *want* you to march. They want you to . . . hang. Please. The London Committees don't know about any marchers coming down from the Midlands; the Home Office has been writing to its magistrates. . . ."

"And how the bloody 'ell do you know that?"

She stood up to better hear what they were saying. But there was such a crush of men around him, she could only see the top of his head, his eloquent hands sweeping through the air as he tried to make them understand.

"Morrice . . . *Everyman's Review* . . . Sidmouth . . ."

It seemed to her that he'd influenced a few men anyway. She could see some heads shake—disappointed, disgusted, or even relieved.

He was keeping his voice low, calm—as he must have learned to do in Spain and France, when he had men under his command. "I saw the provocateur myself. Twice. In Wakefield, with General Byng's valet tipping his hat to him . . . ah, you've heard those rumors, have you?"

A few nods.

But more than a few angry demurrals as well.

"We got ter go tonight, while there's still lads out wantin' to do it. If we're lost, we'll go down in glory, with Brandreth and the boys from Pentrich."

"We ain't lost. Don't believe the Byng story, put out to scare us. But will we be scared, boys?"

Angry demurrals.

Kit's voice again. "I also saw him in London—I think he was meeting with a functionary of the Home Office."

And then more urgently, "You must believe me. It's a plot against you."

But perhaps he'd already dissuaded all of them that he could. Leaving those who were young, those who were desperate. They'd prepared themselves to act tonight. For an instant, she could see it through their eyes, the ragged grandeur of it, each small group of men marching south and eastward through the rain, meeting up with their fellows in an ever-swelling multitude. . . .

And they wouldn't even have to *walk* the whole way, someone was saying, there'd be boats along the Trent to take them to London, for certainly the boatmen would join them in their noble cause, boatmen and bakers too, there'd be cakes and ale, they'd sing the song Brandreth had written for the occasion . . .

She didn't think that Mr. Oliver had promised them cakes and ale. His promises had been of unity, of individual voices raised in chorus.

It was an extraordinary fantasy. Heartbreaking, in its way, when you knew it had been created by a paid agent of a government who continued to reject their petitions.

There were still men trying to buy drinks, on credit redeemable after they'd taken the Tower, but it seemed that the landlord was shaking his head.

Even as it seemed that a number of other men had begun to repeat what Kit was saying, repeating news of the mysterious arrests that had recently occurred in the area, and usually in the wake of a visit from the London delegate.

At least they weren't *all* going to march tonight.

But what of that small group jostling their way up to Kit's right? Boys not quite grown to men, but the tallest of them topping Kit by several inches.

Topping him, but reflecting his looks—seeing the two of them together, she realized that she'd been correct. Nick Merton looked not so much like Kit looked now, but very much indeed like he'd once looked. Not just the expression either, but the cast of his features.

The boy drew back his arm. It was hard to see. For a moment she imagined she saw a pistol drawn. . . .

No, not a pistol—he was standing too close to be firing a pistol. He was simply brandishing a furious, raw-boned fist.

A few blows were exchanged. She thought she could see blood. And then Kit falling, ah, in a way she recognized.

She screamed then, perhaps a bit too dramatically, she thought; good thing Fannie was taking her lead. Right, she'd read Mendoza; she also knew that Kit wasn't really being knocked senseless. But surely one or more of the men standing around Kit would be suspicious, though all the blood pouring from his nose had an impressive effect.

Unless he received a bit of help.

Kit! Christopher! Darling! She pushed her way into the ring of men, dropping to her knees beside him, raising his head into her lap. *Oh, what brutes, what strong, horrid brutes, my husband, my darling, my only love*— the tears (she hadn't known she could produce tears at will) streaming down her cheeks, mingling with the blood dripping over his.

She couldn't find her handkerchief. Fannie gave her a particularly dainty one, trimmed with lace; a barmaid brought a towel that had been used to wipe the counter. The fumes of alcohol rising from it were all for the better, she supposed, though the dirt wasn't pleasant.

Kit fluttered his eyelids a bit.

Just don't grin, she tried to communicate to him. *Yes, I know what I called you, and in public too. Well, it's true. You can gloat about it after we get out of here. Before someone does try to draw a pistol on you.*

Where's the man who did it? she shouted now. *Who's the man who killed a defenseless man who tried to give him good advice, and . . . and wouldn't . . . wouldn't even . . .*

Nick Merton looked frightened, defiant, a bit proud. *You horrible . . . man,* she shouted at him, *man* seeming to be the word he was most anxious to hear.

A pulse, she shouted now, *oh, dear Lord, I feel a pulse.*

And yes, the boy did look relieved.

"You'd better go home, Nick Merton," she told him. "You've caused enough damage for one night."

She couldn't hear what he and his friends were murmuring. But it didn't sound quite so defiant as it had. The crowd in the tavern seemed to have divided into two. Some, she could see, would set out undeterred to meet up with the men from Pentrich. But some, already swayed by what Kit had told them, their pride salved by his fall and momentum broken by her performance, had regained their seats or even wandered out the doors and down the dark country road in what seemed to her was the direction of their homes.

Kit had his eyes open now. In truth, he did look rather dazed—from her histrionics, and from something else as well, that she couldn't quite construe at the moment.

All right, perhaps she'd never called him her *only love* quite like that before.

And all right, perhaps she'd meant it.

"Help me, Fannie," she called, and together they did a fair simulation of dragging him to the carriage and hauling him onto the seat.

"I'll explain later," she whispered to the girl. "But thank you for helping me save him. And to save some of them as well."

Unsatisfied curiosity warring with wounded pride, Fannie took her seat in the back and snapped the big umbrella open.

Mary took the reins. She could hear more singing from inside the tavern. The men who wouldn't be dissuaded, she thought.

"Best to pretend you're still dazed," she whispered to Kit. And they were off.

"How do you feel?" she asked him.

"Like I've taken a heavy fall to the floor," he answered, "and a bit of a knock on the jaw."

She smiled, and he shook his head.

"And like hell that I couldn't stop all of them."

"You stopped quite a few. Perhaps they'll disperse on the road; perhaps the Nottingham magistrate will be reasonable. . . ."

They rode on in silence for a few minutes.

He rubbed his nose. "Not broken, at least."

"That's a mercy. I've always loved it. . . ."

He moved closer to her. "*We* stopped them, together—those that we did stop. We kept a few men from being clapped in irons anyway. For that's what will happen to some of them—I'll wager that the magistrate toward Nottingham will be out, with his troops, to arrest those marching through there when the sun comes up."

She nodded, shivering in the wet.

"He's my cousin, you know," he said a few minutes later.

"Who's your cousin?"

"Well, probably more than one of them, but I mean that boy who tried to punch me, Nick Merton."

"Ah, I always thought of you when I looked at him. But how do you know?"

"I spent an hour reading the parish records. Third cousin, once removed. Of course, he's not the only one—Mr. Greenlee comes from a large family. It gives one a different sort of feeling about the people here."

"I see."

"And what was almost as bad," he said, "was shattering their hopes, when I'd manage to convince one or another of them that it was a sham, that there wouldn't be chartered boats down the Trent or thousands of their cheering fellows awaiting them in London. It's awful to take hope away from anyone."

"You'd hoped for something too from the Home Office."

"I'd hoped for quite a lot. A life's work. A calling, I expect you'd say. I don't like living to amuse myself. I want to know what I'm going to be doing tomorrow, besides writing to Sidmouth to withdraw my application for employment and to protest their use of provocateurs. I wish I could offer you a husband who knew what he'd be doing tomorrow."

"Tomorrow," she said, "you must meet Edward Elyot. He needs your help with an essay he's going to write."

"Elyot? What do you mean?"

"You really don't know? You . . . honestly *liked* what I wrote? But why didn't you tell me?"

She'd flung her arms around him.

"What the devil?" But he hadn't passed spy messages for nothing. "Really, that was you? How extraordinary."

"Yes, and I'm going to write about what happened tonight at the Anvil Tavern and how the men were

wronged, and Richard will publish it. And you must use
your eloquence, and your memory, and your talent for
detail in particular, to make sure ... that I ... that
he ... that we get it right."

"Edward Elyot, eh?"

"You used to call him Cousin Ned when he wore his
bright red neckcloth."

"Indeed. You're a woman of parts, Lady Christopher."

"Will you help me?"

"I will," he said.

"And after tomorrow?" he asked. "Have you any
suggestions for what I shall do after tomorrow?"

"Inquire how we go about building a cistern in the
village—which will be as immediately important to the
women as the vote will be to the men. And of course,
they'll continue petitioning for the vote until they get it.
They could use your help, I think. And someday perhaps you could run to represent the district."

"As my brother's candidate?"

"As theirs, perhaps. Who knows? Perhaps as mine."

"Yes, that *would* be a life work. One would have to
understand everything—rents, prices, new industries,
good roads, and pure water ... in order to make fair decisions. Would you help me, to be sure I ... got it
right?"

"I would, Lord Christopher. I will."

The cloudy sky had become a little lighter, although
the rain still came down upon the gravel road to Beechwood Knolls.

She yawned, and he stroked her wet hair.

"Were these our vows?" he asked.

"I expect they were."

No need to vow to love each other—it felt as though
they always had. It was difficult for either of them to
remember who they'd been and what they'd done before they'd loved.

And no use to vow to stop struggling and squabbling—
for that would never change. But to vow to try to help

each other, imperfect as they were in the far-from-perfect world in which they found themselves.

There wasn't a great deal more to say, and Fannie must be getting awfully wet back there. So they stopped, and Mary managed to convince her to let Kit wedge himself into the little backseat.

"I'll drive home," Fannie said, and so she did, in silence, while Mary admired the grace with which she handled the ribbons.

Fannie stopped the horse, and Kit jumped out of his seat to come help her down. She allowed Mary to kiss her good night, but when she tried to say something to Kit it came out a sob and she turned away quickly.

They stood arm in arm to watch her run up the front stairs.

The door opened. Elizabeth had been waiting up. They could see a golden tress escape from her nightcap before the girls became one form, engulfed in a tight hug, in the dimly lit doorway.

Still, Mary thought, what she'd heard from Fannie had been a sob of mortification and not of heartbreak. A sob of not believing you'll ever be able to face someone again, though of course you will and quite soon too. Mortification, at eighteen, might seem a lot like heartbreak, but it wasn't, thank heaven. At thirty-one, one had learned the distance between mortification and heartbreak, as well as the distance between thirty-one and eighteen.

There's nothing like young people about you to make you feel, to make you know *how old you are,* Mary thought, *and how responsible you are to them*.

"I don't want to stay here tonight," she said. "Fannie needs a day or two without either of us."

"Good," he said, "I want to bring you home to Rowen."

She yawned quite unromantically. It would be nice to get some sleep.

How quiet it was in this still, wet hour before dawn.

He gave her his hand, to help her up to the box.

She raised her foot to climb up and then lowered it again.

For in the quiet, you could hear another of the house's doors opening—the side door, up from the kitchen.

Was no one *safe abed tonight?*

A small figure, looking rather wide in a russet cloak, bonnet, and several shawls, coming through the gate of the kitchen garden and softly closing it behind her, and now picking up her packages and coming quickly down the gravel path. Stopping now, and gaping at the two of them.

Had Peggy been waiting up to see that Mary was home safely?

One doubted it, for she seemed to be dressed for traveling. The sky wasn't quite so black anymore, and one could see—for she continued to walk toward them, though slowly and warily—that she was wearing a large portion of her best clothes piled atop each other, with what looked like the remainder of her possessions wrapped in yet another large shawl and jammed into two of Mary's discarded bandboxes.

A hedge rustled, and an imposing man stepped out from behind it. He carried a shabby valise; his overcoat was brown, his boots Wellingtons, and for a moment Mary and Kit each and simultaneously imagined that Mr. Oliver was making an oddly chosen final appearance.

Only for a moment, of course. For it was a taller and much handsomer man. An honest mistake for people of their station; neither of them had ever seen Thomas out of livery.

"My people in Ripley won't give permission," Peggy explained. "They've got somebody they like better than Tom that they want me to marry, but I won't."

Kit winked, Mary began to laugh, Peggy raised her chin proudly, and Thomas put an arm around her shoulders and drew her close to him.

"Of course you won't, Peggy. You'll marry who you want, with my hearty congratulations." Kit brought some coins out of his pockets and handed them to Thomas, who thanked him gravely.

"Even if it means I'll be left all tied up in my corset?" Mary asked.

Peggy made a hurried and slightly abashed curtsy. "I wouldn't have left you like that, Lady Christopher, if you'd been home earlier. I'd have put you to bed, quite tidy as always."

"It's all right," Mary said, "I meant it as a joke, and anyway, we can depend upon Lord Christopher to put me to bed until you return. He's not as tidy as you, Peggy, but he has other qualities to recommend him. I shall manage. Just don't stay away too long, will you, on your honeymoon? Ah, but on second thought, you must have secured a position with the marchioness, for you'll want to be working with Thomas, I should imagine."

The two servants looked at each other, Peggy finally shrugging her shoulders while Thomas drew himself up to his full, impressive height. "I won't be a footman any longer, Lady Christopher," he said. "And we won't be returning here."

"Been studying about fixing engines, he has." Peggy's expression warred between pride and skepticism. "Talks about steam, says it's good for more than kettles and tea. Says he can earn more than three weavers or two footmen by it."

"Good man," Kit said. "Good night—well, good morrow, I expect—and Godspeed."

"But at least take the umbrella," Mary called, "to make up for how drenched the two of you got in Calais. My husband and I shan't be needing it tonight on our way to Rowen."

Epilogue

The dower house at Rowen had several entrances. One, toward the back, seemed to lead to the kitchen, but if you knew how to slide a certain panel, you'd find a hidden staircase.

It really was a clever piece of work, Mr. Greenlee had thought, when he'd climbed the staircase to the marchioness's bedroom earlier that night. He nodded. *Probably my cleverest piece of work.*

He wasn't usually the sort of man to make a fuss about his accomplishments, but tonight he was feeling in rather a celebratory mood. Estate carpenter at Rowen was an excellent position. He'd loved the same woman for, oh, forty years it must be, shared her bed for most of that time, and weathered the difficulties of a long, hidden, sometimes maddeningly complicated liaison. Good times and bad—the worst, perhaps, her episode with the Prince of Wales, just to draw people's suspicions away from what was really happening. But mostly good.

The best, perhaps, that their son might be finding his way to happiness.

Mr. Greenlee had been thinking these thoughts at about eight at night—before Kit and Mary had interrupted a bad elopement, helped along a more optimistic one on its way, and done what they could do to turn back the tide of an ill-fated revolution. For all Mr. Greenlee had known at eight, their night out in the rain and the wind might have turned out disastrously. But he hadn't thought it would, and as it happened, he was right.

"Emilia?" Rapping softly on a secret panel that led to the bedchamber.

❧

Still, the marchioness thought some hours later, it was a relief to hear the horse, the creaking of wheels, and the jingling of traces.

She'd hoped they'd be back before dawn. For you never stopped worrying about your children.

She thought she could hear a faint sound of laughter. Yes, she was pretty certain of that. It was laughter.

We had fun, Mary had once confided through her tears. *We could always make each other laugh. But I expect that fun and laughter aren't enough, are they, your ladyship?* Poor child, it was when she and Emilia both were waiting to hear the news from Spain.

Fun and laughter make a good beginning, Emilia had answered, thinking of a certain day, many years before, in Martin Greenlee's workshop. Perhaps the most fun she'd ever had, and the only day they'd dared make love there, and possibly the beginning, amidst shrieks of pleasure and whoops of laughter, of what would turn out to be Kit . . .

❧

"They look happy." Martin Greenlee stood by the window in his dressing gown, which hung hidden behind yet another partition during the day. Living in this room, Emilia thought, sometimes felt like living in a conjurer's box, with its trick panels and false walls.

It wasn't what she would have chosen, but it was fun in its way.

She plumped up the pillows behind her, wrapping a

shawl around her naked shoulders. Her white breasts, grown heavy but still very pretty, shone in the firelight. She felt his eyes on her. The room was a bit chilly, but she let the shawl drop open. He nodded, grinning in a way that most people didn't see, and folded his arms in front of him, tapering, squared-off fingers resting on upper arms that still had plenty of muscle and sinew in them.

"He's taking her back to the castle," he said. "They're going to wake up together, eat their breakfast together. . . ."

She sighed. "You would have liked that."

"You know it wasn't only your secret to keep, Emilia. There was also Martha to consider."

Since his wife's death, they'd sometimes wondered if they might be a bit freer about their meetings—being careful, of course, to keep it from Wat and Susanna.

"We could go away together," he said now. "There's a small lodge I know about. We could be alone for a few days."

He'd always enjoyed the sound of her laughter, but just now he didn't know what he'd said to set her off that way. "Well, why couldn't we?" he asked. "Why is that so funny?"

"We should starve. I don't know how to cook."

"Not even eggs?"

"Eggs? You know, I've always wondered what one does to them to get them hard like that. And the shells, however does one . . . ?"

He laughed too. "Perhaps we'd better not. We're all right as we are."

"Even if Kit never knows his father?"

"I think perhaps he does."

"I hope he does," she said. "I think it might help him be a good man, to know . . ."

But sentimentality had never been their way, and so she found it a great comfort that even at his age, he could still leer at her, and very convincingly too.

She licked her lips, which weren't as full as they once

had been, but which still had a sinuous curve to them when she smiled. She nestled back among the swansdown pillows and let the shawl fall away from her.

He'd be leaving in an hour, as he always did. While Kit and Mary would be waking tomorrow, smiling into each other's eyes and still in each other's arms when the busy sun stole through the windows.

Doesn't one always wish one's children to have more than one's self has had?

And anyway, what she'd had—what she still had— was good enough.

She stared across the room to meet his contained, confident gaze. Same way he'd looked at her from the first, when she'd been told to oversee his work on the old paneling, on her way to learning to be a great lady. But now she knew how to return his look—and to value it and everything good she'd gotten from her life and had still to look forward to.

And no, it wasn't really very late. The sun's rays hadn't stretched over the hills yet.

She laughed again.

"Come back to bed, Martin," she said. "There's still time."

Afterword

As far as I know, there was never a village of Grefford in the southeast corner of Derbyshire. But there was and is a town called Pentrich, and on the night of June 9, 1817, a few hundred men did set out in the rain for Nottingham, hoping to continue on to London. A farm servant was shot accidentally; it was the only blood spilled that night. Those of the marchers who got to Nottingham were met by a waiting detachment of cavalry; those who weren't arrested immediately were hunted down in the next few days. Three men were convicted of treason and hanged; fourteen others (knitters, miners, masons, clerks) were transported for life to the brutal penal camps of Botany Bay.

And there was an agent named Oliver (or Hollis, or Richards, or perhaps his real name was something else entirely), in the employ of the Home Office, who presented himself to reformers in the countryside as a delegate from the London leadership, and who urged them toward insurrection. At the British National Archives, you can read a microfiche copy of his reports to Lord Sidmouth, as well as the reports of local informers and Sidmouth's correspondence with the local magistrates.

As the date of the planned insurrections approached, reformers in the countryside grew increasingly suspicious of Oliver; unfortunately no one from Pentrich was present at the Nottingham meeting where these suspicions were aired. Oliver was finally exposed by a Mr. Dickenson, who knew something was wrong (as one would in that society) upon seeing General Byng's servant doff his hat to a man of the lower orders.

Dickenson broke the story to the *Leeds Mercury.* And even as the leaders of the Pentrich rising were tried and convicted of treason, the story of "Oliver the Spy" became a lightning rod for public sentiment against domestic espionage, and helped contribute to the passage of the First Reform Act of 1832, which extended suffrage (though not awfully far) among the men of Britain. As for Oliver, he was spirited away to the Cape Colony in South Africa, where he was given yet another name and an undemanding job with the British East India Company, and where he died several decades later.

While in the village of Youlgreave, a bit to the north and west of Pentrich, there's a cistern, built in 1829 to bring piped water from the local spring, and established through the efforts of the Youlgreave Friendly Society Women.

❧

I wanted to locate Mary and Kit's love story in this world of change and conflict, dark intrigue and incipient popular progress. And I wanted as well to situate them among characters (like Peggy) with love stories of their own. I like to imagine my romantic hero and heroine as one pair among many, their joys and sorrows amplified and reflected among a variegated and brightly hued populace, as though in a country dance.

But there's a pair of actual historical lovers I didn't bring into these pages, for they were too humble to know anyone like Mary or Kit and too desperately poor to afford tickets to a country assembly. Jeremiah Brandreth led the Pentrich marchers, fired the shot that killed the farm servant, and was hanged the following November. His wife, Ann, walked from Sutton-in-

Ashfield (near Nottingham) to Derby to bid him farewell. In his last letter to her, he wrote:

> *I feel no fear in passing through the shadow of
> death to eternal life; so I hope you will make the
> promise of God as I have, to your own soul, as we
> may meet in Heaven. . . . My beloved . . . this is the
> account of what I send to you—one work bag, two
> balls of worsted and one of cotton, and a handker-
> chief, an old pair of stockings and a shirt, and the
> letter I received from my beloved sister . . .*

Read on for an excerpt
from Pam Rosenthal's

THE EDGE OF IMPROPRIETY

winner of the 2009 RITA Award for
Best Historical Romance

and selected as one of the five
Best Romances of 2008 by *Library Journal*

Available from Signet Eclipse

As she'd predicted, the sunshine hadn't held. The next day dawned gloomy, skies steadily darkening. Toward midday the heavens opened, but by afternoon the rain slowed to a pale drizzle from a pearly sky over Bloomsbury.

A few birds chirped in the budding plane trees overhead; fat droplets of water gathered on the branches to splash atop her umbrella and into the puddles at her feet.

The soles of her half boots were hardly waterproof. She'd be glad to turn the corner at Great Russell Street. As at the moment she found herself glad of everything, and everything seemed to glow with misty possibility.

Her first errand of the day—to a shabby office in the City—had brought its usual humiliations: insults from her principal creditor (as she thought of him), her own responses in kind. Still, she was done with it for the month. She'd handed over the bank draft for April, pulled her skirts about herself as the door squeaked closed behind her, and breathed more freely with every step down the steep stairs, out to the narrow street, and into her carriage.

After which the visit to her modiste in Bloomsbury had almost been a pleasure. The green sarcenet was nearly done. Madame Gabri would be sending it to Marina's house in Brook Street in time for tomorrow night's dinner party.

And what a lovely surprise that the modiste would be charging last year's rates, in thanks for the mention of her name in Lady Gorham's last novel, *The Tale of Lord Farringdon.*

The bon ton's *best ladies look all the better for the work of her magic needle,* Marina had written. Which was certainly true of Marina herself, even as the styles grew more horrid with each Season: cumbersome, over-decorated skirts continuing to widen; challenging tight bodices that madame assured her would only become lower and righter; and puffing about the upper arm, what the fashion magazines most appropriately called the "imbecile sleeve"—a yard of fabric for each arm at least. The only good thing about the general effect being the illusion of a smaller waist.

The modiste had disagreed. "Not the *only* thing, my lady," she'd told Marina over tea. "Remember that it isn't everyone who can carry off the wide swath of shoulder and bosom it reveals."

Pleasant to be reminded of her better features, even as she regretted the passing of the fluid, Grecian-inspired white muslins of her youth. And she'd certainly come to the right place to mourn the passing of style *à la Grecque.* Passing through the courtyard to the venerable portals of the British Museum, she snapped her umbrella shut and entered the building.

It was the first collection of precious old objects she'd seen besides Harry Wyatt's own. At his estate in Hampshire she'd wandered about feeling more like an artifact than a viewer—for wasn't he always telling her she was the most beautiful thing he'd found on his travels?

If left to herself during the trying period just after she'd become Lady Gorham, she likely would never have come near this museum. But everyone had to see the great marble sculptures Lord Elgin had taken from the Parthenon in Greece. Counterfeiting an excess of delight, she'd expected to be bored beyond imagining. Surprisingly, she'd found it thrilling—the splendor of the marbles; the bewildering accumulation of other objects intrepid travelers hauled home to Britain; the multiplicity and variety of animal and plant life, fossils caught in rock or amber and displayed in the trays, drawers, and cases divided into what seemed an infinity of little compartments with their tiny, laboriously scripted labels affixed.

Thrilling yet oddly reassuring: the earnestness, the utter absence of dash or *ton* in these galleries a welcome relief to a young woman striving for acceptance in the dashing, *ton*-ish world in which she'd found herself.

And when she'd begun writing little sketches to amuse herself, it had been in these galleries where Marina would sometimes catch sight of an arresting, anonymous face or figure and think of a suitably expressive or humorous name to be affixed. She still salted her novels with amusing minor characters—a shopkeeper, perhaps or a country parson—before moving on to the main plot in the heroine's drawing room.

No new face caught her imagination today. Only a familiar mocking grin and a pair of bright black eyes peering at her from the other side of a glass case.

"Mr. Disraeli." One of the most successful, amusing, and outrageous of Colburn's novelists: Just look how the impish young man had gotten himself up today; he must have danced between the raindrops in his sapphire velvet and narrow, beribboned shoes.

When his novel *Vivian Grey* had been published last year it had rivaled her *Farringdon* in sales—no mean feat, for as a Jew, he'd experienced nothing of the Society he wrote about, concocting his fantastic tale of high life and political intrigue out of the vapors of passionate ambition.

Her smile softened now as she gave her hand to his father standing at his side. "How good it is to see you, sir. And how does Mrs. Disraeli do?"

"Quite tolerable, my lady. She often speaks of how she enjoyed your call upon her."

"I shall come once more, if I may, now that I've finished my latest." The mother was mystified by her son's adoration of a world that didn't want him, but Marina—who understood it completely—had been pleased to assure Mrs. Disraeli that her odd, brilliant boy was bound to make his way.

She must make time to call again. She'd have to find a shortcut to that next novel. Perhaps Mr. Parrey could discover a long-lost identical twin. . . .

Recalling herself, she allowed the elder Mr. Disraeli to lead her among the cases of Persian and Macedonian coins, while his son babbled on about *his* next novel. They'd take their leave of her, they said, at the hall that held the great Greek marbles.

"We've already visited them today," the younger man added. "I insisted we go directly upon our arrival. Papa wanted to save them for last, but I've spent all my patience waiting for the patronesses of Almack's to discover how indispensable I am. And here you are," he now said with a flourish. "The Elgin Marbles."

Pausing to bid her friends farewell, she stood aside to allow a trio of other viewers to enter the gallery ahead of her.

Botheration.

It wasn't as though she'd expected to be alone. One often saw scholars, students, and artists bent over their sketchpads, heard their civilized, respectful murmur of informed or fatuous commentary.

But sharing the Elgin Marbles with a mama and papa and their noisy, fidgety, half-grown child was another matter. Her eyes swept quickly and impatiently over the trio, with their unmistakable air of being up from the country. The tall gentleman with his unusually upright figure had the look of a clergyman.

Odd that he'd bring his child into this hall of naked statuary. Inconsiderate too: The little beast would doubtless be emitting gasps and giggles, sighing with boredom and demanding to be taken out for cakes and ices.

Marina would simply have to close her ears until then—and remain on the side of the hall where the centaurs did battle.

But as if to spite her by proving her wrong, the next minutes passed exceedingly peacefully, with not a gasp, giggle, or demand for more thrilling amusements to be heard. The girl from the country—how old might she be, certainly not thirteen yet?—conducted herself more quietly than had the younger Mr. Disraeli. An occasional raindrop pattered down upon the skylight. And when the child did ask an occasional question, it was in so soft a voice that Marina found that she couldn't make out the words.

If she'd wanted to make out the words. In which—it hardly needed saying—she had absolutely no interest whatsoever.

She moved a bit closer to inspect a group of large standing pieces.

How might a youngster respond to these epic works of art? Marina couldn't imagine. Guiltily, her thoughts strayed to Harry's children. She might have asked to have them visit more often; Lady Isobel must have been sad to lose her own mother.

She hadn't asked. The earl hadn't needed to make it any clearer: Not only didn't he want more children, he had very little interest in the two he had. His nobody of a second wife was in no position to ask for anything; it was astonishment enough that he'd wanted to marry her, rather than simply keep her as his mistress. In truth, she'd counted it excellent luck that people were calling her a *nobody*. They could have been calling her a sight worse—and might still, she thought briefly, if she fell behind on her monthly bank drafts.

But what were the girl and her father whispering about in front of that group of sculpted horsemen?

Now that she'd come around a mass of broken pillars, including the remarkable one shaped like a woman,

she had a better view, and could hear a few words s well.
"Xerxes . . . Persians . . . Panathenaic Procession." Odd
to hear such weighty syllables so eagerly whispered by a
child.

A nicely dressed child, she'd give the family that—
quite sweet how simply but elegantly and expensively
she was turned out, in contrast to the rusty (oh, dear,
even slightly shiny) black that contained her father's excellent shoulders.

(But when, she wondered, had she found the time to
take note of his shoulders? Or to consider—for it
seemed she had considered it, in some sly, hidden part
of herself—whether the legs in their shapeless trousers
might be good as well?)

His hair was thick, cut more closely than was
fashionable—as though he couldn't be bothered with
anything but the simplest arrangement—its color of a
metallic brightness. One could see that it had once
been a sort of sandy brown, now brindled, tipped
with silver. Pale gleams from the skylight shone down
upon it.

Perhaps she might add a country clergyman to the
ensemble of minor characters in her next novel.

Perhaps the clergyman could disclose the mystery of
the twin brothers' birth.

Perhaps . . .

Enough perhapses, she chided herself. It was one
thing to catch sight of an interesting face, quite another
to be making patent excuses for ogling strange, even if
well-built, gentlemen behind their backs.

It must be the proximity of the exquisite bodies the
ancient sculptors had rendered so perfectly, she thought.
Or perhaps some not so pleasant memories stirred up
by her visit, earlier today, to that baleful office.

Whatever the mix of confused affect that had caused
her. to stare at him so shamelessly, she'd better stop it
immediately. Had she forgotten that his wife was also in
the hall? For all Marina knew, the lady could be entirely aware of the attention her husband had been

attracting—and would most likely, and quite correctly, have found it outrageously impolite.

She peered down the gallery: Where *had* the lady taken herself? There she was—in front of the formidable, recumbent Dionysus from the temple pediment, done in the glorious round. But upon closer scrutiny it had become clear the tall, plain, angular creature, gown drooping where it ought to cling, was far too young to be the child's mother.

Silly of her. One hardly needed an author's powers of observation to discern that the woman gazing so avidly and unselfconsciously at the god's splendid, muscled torso (and downward too) hadn't celebrated very many birthdays beyond her twentieth. And that she was too completely, naively fascinated by the masculinity sprawled out before her to be *anyone's* mother, or, for that matter—one dearly hoped—anyone's wife.

A governess then, quite as the unbecoming gown and austere bonnet proclaimed her. An unusually well treated governess to have leave to wander among the antiquities as her fancy dictated, while the gentleman took his daughter about and answered her precocious questions.

Impatiently, Marina moved past a row of marble panels, turning her eyes back to the gentleman and to the child by his side, the dress of pale blue cotton that was only a little spattered about its hem from the rain, the white apron, good boots, bonnet dangling at the back of the neck, and sky blue grosgrain ribbons in the girl's thick fair hair.

One of the ribbons was coming loose.

Irksome. She found herself wanting to fix it before it slid to the floor.

She needn't have concerned herself. Because even while the eager murmur continued—"Athena . . . handmaidens . . . goddess's ritual garment rewoven every year . . ."—the gentleman reached down to retie the ribbon. The bow he made was merely serviceable, but his gesture was so quick, so sure and practiced, so quotidian, plain, and entirely to be taken for granted by a girl lucky enough to feel herself so cherished, that his daughter might not have been quite aware of it.

Marina felt herself go short of breath. But the child didn't change the tilt of her head. Continuing to stare above her, at the figures raised in low relief upon the slab of marble fixed onto the wall, she whispered something that Marina supposed must be another question.

Impossible to hear: The girl must have been carefully schooled not to disturb her fellow knowledge seekers within the sacred confines of a museum.

And so it was the gentleman who finally broke the silence, when it seemed that he couldn't suppress a low rumble of laughter that suggested pleasure rather than ridicule.

Less restrained in the wake of his outburst of mirth, his voice came a bit louder now, the words at long last audible to Marina. "But that's a very good . . . my word, that's a most *excellent* question, Sydney. The best kind of question, the kind no one knows the answer to—well, not *these* days, anyway, perhaps someday if . . . But let's move on, shall we, to the parts that originally faced east? It'll make more sense if I show you. . . ."

He swiveled his long body at the waist to point to some figure on the frieze directly above Marina's head. Catching sudden sight of her, he halted in midgesture, his smile apologetic and a bit self-mocking, his surprise evidently quite genuine. It seemed clear enough that he'd thought himself and his family group alone in the gallery.

Which meant, Marina thought, that until this moment he hadn't been in the least bit cognizant of her presence. While she'd been rather making a cake of herself tiptoeing about the room with her eyes on him and an ache in her chest.

She might have found the situation more humiliating still if his smile hadn't been so engaging.

Odd—she'd expected a scholar's pallor. Perhaps his skin seemed browner than it really was, in contrast to the brightness of the hair at his temples, the gleam of copper-rimmed spectacles.

No, he really was that dark: The hand that had fixed the hair ribbon had been burned by the sun and hardened by some sort of labor.

A light on the wall caught the glass of his spectacles, rendering them opaque. Breathing calmly (yes, that felt better), Marina inclined her head to change her angle of vision. The large blue eyes behind the lenses were warm, friendly. A sunburned hand moved to the bridge of his nose to bring the spectacles into a different alignment.

The young person had begun to fidget and now to glare. Jealous, possessive, moving a step closer to her father, she stared smugly up at Marina.

We were very well by ourselves, thank you, her expression seemed to proclaim, even as she dipped and bobbed back up in a polite enough curtsy, while the gentleman continued to gaze at Marina from above the rims of his spectacles—and while Marina did her best to assure that he continued to do so.

Unworthy, she'd reflect later, amid a twinge of guilt and a glow of satisfaction. She'd acted most unworthily.

If you could say that she'd really acted at all. If you could call the merest of smiles an *act.*

Except that it hadn't been the *merest* of smiles that had stolen across her face. Useless to wonder why and pointless to deny having done it: Marina had returned the gentleman's casual, affable smile with one of a brightness last seen when Sir Thomas Lawrence had painted her portrait fourteen years earlier—and taught her to put the whole of her body behind what might seem like a momentary flicker of pleasant emotion.

And damn anyone, she thought now, who might find the body behind the smile too old or too fat; they were the only smile and the only body she had. And if she were to put every bit of candlepower she had into a flirtatious glance at a country gentleman she'd never see again, among Lord Elgin's collection of marble sculptures in the British Museum on a rainy London Wednesday afternoon, well, what of it?

Except that he'd held her glance with a keen, critical, highly amused one of his own. If they'd been gamblers one might wonder if he might still hold a trump card.

She'd wonder later how much time had elapsed. Ten seconds? A minute?

But if she didn't care to see his hand . . .

"I beg your pardon," she murmured. "I expect I'm in your way." Whereupon she quitted the hall in a loud swoosh of skirts, and left the family group to sort themselves out among the marbles.